Broadway Christian Church Fort Wayne
Riders Of The Pale Horse
Bunn, T Davis
F Bun
0000 2977
P9-EMG-808
RIDERS OF THE PALE HORSE

Books by T. Davis Bunn

The Maestro
The Presence
Promises to Keep
The Quilt
Riders of the Pale Horse

The Priceless Collection

Secret Treasures of Eastern Europe

1. Florian's Gate
2. The Amber Room
3. Winter Palace

Rendezvous With Destiny

Rhineland Inheritance
Gibraltar Passage

RIDERS OF THE PALE HORSE

T. DAVIS BUNN

BETHANY HOUSE PUBLISHERS
MINNEAPOLIS, MINNESOTA 55438

This story is entirely a creation of the author's imagination. No parallel between any persons, living or dead, is intended.

Cover illustration by Joe Nordstrom

Published by Bethany House Publishers
A Ministry of Bethany Fellowship, Inc.
11300 Hampshire Avenue South
Minneapolis, Minnesota 55438

Printed in the United States of America

Library of Congress Cataloging-in-Publication Data

Bunn, T. Davis.
Riders of the pale horse / T. Davis Bunn.
p. cm.
1. Islamic fundamentalism—Middle East—Fiction.
2. Nuclear nonproliferation—Fiction. 3. Americans—Middle East—Fiction. I. Title.
PS3552.U4718R53 1994
813'.54—dc20 93-45734
ISBN 1-55661-346-6 CIP

This book is dedicated to

Cyril Price

with heartfelt thanks for the
wisdom and humor which helped me
learn and survive in the Arab world.

And to his wife, Nancy,

for the splendid gatherings
through which we keep these memories alive.

T. Davis Bunn, a native of North Carolina, is a former international business executive whose career has taken him to over forty countries in Europe, Africa, and the Middle East. *Riders of the Pale Horse*, his ninth novel for Bethany House Publishers, is based on extensive research as well as recent travels in Jordan and Russia. He and his wife, Isabella, currently live in Oxford, England.

For 100 years the West failed to understand communism. In the end it did not matter, there was nothing left worth understanding. For more than 1,000 years the West has failed to understand Islam. This time it matters: a system driven by God will always be more subtle, durable, and rational than one driven solely by economics. In the calculations and fears of many, Islam is now on the verge of replacing communism in the front line of global opposition to Western liberal democracy.

Bryan Appleyard

We must reject democracy in favor of Islam, which is the unique political system worked out by the Almighty.... Our march has just begun and Islam will end up conquering Europe and America.... For Islam is the only salvation left for this world in despair.

Sheikh Saeed Sha'ban
Leader of the Sunni majority
in Tripoli, Lebanon

If one allows the infidels to continue playing their role of corrupters on earth, their eventual moral punishment will be all the stronger. Thus, if we kill the infidels in order to put a stop to their activities, we have indeed done them a service.... To kill them is a surgical operation commanded by Allah the Creator.... Those who follow the rules of the Koran are aware that we have to apply the laws of retribution and that we have to kill.... War is a blessing for the world and for every nation. It is Allah himself who commands men to wage war and to kill. The Koran commands: "Wage war until all corruption and all disobedience are wiped out!"

Ayatolla Khomeni

Blessed are the peacemakers,
for they will be called sons of God.

MATTHEW 5:9

SWEDEN
FINLAND
WHITE SEA
Helsinki
Leningrad
Stockholm
BALTIC SEA
Tallinn
ESTONIAN S.S.R.
Riga
LATVIAN S.S.R.
LITHUANIAN S.S.R.
Volga R.
Moscow
RUSSIAN S.F.S.R.
Kaliningrad
Vilnius
Minsk
BELORUSSIAN S.S.R.
Warsaw
POLAND
Kiev
UKRAINIAN S.S.R.
Khar'kov
Don R.
Dnieper R.
Dnepropetrovsk
CZECHOSLAVAKIA
MOLDAVIAN S.S.R.
Budapest
HUNGARY
Kishinev
Rostov
ROMANIA
Odessa
SEA OF AZOV
Belgrade
Bucharest
Sevastopol
Constanta
Danube R.
YUGOSLAVIA
Varna
BLACK SEA
Sofia
BULGARIA
Istanbul
ALB.
GREECE
Ankara
AEGEAN SEA
TURKEY
Izmir
Athens

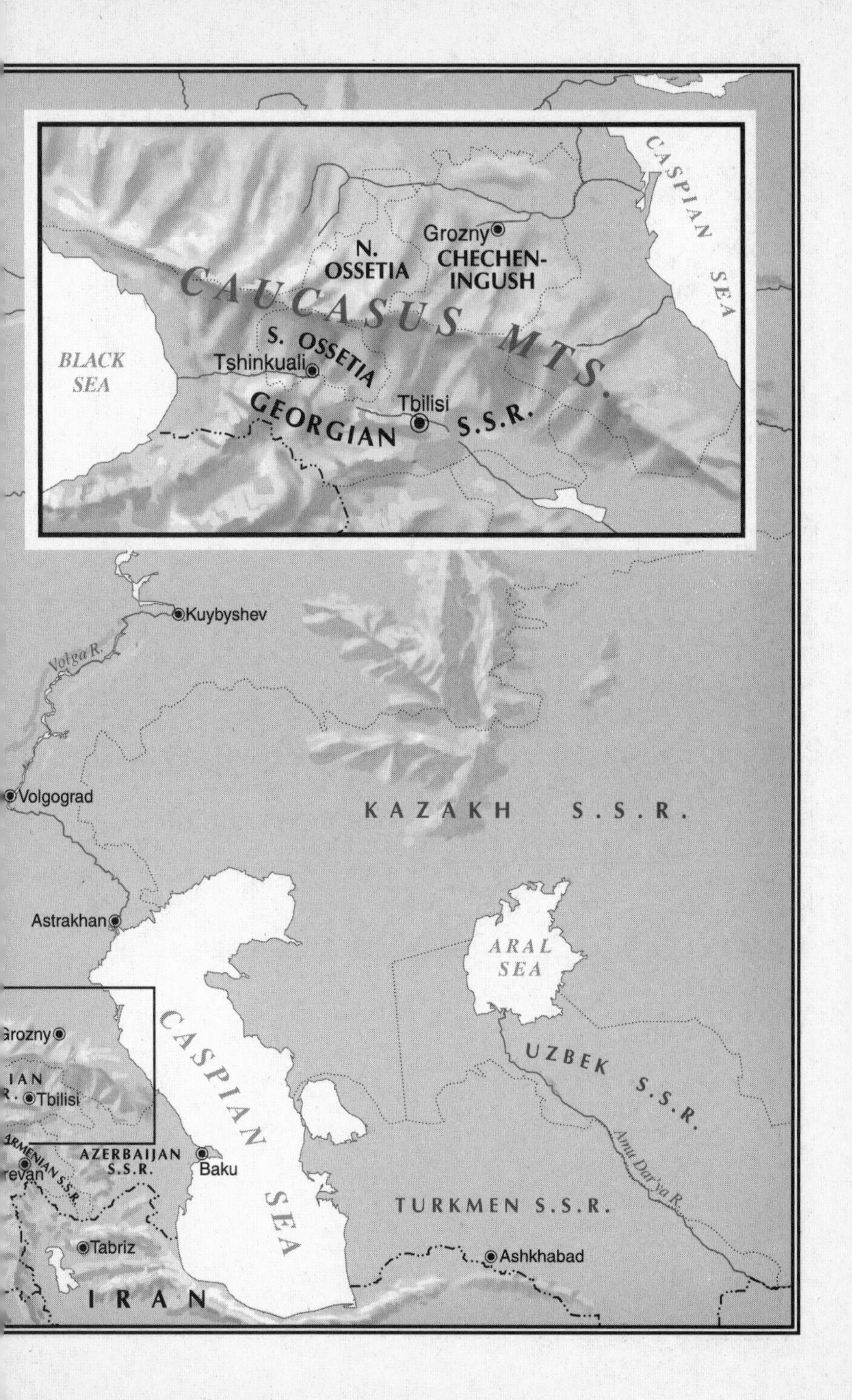
CASPIAN SEA
Grozny
N. OSSETIA
CHECHEN-INGUSH
CAUCASUS MTS.
S. OSSETIA
BLACK SEA
Tshinkuali
Tbilisi
GEORGIAN S.S.R.
Kuybyshev
Volga R.
Volgograd
KAZAKH S.S.R.
Astrakhan
ARAL SEA
Grozny
CASPIAN SEA
UZBEK S.S.R.
Tbilisi
Amu Dar'ya R.
AZERBAIJAN S.S.R.
Baku
ARMENIAN S.S.R.
TURKMEN S.S.R.
Tabriz
Ashkhabad
IRAN

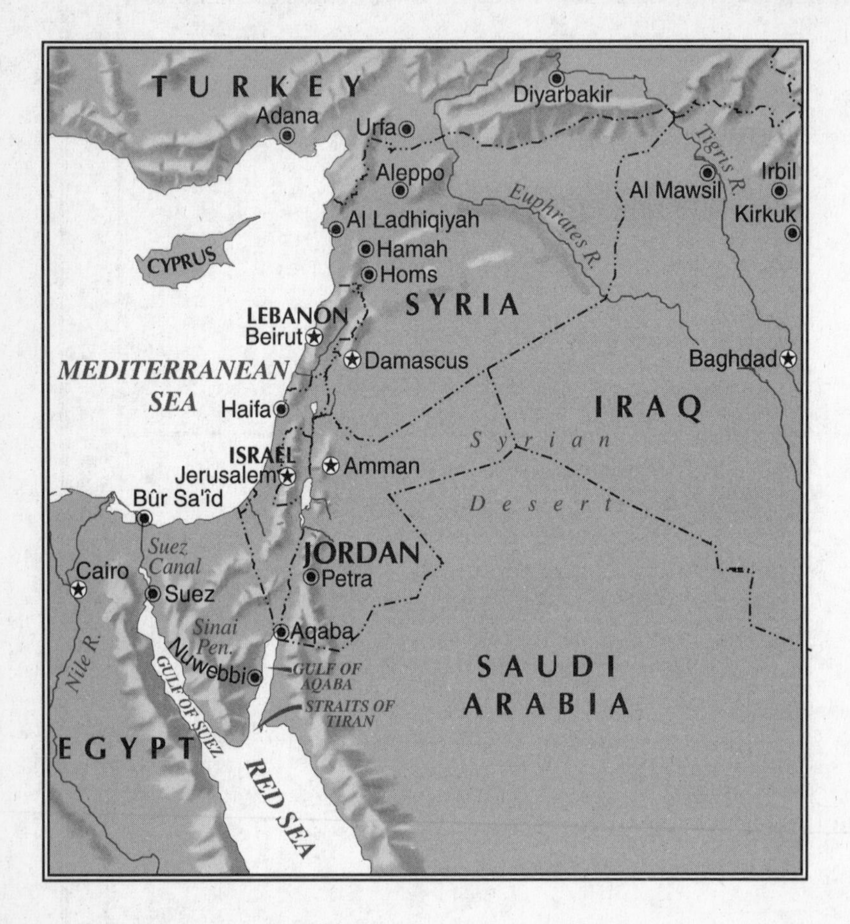
TURKEY
Adana
Urfa
Diyarbakir
Aleppo
Tigris R.
Irbil
Al Mawsil
Kirkuk
Euphrates R.
Al Ladhiqiyah
Hamah
Homs
CYPRUS
SYRIA
LEBANON
Beirut
Damascus
Baghdad
MEDITERRANEAN
SEA
Haifa
IRAQ
Syrian
ISRAEL
Jerusalem
Amman
Bûr Sa'îd
Desert
Suez
Canal
JORDAN
Cairo
Petra
Suez
Sinai
Pen.
Aqaba
Nile R.
Nuwebbi
GULF OF
AQABA
SAUDI
ARABIA
GULF OF SUEZ
STRAITS OF
TIRAN
EGYPT
RED SEA

Prologue

IT WAS THE QUIETEST argument in the history of Russian nuclear science.

They were quarreling softly not for fear that people in the other labs might hear them. There was no chance of that. Despite the exterior walls being over two feet thick, the wind had such force that the entire central lab building rumbled like a huge bass drum. No, they were quiet because they did not want to wake their sleeping child. The wind did not bother her, for she was a true child of the Russian steppes. But she always cried when her parents argued. Their impending departure was hard enough without her wails.

They crouched behind the particle analyzer, which like most of the other lab machinery did not work. Their cramped alcove was carpeted with litter and dust. The cleaners had not ventured back there since the downfall of the Soviet Empire. Why should they, when their pay had slipped to twelve dollars a month and their families were slowly starving. At least the scientists were still fairly well fed.

"I am not leaving without you," the woman quietly declared.

The scientist still wore his lab coat and cloth-soled shoes. His lank blond hair framed a face that looked perpetually hungry. Months of fear and worry had turned his cheeks cavernous and drawn his eyes back in their dark-ringed sockets. He hugged the sleeping child closer to his chest and softly replied, "If they find me, they shoot me. Is that what you want?"

"I want our daughter to have a father," the woman replied, her voice a faint wail. "I want a future together with my husband."

"This also do I want," the scientist replied. "It is for this and only this that we risk all."

"But together, Alexis," she pleaded, the words so often spoken they had long since become a litany.

"We shall be together," he replied, all force drained from his voice. He droned the words, his attention as much on the slumbering girl as on what he said. His daughter was three days from her fourth birthday and shared her mother's dark coloring and almost Oriental features. Her blood carried the heritage of ten generations of Mongol raiders. "It is all planned," Alexis told his wife. "You know this as well as I."

"Yes? So you force us to travel four thousand kilometers alone, hoping against hope that you will send for us?"

Alexis searched his wife's face. Despite the harsh demands of the past two years, her dark features still sparked with youth and passion and beauty. He eased his finger from the child's clutches, reached over and stroked her cheek. "You have been my life's only love, Alena."

Angrily she shook her head, casting his hand away. "And down south? They do not shoot escaped scientists in the south?"

The lab's outer door squeaked on rusting hinges, and they froze into terrified stillness. Footsteps scrunched across the grimy floor, and when the guard's battered cap came into view they heaved vast sighs of relief. "You are ready?"

"We are."

"Loading has commenced. I will come for you in five minutes. You must move swiftly."

"Thank you, Ivan Ivanovichu. You are a good friend."

"I am a man with four starving children, and for ten rubles more would flee with you." He inspected them nervously, then withdrew, saying, "Be on guard. They are a strange lot, these gypsies of the road."

When the door had creaked closed, Alena grasped his arm. "Answer me," she hissed. "You will answer me or I will return to our quarters."

"And do what," he replied calmly. He could not return her anger. Not now. His entire world began and ended with these two precious ones. "Wait for our daughter to starve?"

"Things might improve."

"We have been living on that myth for over two years now. It is time to face facts. The life here is meaningless. The situation here is beyond hopeless. To stay is to accept death."

"Then come with us," she pleaded, her fingers digging into the flesh of his arm. "Without you I am nothing, have nothing. I beg you, come!"

"What can I tell you that I have not already said?" He brushed a feather of dark hair from his daughter's sleeping face and felt his heart squeezed by the impossible beauty of her. "To the south there is war. War upon war. There are no controls on the southern borders."

"Then take us with you!"

"I cannot," he replied softly, yet as unbending as the Siberian soil locked in winter. "I will not. It is too dangerous."

"Too dangerous for us and not for you?"

"Too dangerous for you and our daughter. From Grozny I travel with Ilya and Yuri. This you know. The guides have instructed us to travel without our families. It is not a route for children. This you also know. Each additional person adds to the risk." He looked up, willing her to see the love in his gaze. "I must go alone, Alena. For us."

The door creaked open once more. The guard called quietly over the wind's deep drone, "It is time."

"We come," Alexis called back.

"Tell me again," she pleaded desperately, rising with him. "Let me know your hope since I have none of my own."

"Tbilisi," he repeated, the words a soothing chant. "We escape over the Caucusus into Georgia. From the capital Tbilisi we fly to Jordan. Amman, Aqaba, then a boat to Iraq. Then work and money, Alena. Enough money for a life. Enough money for hope."

She searched his face with a feverish gaze, her defiance slipping away to the agony he knew it covered. A tear escaped from the side of her eye and trickled down the face he had come to know and love so well, so very well. She whispered shakily, "And us?"

"Graz," he soothed, saying the word as he would an intimacy. "You travel to the detention camp in Austria. Processing takes six weeks. This is well known. By then I will send for you." With both arms now supporting his daughter, he leaned forward and stroked Alena's cheek with his own. He drank in the scent of her, willing himself to etch the memory deep. "Go. Await my word. I will contact you. I *will.*"

"Come now or they go without you," hissed the guard.

"Take the satchels," Alexis said, and slipped out from behind the machine, giving silent thanks that his daughter still slept. "We are ready."

As with all personnel in these days of want and misery, the guard's uniform was little more than rags. His cap was battered and sweat-stained, his coat lacked buttons, his trousers were so worn they had been washed of their color. His shoes flip-flapped as he walked out and scanned the corridor, then returned to wave them forward. "All clear."

The three of them hustled down the long central hall.

Mildew and ancient spider webs clustered in the ceiling corners. Their footsteps rang overloud as they hurried past what once had been the centerpiece of Soviet scientific achievement, now as desolate as a forgotten mausoleum.

They turned the final corner, and the wind grew so loud that it covered the sounds of Alena's weeping. They pushed through the inner doors, and instantly the noise became a ferocious howl.

His daughter stirred sleepily in his arms. "Papa?"

"Shh, little one, all is well. We must go outside." He turned to his wife's tear-streaked face. "The towel, Alena."

His daughter was indeed a child of the steppes. At four years she knew enough to remain still as the dampened towel was tucked in around her eyes and nose and mouth and ears. Alexis gripped her more firmly, then nodded to the guard. "Let us go."

As soon as they opened the outer doors, the wind sought to rip them apart.

Russians called their steppes the earthen sea. There in the Siberian borderlands it lay flat and featureless from the Arctic forests to the southern mountains, three thousand kilometers of aching emptiness. In such autumn days as these, Arctic winds came shrieking down from the north, with nothing to slow their fierce blasts until they struck the Caucasus mountains another thousand kilometers farther south. The soil was dry and bare of snow to hold it in place. The wind plucked up giant fistfuls and flung it with such ferocity that paint could be stripped from a car in a matter of hours. It was a maddening wind, a blinding force that could lift entire trees and send them whipping unseen onto houses and trucks and people.

Arms interlocked for added strength, together they fought their way across the laboratory compound to the outer loading platforms. There was no way for them to visually check their progress. Around them swirled impenetrable clouds of yellow-black dust. They walked by memory alone.

Suddenly above the wind's blast came the roar of great diesel engines, and Alena wailed in her husband's ear. He forced her forward until the first great dark beast appeared in front of them. The guard shouted words that were lost in the wind, but his signals were clear—this was Alena's truck.

Alexis felt the child in his arms stiffen with fear from the strange roaring shape in front of them. He bent over and buried his face in the towel that protected her face, then straightened and allowed his sobbing wife to clasp his neck. He placed his lips upon her ear and shouted as loud as he was able, "I am ever with you, Alena!"

Together with the guard he forced his wife up into the truck's open door, then lifted his daughter up to her. The satchels came next. He climbed up the step, and in the cabin's relative calm he embraced them again once more. Then he stepped back and slammed the door, searching through the yellow storm for a final glimpse of his world beyond the grimy window.

His daughter pulled the towel free and instantly realized that she was on the inside and her father on the outside. She flung herself at the closed window and screamed at the top of her voice, *"Papa!"*

He stepped down from the truck and watched his daughter claw at the glass, shrieking the single word over and over. *"Papa!"*

The truck roared its defiance of the storm and pulled away. Alexis stood and faced the tumult until his daughter's screams had faded to meld with the wind's shrill blast.

The guard gripped Alexis' arm and pulled him to the next truck. They embraced in the way of friends in the Orient, a swift hug to either shoulder, and Alexis was surprised to find tears streaking the guard's seamed features. In order to keep the moment untainted, Alexis did not place the final payment into his hand, but rather shoved it deep into the man's pocket, then gripped him by the neck. He shouted, "You are indeed a friend, Ivan Ivanovichu."

"My world collapses and sweeps away all of value, even friends," the guard replied, then shoved him brusquely toward the truck. "Go while the portal is open. And when your way is clear, remember me."

Alexis climbed aboard, slammed the cabin door, and looked down at his friend. The man stood defiantly against a wind so fierce it threatened to blast him from the earth's surface, and shouted up a single word of farewell.

Remember.

Autumn's first frost fell early upon Munich, but the two smugglers did not complain. The chill kept prying eyes away.

The freeze had arrived on the heels of two weeks' hard rain. The clouds dispersed soon after dusk when the wind drifted around to the north and breathed an icy whisper straight from the frozen Arctic tundras. Stars made their appearance in a night sky washed so clear that not even the massed lights of downtown Munich could block their brilliance.

The central Munich train station closed at midnight. Soon after, police patrols made sweeps for Romanian gypsies fleeing forced deportation. By that time, the temperature had dropped below zero. Cars entering the thoroughfare fronting the station skidded upon sheets of dark ice and danced for frantic seconds with their brake lights marking time.

As the city slowly quieted with the deepening of night, clusters of people began gathering in the central train station's side parking area. They were travelers long accustomed to the vagaries of nature. Undaunted by the cold, they settled in to wait. Portable cookers were lit, water was poured from plastic thermos bottles, teas were brewed.

From a distance, the gathering seemed to possess a mystical aura. Tendrils of mist hung in the bitter breeze, muting the harsh streetlights. The several dozen cookers softened the faces of those who huddled around them, changing into gentle, inward-looking gazes. Countless mugs drifted smoke like hand-held incense burners.

But the magic vanished at closer inspection. The clouds of breath exhaled over steaming mugs reeked of vodka or homemade grain alcohol. Dark eyes glittered suspiciously as they inspected each newcomer for signs of weakness or threat. Families kept vigil over flimsy cases bound with twine and layers of tape. The cookers illuminated faces furrowed by hard winters and a harsher life.

The first bus arrived around two in the morning. It wheezed into the lot, taking the entrance ramp in weary, rolling motions. It puffed into the parking lot with oily exhalations of relief. The vehicle had an old-fashioned round-shouldered shape. The number plates were crudely fashioned, the windows streaked from a thousand miles of dusty roads. The brakes squeaked, the door groaned as it was thrust open, the round headlights dimmed as soon as the motor was cut. Passengers dismounted with the stiff-legged gait of those long imprisoned.

By four o'clock, the lot was full. Throngs milled about ancient buses bearing plates from ancient lands whose names now sounded strangely new. Romania. Bulgaria. Hungary. Estonia. Uzbekistan. Albania. Latvia. Belarus. Georgia. Ukraine.

As yet another lurching vehicle arrived and the first passenger wobbled down the steps, the two men in bulky overcoats separated themselves from the station shadows. The pair hovered outside the gathering of travelers. They watched as the bus driver hefted the doors from the lower luggage holds, then swiftly stepped back and away from the frantic rush for belongings.

The young woman they awaited stepped out last, rubbed fatigue-smudged eyes, and walked over to where they stood. The shorter of the pair said in greeting, "You're so late I almost froze."

"Four hours at the border," the woman replied. "The Germans are cracking down."

"No trouble, I hope."

"I'm here," she replied flatly. "But we will have to find another route. These buses will soon be history. Germany is cracking down on refugees from the East."

"Shouldn't you be seeing to your goods?"

The woman grimaced. "If you see somebody trying to run away carrying an eighty-kilo case, stop him."

The shorter man motioned to his companion, who walked over to the bus, forced his way through the jostling throng and extracted what appeared to be an utterly normal suitcase. Yet the weight of it bunched his shoulder muscles and canted him to one side despite his best efforts to remain upright.

Closer inspection revealed that a cardboard frame had been glued over a metal inner case, and a rough fabric applied to the cardboard backing. Imitation leather framed the edges and the opening for the handle. The snaps were fake; there was no way to open the case without first tearing off the outer covering.

As the big man started for a car parked at the end of the lot, the woman's hand slipped into her purse. "You are forgetting something."

The shorter man looked pained and signaled for the other man to stop. "We agreed it would be safer to make payment later."

"I agreed to nothing."

"It is too public here."

"Then it is too public for the transfer," she replied, her hand hidden in the folds of her bag. "I do not care to see either of you again, but if I must, I will hold on to the merchandise until then."

The shorter man sighed in mock defeat, slipped a hand into his coat, and produced a bulky envelope. Offering it over, he muttered, "And to think you were trusted with our cause."

"I was trusted because I would get the job done." She gestured with the hidden hand. "Open it and fan the contents. Slowly."

He did as she instructed, sheltering the motion with his body from the milling crowd behind him. A thick sheaf of five-hundred-mark bills slowly flickered by under the woman's watchful gaze.

"Again," she ordered, and ignored his exasperated sigh. Then, "Enough. Set the envelope on the ground in front of you and be off."

"I shall remember this offense," the shorter man replied, but he did as he was told. "Your superiors will not be pleased."

"My superiors told me to do exactly as I have." She stepped forward and set her foot on the envelope. "Back away and keep your hands in sight."

Only when the pair had arrived at their car and were busy hefting the weighty case into their trunk did she glance swiftly around, then bend over and pick up the envelope. Her hand still hidden in her bag, she turned and walked quickly away.

Across the street, in a darkened third-floor room inside the Hotel President, two men by the open window watched the woman depart and eased taut muscles. The man on his knees stripped off his earphones and gently settled his bulky apparatus to the floor. It looked like a standard television satellite dish connected on the back to a pair of padded hand grips. Sprouting from the center of the bowl was a slender plastic tower. The purpose of the dish was to gather sound and focus it upon the ultrasensitive long-range microphone set at the peak of the tower. He reached over and shut off the tape recorder.

His partner snapped one final pair of photographs as the car wheeled away, then straightened from his tripod with a silent groan. The solid aluminum frame held two Nikon F4 automatic-focus cameras connected by a parallel trigger. The lens on the top camera was only three hundred millimeters, but its outer edge was a full fifteen inches in diameter—a low f-stop professional telephoto lens made for shooting precision pictures under low lighting conditions. That camera held Kodak Ektar 1000 film, the finest-grain light-sensitive film in the world.

The second camera used a thousand-millimeter lens, allowing for closer filming but cutting down the amount of light gathered by a factor of thirty. It made up for this by using film sensitive to the infrared spectrum. The resulting grainy prints would be adequate if they were not blown up too large. The two cameras between them should have recorded the transfer in intimate detail.

The sound man blew on his hands and rubbed circulation back into chilled limbs while the cameraman strode to the telephone, dialed a number from memory, and spoke with a crisp British accent. "Mr. Price? Reporting in as ordered, sir. Yes, sir, without a hitch. Should have everything you wanted. Right, sir, we're on our way."

The cameraman hung up, nodded to his companion, and pulled his apparatus away from the open window. Then they shoved the stubborn window closed, pulled the drapes, and began packing. Much work remained to be done before they could call it a night.

1

HE STEPPED ONTO THE runway of the Chechen-Ingush airport and paused to sniff the steamy September air. A swarthy soldier in a decrepit uniform watched him with eyes as dark as his moustache. The new arrival smiled blandly, took in the well-oiled machine gun, and announced to no one in particular, "There's money in the air and riches in the wind."

The soldier barked a guttural command and swung his weapon toward the arrivals hall. Robards replied with a full-fledged grin, shouldered his battered satchel, and sauntered off.

In his thirty-seven years, Barton Jameson Robards had won and lost more fortunes than many small countries. In a barroom confession to a buddy too drunk to remember, he had once said, "Finding it isn't near as much trouble as making it mine. Losing it isn't any trouble at all."

Robards stood a hair over six-foot-six and sported a jaw like the front fender of a Mack truck. His hair was black, his eyes steel-gray, his way with women indifferent or demanding, depending on his mood of the moment. His friends, and they were almost as numerous as his enemies, called him Rogue, after the bull elephant who preferred his own company unless the heat was on him, and who reigned supreme over whatever turf he decided to claim as his own.

Rogue Robards didn't consider himself a particularly greedy man. All he wanted was his own yacht, his own tropical island, his own Rolls, his own Swiss bank account sporting some number followed by at least nine zeros, and a string of nubile secretaries to smile adoringly as he dictated his autobiography. He had long since decided on the title—Laws Are for Little People.

The arrivals building, a converted airplane hangar of World War II vintage, was as cheerful as an empty morgue. Voices splashed like a heavy rain off distant metal walls and roofs and concrete floors.

Robards clumped his leather satchel down on the steel customs table and opened it without being asked. Experience had taught him that anybody as big as he was, dressed in flight jacket and laced-up boots and pressed cords while everybody else wore either the local garb or grimy business suits, was going to get searched. Opening his luggage unasked usually saved a few minutes and disarmed the worst of the questions.

"Anything to declare?" the officer asked, his accent mangling the English words into insensibility.

"Merely sixteen smidgens of ground worm food and a can of green guppies," Robards replied, certain the man had memorized the question and knew no other English at all. He shook his head and lifted out his shaving kit; holding the bag toward the man and his confused expression, he said in a casual drawl, "I left my pet catfish on board with the baby alligator. I hope they get along."

The customs guard released him with a curt wave and turned to the next passenger. A bald-headed businessman raised his multilayered chin to give Robards a thoroughly confused look. Robards replied with a buccaneer's grin, hefted his satchel, and sauntered toward the exit.

There was a good deal of the pirate in Rogue Robards. Once a solid deal had taken him to New York—a solid deal being one that allowed him to walk away with his money and his life. His lady of the hour had used a costume ball to dress him up in pirate garb; fold-down boots, baggy black trousers, drawstring shirt, sword, and ostrich-plume hat. Standing on a chair to tie his eye patch into place, she had examined his reflection in the full-length mirror and declared, "You were born four hundred years too late."

"I've always had a soft spot for hidden treasure," Robards had agreed.

"Now the question is whether I'm going to risk letting you loose in a roomful of New York women," the lady had added, getting as much of his shoulders and neck as she could manage in a full nelson. "After a steady diet of Wall Street yuppies, they might just eat you alive."

Rogue Robards described himself as a product of the Florida property boom. His daddy had been a swamp creature lured from the Everglades by Gulf Coast developers, who feared rolling out their blueprints on a log that suddenly grew fangs and a tail and showed a marked desire to eat them, Ray-Ban specs and all. His momma had been a washed-out woman decked in shades of gray, whose days had been filled with the drudgery of hard work and the happy sounds of a drunk husband beating the living daylights out of their only boy. Thankfully, the boy had grown up fast enough to keep his pappy from inflicting permanent damage, and left home at the ripe old age of fourteen, after landing a punch that drove his father through the front wall of their two-ply home.

Next had come three years of roaming the drier reaches of Texas and marking time in a variety of oil fields and other places too remote to feel the nosy influence of social workers and child-labor investigators. Then Rogue Robards had come into town one evening with a paycheck burning a hole in his Levi's, and the next morning he had sought refuge from a monumental hangover in a Marine recruiting office. The spit-and-polish NCOs had taken one look at his strapping physique, ignored his somewhat off-center list and the way he shaded his eyes from the glare of their fluorescent overheads, and practically begged him to sign on the dotted line.

Vietnam had swallowed up Robards, chewed him up, and spat him out. He was left scarred down deep, pitted with wounds that stubbornly refused to heal. He had then taken the only step he saw as both open and sensible, given the circumstances.

Rogue Robards had become a mercenary.

Sunlight hit him like metal striking an anvil as Robards emerged from the hangar and sauntered toward the rank of taxis. Rank was definitely the right word here—the newest car in the lineup was a DeSoto of late fifties vintage with more rust than paint. But Robards liked the look of that vehicle and its driver, who had parked his car beneath the lot's single sheltering palm. The man leaned silently against his car and watched while his compatriots started a raunchy chorus of pleas for Robards' business. The man's only reaction to Robards' approach was a slight stiffening of his spine.

Robards dropped his satchel at the man's feet. "Hot day."

"I await a fare," the man replied in oddly formal English.

"Your fare's just arrived," Robards said.

The man inspected him frankly. "You are representing the Siemens Company?"

"If that's what it takes to get a ride."

"Why me? You can see, twenty other cars are here, and they are all eager to take you anywhere you want to go."

Robards stayed put. "Where did you learn your English?"

The driver inspected him for a long moment, then replied, "I worked for an American base on the Turkish side of the border. A sergeant at the post, he had a multitude of books. I read them all."

"Impressive. Might have been that we knew the same man."

The driver was clearly skeptical. "And yours—he had a love affair with his bunk?"

"And a crew cut gone gray, and eyes filled with unlived passions. He lived for his books and cultivated a belly more like a cauldron than a pot." Robards wiped at sweat. "Shakespeare and Tolstoy in battered paperbacks. Wooden packing crates filled with everything from Dickens to Harold Robbins."

"It might have been the same man," the driver conceded.

"Or maybe just a kindred spirit. The Marines breed a lot of strange characters in the seasons between wars."

The driver smirked. "So you were one of those few good men."

"At least until I enlisted. Afterward they called me something else." Robards reached down and tossed his satchel into the car's backseat. "What is your name?"

"Anatoly. And you?"

"Barton Robards. My friends call me Rogue."

"You can afford to pay a driver?"

"Pay him well now and promise more later."

"Later does not often arrive in this country, in this time."

"If it doesn't for me, you'll hear about it soon enough," Robards assured him. "My generosity increases in time to my wealth. It is my greatest failing."

"Not to me." Anatoly gave Robards' face a close inspection. "A hotel, you need?"

"With more charm than glitz," Robards agreed. "I have no need of newness, and too much air conditioning gives me the hives."

"A taste of the old world, perhaps."

"Clean would be a plus. And fresh sheets."

"Food without gristle," Anatoly said, walking around

the car and climbing in. "I comprehend."

"Also a minimum of flies and other winged creatures," Robards said, joining him in the front seat. "I have grown attached to my own blood."

The ancient auto groaned and creaked but ambled forward in a rocking good humor. The slender driver handled the vast steering wheel and its chrome-plated horn with ease. "What brings you to our formerly fair land?"

"I heard rumors of several small wars."

"No war is small for the ones involved."

"True. But so long as foreign powers are not involved, it cannot be called large."

"Also true. You seek small wars? It sounds like a risky life."

"No. It is not the war I seek but the opportunity. And yes, it's a risky life."

"And you call such wars an opportunity. Interesting."

"A war often makes holes. Or windows. Or cracks in the woodwork, whatever you like to call them. Places for an agile man to slip through."

"I prefer to join with surer things these days. Life alone has more risks than I care to take."

"The war has not been kind to you?"

"War and kindness are words that mingle like oil and water." Anatoly drove with as much pressure on the horn as the gas pedal. He swerved deftly around an overloaded ox cart.

"I have heard that these wars have left certain people in great need of certain items."

"That too I have heard."

"Put out the word," Robards insisted. "Speak of a man you have known for ages—"

"Minutes, even," Anatoly corrected.

"—long enough to trust," Robards continued

smoothly, "who has interest in helping resolve the problem."

"Which one?"

"Whichever has been left undone. Whichever pays. Delivering the odd container. Finding the lost. Rescuing the captured. Healing the rift. Righting the wrong, or if not, wreaking havoc upon the wrongdoers."

Anatoly was silent for a long moment, then mused aloud, "There is something."

"There usually is."

"It is, of course, quite dangerous."

"Of course."

"And not entirely legal," Anatoly continued.

Robards merely shrugged.

Anatoly slowed at an intersection manned by troops stationed by an armored personnel carrier. Once safely through, he asked, "Would you consider working for a church?"

Robards tried to mask his shock. "It would make for a certain change."

Anatoly pulled up in front of a decidedly third-rate hotel, honked his horn, and said to Robards, "Then see to your bath and meal and rest while I return for my sweating passenger. I shall then speak with the church people and see if perhaps they are ready to meet with the likes of you."

Rogue Robards lay drifting in and out of sleep in standard jet-lag dozes. Through his window drifted the cacophony of a third-world city—revving motors and blaring horns and diesel fumes and shouting voices and strange music played through speakers shattered by the constant load. To Robards the din played itself out like a familiar lullaby.

The tentative knock came as a welcome relief. He rolled from the bed, crossed the room, and opened his door. The young man who faced him looked so much like a fish out of water that Rogue could not help but grin.

"Mister Robards?"

"The one and only. What can I do for you?"

The young man acted uncomfortable with his own skin. "Your taxi driver? Anatoly? He said you might be able to help us with a problem we have?"

Robards crossed bulky arms across his chest. "Do you make a habit out of turning every sentence into a question?"

"Only when I'm nervous." The young man scratched his cheek, caught his hand, and brought it back down under control.

"Which must be most of the time around here."

"It's not much different here than any other place," the young man replied. "At least, not as far as my nerves go."

"Watch it, now," Robards said. "Keep that up and I might decide underneath that mild-mannered exterior lurks what'd pass for a sense of humor."

Brown eyes drifted up long enough to inspect Robards' face for derision. Finding none, they settled back on the floor. "My name is Wade Waters."

"You don't say. What's your middle name?"

The young man hesitated, then answered resignedly, "Donald."

"Wade D. Waters." A grin stretched the leathery skin of his face. "Yeah, I'd say you had a pretty good reason for running. Don't know if Russia was far enough, though. You from the States?"

"Illinois. But now I work at the clinic of a local mission."

"Mission as in religious?"

"A Christian mission, yes. Is there a problem with that?"

"Not from my end," Robards said evenly. "But not many of you people want to have much to do with the likes of me."

Wade Waters started to say something, then stopped and asked, "Would you mind coming and having a talk with our director?"

Robards reached to the bedside table for shades, keys, money clip, and knife and pocketed it all in practiced motions. "Lead on, Sanchez."

"Who?"

Robards showed genuine surprise. "Don't tell me you've never heard of Don Quixote."

"Oh. Sure." The young man rattled down two flights of rickety stairs, crossed the scuffed lobby floor, and entered the bright afternoon sunlight. "I might even prefer it to Wade."

"Watch it there," Robards said, slipping on mirror shades. "You gotta learn to trap that humor, keep it outta sight."

In the lowlands around Grozny, the capital of Russia's Chechen-Ingush region, autumn held on long and surrendered only after a hard and dusty struggle. The Caucasus foothills were a world unto themselves; even nature seemed to accept that no normal rules applied here. When winter finally did arrive, it landed with a ferocity so sudden that every year a few people were caught unawares and left frozen to an iron-hard ground. But this year autumn had fought a more valiant battle than usual, with temperatures remaining in the eighties for weeks after the first snow normally would have fallen. The locals responded with customary pessimism and predicted that the snows when they came would be heavy enough to bury houses.

The town's Christian sector was busy, but no busier than usual for that time of day. Buses from all the nearby villages made their disgruntled way across desolate roads soon to be lost beneath the ice, and deposited their hot and stinking and tired passengers at the market gates.

Robards stepped lightly alongside Wade. He moved easily through the tightly packed throngs, granted room by his obvious foreignness and his imposing size.

The marketplace cracked with sounds like gunshot as young boys popped open paper bags. The boys whipped the bags open with a snap that resounded through the market. Hundreds of these boys, dressed in traditional baggy vests and trousers that were little more than filthy rags, wandered through the market selling bags. The continuous pops were louder than the traders' cries and the buyers' answering complaints. Popping bags was the only game many of these boys had ever known. They had been assigned to the task of earning much-needed pennies since they could walk. They flicked the bags open over and over and over with grim boredom.

The mission stood at the far end of the market from the mosque. Despite the cool shade visible through its wide-open doors, the church was an island of empty calm. The mission was surrounded by a chest-high, lime-daubed wall with a portal of rough-hewn timber. The gate was manned by beggars who won coveted holy spaces by right of age and infirmity. Robards dropped a few pennies into a clawlike hand emerging from a filthy burlap cloak. He was rewarded with a twitch of life and the traditional groaned blessing.

At that moment a nearby rag heap erupted into life. The crone's eyes spit a brilliant light as she pointed one shaking finger directly at Wade Waters and began screaming words Robards could not understand.

With the swiftness of a world whose only entertainment is the public spectacle, people gathered. Faces examined the pair with chattering curiosity. The crowd clustered close, leaving sufficient space for the old woman to dance. The two westerns were trapped within a vacuum of heat and dust and isolation. What amazed Robards as much as the woman's screaming was Wade's reaction. He positively cringed, as though embarrassed by some act he himself had committed.

"Are you the man they call Robards?" Another white face emerged from behind the nearby wall and shouted to Robards over the crowd and the old woman's continual din. "I am Reverend Phillips. I say, wouldn't you be more comfortable in here?"

"Friend, that's one invitation I don't need to hear twice." Robards grabbed the wall and leapt over it, landing with a thud in the dusty yard, then turned and helped Wade.

The crone danced in through the open gate. She stopped and leveled her scrawny finger within inches of Wade's chest. The crowd pressed in around the wall and watched with joyful curiosity.

"Let's go inside, shall we?" The frocked little man motioned toward the church. His accent was thoroughly British, his manner delicate and offended by all the furor. "They won't follow us any farther than here. The mullahs don't allow it. We are right on the border with the Muslim district, you see, a sort of no-man's-land. It was the only area where we found space large enough for our mission. Which means, of course, that we are constantly being harassed by the pestilent mullahs."

Once inside the mission portals, Robards found himself surrounded by relative peace. Outside the crone continued her screeching invective. "That old lady was making my skin crawl."

"Yes, they do tend to have an unsettling effect," the parson agreed. "When they're like that it's hard to tell when they will go from happy and gay to nasty and dangerous."

"Could you tell what she was saying?"

"Step up here where they can't see us." The parson led him up to the front of the church, where a narrow doorway led to a closet-sized vestry. He paid absolutely no mind whatsoever to the sweating Wade. "Oh, she was saying what they always do."

"They? Who is they?"

"I'm sure I don't know." Reverend Phillips was clearly

distressed by the whole line of discussion. "Some group of troublemakers the local mullahs sent over, no doubt."

"They are Christian," Wade protested in his ever-soft voice. "This side of the market borders the Christian section."

"Christian in name only," the parson countered crossly. "And this close to the border, they pay more attention to the mullah's orders than they do any priest or parson. Besides, with these beggars you can't make any such generalizations. They know no borders."

"But what did the woman say," Robards pressed.

"Oh," Reverend Phillips waved distractedly in Wade's general direction. "They call him a healer of nations."

Robards cast an astonished glance toward Wade. "This happens every time you come around?"

Wade nodded, trapped in painful shame. "I gave her some medicine for a sore on her foot."

"Yes," the parson replied testily. "And look what happened. Just as I warned. You should never have started all that nonsense."

Robards looked from one to the other, asked, "What nonsense?"

"He insisted on going out and treating beggars where they lay on the street," the parson said, positively incensed by the idea. "As if we didn't have enough trouble already with those insufferable mullahs and all their idiotic restrictions. I ask you, why on earth would anyone bother to go against their orders and enter our mission if this, this *boy* is going to turn around and treat everyone he can find out in the gutters?"

Wade made no attempt to defend himself. He stared silently at the floor by his feet.

"Oh, my goodness, where on earth are my manners." Reverend Phillips waved a delicately veined hand at one of his rickety chairs. "Have a seat, won't you. As big as you are, when you're standing in these confines it doesn't leave room for us to breathe."

Robards did as he was told. "Aren't there any local doctors?"

"Not anymore," Wade replied.

"All the professionals were Russians," the parson explained. "The Chechen are making the local Russian population extremely nervous. They threaten them on the streets, in the markets, wherever. Those who have the opportunity to make a life for themselves elsewhere have long since departed."

"They say it is because they wish to make the Chechen state truly Chechen," Wade added. "But really it's just a way of robbing people. They force the Russians to leave in a panic, then steal everything they leave behind and sell rights to their empty apartments on the black market."

Robards nodded. It was a story as old as war. "I hear you have a problem."

"Quite a large one, actually. You see, there is this rather irritating little war just to the south of us."

"Several of them, if I've heard correctly," Robards said, focusing in.

"Yes, well, for some reason known only to God and some unnamed officials in London, we have been selected as a drop-off point for medicines intended for a Red Cross center that serves stranded villages."

"Where?"

He waved a vague hand toward distant blue-clad mountains beyond his window. "Somewhere in the Caucasus. I'm sure I don't know where, exactly."

"In the highlands, near Carcash," Wade said quietly. "In the tribal borderlands between Georgia, Ossetia, and Russia."

"Not a healthy place to be raising a family just now," Robards offered.

"As you can see," the parson interjected, "that leaves us with quite a problem. There were supposed to be some people coming down from the center to collect these medicines. They are five weeks overdue—"

"Nine," Wade corrected mildly.

The parson shot him an irritated glance. "What it all boils down to, Mister Robards, is we have a large portion of our mission space going to medicines that are not ours in the first place."

"I'm afraid they're in trouble," Wade said, his eyes on his shoes.

"Nonsense," the parson snapped. "No doubt they are simply too busy to come down and see to things. Either that or they already have everything they require."

"I've sent three messages up by local transport," Wade persisted softly. "I haven't heard anything back."

The little parson looked ready to boil over. Robards interrupted with "Just how much medicine are we talking about."

It was Wade who answered. "Three tons. About two truckloads. Mostly medicine, but there's a spare generator and equipment for a portable surgery."

"Be that as it may," Reverend Phillips snapped, "what is important is that I simply cannot permit this massive pile of goods intended for someone else to continue to clutter my establishment. You cannot imagine the problems this amount of goods has caused. I have had to spend simply staggering sums for twenty-four-hour guards."

"Speaking of which," Robards interrupted smoothly. "You gentlemen might work out of the goodness of your hearts, but I operate from baser means."

A gleam of hope appeared in the parson's eyes. "Then you will deliver it?"

"If we can work out a suitable arrangement," Robards replied, "I don't see why not."

"We were also left a certain sum intended for the Red Cross center," Reverend Phillips said. "If we continue to wait for these miscreants to arrive, the guards will use it up in a matter of days."

"Months," Wade corrected. "It was a pretty large sum of money."

The parson stifled a rebuke and instead ordered, "Go find the manifest. I am sure our Mister Robards would like to see what we wish for him to carry."

As soon as the door closed behind Wade, Reverend Phillips leaned closer and said, "I want you to take that young man with you."

"Insurance, sure."

The parson showed confusion. "I beg your pardon?"

"As insurance that the goods arrive where they're supposed to," Robards said. "No problem."

"Oh yes. Of course. Of course." The parson gathered himself. "I absolutely must have some peace and quiet around here. You saw the disorder he causes. It is the same, day in and day out. I simply cannot carry out my work under such conditions. Things simply cannot continue as they are."

Wade D. Waters would have never described himself as a missionary. A missionary in his eyes was somebody who knew enough about God, the Bible, and plain simple faith to feel a sense of purpose. Wade was far too honest to consider himself a good Christian. He admitted to his faith publicly only because the Bible said he had to. It wasn't that he was ashamed of God. On the contrary, Wade was fairly certain God was ashamed of him.

Wade's few friends at college had dubbed him CD—Wade D. Waters and CD Lord. The name had been one of many aspects of his former life that Wade had been happy to leave behind when he came to Russia. Another had been his family.

Wade's mother had spent his early years convincing everyone within reach that she was a legend in her own time. Dinner parties were a chance to place Wade on a pedestal and proclaim, see what I raised, the missionary-to-be, no doubt he'll go off somewhere and give his life to the unwashed heathens. She had made monumental scenes at family gatherings over her baby boy's upcoming demise in darkest wherever. Wade had endured it all with quiet resignation and the feeling that he had learned to hold his breath for hours.

His father was a lab technician, a nearsighted, quiet little man who felt distinctly ill at ease with anything that could not be studied through the safe distance of a microscope. He had watched his son grow from embryo to teenager with rising confusion, never interfering with his wife's ideas of child rearing.

In his final year of high school, Wade had emerged twice from his own protective shell of silence. The first time had come after a ringing sermon from a visiting minister, on a Sunday when his mother had been bedridden with the flu, when he had walked forward and given his life to Christ. The second time had been when he had adamantly refused to go to the local university and thus remain at home, opting rather for an upstate Christian college. His mother had stomached this surprising burst of independence only because such an education would prepare her boy for his chosen destiny.

But at college, few of the glories professed by so many of his so-called brothers and sisters in the Lord ever came Wade's way. He never felt an infusion of the Holy Spirit. He never sensed the Word of God light up before him. Throughout his college days, Wade felt as if he was a little gray shadow flitting through a scary gray world. He didn't fit in anywhere. He never felt God's guiding hand. In fact, Wade was basically convinced there was nothing inside him of any real interest to anyone—not to his parents, not other students, and certainly not to God. He looked into other students' shining eyes, heard the fervor and joy in their voices, and decided he just wasn't important enough for God to waste much time over.

Strangely enough, however, he never saw in any of this a reason to doubt God's existence. Nor did he question his own sense of eternal salvation. Wade more or less decided all he had to do was endure the next sixty or seventy years, and then eternity would be as much his as the next guy's. In his darker moments of lonely wishing, it was almost enough.

Pushed by feelings he could not understand, Wade studied public health and minored in French and Spanish. Having nothing better to do, he signed up for optional courses at the local college of nursing. To his surprise, Wade showed a strong aptitude for the work. He loaded up his last two years, and earned dual degrees in public health and nursing. His mother survived the embarrassment of her son becoming a male nurse by declaring that he was doing vital research in the medical field.

Wade proved to have a true gift for working with sick people. He was incredibly patient and infinitely gentle. He took time for the old and the lonely and the frightened. He accepted the most menial of duties without objection and carried them out professionally. When a local hospital gave him a six-month-trial contract, Wade spent more time on the wards than any other nurse and many of the doctors.

But Wade's mother stayed after him constantly to fulfill his destiny, as she put it. Wade remained silent and did nothing. Exasperated beyond speech, she finally mailed off for missionary application papers herself. During one Sunday afternoon visit, she slammed them down in front of him and demanded he complete the forms then and there.

Wade did not mind. He knew the whole thing was an exercise in futility. He had barely passed the college's Bible courses. He had absolutely no aptitude for the ministry. Anybody but his mother would see that immediately, and send him packing. So Wade filled in the papers for peace's sake, and when it came time to select his destination, he checked the most exotic name on the list.

Grozny, capital of The Autonomous Republic of Chechen-Ingush, The Russian Federation.

The review board, however, decided to pay more attention to the nursing director at Wade's hospital than to their own impressions of the young man. The nursing director wrote and then followed the letter up with an unsolicited telephone call. She said that the young man had the power of a true healer. He held hands and people simply felt better. He did the work of ten and did so without complaint. She actually had been forced to send the young man home on several occasions. He would be missed at the hospital, but the nursing director was a Christian and would never stand in the way of someone called to service.

It was only at the airport, on the day of his departure for Europe and final mission training, that his mother-the-soap-opera-star had become just a mom. By then it was too late. The fact that Wade was actually leaving hit her with the force of John Henry's hammer, and she had fallen apart. She had sent him down the departures tunnel with her sobs echoing in his ears.

Wade had never in his life run across anybody like Rogue Robards. Not even close.

Robards was as solid as he was big—a rock-hard man with skin the color of a well-worn saddle. Though he was in his late thirties, the sheer power of the man made the number of his years unimportant. He exuded an unquestionable confidence, a complete reliance in his own ability to overcome whatever rose up before him. His smile came as easy as the sunrise, but contained neither warmth nor friendliness. It was as cold and confident as the gleam that lit the depths of his dark blue eyes.

"What do you make of all that fuss raised over you back there?" Rogue demanded.

Wade shrugged. "I guess it's like Reverend Phillips says, they know I tried to help them."

"You a doctor or something?"

"A nurse."

"Why didn't you get qualified as a doctor if you knew you were gonna come over?"

Wade shrugged. "Maybe I should have."

"Well, there hasn't been a man born who's learned how to backtrack," Robards said easily. "Might as well bury past mistakes and get on with life, right?"

"I guess so," Wade said, marveling at the idea that it could really be as easy as that for somebody. Not for him, of course. Just for anybody.

Wade directed their course along the winding, crumbling streets that skirted the central Muslim market. The city was split distinctly in two, and the Muslim section contained the largest market. The local Chechen tribe, who were Muslim, were also great traders. The Christian area contained all the modern stores, because the Russians living in Grozny had never become comfortable with the lengthy bickering required to make a purchase in the Muslim market. The city's remaining Christians were mostly Ossetians, citizens of the neighboring region who had traveled to Grozny in search of work. They loathed all Muslim hill tribesmen equally and would rather travel the two thousand miles to Moscow than shop in the local Muslim market.

Here in the lowland capital, Russian soldiers massed at street corners and held the city to a grim semblance of order. Armored personnel carriers, their flat metal roofs sprouting machine-gun turrets, guarded major intersections. The key thoroughfares leading to and from the central city were defended by tanks, always in pairs, always with soldiers camped on neighboring verges so that the guns were manned round the clock.

With this show of force, and with more soldiers pouring into the city every day, peace reigned in the lowlands with the deceptive calm of a caged tiger. But at night, startling flashes of orange and yellow and red lit the outlying hills, and manmade thunder rolled down from cloudless, star-flecked skies.

"Hold it a second," Robards said. He halted before a

rickety street stall. The trader, a bearded hill tribesman, wore the traditional black-knit cap with a little top button. The tribesman did not need girth to look imposing. A knife scar slashed down from a mutilated ear to his dark and scraggly beard. An empty bandolier crossed over his shoulder and fell to his waist, hanging with the ease of one long accustomed to its presence.

Robards asked, "You speak the lingo?"

"Some," Wade admitted. "Russian mostly. I only know a few words of the hill dialects."

Robards eyed him anew. "How long did you say you'd been here?"

"A little over a year."

"You study Russian before you came?"

Wade shook his head. "I've been taking lessons here, though. Every day."

The big man nodded his approval. Once. "Well, ask the fellow here if he understands the tongue of his oppressors—or whatever's the right way to go about it."

"He probably speaks it fairly well. Most city traders do."

"Good stuff. Okay, then ask what his tribe is."

"Chechen," Wade answered instantly.

Robards looked down on him. "You gonna let me talk to the man or not?"

"I can tell the tribe from his clothing," Wade explained. "If you ask questions that you should already know the answer to, he'll assume you won't know the proper price to anything and charge you more. He will anyway, since we're foreigners, but this would raise them even higher."

"You know something?" Robards said. "I'm beginning to think that parson of yours is a purebred fool."

Wade covered his embarrassed confusion with a glance at the stall's wares. The splintered boards were covered with a vast array of tools. "Don't you think we should find the trucks before we worry about repairs?"

"You know so much," Robards replied, "maybe you

can tell me whether the Chechen is one of the tribes at war."

"Yes. With the Ossetians and the Ingush. That's why the Russian soldiers are here. The Chechen control a lot of the Caucasus highland south of here, and they are battling with the Ingush, the other hill tribe of that region. Then both the Chechen and the Ingush are fighting with the Ossetians, who are the only Christian tribe in the north Caucasus."

Wade motioned toward the southern mountains rising through the afternoon dust. "Some of the Muslim tribesmen are fighting with the Abkhazi farther to the southwest. A couple of the bigger Chechen warlords have decided to join with the Abkhazian and Svaneti to fight for independence from Georgia."

Robards inspected him frankly. "How do you know all these things?"

Wade shrugged, examined the dust on his boots. "I listen."

"Chechen is Muslim, right?"

"Sunni," Wade agreed. "And one of the most militant tribes."

Robards turned his attention to the stallkeeper. The bearded man had followed the incomprehensible conversation with glittering black eyes. He was accustomed to long and bickering arguments over prices before money exchanged hands, and had the patience of one with nowhere better to go and nothing else to do.

Robards said, "Go ahead and give the gentleman the proper salute."

Wade turned and bobbed his head. "Peace be upon thee and thy family."

"And upon thee, stranger to our lands," the man replied, clearly taken aback by the words coming from the mouth of one so alien. "This is indeed a day of miracles."

"I apologize that I do not speak thy own tongue," Wade continued in Russian, but using the formal tone of the Muslim tribes.

"It is nonetheless an honor to deal with one who has the gift of proper speech," the tribesman replied. "And makes a change from the pestilent soldiers who surround us on all sides."

Robards watched carefully, noted the man's surprise, and knew he had gained an advantage. "Ask him if he's got other goods for sale."

"My friend wishes to know if all thou carest to share with us this day is here on display."

The gleam sparked. "That would depend both upon what is sought and who does the seeking."

"He says, maybe," Wade translated, not understanding the parley at all. "It depends on whether he trusts us or not. What is it you're after?"

"Tell him I'm looking to keep my skin in one piece when we travel into the hills."

"My friend wishes to know if he might acquire safe passage through thy homelands."

The tribesman again showed surprise. "Thou goest into the highlands?"

"If thou and thy peoples might permit us, we would wish it."

"Then make thy peace with Allah," the tribesman replied with no malice to his voice, "for all who enter have great chance of seeing his face. Especially strangers."

"He says we don't have much hope of surviving," Wade said, his pulse racing with fear and something more. There was the scent of adventure here. The touch of the unknown. The drug called danger.

Robards gave an easy shrug, as though expecting nothing more. He reached across the counter, plucked up a dark metal object from among the litter of tools. It was only when he held it up that Wade recognized it as a rifle clip, about fifteen inches long, curved like a saber blade, black and deadly.

"Tell the man that in that case, maybe we ought to buy ourselves a couple of passports."

Wade could not help but glance up at Robards. The

man's face had undergone a sudden transformation, as though a mask had been set aside to reveal a brief glimpse of what lay beneath. The confidence of the man was no longer a calm and resting strength. The power was laid bare.

He found himself slightly breathless as he said, "My friend wishes to ask thee if perhaps articles such as this might assist us with our passage."

The tribesman had also noted the change in Robards. Yet instead of alarm, there was only respect in his eyes. A recognition of something shared, something Wade could not fathom. "A wise man always trusts in Allah and then ties his camels carefully," the tribesman replied.

"Kalashnikov AK-47," Robards said, not waiting for the translation. "Probably the updated AKM version. Extensive usage of plastics and metal stampings to reduce weight. Nice to see you guys are using the latest in weaponry. Fires forty rounds per minute in semiautomatic mode, accurate to four hundred meters. Cyclic rate reducer and compensator, can be fitted with an NSP-2 infrared sight. One of the finest automatic rifles ever made."

The tribesman nodded slightly as Wade translated loosely. "Truly your friend knows quality wares."

"And this," Robards continued, fishing through the tools and coming up with a second, stubbier clip. "Druganov SVD sniper's rifle. Best in the world. Ten-round magazine, fires long 7.62 millimeter rimmed bullets. Muzzle has flash suppressor and recoil compensator for a level second shot. Uses a PSO-1 sight with times-four power. Accurate to twelve hundred yards plus, in the right pair of hands."

"It is indeed as he says," the tribesman said, nodding to the words Wade was able to remember. "Of course, such items are outlawed in these quarters. The pestilent Russian invaders have orders to shoot an armed man on sight unless he is a licensed private guard and on private grounds."

"Tell him we'd be happy to take delivery after dark."

"The veil of night covers many transactions," the tribesman agreed when Wade was finished. "Would it be possible to ask what takes thee along such an uncertain course?"

"We seek to deliver medicines to a clinic in the hills," Wade explained.

The dark eyes turned blank. "One whose flag has a cross of blood upon a white surface?"

"Red Cross, yes," Wade said, his pulse surging. "Thou hast seen them?"

"I have heard only," the tribesman replied, his tone a blank wall.

"We are concerned for their safety," Wade pressed. "It has been too long since we had word from them."

"Of such things I know nothing," the tribesman replied. "I am a simple trader only."

Wade turned to Robards and said disconsolately, "I think something's happened at the clinic."

"He tell you that?"

Wade shook his head. "He just refused to talk about it, like he knows something but doesn't want to say."

"Well, maybe you're right," Robards answered, not concerned by the prospect. "But worrying about it now won't solve a thing. That news just makes it more important to get started." He focused once more on the tribesman. "Tell him we'll be back in touch about the goods."

The tribesman saw them off with the three-pointed hand signal of the devout—first to heart, then lips, then forehead. When they had rejoined the crowds jostling good-naturedly down the rutted way, Wade asked Robards, "How can you trust him?"

"Only way you can trust anybody once you've left civilization behind," Robards replied, moving forward with deceptive speed. "By sleeping with one eye open and not ever trusting anybody completely. Come on, let's go take a look at those trucks."

2

THE STORM RAGED SO HARD the night of her meeting with the infamous Colonel Mendez that Allison could feel the entire United States Consulate building shake on its foundations. But she had no time to worry about her own safety. Papers representing a dozen different crises were spread across her desk, all screaming a silent warning of the coup that was about to happen.

Lightning blasted outside her window, illuminating the stark and frightened features of her two assistants. They stood helplessly, waiting for her to make her decisions and order them into action. But she could not focus. There was too much going on.

The phone rang. She picked it up. It was her boss. Or her father. She could not be sure. "There's been a cable from Washington," he reported. "Your budget has just been cut by fifty percent. And your mother wants to know why you haven't called her in almost a month."

Allison struggled to keep her voice calm. She knew that it was important to remain calm in such circumstances. The examiners were always watching for the applicants who broke under pressure. "But I have a government to prop up here."

"You'll think of something," her boss replied and hung up. "And call your mother."

As she hung up the receiver, another lightning blast

split the night, illuminating scores of dark-clad men scurrying under the trees beyond the consulate compound. They were all headed her way. They carried weapons.

"What do you want us to do," her number one assistant whispered, fighting back panic.

"I want us to all stay calm," Allison replied. Stay calm above all else, they had told her.

Her secretary chose that moment to burst into the room. "My typewriter," she squalled. "My typewriter has broken down again!"

With a horrendous groan, a corner of the roof was lifted by the wind. A massive tree limb crashed through the window. Wind and rain whirled a maelstrom of paper around what before had been her office.

"I have all those orders to type," the secretary wailed, "and now it's broken, and you told me I would have a new one, and now it's too late! Too late! Too late!"

Allison was just going to tell her that it couldn't be right, it wasn't too late, she still had another twenty minutes before the exam ended, when she realized that the secretary's chant had changed: "Raggedy Ann, can't keep a man.... Raggedy Ann, can't keep a man."

Then the intercom on her desk suddenly crackled to life and announced, "Ladies and gentlemen, we have now begun our descent into London's Heathrow Airport. We ask that you now return to your seats, extinguish all cigarettes, bring your seat backs to an upright position, and make sure that your seat belts are securely fastened."

Allison opened her eyes and smiled away the last bits of her dream. It was a familiar pattern, one she replayed at least a couple of times a month. Four years since she had passed the Foreign Service Exam and entered the Commerce Department, and still she had nightmares over the high-pressure crisis control test.

She watched as the plane swept through the cloud covering and London appeared beneath them. It could have been worse, she reflected. At least this time the dream was over before she got to the part where she looked down and realized she wore no clothes.

To her everlasting delight, there was a uniformed chauffeur holding up a sign for her as she exited the Customs hall. Allison walked toward him, very glad she had stopped long enough to repair her makeup. She felt as though every eye in the building was upon her.

"I am Allison Taylor," she said.

One gray-gloved hand rose to touch the bill of his cap. "Good morning, ma'am. I am Jules, Mister Price's driver. May I help you with your luggage?"

"Thank you." She let the chauffeur lead her around clusters of foggy-eyed tour groups who whispered among themselves as they tried to figure out if they recognized her. They walked down the passage toward the parking garage, then detoured by a guarded barrier and entered a signposted VIP lot. This is just too cool, Allison decided silently.

"Mister Price has made a reservation for you at quite a nice establishment on the outskirts of Oxford," Jules reported, once they were under way in a royal blue Daimler. "But I suppose you have already been informed of these arrangements."

"I wasn't told anything," Allison replied. "Everything was so rushed." There had been a mere forty-eight hours between notification and departure. Not that she was complaining. The offer of a three-month assignment in Europe had come at the perfect moment, as both her personal and her professional lives were in a major slump. "I just hoped somebody would see to things on this end."

"Indeed he has, miss. Mister Price has given his personal attention to your needs."

Allison tried to recall what she could of her father's old friend. Cyril Price held some important post with the British government, but exactly what she did not know. When she was younger, he had been chargé d'affaires at the British Embassy in Washington, D.C. Since his departure from that post, his visits had been infrequent and had consisted mostly of being closeted away with her father for long and serious discussions. Still, whenever his attention turned her way, Cyril Price had always displayed great charm and a genuine affection.

Despite her best efforts, her eyelids refused to remain open. Scarcely did it seem that she had settled into the Daimler's luxurious backseat before she was being jolted awake. The car scrunched down a graveled path and halted before a vast ivy-covered manor house. Allison rubbed the sleep from her eyes, took in the diamond-shaped lead-paned windows, the dual turrets, and the liveried butler hurrying toward them. Her smile returned.

Once Allison had been bowed through the registration process and shown upstairs, the chauffeur busied himself at the telephone while Allison admired her two-room suite. "Miss Taylor?" The chauffeur offered a telephone. "Mister Price is on the line."

Allison accepted the receiver. "Cyril?"

"Hello, my dear Allison." The familiar upper-crust voice brought back a flood of memories. "I am terribly sorry not to have been able to greet you myself, but something rather unexpected came up this morning."

"Your driver has taken the very best care of me."

"Splendid. I do hope the accommodations are up to your standards."

Allison glanced around the palatial suite, and replied, "It's almost enough for me to forgive you for forcing me to come."

"Not force. Please. Nothing so drastic as that."

"I don't know what else to call it. My own boss hears from her boss's boss that I'm ordered to drop everything and fly to England for a conference with you."

"Call it the application of appropriate pressure," he replied smoothly. "Unfortunately I could not spare the time for lengthy and roundabout requests."

"So what is this all about?" Allison gave a little wave

as the driver tipped his hat and bowed himself from the room.

"Perhaps it would be advisable for you to take a rest just now," he countered. "I shall join you in three hours, if that is suitable. We shall then discuss all matters great and small over dinner. Is that acceptable? Splendid. Until then, my dear."

The dining chambers were straight from the tales of King Arthur—forty-foot ceilings, Cotswold stone walls, medieval tapestries, paintings of grim-faced royals, vast chandeliers, candles everywhere. Allison felt like a little girl playing grown-up as she sat across from Cyril and listened to him discuss their orders with three hovering waiters. Three.

Allison caught a glimpse of herself in a mirror hanging upon the opposite wall. She was tall and slender and crowned with abundant red curls. She had worked hard over the years to make the most of her beauty. It was the only way she knew of masking how she felt.

In her younger days, tall and slim had meant skinny and gawky. She had been called Raggedy Ann for years, until braces had earned her the label Metal Mouth. Allison had learned not to smile. She had learned to bend her legs and crouch slightly when standing in line, so she would not be taller than everybody else, including the boys. She had learned not to lie out in the summer, since fifteen minutes even with sunblock was enough to turn her lobster-red. She had learned not to pay her hair any attention at all. She had learned to retreat into her books, staying at the top of every class. She had learned to keep her loneliness hidden deep.

Allison smiled nowadays with ease, a beautiful even-toothed smile. Fair skin was suddenly fashionable. Women singed their hair with chemicals in a vain attempt to copy her curls. Lean and rangy figures were in.

Nowadays, her friends spoke of Allison's ideal beauty. Allison learned ways to divert the attention, laugh it off, turn the compliment into something intended for someone else.

For when Allison Taylor looked into the mirror, her heart still told her she was seeing Raggedy Ann. She was precocious, intelligent, able, eloquent. But on the social side, Allison Taylor walked with two left feet.

"I think a claret would be best with the duck," Cyril had decided. "Would that be acceptable, my dear?"

"Perfect." Allison glanced about the room, immensely glad she had decided to bring her only formal dress.

Once the serving entourage had departed, he said, "Tell me what you've been doing with yourself all these years."

"You probably know more about that than I do."

"Nonsense." Cyril was a tall, slender man whose glossy silver mane and perfectly tailored dinner jacket gave him a sleek, aristocratic elegance. He carried his polish with that astonishing ability of the English upper class to be courtly without the slightest hint of effeminacy. His jaw was cleft as with a hatchet. His immaculately manicured hands suggested a steely strength. "I would find it most fascinating to hear your perspective."

"Nothing could be more boring, I promise you."

"Try me. Please."

"I assume you've heard that I work with the Office of Export Administration. Talk about a snooze."

"On the contrary, I am positively riveted."

She smiled at a sudden memory. "Pop always did say you could charm the pants off the Prime Minister."

"What a horrid thought. I'm quite sure he said no such thing. Do go on."

"I was actually supposed to be somewhere else, but the export people were tremendously understaffed. Commerce assigned me there 'temporarily.' "

"I see. And that was . . ."

"Three and a half extremely long years ago."

"Once they realized just how good you were at your job," Cyril interpreted, "they insisted on keeping you."

"There are statutory deadlines for when they have to act on all export license applications," Allison went on, "but the deadline is suspended if Commerce requests more information. So just when the deadline arrived, they began sending out letters asking the manufacturer for more data—maybe something that had already been sent, most likely something they didn't really need in order to make a decision. That gave them a chance to extend the time limit. By the time I arrived, it was a racket, with some companies waiting six months or longer for a permit that should have been completed in a couple of weeks."

"I would imagine the companies did not take this sitting down."

"Not on your life." Allison paused as the wine waiter presented the bottle to Cyril. While the wine was being opened, tasted, and poured, their duck arrived. Each plate was carried by a different waiter—two for the duck, two for the side plates of lightly steamed vegetables. The main ones were set into place and the silver covers raised in unison to reveal thinly sliced fowl in a rich Madeira sauce.

"If this is the way I'm going to be treated for the next three months, I may never go home."

Cyril hid a smile behind a polite dabbing of his moustache, then lifted his glass and said, "To the success of our mission. Thank you so much for joining me."

She clinked glasses, sipped, smiled approvingly, then asked, "Just what is our 'mission,' anyway?"

"Be so good as to indulge me and continue your story, would you? I assure you that all your questions will be answered in due course." He picked up his knife and fork, said, "Bon appetit, my dear."

She took a bite, declared, "Delicious."

"I'm so glad you approve. Now you were saying about the business community's rising tide of discontent."

"A few months before I was brought in," Allison continued, "the President started his massive export push. Companies responded with an uproar over how long it was taking for their export licenses. Talk grew of bringing in an outside GAO team to do a full audit. Alarm bells went off all through the department. Suddenly there was this huge clamor for more speed, more personnel, better service."

"So what do you do," Cyril said, picking up the thread, "within six months of your arrival, no less, is to devise a computerized interagency tracking system—"

"How did you hear about that?"

"—whereby any would-be exporter could call in and find out exactly where his application is in the process, what else would be required, and when his approval might be expected. A system, I might add, which proved so successful that you were then seconded to three other agencies to adapt the same system to their needs. All the while you were still held on to tightly by the Export Administration, who by this time had awakened to the fact that they had stumbled upon a real prize."

Allison did not contradict him. "So how did you pry me loose?"

"By appealing to a higher authority," he replied. "Much higher, as a matter of fact."

"But why?"

"Because your country and my own," Cyril replied, "require the services of an intelligent, resourceful, courageous young woman."

She gave him a look developed during years of sorting through Washington baloney. "And just what special ability am I supposed to have that no one else does?"

"Please do continue with your meal, my dear."

"I'm waiting for an answer."

"Before I can clarify that point," Cyril answered, "I must supply a few details which I assure you will not mix well with your dinner."

Allison set down her utensils. "I've finished."

"Very well." Cyril signaled for the waiter to clear the table. "The situation, as you Americans would say, is beyond critical."

He fiddled with his glass until the waiters had departed. He then leaned across the table and said quietly, "At present, there are only nine countries who publicly acknowledge having nuclear weapons: they are Great Britain, France, Russia, Ukraine, Belarus, Kazakhstan, Uzbekistan, China, and the United States. South Africa recently claimed to have developed four nuclear bombs, then dismantled all of them. Three other nations are widely believed to possess such bombs—Israel, India, and Pakistan."

His words struck hard. "Nuclear weapons?"

"Now there are another eight countries actively seeking to acquire nuclear weapons through the new international black market," Cyril continued unabated. "They are Brazil, Argentina, North Korea, Iraq, Iran, Egypt, Syria, and Libya. One great concern within the Arab nations is that the rising tide of Islamic fundamentalism may fasten upon these weapons as the ultimate terrorist weapon."

Allison protested, "What on earth do I have to do with nuclear weapons?"

"Bear with me," he replied crisply. "I will get to that soon enough. Iraq was most willing to use chemical weapons on its own people. Syria bombed a village suspected of harboring radical fundamentalists, massacring thousands of innocent Syrian women and children. Iran has sacrificed millions of its own children on the altar of war. If such countries are so careless with the lives of their own citizens, what concern could they be expected to show for others outside their own borders?"

"None," she murmured, so confused she found it hard to pay attention. Nuclear weapons.

"Three bombs the size of Hiroshima's would be sufficient to destroy two thirds of Israel's entire population. Or imagine a holiday launch boating up the Thames, docking just opposite Westminster, and igniting a small warhead. Think of what such a bomb and the resulting fallout would do to Manhattan, or Washington, or San Francisco." His gaze was bleak. "Terrorists would be able to threaten any of our coastal cities with annihilation."

"I thought the whole reason behind the UN inspectors in Iraq was to make sure they don't have the capability to build bombs."

"It was. Still is, I suppose. But for some time we have had unconfirmed evidence." Cyril then permitted himself a small smile. "As you are new to the game, my dear, I shall interpret that for you."

"Some game," Allison said softly.

"Yes, well, better than other names I might use. In any case, what we call unconfirmed evidence normally resides somewhere between bizarre gossip and a bald-faced lie. But this time we have been able to substantiate at least some of the rumors. As of three nights ago, to be precise, our agents obtained the most concrete evidence possible. They witnessed the delivery of materials smuggled out of the Ukraine to buyers in Munich. The only thing that has saved us thus far is the incompetence of the people involved."

"At least," she amended, "of those you caught."

"Well, there you are. For the moment, you and I are concerned with the independent entrepreneurs seeking to make a killing, if you will forgive me for making such a poor pun. Other, more concentrated resourses are being put to bear upon the established governments and their minions."

Cyril studied the depths of his glass. "It is all so unprecedented, you see. The Soviet Union's dismantling itself in the space of just ten months. The largest spy network on earth becoming such a laughingstock they couldn't manage to find their own toes with their shoes off. Terrorists the world over presented with offers to buy fissionable material as though ordering from Harrod's."

"Who in their right mind would ever have imagined it?" she agreed.

"Precisely. If two years ago one of my own men had suggested such a state of affairs, I would have sacked him on the spot."

"I still don't see where I—"

"Permit me to continue at my own pace," Cyril interrupted. "There is now evidence that a second route has opened. Perhaps not for fissionable materials, but rather for engineers. You see, just as worrisome to us as the transport of material is the transport of people."

"Know-how," she interpreted. "Transfer of brain power."

"Quite so. In 1992 the West received its first confirmed reports that Iran and Iraq were offering jobs to Soviet nuclear scientists."

"With higher pay than what they'd earn back home."

"A skilled technician," Cyril confirmed, "working in one of the ten sealed cities where the Soviets did their nuclear testing, currently earns one thousand rubles per week. At today's exchange rates, that works out at less than fifteen dollars a month. A trained nuclear scientist earns at the very outside ten thousand rubles, or about thirty dollars, per month."

"Versus how much, maybe ten thousand dollars a month in Iraq?" Allison shook her head. "Hard to pass up."

"Russia is doing what it can to stem the tide," Cyril continued. "Travel for even the lowest-level technician is highly restricted, despite the fact that passports are now freely offered to the rest of the Russian population. The United States has joined with Western Europe in offering Russia sixty million dollars to build a new institute for nonmilitary nuclear research. But it will prove to be too little, too late, I fear. It will take years before the institute is built and staffed, while the emergency is *now.*"

"So there is one route for people," Allison said, her interest piqued despite herself, "and another for bombs."

"Fissionable material, my dear; please call it by its proper name. Nobody in their right mind would dream of carting a nuclear warhead over such terrain."

"To be honest, I'm not sure how people in their right minds allowed such a situation to develop in the first place."

"Yes, well, water under the dam and all that." With one finger Cyril began tracing a map-line down along the tablecloth. "On the opposite side of the Caspian Sea from Turkmenistan lies an extremely volatile region shared by the Ukraine, Georgia, Azerbaijan, and Armenia. It appears that the Chechen-Ingush region of southern Russia is now being used as a jumping-off place for this modern-day traffic in people. The product is taken overland through the high passes of the Caucasus Mountains and down into Tbilisi, which is the capital of Georgia."

"Product," she repeated. "It sounds inhuman."

"Not so inhuman, I would imagine, as calling them the creators of atom bombs. Or the perpetrators of mass destruction."

"Where is it all headed?"

"Again we have only rumors to go on," Cyril replied. "But an increasing amount of evidence suggests that an international smuggling ring, dealing in both fissionable material and nuclear engineers, is operating in Jordan. Jordan is an ally of Iraq, yet at the same time it remains a friend to the West. Quite a feat of political juggling, as you can imagine. Iraq is prohibited by UN sanctions from using its aircraft or from letting foreign flights in or out of the country. Yet Jordan, which borders Iraq, remains open to the outside world. Once the product is there, then, further overland transport would be quite feasible."

Cyril watched Allison carefully and added, "This group is purported to be located in Aqaba, to be precise."

Allison straightened as yet another flood of memories surfaced. "Aqaba! Isn't that where—"

"Exactly," Cyril interjected. "Ben Shannon has kindly

agreed to allow us to place someone within his compound. Unfortunately, we made the error of initially assigning him an agent from our embassy in Amman. Let us simply say that they did not get along. He has now taken the liberty of telling us whom he will work with." The stare intensified. "He is willing to work with us only if you will go in as our agent in the field."

3

LOADING THE TRUCKS proved to be a dangerous affair, especially after Rogue ignored the guards' warning.

They had taken their purchases back to the mission compound later that morning, with Robards driving one canvas-topped truck and Wade the other. The trucks were a pair of discarded army-issue troop carriers, noisy and cantankerous as old camels and much less comfortable. Wade's seat was covered with a thin strip of padding that had long since been mashed into something resembling plastic-covered concrete. The steering wheel was a giant affair that bucked and trembled and demanded a steel grip. The gears were spaced three feet apart and ground out a wailing protest at each change. Both trucks stood high and top-heavy on bald tires and bad shocks. The windshields were cracked, the paint blistered, the bodies badly rusted. The trucks shook and rocked and creaked and chugged noisily, even when standing still.

Wade could hardly wait to start their journey.

The seven men guarding the compound were from the town's Christian population, members of the Ossetian tribe. They were slightly fairer in complexion and lighter of eye than the Chechen, yet displayed the suspicious squint of the southern folk, and the same hostility toward all but those fully accepted by the clan.

The pair on gate duty barred the way with rifles raised

until they spotted Wade, then opened the portals and allowed them through. As Wade stepped from the cab, there was a moment of solemn greetings quietly given, a series of nods and respectful words that raised Robards' eyebrows. Wade answered with his customary embarrassed hesitation.

Yet as soon as Wade and Robards made preparations to load the wares, the atmosphere turned ugly. Murmurs became angry protests as Robards slid down the loading ramp and fastened the hinges into place. When he helped Wade do the same for the second truck, the volume rose to dangerous levels.

"What on earth is going on here," the parson demanded. He scuttled over from the parish office, his cassock raising fitful dust clouds. "Oh, it's you. Back already?"

"No reason not to go ahead and get the job done," Robards said easily, dusting his hands on the sides of his trousers and paying the angry guards no mind. "Who's got the warehouse keys?"

"It's the schoolhouse, actually," Reverend Phillips said, distracted by all the angry shouts and arm waving. "Wade has the keys. What on earth are those guards saying? I can't make it out when they talk among themselves."

Wade selected his words with delicacy. "They don't like to see the medicines moved."

"Stands to reason," Robards said, giving the sky overhead a careful inspection. "They're not going to be overjoyed to hear their jobs just took a hike."

"But I explicitly told them when they were hired that the work was temporary," the parson said petulantly.

"Hearing is one thing and letting go another," Robards said, and pointed at the northern horizon. "I'm not too pleased with the look of those."

Reverend Phillips squinted, searched the heavens, said, "I'm sure I don't know what you're speaking of."

Robards dropped his gaze and inspected the guards

who were quieting somewhat under his studied calm. Then he pointed toward a gray-bearded elder who stood by the back wall and watched the proceedings with lively eyes. "That the head honcho over there?"

"He's sort of in charge of the day crew," Wade replied. "At least the others seem to listen when he speaks. His name is Mikhail."

"Ask him what those clouds mean."

Wade did so. The elder neither looked upward nor turned away. He replied with one croaked word, which Wade translated as "snow."

"How long?" Robards demanded.

There was another exchange, then, "Four, maybe five days."

Robards nodded his thanks toward the old man, then asked, "When were they last paid?"

The parson protested, "I really don't see—"

"End of last week," Wade replied.

"Tell them anybody who gets in the way won't be paid for this week," Robards commanded. "But if they'll help us load the trucks, each will receive a two-week bonus, cash, when we pull out of here. Tell them our destination is the highlands and we're racing the clouds."

The news of a bonus satisfied all but one burly man with bad teeth and a wandering eye. He gestured threateningly with his rifle, stationing himself between the trucks and the schoolhouse.

Reverend Phillips said worriedly, "Perhaps it would be best if we went inside and discussed this a bit longer."

"That's a great idea," Robards agreed, his eyes on the man blocking his way. "You go right ahead, Reverend. We'll be along directly."

The parson took a step, realized no one was following his lead, hesitated, and stopped.

The courtyard grew very still. Robards stared at the truculent man, and for a second time Wade saw the casual veneer stripped away. So did the man, and for a moment his resolve weakened. He cursed the other guards for leaving him isolated. Then he swung his rifle around to the ready.

Robards held out a hand toward Wade without taking his eyes off the resistant guard. "Give me the keys," he said quietly.

The keys danced slightly in Wade's trembling hand, sounding like little bells in the suddenly still air.

The guard's gaze slid away from Robards at the sound, a glance lasting less than half a heartbeat, but it was all Robards needed. He moved so fast that his actions melted into one continuous flow. Suddenly he was standing with the rifle in his hands, and the guard was lying unconscious at his feet.

The elder laughed a creaking bark and clapped his hands at the feat. Robards tossed him the rifle, which he caught one-handed, as though expecting it all along. Robards said, "Tell the old man he's welcome to join us if a guide's pay would interest him."

"Truly I could find the passes in fog or blinding snow," the tribesman replied smoothly, and swept a hand out to include all his clansmen. "Alas, I must see to the well-being of those who rely upon me for bread and hearth."

"He's just upping the price," Robards said when Wade had translated. "Tell him we've got to get these trucks loaded. Then we'll get down to brass tacks." He pointed to the clouds gathering among the high peaks and said, "His first duty is to make all these guys understand that we're racing the wind."

They left in the late afternoon, less than two hours after the trucks were loaded.

Once the loading had begun, Robards had settled himself on one of the trucks and directed traffic, sending his chosen band out on a score of errands and in the process firmly establishing himself as leader. Mikhail had been persuaded to join them as guide. The other guards had been paid off and sent packing, with Mikhail standing next to Robards to back him up. The taxi driver, Anatoly, was summoned and then dispatched again—first to collect Robards' belongings from the hotel and then to purchase food. Wade was sent to set up a rendezvous with the Chechen trader, then to buy maps, and finally to purchase a money belt for all the remaining dollars.

The parson was loathe to see the Red Cross funds drive off into the hazy distance with a total unknown, but Robards was insistent. If there was trouble, he explained, either for themselves or the ones they were being sent to supply, their only hope of escape might well be a ready fund of *valuta*, or folding money. Wade ended the hand-wringing argument by simply walking away from it and going to do as Robards had instructed.

The caravan passed the blockhouse apartments ringing Grozny just as the sun touched the horizon. As promised, the Chechen trader was waiting for them in an outcrop of trees beyond the only petrol station on that side of the city. While Anatoly and Mikhail took the trucks and waited in line for fuel, Wade acted as translator for Robards and the trader.

They were still at it when the trucks returned with both the tanks and the string of canisters tied along the canvas sides brimming. The Chechen trader watched with narrowed eyes as the Russian taxi driver and Ossetian elder appeared through the gathering gloom.

"Ask our Chechen friend if he's willing to come along as one of our guides," Robards instructed as he stacked the purchased weapons and clips and waxed bullets.

His eyes still on the new arrivals, the Chechen replied, "Alas, I am unable to depart from my responsibilities, much as I regret the need to decline such an invitation."

Robards accepted the news with the barest of nods. His voice purposefully casual, he asked Wade, "You think this is a ploy to up the price?"

"He sounds pretty definite," Wade replied. "And he doesn't appear to like the looks of our companions. The

Russians are fighting a couple of skirmishes with the Chechen tribes right now, and the Ossetians are seen as usurpers on their ancient homeland. Not to mention the fact that they're Christian."

"Then ask him which in his opinion is the best road for us to take from here to the passes," Rogue said, motioning for Mikhail and Anatoly to carry the purchased arms back to the trucks.

"The Georgian Military Highway begins in Vladikavkaz, the Ossetian capital to the southwest," the trader replied, waving casually toward the night. "The Russian soldiers and the Ingush are fighting there, and the city is no longer a haven of safety for strangers. However, this very road skirts the city and joins with the highway farther south, before the mountains begin."

When Wade had finished translating, Robards gave the trader a friendly nod. "Tell him we're really grateful for the advice, which we'd be foolish not to take. Ask him if we were to drive all night, how far we could get."

"Truly," the Chechen replied, his dark eyes gleaming in the trucks' headlights. "All such undertakings are in the hands of Allah, especially in such troubled times. But if thy way remains safe, then thou shouldst arrive upon the highway with its guards of Russian soldiers before the sun rises yet again."

"Then we'd better get started," Robards said with great cheer, shaking hands and waving the Chechen off with jolly fanfare before climbing into the truck. Under his directions, Wade drove with Anatoly while Robards took the lead position with the elder Mikhail alongside. As they started down the road he hooted his horn and waved and shouted another round of thanks to the silent Chechen.

Once around the second bend, however, he pulled off and stopped. Wade walked up to the lead truck, climbed onto the running board and grabbed hold of the mirror mounting. Through the open window Robards said, "Ask Mikhail here if we can trust the Chechen's advice."

"We can trust him to greet us a second time just as soon as we are far enough removed from Grozny to escape the Russian's surveillance," the old man replied, his voice creaking with vehemence. "We can trust him to bring along a vast number of his Chechen thieves, for they are cowards and lower than the dust beneath our feet and will do nothing unless they outnumber honest men by a hundred to one. Then we can trust them to steal everything we carry, and cut our throats and leave our offspring to mourn us in poverty."

"Sounds about right to me," Robards declared. "Ask him if there is a pass to the east of here."

"There are only a few other passes below the level of the eternal snows in all of the great Caucasus range," he replied firmly, "and they are very distant. There you will find wars as well, and without Russian soldiers to grant a shred of order."

"Then we'll just have to circle around and hope the weather holds," Robards replied. "Ask him what lies directly east of here."

"The territory of the Ingush," the Ossetian elder replied, "who are as treacherous and cowardly as the cursed Chechen, if not more so. But they at least will not be expecting our passage." He pointed ahead. "There is a turnoff to the left coming soon."

"That's it, then," Robards said, grinding the gears. "Let's make tracks."

"Wait!" A voice called out from behind Wade. Anatoly appeared from the shadows. "I have been thinking."

"A dangerous occupation," Robards replied easily, as though expecting no less.

Anatoly hesitated, then confessed, "I see danger on all sides."

"Except within the safety of the known," Robards added.

"It would appear to be the wiser course for a man of responsibilities." He motioned vaguely at the second truck. "I am unused to traveling with weapons at my feet.

The thought of having to fire them fills me with dread."

"You will excuse us if we keep our farewells to a minimum," Robards said. "Wade, pay the man."

"I shall guard your destination with my life," Anatoly promised.

"Let's hope it doesn't come to that," Robards said, watching Wade peel bills from his money belt. "But if anyone asks, it'd be great if you had a lapse of memory."

"North," Anatoly promised, pocketing the money. "I will say you had a change of heart and headed for the Crimea."

"Guard your own steps home," Robards warned. "The forests are full of brigands."

"And the steppes a haven for wolves who walk on two legs," Anatoly replied. "I shall await the dawn at the petrol station." He lifted his hand. "You are indeed a singular man, Rogue Robards."

They watched as Anatoly vanished into the darkness. When he was gone, Robards said, "Time to be heading out."

"Mikhail says the road up ahead ought to be safe," Wade said.

"Hope he's right," Robards replied. "Nothing on this map but a great big blank. Reminds me of those ocean charts from a couple hundred years ago. Get away from civilization and they start drawing in dragons and sea monsters."

Wade asked, "How much farther do you expect to take us out of our way?"

Robards restarted his engine, let it roar long and hard, then replied, "Far enough to keep us alive."

4

"IT'S TOO MUCH," Allison murmured as they passed through another timeless university courtyard. "There's no way I can learn everything."

"Of course not," Cyril soothed. "No one expects you to, my dear. What we wish to do is merely introduce you to the topics and terms."

The day had proved to be long and draining. Cyril had accompanied her to Oxford, where he had introduced her to one expert after another. By midafternoon her eyelids weighed ten pounds each, and the voices had begun taking on the consistency of strawberry jam.

Cyril examined her weary features and announced, "I believe we should declare that lecture our last."

"I'm fine, really," she protested feebly.

He shook his head. "Nonsense. You are still fatigued from your trip. Besides, even I find some of these experts to be as interesting as watching snow melt."

At Cyril's direction, Jules brought the car around, and Allison sank back with a sigh of relief. As Jules guided them smoothly through the snarled traffic, she said, "I've never felt so ignorant in my entire life."

"Perfectly understandable, given the circumstances." Cyril switched on the car's reading light. "You will no doubt be delighted to hear that there remains only one more item for us to discuss today."

Allison struggled to clear her mind of the fog of fatigue. "Let's have it then."

"If the smuggled items are what we might call traditional fissionable material," Cyril Price replied, "nothing would be visible but a metal case, and that would most likely be disguised. We will outfit you with an instrument which will give you radioactive readings. But there is also one particular canister for which you should remain on the lookout."

He slid his red-leather Dunhill briefcase onto his knees, snapped open the gold-plated locks, and handed over a folder. "Mind you, this is only a best guess. It could come in a variety of forms."

Allison opened the folder and inspected a black-and-white photograph of a metal canister set beside a simple measuring stick. The canister was thirty inches high and bore two metal plates upon its painted surface, one in Cyrillic and the other in English. She read the top English words as a question, "Red mercury?"

"We have reason to believe," Cyril explained, "that the material may be used to create compact atomic bombs."

"You're not sure?"

"Some scientists are absolutely certain, yes. Others, well, let us say that at present we are having difficulty determining who is seeking to protect a reputation and who really believes that red mercury is a harmless hoax."

She leaned back in her seat. As the car left the spires of Oxford behind, Allison felt a deep familiar ache. How much this day would have meant to her dad. If only, she reflected sadly, he could have lived long enough to be a part of this with her. As the veil of fatigue rose once again, she found herself recalling another evening, one where Ben Shannon and Cyril Price had gathered with her father. It was the evening when Allison had come to realize that her father was more than the gentle, pipe-smoking professor. That John Taylor had a past filled with mystery upon mystery.

"Experts at your Los Alamos National Laboratory

have categorically stated that red mercury does not even exist," Cyril went on. "The samples they tested supposedly contained mercuric oxide with a radioactive level a thousand times below what is required for weapons. Your nation's secret service agencies have based their official policy upon this statement. They say that without the slightest doubt the story was concocted by arms dealers intent on making an easy killing. It is, they claim, nothing more than a nuclear scam. There are, however, Western scientists who disagree. A growing number, I might add."

Allison Taylor had positively adored her father. She had been born long after her parents had given up hope of ever having children. From the very beginning, Allison had been her daddy's girl. Her father had been an analyst for a Washington think tank, and had taught international economics at Georgetown. Allison had decided she was going to be an analyst soon after she learned to say the word. Analysts had lots of interesting friends who dropped by day and night. They came from all over the world, and they sat and listened while Allison's father talked in the same soft patient voice he used to answer her own questions.

"Western technology has concentrated upon manufacturing bombs from enriched uranium and plutonium," Cyril began. "In such a weapon, explosives such as TNT are ignited to create what is known as an implosive force. This crushes the inner ball of radioactive material, creating an unstable critical mass. At that very instant, an electronic gun fires a burst of high-energy neutrons into the plutonium. This in turn creates the atomic explosion."

Allison was seven when she learned of her father's mysterious past. She had discovered that if she hid in the tiny crawl-space behind his filing cabinets, he would sometimes forget that she was there. That afternoon, Cyril Price had come to visit and found her father seated in the study with Ben. Cyril had brought with him a problem so serious that it had creased her father's face in unnaturally severe lines. For several months after, she had suffered nightmares which began with the words Yom Kippur War. Allison had not understood much of what was said that day, but her young mind discerned that Ben and Cyril placed great weight on what they called his experience in the field.

"The complexity of this process has been the West's saving grace in limiting nuclear proliferation, far more than any oversight committee. But a growing body of evidence suggests that red mercury operates on an entirely different principle. It is safely transportable as a powder, but can be altered to liquid form by a combination of pressure and radiation. When this conversion takes place, the resulting substance contains explosive properties all its own. This does away with the need for the complex trigger mechanism of Western bombs. It also can have a tremendously magnified result when combined with other elements, called actenides, which are strong neutron transmitters. These actenides are quite easily obtained."

There had never been any question of what Allison would study at college or what she wished to do with her life. She had yearned for the days when the two professors, father and daughter, would stroll across campus, caught up in their glorious shared world of thoughts and dreams and ideas.

Cyril tapped a worried beat against the side of his briefcase. "The Russians are quite open in their declarations that we now face an enormous danger of widespread nuclear proliferation. According to them, Alkor Technologies of Saint Petersburg developed the technology. Promecology of Moscow and Ekaterinburg has been made the official international sales group. But recent estimates indicate that less than one third of current production is being disposed of through legal channels."

Allison had reveled in college life, reinventing herself with people with no memory of her Orphan Annie days.

But once a month she had eagerly returned to the easy routine of home. Her mother had stuffed her like the Christmas goose and asked about young men, questions Allison had always avoided. Her father had taken her for long rambling walks in winter-clad forests; she had returned with her cheeks burning and her ears numb and her mind filled to overflowing.

Deftly Cyril slid out the bottom document from the folder she held. "This is the single piece of evidence from Western research. A scientific paper published by Du Pont in 1968, simply stating that a new compound had been synthesized, $Hg_2Sb_2O_7$, better known today as red mercury. It was duly registered as number 20720-76-7. No document was included to explain what the compound did, which is most peculiar. However, Du Pont is one of the key manufacturers of compounds within the US nuclear weapons industry." Cyril let the paper drop in exasperation. "We have been through channels both official and unofficial and gotten absolutely nowhere. It appears that the people responsible have all departed for parts unknown and all records have been lost. They do not even show records of having registered the compound in the first place."

And then her father had dropped dead of a heart attack three days after her final examinations. As soon as Allison had heard her mother's broken voice, she had known. Even before the words were spoken, she had known. The dream of sharing her father's world had been shattered just as it had approached her grasp.

Allison sighed shakily, filled with the ache of wishing for the impossible.

"My dear, is everything all right?"

"I think maybe I've gotten a little too tired."

"Of course you have, and just listen to me prattle on." Cyril plucked the folder from her hands and closed his briefcase. "All of this can very easily wait until tomorrow."

She pushed away the hurt and said, "It will be nice to

see Ben again. Pop thought the world of him."

"They met in college, I believe," Cyril offered.

"My father always spoke of him with awe," Allison said. "One of the most brilliant minds of their generation, that's what Pop called him."

"Yes, I remember those words. I did not believe him at the time, but nowadays I think perhaps your father was correct."

"Was that where you two met as well?"

"Who, your father and I?" Cyril shook his head. "No, our own beginnings were not so commonplace. Quite the contrary. Your father happened to save my life. Not once, but on three different occasions."

"He never told me—"

"Now is not the time, my dear. Suffice it to say that the bonds which tie us together, your family and mine, are there for life."

" 'Shared ideals and fates,' " Allison recalled.

" 'The makings of lifetime bonds,' " Cyril finished, nodding. "I shall always recall your father's favorite toast with fondness."

"My mother detested Ben, you know," Allison said. "Still does, as far as I know."

"That they did not get along is a matter of record," Cyril agreed.

"When I was a kid, I used to think of him as 'that man.' Mom used to call him that before he arrived, and then inserted a word after he left." Allison smiled at the memory. "It was either that loud man, or that overbearing man, or that stubborn man, or that rude man. I used to imitate her when Pop and I were alone. It always made him laugh. She never could understand how you two saw anything of interest in him."

"Let us simply say that his gifts and his altruism humbled us," Cyril replied, "regardless of the fact that neither of us shared his faith."

"He finished at the university in two years, didn't he?"

"That is correct. Then he entered medical school at

the ripe old age of nineteen. When I heard of his rabid conversion, as I used to call it at the time, I simply assumed it was a result of his relative youth and his obvious loneliness. I made the error of referring to him in your father's presence as the James Dean of mental giants, made outcast by his intelligence and his age. Your father was sharper with me than ever before or since. He told me that medical school had forced Ben into contact with suffering and that in suffering Ben had found the one thing on earth which intelligence alone could never fathom."

"That sounds just like Pop."

"Your father's wisdom is the salve I place upon his absence from my life," Cyril said.

The comment brought a burning sensation to the back of Allison's eyes. She said quietly, "I miss him, too."

Cyril briskly changed the subject. "You have not seen Ben in quite some time, I take it. No, of course not. He has not returned to Washington since your father's funeral, as far as I am aware. Well, my dear, you will find him much altered. More than either of us might have thought possible."

"In what way?"

"His wife certainly has a great deal to do with it. Leah is quite a formidable woman in her own quiet way. She is a Palestinian Christian. But I am quite certain there is more than just a woman's hand at work in Ben's transformation."

"What do you mean?"

"That is for you to decide. But I suggest you do not expect to find the same person you recall." His gaze became distant. "The desert tends to pare men and women down to the basic components of their nature. For some, it brings out the essence of evil; for others, the essence of good. Nowadays I find being around Ben Shannon a very unsettling experience. There is much to him which I wish I had gathered for myself."

5

DAWN FOUND WADE already up and moving.

They had overnighted at the edge of a small village, where an enterprising Ingush had built a roadside cafe in the hulk of a burned-out bus. They had shared camp with seven other trucks, all laden with farm produce and gathered into a separate enclave. Upon their arrival Mikhail had exchanged formal greetings, to let the others know they were no threat. Since then the two trucks of medical supplies and their couriers had been left alone.

Rogue had wakened them when the coming light was a glimmer on the horizon. Now he squatted next to the road with Mikhail, a greasy map unfolded on the ground in front of them. While Wade broke camp, the pair shared one of Robards' slender cheroots and a tin mug of steaming coffee. They spoke in hand signs and nods as the old man described the rutted road that led toward the hills.

The Caucasus Mountains dominated the distance. Their bases were lost in mists that drifted in the still air. The dawn light tinted their looming, snow-capped peaks with hues of rose and gold. They rested on earthbound clouds and stretched from horizon to horizon, a serrated nine-hundred-mile wall that divided two separate worlds. To the north lay the endless steppes, the Arctic, the brutal

Siberian winds. To the south spread balmier Mediterranean realms.

Rogue waved Wade over. When he hunkered down beside the pair, Rogue said, "Tell me about the conflict up ahead."

"There are wars up and down the Caucasus range," Wade replied. "But as I mentioned before, the ones which concern us are between the three main local tribes. The Chechen, the Ingush, and the Ossetians."

"Ossetia is the state next door, right?"

"Right," Wade agreed. "Well, technically, it's North Ossetia, or Severnaja Osetija. They're another autonomous republic, part of the Russian Federation just like here. Then there's South Ossetia, below the mountain range, which is a part of Georgia."

"And these three tribes don't get along."

"Not for centuries," Wade agreed. "Chechen and Ingush are Muslim; Ossetians are Christians. They hate each other. Then there is the local Russian population, brought in by Stalin to dilute the tribes during his policy of Russification. They make up almost forty percent of the population. But as far as the tribes are concerned, they don't exist. Since the downfall of communism, the Russians do not dare even enter the Muslim market areas. The Chechen warlord recently vowed death to all Russians who attempted to remain in his homeland."

"Chechen warlord," Rogue mused aloud. "This place is getting more interesting by the minute."

Wade took a moment to translate for Mikhail. When he was finished, the old man waved a veined hand toward the mountains. "The Chechen are traders and sheep farmers and cleverer than the Ingush," Mikhail began. "The Ingush tend to hug the land. They put down deeper roots. They raise cattle. They and the Chechen were neighbors and only sometime enemies until Stalin, may his name be erased from the earth, stole their lands and brought in the Russians. More Russians now live on Chechen land than the Chechen themselves. More

Chechen died in Siberia than survived to tell the tale. Ingush as well. Now they taste the wind of liberation and seek to steal both what was theirs and what their neighbors have managed to settle—neighbors such as my own Ossetians."

The old man ran a knotted hand around the back of his neck as Wade translated. "The winds of change are not always kind. I myself have lost sons and grandsons to a war that means nothing except misery for everyone."

"Which war was that?" Robards demanded, nodding to Wade for the translation.

"The war beyond the count of man's days. The war that has continued since before the birth of my father's father."

Mikhail stooped, picked up a stick, and drew a crude map in the dust at their feet. "This long line is the Caucasus range, separating Russia from Georgia for all of time. Here to the west of us lies the Black Sea, where the mountains begin their eternal march. The lands bordering sea and western hills belong to the Abkhazi, or those whom Stalin left alive. Next to them, south of the mountains still, are the Svaneti, then the Ushguls, then the Ossetians. The Ossetians are the first tribe both north and south of the mountains, because here lies the first great Caucasus pass. We are also the only Christian hill tribe. You as a warrior will understand what this means. Here in the heart of the mountain tribes stands the Ossetian stake, which the Muslim tribes are sworn to tear from the earth and burn on the fires of their hatred."

"What is there to the east of us?" Robards demanded, focused upon the map at his feet.

"North of the mountains, the Chechen and Ingush, as I have said," Mikhail replied, almost chanting the words. "In the southern highlands, some Chechen and Ingush still, but not many. Mostly Tusheti tribes. Some Karachai also, but most Stalin deported to Siberia. They have not returned."

"Is there trouble in that area?"

"For the modern man, there is trouble everywhere," Mikhail replied, "but more here than elsewhere. Farther east the mountains curve down southward and fall into the Dagestani lowlands, which in turn slide into the Caspian Sea."

Robards pointed with the toe of his boot to the region where the mountains begin their curve. "What about to the west here?"

"The Kasheti region of Georgia," Mikhail answered once Wade had translated. "Though they are more a name than a tribe in these days. Stalin had a special hatred for them. Why, no one knows. But almost the entire tribe was scattered. On the other side of the Georgian border here to the southeast lies Azerbaijan. To the south, Armenia. To the southwest, Turkey. There again one finds the battle between Muslim and Christian, especially in the Christian enclave inside Azerbaijan."

Robards nodded approvingly. "Your knowledge is great, old man."

"In my youth I journeyed far and wide," the elder replied proudly. "I was a trader, and a good one. Dagestani carpets were my specialty."

"Are there passes down through the Caucasus range to the southern lands?"

"None that are not fiercely guarded by tribesmen." Mikhail squinted. "Was not our objective the highland hospital?"

"Always best to know where the back door's located," Robards replied. "Ask the gent how old he is."

"I am about to see my seventieth year." He cupped his arm close to his chest, and made as though holding an invisible gun. "Yet remain strong enough to hold a Skorpion with one hand and shoot a level line."

"Skorpion's a machine pistol with the kick of a mule," Robards explained to Wade. "Says a lot about the world we're in when an old guy uses that as the symbol of his health. Tell him I hope I'm in such shape at his age, if I make it that far."

"Your friend carries the scent of good fortune with him," Mikhail replied. "That is why I agreed to come. He should choose to remain and make his home here. There is much work for one such as him, and the hillsmen are known for their long lives. My father still tends his sheep, and my great-uncle swears he will see his two hundredth year."

"We oughta talk once this little jaunt's over," Robards replied. "First I need to see how much chance there is of me walking into somebody else's bullet." He stared at the crude map drawn in the dust and said, "Tell me about the pass we'll be taking."

"We shall join the Georgia Military Highway south of Vladikavkaz, North Ossetia's capital city," the old man replied. "This follows the central and clearest pass through these jutting peaks. It winds through gorges and hairpin turns and drops and ravines before descending into Georgia. The road is the single paved Caucasus artery not often either washed out or bombed. Too many trucks carrying far too many goods have ground the road's surface to a trail of cracks and bumps and gravel and dust. But at least we should be safe. Russian military convoys travel its length, followed by civilians who bribe the transport officers for the right—"

A swiftly moving cloud brought them all around. Wade searched the windless horizon and realized with a start that the approaching cloud was alive. A sound of honking strengthened as the cloud became hundreds of thousands of migrating waterbirds.

Robards looked an astonished question at Mikhail, who replied through Wade, "North of our campsite is the Volga Delta, a remnant of the wilderness that once held all of Russia in its grasp. Where the great river joins the Caspian Sea, there lies a maze of marshes and streams. Three hundred species of birds live there. Plus the Saigar antelope. Wolves. Wild boar. Steppe eagles."

The cloud of birds arrived overhead, throwing their campsite into fleeting shadows. The bird cries became so loud that the old man had to shout to be heard. "In my father's time, the birds formed flying walls that went on for hours and days on end. Now the flocks pass only in morning and in evening, and only for two days, three at most."

Robards listened, nodded, and watched the sky. There was nothing to see save the cloud of birds. He called the question, "Same time every year?"

When Wade had translated the old man shook his head emphatically. "There is no set time to their pattern, no date upon which the giant gatherings begin. Yet the birds know, as do the Saigar antelope. On a certain day each autumn, as early as the first week in September or as late as November, the herds join and begin to move. And then, a few days later, the first Siberian wind arrives."

As quickly as it began, it ended. The last of the birds passed overhead, and within a few seconds their raucous cries blended with the gathering wind.

"In the autumn," Mikhail continued in a normal tone of voice, "the steppe's silver featherwood stands burnished by the sun like ripening wheat. It shivers in these gathering winds as though knowing what the birds and the animals know—that soon the wind will turn and howl in icy fury from the north. Here in the south we have only the slightest taste of Russian winter. But I have traveled. I know. Not so far to the north, the land will soon turn to iron, its coat of ice so hard and jagged that tires can be cut to shreds. Then the land is empty as only a Russian steppe can be, lost to the vacuum of unconquered winter, its isolation accented by a lone wolf's howl."

"A good time to be somewhere else." Robards raised his boot and deliberately erased the map scratched into the earth. "Let's move out."

The Caucasus, one of the world's youngest mountain

ranges, were not yet worn down and softened by nature. They did not rise gradually from plains to foothills to high reaches. Instead, they *leapt* into being. The world was flat, an endless steppe, and then came the walls of rock crowned by ice and snow. Waterfalls thundered down from all sides. Among the silent giants loomed a dozen peaks higher than Mont Blanc, Europe's tallest mountain. Two thousand glaciers locked the highlands beneath frozen seas a mile and more in depth.

The southern Kalmyk Steppe was a sweeping earthen sea, bound on the south by the Caucasus Mountains, rimmed to the east and west by the Caspian and Black seas. To the north there was no boundary, no ending, no rise nor fall nor physical landmark. The name changed with distance, from southern to central to northern, yet in truth the steppe continued in one flat empty stretch from the Caucasus to the Arctic wastelands, a distance of over three thousand kilometers. Winter winds generated in the depths of Siberia howled unchecked down its length until they crashed in frustrated fury against the unyielding Caucasus range.

Today, however, the weather was with them. Warm sunlight marked their traverse along the steppe's southern edge. They kept to byroads which were little more than rutted tracks, circling around several Chechen enclaves, heading ever closer to the mountains that dominated the horizon.

Their journey was noisy and dirty and slow. As the day progressed, the wind became their constant companion. Several miles after they joined the highway, they passed another petrol station. Robards insisted they stop and top up their tanks. They sat in sweltering heat, trying to breathe through the diesel fumes and dust clouds as inch by inch the mammoth line crawled forward.

"Take a look at those," Robards said when Wade climbed upon his running board during the wait. He jutted his chin toward the meadow flanking the station where a flock of shaggy beasts cropped meager grass.

"They're called yakaws," Wade explained. "A cross between yak and cattle. You see their milk a lot in the markets."

"This place is right from the storybooks," Robards declared and pointed in another direction, to where the shepherds stood watching their flocks, totally oblivious to the station's noisy cacophony. "What tribe are they?"

"I'd guess Ingush," Wade said after a moment's hesitation. "The Chechen generally have sharper features. They are said to be a Persian tribe. The Ingush are probably of Turkish descent. Some say Afghan, though. They are swarthier, a lot with the hawk noses and full features of the Himalayan tribesmen. They're considered the more easygoing of the two, but that's only a matter of degree. As Mikhail said, the Ingush farm and tend cattle. A lot of them wear expensive sable hats or fedoras."

"So basically what we got here are a pair of tribes who love to carry steel, fight, sneak across borders with contraband, pass down grudges for centuries, and wear fancy headgear." Robards gave a satisfied chuckle. "The more I hear, the better I like this place."

Within a half hour of leaving the station, they began a steady climb. Their speed slowed even more, seldom creeping above twenty miles an hour.

Streams and rivers crisscrossed the highway every mile or so. A dozen waterfalls glistened in the distance. As the two trucks crossed one makeshift wooden bridge, Wade spotted the metal girders of a more modern construction. It was upended and embedded in a monstrous pile of debris, testimony to the spring floods that roared down from above.

The mountains' lower reaches were dreamlands of mist and silver birches. As the trucks ground relentlessly higher, the mists gave way to aching blue-black skies, the birch to ancient firs and then to silver-green meadows.

They rounded yet another curve and a broad, rushing river came into view. At the top of the rise they pulled into a lay-by crowded with trucks and buses and people taking a break from the heat. With his first step into the icy torrent, Wade lost all feeling in his feet. He continued out until the rushing current threatened to pluck him away. The mist hanging above the river dropped the air's temperature by fifty degrees. Wade stood and reveled in the coolness until he saw Rogue wave for him to return.

When he arrived back at the trucks, the old man said with pride, "That is the River Terek. We follow its path all the way to the Krestovy Pass. Pushkin called it the laughing waters. Tolstoy called it the river of smoke."

Mikhail then pointed off to his right to where a rutted track broke off and meandered into a heavily wooded glen. "The entrance to the Fiagdon Valley. There lie the remnants of the Ossetian city called Tsimitar. Beyond that stands the City of the Dead, where until the Middle Ages my people came and buried their kin in family towers built over a thousand years ago. Now there is nothing. Stalin, the killer who was half-Ossetian himself, succeeded where even Tamerlane had failed. Today our valley is empty of life."

Rogue grinned at the news. "Tamerlane and the Mongols and a battleground for over two thousand years. Makes me wish I could strap a sword to my side and go riding off on a great white charger."

"It doesn't bother you," Wade countered, "hearing about all the tragedy this land has known?"

Robards gave his easy shrug. "They lived, they died. Same as you and me, sport. Life's only a tragedy for those on the receiving end, a place I avoid." He tossed an empty Pepsi bottle toward a colossal pile of trash. "Come on, time to head for the hills."

At the highway's turning around the next cliff, the trucks slowed to a crawl. Robards inched slowly forward. A protruding rock outcrop crumbled as the truck's right side hugged the wall for safety. Wade braked his truck and waited for Rogue to manage the turn. He swiveled in his seat and looked back. To his left the course they were following fell away to nothingness. A mountain eagle drifted on an unseen current, its four-foot wingspan unfurled and stable as it screamed at these human interlopers.

Beyond and two thousand feet below, a valley expanded as it left the mountain fastness. The earth was mirrored silver in the harsh afternoon light. Richer bands of green ran alongside delta rivulets which tracked over the burnished autumn steppe like life-giving veins. Here and there the utter flatness was broken by solitary foothills that rose and fell like tiny waves upon a silver sea. Winds whistled and moaned, the constant voice of this alien land.

The roar of Rogue's engine signaled Wade that the way was clear. He ground the gears and started forward, inching his way around the bend. Halfway around the curve, he turned back once again.

At that moment, before his vision was blocked by the cliff wall, Wade knew a moment of utter clarity. He felt his own life yawing forth in an instant of realization, a glimpse of choices soon to be forced upon him.

On the one side was the terror of open space with no visible support whatsoever. On the other the strength and power of visible and solid cliffs.

Yet for some reason, the cliffs frightened him most of all.

6

THE DAIMLER SWEPT THEM toward Heathrow Airport, which was as far as Cyril Price would allow them to be seen together in public. Once on the plane, for all intents and purposes, she would be on her own. Allison watched the windshield wiper clear away the misting rain, and felt her own emotions sweep back and forth, back and forth, between the thrill of adventure and the fear of unknown dangers.

Allison clenched her hands in her lap to keep them still, and worked to keep her voice calm as she commented, "I don't see why you were the one who approached me about this."

"Because Ben Shannon contacted me," Cyril replied patiently. Years of experience with field agents had clearly taught him how to handle cases of last-minute nerves. "Personal contacts mean a very great deal in this trade. It is one of your greatest assurances of safety. Especially when one is standing so close to the danger zone as Ben is."

The danger zone. "I think I see."

"Oh, the Americans are all too pleased to have our assistance. We British have ever so much more experience at this sort of hands-on work. There is only so much your lot can gain through eyes in the sky. Since we did not have the cash lying about to heft up those great rockets, we have focused our attention on running agents on the ground."

"But when something like this came up, the Americans were left empty-handed."

"Not entirely, but more than they might wish to be. Distant eyes can see only what is large enough to be identified. And technical ears can hear only what is sent out over radio waves or spoken by telephone—unless there is an agent on the ground to carry a microphone, of course. When groups are limited in size to small terrorist cells that gather only in caverns and mosques, then all the technology in the world becomes, well..."

"Useless," Allison finished for him.

"Mind you, when such decisions were being taken, the American agencies saw their Middle Eastern foes as limited in the amount of damage they could produce—limited both by their small numbers and the conventionality of their arms."

"But with more deadly weapons, all this changes."

"Precisely. Place small, portable nuclear armaments in the hands of certain governments or terrorist groups, offer them missiles capable of transporting these bombs from the decks of small boats to our cities, and the situation is transformed. It is then an explosive situation that requires our direct, on-the-ground, dirty-hands involvement."

"Which is where I come in," she said, finding it difficult to force air into her lungs. "I just hope I can do it right."

"You will, my dear. Of that I have not the slightest doubt." His tone turned brisk. "As was explained yesterday, you have an introduction to someone within your embassy in Amman. Her name is Judith Armstead. But I would prefer that you hold off contacting her for the first few days, granting us an opportunity to establish your cover, so to speak. I shall meet with you myself as the occasion arises. But not at our embassy. I intend for you to have as little contact as possible with my own number inside the British Embassy."

"Why is that?"

"As Ben discovered to our mutual distress," Cyril replied, "he is a gentleman of impenetrable ignorance."

"How terrible," Allison said, pleased to have a reason to smile.

"Quite. He also has an extremely well-developed trait of rubbing people the wrong way. Your work shall be difficult enough as it is without having to deal with someone as thick as a venerable oak tree." Cyril picked at an imaginary fleck on his trousers. "As I was saying, to succeed—that is, to survive—you must be extremely alert and ready to abandon all whenever the situation turns against you."

"You're about to frighten me. Again."

"Fear can be quite useful, so long as you do not allow your fear to make you incapable of functioning." He stared at her with utter gravity. "Make no mistake, my dear. We are battling an enemy as dangerous as the dark king himself. You must be alert at all times. If fear helps you to do so, so be it."

The car pulled up in front of the terminal. Jules climbed out and extracted her cases from the trunk. Allison took a suddenly shaky breath. "I guess this is it, then."

Cyril grasped her damp hand with both of his. "Your father would be very proud of you, my dear."

There it was, the very right thing at the very right time. Allison felt herself steady. "He was a spy for a while, wasn't he?"

Cyril smiled with genuine fondness. "When this is behind us, we shall find a quiet corner, you and I. And I shall fill you to the brim with tales of daring and intrigue."

"Once my initiation is over, right?"

"Come." He reached across her and opened her door, then slid out behind her. When they were standing beside the car he offered his hand once more. "Remember, my dear. Intelligence is not concerned with stopping threats. It is involved solely in *warning*. Our task is to ensure that our governments are never surprised. Leave the actual intervention to others with the proper expertise. You are the eyes and the ears, nothing more, nothing less."

It was hot in Amman, hotter than Allison had imagined possible for early autumn. The sun was a blazing orb overhead. Shadows cut spiked angles from the ground. There were no clouds. The air was dry and dusty and sucked the moisture from her skin. Allison walked down the sidewalk outside the airport terminal and searched desperately for a familiar face.

"Over here, Miss Taylor," a testy voice said.

Allison squinted through the glare and found herself looking at a squat little man in a sweat-stained white shirt, a handkerchief knotted over his bald head. "Were you talking to me?"

With an exasperated sigh the little man waddled over, grasped her two cases, and lugged them toward a vintage taxi. "I said come along."

The car had the suspension of a trampoline. Every bump in the road threatened to send her through the roof. The driver was a dull-faced Arab who neither returned her greeting nor looked her way. He drove with more use of his horn than his brakes. They careened out of the airport complex, took the highway turnoff on two wheels, and barreled southward at speeds Allison did not care to think about.

The little man swiped the handkerchief from his head and used it to mop his peeling red face. "There was a problem at the clinic," he said with undisguised annoyance. "I was appointed stand-in."

"I'm sorry; I don't believe I caught your name..."

"Smathers. British Embassy. Doesn't matter, really. With luck we shall never need to see each other again."

He reached down by his feet and drew out a battered case. "I suppose we might as well get this over with."

"You would have preferred that I had not been sent here," Allison guessed.

"I have long since given up dwelling upon the decisions of the powers-that-be," he said with asperity.

"This wasn't my idea," Allison told him.

"You cannot imagine how much reassurance I find in that," he snapped. "Now can we please get down to business?"

Allison cast a glance at the driver, who paid them no mind whatsoever. "If you say so."

"Then pay attention." He flicked the locks, opened the lid, and brought out what looked like a thick portable telephone without the aerial. "This is a radioactive monitor. It has been reworked so that all you need do is switch this lever here when you want to begin."

"They showed me one like this in Oxford," she informed him, "and they said it would be safer to have someone deliver it to me than try to take it through customs."

"All of which is decidedly more than they told me," he said angrily. "Now pay attention. The monitor has a range of fifteen meters. This little screen will give you a continuous reading, but you will most likely not have need nor opportunity to use it. This particular machine has been designed to supply you with a printout."

"Readings taken every twenty minutes," Allison recited, "or three times an hour."

"Do be kind enough to bear with me. You will need to make a note of where you are every twenty minutes. Each evening you must write down beside the readout where you were. Any reading over three is of interest to us."

"And if I find any place that gives me a reading higher than five," she persisted stubbornly, "I have to report immediately to the American Embassy in Amman."

He turned the apparatus over, slid out a small panel,

and revealed a paper roll. "This will last you three days, assuming you will not have it on for more than twelve hours each day. There is a box of rolls in this case that should last you for a month." From the case he extracted a battered black doctor's bag. "This has a false bottom. You shall place the monitor in here before you leave the compound. Do try to keep a good grip on it in your wanderings; we would very much like to avoid the nightmare of a street thief discovering this monitor and turning it over to the wrong hands."

"You don't think this is a good idea, do you?" Allison demanded. "Bringing in an outsider like this."

"Quite the contrary," he replied acidly, bundling the monitor and bag back into the case and slamming it shut. "Since professionals have been chasing down these absurd rumors for more than five weeks and found absolutely nothing, naturally we are grateful for the assistance of someone as qualified as you."

Allison gave up. She leaned back in her seat, bracing herself with both arms against the jouncing rocking ride. The little man settled the case back under his feet and did not say another word.

The highway was a narrow man-made band running through utter desolation. Rock and scrub wilderness stretched out in every direction. Wherever patches of dusty green signaled the presence of underground springs, people appeared. Bedouin tents reached out a variety of multicolored arms as wide as houses. Flocks grazed nearby—sheep, goats, donkeys, camels. Towns were clusters of square concrete blockhouses connected by packed earth tracks. There was little vegetation to soften the harshness of this desert world. The few trees grew stunted and dry and gnarled. Roads to distant settlements were not roads at all, but dusty tracks that rose and fell and twisted like yellow veins on the hard surface.

Closer to Aqaba, the mountains closed in on both sides. Pink and yellow and ocher sandstone cliffs were striated with black volcanic ash and white quartz and brown iron ore, carved into weird shapes by a hundred million years of wind.

On the city's outskirts they were stopped by a heavily armed police blockade. Allison caught the word *tourist* in the exchange between soldiers and driver, then their car was waved through. The little man beside her muttered a relieved sigh and mopped his peeling brow.

The doctor who came out to greet her arrival was both the man she remembered and a different man entirely.

"My dear Allison," Ben Shannon called out, approaching through the compound's open gates. "After all these years. What a delight to see you again."

Allison recalled Ben Shannon as an unpleasant man—pesky, arrogant, loud, impatient. Inviting him to dinner had meant listening to a boring monologue. Either that or somebody had to argue with him, for the only way to make him stop talking was to push back hard.

Her mother had detested the sound of his name. Her father, however, continually referred to the man with awe. Allison never could understand why. Her only contact with religion as a child had been through Ben Shannon. Because of his personality, she had come to associate religious belief with a constantly open mouth.

But none of those memories seemed to have anything to do with the man who now stood before her.

"Hello, Ben," she said uncertainly, disarmed by his smile.

"Right." The little man from the embassy deposited her two suitcases and his own battered case at her feet. "Break a leg and all that." He climbed back into his taxi and screeched away with a plume of oily smoke.

"He was about the most unpleasant man I've ever met," Allison said, her eyes on the departing taxi.

"The result of a continual diet of subterfuge," Ben replied. "Our friend Cyril Price shows the same irritating strains. He refuses to ever come here, you know. Says it would destroy my value as an asset, whatever that means."

"At least he says it politely," Allison observed.

"Yes, but Cyril has not seen his professional worth challenged by an outsider," Ben replied. "The fact that I may be able to grant you access to areas that are barred to him and his kind does not make the pill any easier to swallow."

She couldn't stop staring at him. He was strong yet worn to a fine and delicate edge. His face was a chiseled set of firm lines and determined action, his body wiry yet fragile. His eyes, though smudged with weary shadows, were full of peace. "You're not like I remember you. Even your voice is different."

"Ah. That is the Arabic, I suppose. The language is so demanding that it tends to wipe the slate clear as far as other accents are concerned."

Allison listened carefully for the aggressive pushiness. But the argumentative nature she remembered was gone. Not simply tamped down and controlled. Erased entirely.

"You will be a most welcome addition here. Our level of expertise is high, but as with all such clinics, we are underfunded and understaffed. There is always a need for volunteers."

"You expect me to work at the clinic?"

He nodded. "You will be watched constantly. It is the Arab way. Our only protection is to have you carry out normal duties."

She glanced through the compound's entrance. "What kind of problems do you face here?"

"Stomach and intestinal diseases," he replied instantly. "Infected skin lesions. Infant and childhood ailments. Dehydration. Eye problems. Tooth and gum disease. Some bullet wounds, some beatings, some bomb fragments. But mostly our problems are the result of overcrowding, lack of clean water, and poor sanitation, not war."

"I still don't see what use I'm going to be to you."

"You will." He gestured toward where the clinic's outer wall was festooned with Arabic spray-painted murals. "Your education begins here. This wall is a sort of running weekly news journal. I say weekly because we whitewash the walls every Sunday. There are strike announcements, new reasons given to hate the West, ditto for the Israelis, notices of political activities and planned protests supporting the struggle in the occupied territories—that sort of thing. Most families here have relatives in camps or settlements across the Israeli border. Also, a remarkable number of the graffiti announcements these days are calls for people to return to their Islamic roots."

"Fundamentalists."

"Perhaps. Or perhaps just angry young men willing to pay any moral price for a taste of hope and a chance of victory against the oppression of poverty."

He turned and gestured behind him. A neighboring hillside was covered with a dense cluster of yellow, dusty buildings. "That is a fairly typical camp. It is crowded, squalid, poor. It has bad sanitation, few schools, fewer jobs, less hope. The middle class live in those overcrowded, crumbling apartment blocks. Poorer families gather in concrete huts with straw thatch or metal sheaves for roofing. Richer homes have high, enclosed walls and solid steel doors. The camp is lined with open sewers and populated by rats and flies."

"It sounds horrid," she said quietly.

"It is," he agreed. "But within those confines are also some of the finest people God has placed upon this earth. You must be careful never to condemn an entire population for the crimes of a few." He hefted the heavier of her cases. "Come. Let me show you around."

Within the clinic grounds, families had gathered. They had set down mats and rugs beneath the trees' meager shade or alongside the building or on the covered walk and set up temporary housekeeping. Women in black tentlike *djellabas* and head scarves fed squalling children while other youngsters squealed and ran and played in the dust. The compound was as noisy as a schoolyard.

"Last week I had a child tell me before he was anesthetized for surgery that he hoped to have a vision of Saddam Hussein while he was under," Ben said as he guided her through the chaos. At every step, families looked up and smiled and murmured respectful greetings to him. "I told that to a visiting American doctor, and she was disgusted. How can these people continue to believe all those lies about such an evil man, she asked. I agree with her about Saddam, yet I also feel the incident shows the state of mind within the Palestinian community. Here was a child who felt he could find no hope of a better life anywhere. Not from the West. Not from God. Only from the president of Iraq."

He led her up the crumbling brick stairs and into the relative cool of the crowded front porch. Rusty metal posts held up overlapping sheets of plastic roofing. The simple concrete floor was packed with mothers tending babies. Men gathered and fingered worry beads and talked in undertones. Everyone paused to inspect Allison as she passed.

"It's something of a rambling structure, I'm afraid. We've had to make do with what we had. When there was money, it always seemed there were few construction materials to buy. When we were poor, the market was naturally flooded."

He opened a sheet-metal spring door and ushered her inside a corrugated metal hall with simple benches stretching down both sides. Notices in Arabic plastered the walls. Three large windows had been cut with a torch and then screened. A desultory breeze shifted the heat back and forth through the chamber.

"Our entrances and waiting chambers are castoff shipping containers. They are fine in cooler weather but like ovens in the summer. As you saw, most people prefer to remain outdoors."

He took her through a second door, this one marked "Private," which brought them to an open-air walkway roofed with the same plastic sheeting. Ahead was an ocher-colored building. They walked through the entrance, across a cramped parlor filled with rickety furniture, up a narrow stairway, and down a hall. He stopped before a door marked with an Arabic number. A key dangled from the lock. He opened the door to reveal a clean but austere chamber with an unmade single bed, a sink, a writing desk and chair, a grit-encrusted window, and a bare bulb.

"No doubt it is far from what you are accustomed to," he explained, "but for you to live differently than the rest of our staff would only cause questions."

"It's fine," she said, and meant it. In her weary state, the bed looked immensely inviting.

"Sheets and towels are in the cupboard down the hall, as is the bathroom." He set down her case and said solemnly, "I hope you will be happy here, for as long as it is necessary for you to stay."

She looked at him. "Why are you doing this?"

He looked at her with grave eyes. "There is danger here for us and for all our world. Very great danger. Not just today, but for many years to come. So long as we do not help these people gain a peaceful purpose and clearer vision, we are allowing their world to remain a breeding ground for terrorists."

He looked through the dirty window and continued. "Some people out there seek to take advantage of this misery. They use the guise of their faith to preach of hate and pain and death. Them I oppose—with all that I have, with all that I am."

7

ON THE EVENING of the third day, Wade's truck crested a rise to find several hundred campfires flickering in the distance.

Within another hour the trucks had wound their way into an encampment filled with roaring engines, shouting men, diesel fumes, dust, the smoke of cooking meat, and the bleating of animals. Wade wrestled the oversized steering wheel with numbed hands and followed Robards to an empty space. He backed his vehicle so that the rear was close to the escarpment, facing out toward the myriad of flickering shadows.

Robards pulled in beside Wade, drawing so close the side fenders groaned as they meshed together. Then he cut his motor and said through his open window, "This way we'll feel if somebody decides to pay us a visit."

Wade translated for the old man seated beside Rogue.

"Tell the warrior that Chechen traders will come by with food and drink and eyes hunting the unwary. It would be best if I spoke for us."

"Time to either fish or cut bait," Robards said when Wade had translated. "You want to trust him?"

"Why are you asking me?"

"Because it's your show, sport. You're what they call the payer. But if you want the advice of your payee, I'd say let the old man handle this."

Wade called through the open window to where the old man sat beside Robards, "We would be grateful for your assistance, uncle."

Without further speech, Mikhail pulled the gun from behind his seat and slid from the truck. He walked out in front, cradled the gun across his chest, and settled into the position of one accustomed to waiting for hours. Light from neighboring fires turned the old man's weapon the color of burnished copper.

"Come on, sport," Rogue called, sidling from his truck. "Let's see to the grub."

Following Robards' lead, Wade set up camp in a small hollow behind the two trucks. From his kneeling position he watched under the high-riding wheels as three pairs of scruffy legs approached the old man. One of the newcomers led a bleating sheep by a rope bridle. "Visitors," he whispered.

"I hear," Rogue replied softly from inside the back end of his truck. "Can you catch what they're saying?"

"No."

The men squatted down by Mikhail, and their faces came into view beneath the truck. All of the strangers were of a type—black hair and unkempt beards and vests with bullet pockets and the knit skullcaps of the mountain Chechen. Their guns fit their hands with the ease of a lifetime's practice. As glittering black eyes searched him out, Wade dropped his gaze to the flickering cooker. "They see me."

"Good," Rogue said for his ears alone. "Here, take this."

Wade accepted their three bedrolls, set them down, then took the extra ones Rogue had insisted they pack in case the others became wet. "What are you doing?"

"No need for them to know how few we are," Rogue said. "Spread the beddings out. I'll just stay up here out of sight for a while."

Wade did as he was told, saw that his motions were followed by the men up front. He pretended a calm he did not feel and did his best not to look their way. He poured water from one of the drinking canisters into a pot and set it on to boil. The hollow where he worked had been formed by what once had been a very large tree that had long since been cut down. The knee-high stump was a full four feet across and made an excellent work surface as he went about preparing their dinner.

Eventually the old man returned, a ghost of a smile on his features. "That was very wise, setting out the extra beddings."

"It was Robards' idea," Wade confessed.

"Of course."

At the sound of the old man's voice, Robards sprang lightly from the truck. Wade handed him a plate of canned stew and a fork. He blew on the steaming food and demanded, "Ask the old man if there was any trouble."

"There is trouble everywhere," Mikhail replied, accepting his food with a nod. "Life itself is trouble. But they did not appear overly interested."

"What did he say we were carrying?"

"Parts for these cursed Russian trucks," the old man replied. "Items too heavy to be stolen with ease and not valuable enough to fight over unless the takings were easy."

"One of us will be on duty all night," Robards announced. "Two hours on, four off. I'll take the first watch. One will sleep in the front cab, one in back, one on top."

"I'll take the top position," Wade said quickly.

Robards showed the glimmer of a smile. "Like to do a little stargazing?"

"I'd just like a little fresh air. I feel as if I've been eating dust all day."

"Well, take a couple of extra blankets. The night will get cold up there."

It did. But Wade found he did not mind at all. Robards woke him for his watch with a steaming mug of oversweetened tea and the words, "Be sure and sit up the whole time. Otherwise you might fall back asleep."

Wade sipped and sighed sweet smoke and wrapped the blankets up close around his neck. The camp spread out in front of him for a half mile or more in three directions. Silent, still forms huddled around many smoldering fires. Shadow figures walked in quiet vigilance around trucks, tall guns jutting like spears from their shoulders or hanging down alongside their legs. Drunken laughter drifted up from points unseen. Overhead the stars stretched out like a glittering silver blanket, bright enough to paint the entire scene with ghostly luminosity. The peaks surrounding their escarpment sliced sharp edges from the sky, silent sentinels overlooking the madness of man.

Morning was little more than a smudge across the eastern sky when Robards had them break camp and get underway. As usual, the old man rode in the front truck with Robards, while Wade followed close behind and ate the front truck's dust. The morning was cold; Wade's fingers were numbed by the steering wheel in the unheated cabin. His breath frosted the inside of the windshield, each dip in the road jarred his spine, the engine roared so loudly Wade could scarcely hear himself think. But he did not mind.

Every turn in the road brought new vistas. The mountains had the raw, untamed look of a new creation. The sun crested distant peaks and flashed fiery illumination into the morning, transforming the road into a molten river of gold and the dust into fairies that coalesced and beckoned and vanished and reformed. Wade shouted a laugh as the next curve revealed a flickering stream from which a flock of sheep drank, oblivious to the thundering motors. He waved to the bearded shepherd with his trio of dogs and ancient rifle and pair of crossed bandoliers. He had never felt so alive.

• • •

By the time they approached the outskirts of Carcash, however, the thrill of adventure had long since faded beneath a blanket of fatigue and dust and heat. The sun poised mercilessly in a cloudless sky. In his cracked rearview mirror Wade inspected a face caked with white dust and a pair of red-rimmed eyes. His mouth tasted of grit and diesel fumes and the road. He was glad their mission was almost completed.

He followed Robards toward the truck compound that dominated one side of the village. Their passage garnered only a few disinterested glances from passersby; they were simply two of an unending stream of vehicles.

At Robards' insistence, they paid a premium for spaces against the windowless warehouse wall that formed the compound's southern perimeter. Robards backed his truck in at an exaggerated angle, blocking out space for both vehicles. Then they had a quick cold meal and left the old man on guard duty as they set off once more in the second truck.

The village of Carcash filled a shallow, bowl-shaped valley with tumbledown shanties, warehouses, bars, stores charging vastly inflated prices, more bars, restaurants, still more bars, and hotels that were little more than bunkhouses. The buildings that fronted the main highway made a feeble attempt at respectability, with walkways raised to escape both mud and snow. There were only two other passages large enough to be granted the names of streets, and away from the highway they soon were reduced to rutted tracks. Most buildings were reached via unnamed, unlit alleys that wandered in haphazard fashion around dusty garden patches, lines of laundry, corrals for seedy-looking horses, scampering children, and outdoor privies. Few women were visible on the streets, and none walked alone. Many of the men were falling down drunk.

Everyone carried weapons of some sort, from antique blunderbusses with stocks sporting hammered silver plates to sniper rifles with scopes as long as Wade's forearm. The Kalashnikov with its sickle-shaped clip was clearly the weapon of choice. Knives, some as long as short swords, sprouted from belts, from thighs, from boots, from backpacks. Bandoliers were worn like badges of honor.

Following vague instructions Wade had brought with him, they tried to find the track that led to the nearest Ingush mountain fastness. They had to ask repeatedly for directions; the first several times their requests were answered with hostile stares and indifferent shrugs. Finally Robards halted the truck, grabbed his gun, and climbed down. The next passerby was stopped by Rogue, looming large and stone-faced directly in his path. That time, when Wade asked, the man answered. But when Wade asked if all was well with the Red Cross camp, the man pretended total ignorance. After having the directions confirmed twice more, they set off.

"It doesn't look good," Wade shouted above the engine.

Robards shrugged his unconcern. "No use worrying," he replied. "We'll find out soon enough."

Their way took them along the valley's western side. The rocky promontory clung to a steep cliff and sidled around a series of hair-raising drops. The roadway was mild in grade, clearly designed so that it could be managed in snowy conditions. Around the curves the track was barely wide enough to keep all four tires on the surface. To one side was an unyielding rock wall. To the other was nothing but a swooping drop. Wade found it best not to look out his window at all.

At one level passage Robards braked. He pointed back to tracks curving off the main path and scrunching along an indentation in the wall. Wade followed the pointed finger but did not understand. "What am I supposed to be seeing?"

"That hollow was made so trucks or carts coming from opposite directions can pass each other."

Wade imagined having to back up along that incline.

"I'm glad we haven't had to do that."

"That's not what I meant," Robards answered, searching behind them. "Nobody's used that passage in quite a while, by the looks of those tracks."

"So?"

Robards swung back around. "So maybe nothing. Let's go see."

An hour passed before the road broadened and began a sharp descent. As the sun touched the distant western peaks, they rounded a corner and saw what once had been a large pastoral community. Now it was nothing but a blackened shell.

Crumbling rock-walled houses were surrounded by sooty shadows of corrals and hay barns. Nothing moved except large mountain crows riding the high currents. The place was utterly still. Lifeless. Robards halted beyond the village outskirts and slid from the truck. "You drive."

Wordlessly Wade took his place behind the wheel. Robards swung into the passenger seat, hoisted his weapon, rasped the cocking arm, and set the barrel on the window ledge. "Take it slow."

The closer they drew, the grimmer the picture became. What had been wood was burned to cinders. What had been made of stone was blown to bits. The place reeked of ashes and decay.

They found the clinic by its flagpole. It had stood just north of the village center, just as Wade's directions described. A blackened pole rose before the burned-out hulk of what once had been a long, low structure surrounded by an open veranda. Wade stopped the truck, walked down the ash-strewn path, and climbed the trio of blackened stone steps. There was no movement, no sound save the wind and the cawing crows.

"What happened here?" Wade murmured.

"Somebody got unlucky," Robards replied, climbing the stairs behind him. "Might happen to us too if we stick around here."

Wade turned to scout the silent valley. "You think they could come back?"

"This is a killing ground." Robards kept his eyes trained back toward the village. "Never want to stay in one longer than absolutely necessary. Somebody comes looking for revenge, or for a lost friend, or loot, they might decide to add us to the list."

"All right, I'm—" Wade stopped, his attention caught by the wind flickering a page tagged to the side wall. He walked over and tore the sheet from the nail.

"What does it say?" Rogue demanded.

"It's in French, and I don't read it very well," Wade said, squinting over the smudged script. "Something about, they came in the night. All the staff managed to escape, but one was wounded. Something about the patients I can't figure out. They think they heard Russian and saw uniforms, but they're not sure. They've decided it would be safer to head for Tbilisi." Wade looked up. "That's the capital of Georgia. It marks the southern end of the Trans-Caucasus Highway."

"You get back to the truck," Robards instructed. "I'll make a quick reccy around this joint."

Five minutes later Robards returned, his face streaked with ash. "All right, time to head on back."

"Did you find anything?"

"Nothing you need to see. You drive."

They left the silent village behind and began the lonely trek back to Carcash. Wade asked, "They were dead, weren't they?"

"Who?"

"The patients. Whoever else you found back there in the clinic."

"Best not to dwell on what you can't help," Robards replied.

"I guess you've seen a lot of stuff like this," Wade said thoughtfully. "I see a little of it in my work. But I don't think I could ever get so casual about death. I think it's important to, well, respect a person's passage."

"Tell you how I see it, sport," Robards said, his tone clipped. "You're here until you're not. Respect don't change it any."

Wade was quiet for a minute, struggling with a question he hesitated to voice. "Is that the way you feel about faith?"

"You mean religion?" Big shoulders bounced once. "If it helps you get through the day, fine. Otherwise it ain't nothing but excess baggage."

"So you don't believe in anything?"

"You know, I've met guys like you everywhere I've been," Robards replied. "They get close enough to smell death, they start talking about all that God stuff."

"I told you, I've seen people die before. You're not answering my question."

"What difference does it make, whether or not I believe in something?" he countered. "How is that going to make it any more or less real? Let me tell you something, sport. It's a great big world out here. A lot of questions just don't have answers. One place I've been, they keep an empty chair at the table for the dead, leave it there for a year. Another place, folks make up this hefty wooden tablet, cover it with words, keep fruit and fresh flowers in front of it, and bow down to it every time they pass. After a month or so they take it out and burn it, then the spirit's been released to wherever it is spirits are supposed to go. Far as I can see, all that stuff's meant to help the ones left around here, not the spirits."

"You don't think people have souls?"

"Maybe they do and maybe they don't, but what I think's not gonna change a thing, now, is it," Robards replied testily. "You just keep your mind on the road up ahead, sport. Whoever it was that didn't make it out of there is weeks beyond the point of no return. Talking about it with me ain't going to change things a bit."

Wade drove for a time in silence, then asked, "So what do we do now?"

"That's for you to decide," Robards replied. "But you

gotta know that my nickel ends when we get back to the compound."

Wade eased them around a cliff side, determinedly not looking out into the void. "You'd just leave me there alone with two trucks?"

"This is the age of capitalism, in case you haven't noticed. You're just lucky you got yourself somebody who stays bought."

"An honest mercenary."

"There are more of us around than you'd imagine."

"I don't have enough money left to pay you more than what we already agreed on."

"That stuff we're carting around is worth its weight in gold to the right buyer. You give me a script for payment, with a note saying I can take medicines instead of money if that old geezer back in Grozny decides to make trouble." Robards pulled the clip from his gun, flipped out the round in the chamber, and dry-fired the trigger. "So what's it going to be?"

"I've got to think."

"You do that, sport," Robards said, and set the gun down behind the seat. "Just keep in mind, the meter's running."

When Mikhail saw them coming, he hefted his gun high and shouted something that was lost beneath the engine's rumble. Rogue climbed down, walked to the other truck, maneuvered it around until it was straight, then motioned Wade to back in beside him. As soon as Wade cut the engine, the old man climbed up on his running board. "I have a favor to ask of you," he said formally.

Surprise filtered through his confusion and fatigue. "Of me?"

The old man nodded. "There are members of my clan who live here. One has a sickness, another a cut which has not healed clean."

The old man's gaze was strong, direct. "I and my families would be in your debt."

The stars were welcome strangers when Wade returned from treating Mikhail's kin. He unrolled his bedding behind the truck, and lay enclosed by its captured warmth, too tired to sleep. He searched the silver river overhead, wishing he could leave behind his uncertainty and live with the assurance that ruled Robards' days.

Perhaps the man was wrong, but at least he lived by what he felt to be right. There was no wondering where Robards stood on anything or where anyone stood with him, and this assurance gave him a solid strength.

Wade allowed his eyes to finally close as he wondered how it would be to feel such strength about anything. He then surprised himself by praying for the patients who had not made it out of the clinic and for the village as a whole. He had seldom felt strong enough in his faith to pray for others. He lay and recalled Rogue's words, and wondered if he was only using prayer as a way of handling the presence of death, until sleep crept up and swept him away.

Wade did not awaken until the sun rose over the truck and lanced directly into his face. He squinted against the sudden brilliance, rolled over, and found Robards leaning against the compound wall and cradling a steaming mug with both hands.

"It's almost noon," Robards announced. "Ready for some coffee?"

Wade rolled from his bedding, struggled to his feet, rubbed his face. His three-day growth felt rough as sandpaper. "Noon?"

Robards handed him a mug. "You were doing a right fair imitation of the truck engine. Both of them, matter of fact."

Wade sipped the scalding brew, rolled the ache from his shoulders. "I was pretty tired."

"There's a bathhouse down the street. Not the cleanest place on earth, but there's plenty of hot water."

Wade scratched at his matted hair. "I could use a shower."

"Better hop to it, then. There was a reception committee here an hour or so ago, but I wouldn't let them wake you."

"What are you talking about?"

"One of them spoke enough English for me to work out the basics. It appears that word has gotten around about your deft touch as a healer," Robards replied. "Looks like there are a few others who could use a helping hand."

"I'm no doctor," Wade protested, fully awake now.

"You're the closest thing they've got," Robards answered, "and a darn sight better than nothing."

Wade bent over the cooker, poured himself a second cup. "We still haven't talked about what comes next."

"There's time enough for that after you see to your new friends. You go get cleaned up. They ought to be back before long."

The bath stalls were rudimentary in the extreme. Generations of insects nested in every corner, and the floors were blanketed with slippery green slime. Still, the water was hot and plentiful. Wade stood and let the water drum down on him and savored the simple pleasure of washing.

The Carcash compound covered the better part of twenty acres and contained almost a thousand trucks. As Wade walked the central avenue, he passed vehicles of every make and vintage. Many had their cowlings opened while grease-stained arms and heads busied themselves with repairs. Guards strung with bandoliers and well-oiled guns lounged with deceptive ease.

The dusty concourse was packed with hawkers. Shepherds tugged at bleating sheep, stopping to haggle with the timeless patience of Asian traders. When a bargain was finally struck, the sheep was lifted and its throat cut with a single motion of a razor-sharp knife. This was done before the buyers to assure the meat was fresh and the blood properly drained according to Muslim tradition. The smells and sounds of death caused a momentary panic among the sheep and chicken not yet sold. Their bleats and shrill cries joined with the laughter and shouts of the buyers, the engine noise, the drunken revelry, the heat, the dust.

As Wade walked the busy passage, he noticed that more attention than normal was being cast his way. Bands of drivers paused in their talk, opened their assemblies to permit his passage, murmured greetings. Wade returned the quiet words and wondered at this courtesy offered to one so evidently a stranger.

Robards waved to him from the midst of a group clustered before their two trucks. "Far as I can make out," he said when Wade walked over, "this is a delegation of drivers. Maybe you'd better take over."

Wade offered them a greeting and saw relief appear on their faces. A gray-bearded man with the unbroken whiteness of one blinded eye said, "It is indeed the blessings of Allah that we find a healer among us who speaks our tongue."

"I am not a doctor," Wade warned.

"Doctors are bloodsuckers," spat a younger man.

"It is said you have the touch of a healer and the voice of a trusted friend," the elder continued. "There are those among us who suffer much."

Wade glanced at Robards, who responded with a grin and the words, "You best get busy making friends and influencing people. We'll leave Mikhail here with the trucks, and I'll tag along long enough to make sure everything's straight."

Wade turned back to the elder and said, "I will come."

In the course of a day, Wade found that his basic medical skills were enough to grant him entry into a secret, unseen world. Entire families, whole clans, traveled together in scores of trucks. Their tales came out in bits and pieces as he worked. They remained banded together through desperate need. Petrol and spare parts were often impossible to find. Bandits and thieves preyed along the length and breadth of the crumbling empire. Food was a constant problem.

Children were everywhere—silent, watchful, solemn-eyed, never far from an adult. Wade counted it a major accomplishment when he was able to make one smile.

He would be brought in for one problem and find a dozen others. A child with a lingering cough had pus-covered scabs on his legs. A young woman with a poorly set finger had infections in both eyes. Pains that would have crippled a Westerner were endured in silence; here there was no other choice. Wade offered what help he could, and for a time forgot all but the pleasure of giving, of helping, of doing the only act that brought him peace.

They spoke because he showed them the quiet patience of a good listener. They spoke of a country that was falling apart at the seams. They described voyages over thousands of miles of empty wilderness, the convoy guards ever vigilant for bandits who hunted prey from horseback because of a lack of petrol. They talked of distant lands where the Siberian bears and leopards prowled around city perimeters at night and filled the air with their howls. They shared their fears, which were many, and their hopes, which were few and dealt mostly with their children. Their gratitude was humbling in its intensity.

It was dark when Wade made his weary way back to

the trucks. Robards received him with open arms. "Got us a regular gold mine here."

Wade dropped down beside the softly glowing stove. "Is there anything to eat?"

"Anything to eat, the man asks." With a flourish Rogue swept back a canvas tarpaulin to expose a vast pile of wealth. "We've got smoked ham. We've got dried beef. Roast lamb, boiled lamb, lamb stew. Two Turkestan carpets. Motor oil. Caviar. Pity you're not a drinking man, on account of we got ourselves almost a case of vodka and some premium Russian champagne."

"It's too much," Wade protested. "These people don't have enough even to feed themselves."

"They're traders," Robards said, settling the canvas back into place. "Traders are the same all the world over—they hate nothing worse than an unpaid debt. Let these people say thanks the only way they know how, sport."

Before the meal was completed, a group of men appeared from the gathering shadows and demanded, "Is this the place of the healer?"

Wade raised his head from his plate and asked wearily, "Can it wait until morning?"

"Perhaps," one of the men replied, coming into the lamplight. He was heavily armed and bore a deep cut running from forehead to chin. The eye that lay in the slashed path was matted shut. "But there is also a chance that he may not see another dawn."

"Careful with this one," Robards hummed with deceptive calm, his eyes remaining on the cup in his hands.

"He's got somebody who may be dying," Wade replied.

"Man's gotta do what he's gotta do," Robards said, his tone almost bored. "Take Mikhail with you for safety's sake."

Wade thought it over, then declared, "One of your men must remain here until my return. And one of my own will accompany me."

The man hesitated only a moment, then nodded. "It will be as you say."

Their way took them far beyond the compound's periphery and into the gloom of a night untouched by public lights. Their flashlights bobbed and wove down litter-strewn paths. Twice they gave way to crowds of drunken men shouting obscenities and seeking trouble. Wade and Mikhail followed the example of their guide and stepped quietly into the waiting shadows.

Their destination was a hovel that was part wooden shack, part well-patched tent. A surly voice challenged them as soon as their lights came into view. The guide shouted back and led Wade and Mikhail to where a trio of fully armed guards kept vigilant watch.

The guide motioned Wade through the low doorway. "In there. Your guard remains here."

Wade hesitated, until a soft groan from within spurred him forward. He nodded to Mikhail and stepped through the door.

The stench that greeted him almost drove him out again.

Wade took a gasping breath and forced himself forward. In the candlelight he saw a form curled upon a makeshift bed of burlap matting. There was no furniture. The room's only light came from a sputtering candle. The stench came both from the still body on the bed and from a bucket by the far wall. Two other men remained huddled in the far corner, watching him with the dull eyes of bone weariness.

Wade squatted down beside the inert form, gently eased the body over, and saw a young man with pale European features. He turned to the pair against the opposite wall. They too had fair features and watchful Western eyes.

Wade asked, "Do you speak Russian?"

That brought a glint of humor. "What else would we be speaking?"

"What is wrong with this man?"

Instead of replying, the man cocked his head to one side and said softly in heavily accented yet understandable English, "Could this truly be an American who has found his way here?"

The scarred man stepped through the doorway, and immediately the glimmer died in the other man's eyes. He lowered his head to his knees and went on in Russian, "He has food poisoning. You would too if—"

"You talk too much," the guard hissed.

"How long has he been like this?" Wade demanded.

"Four days," the guard replied, his eyes on the other man.

"He has not been able to eat or drink anything for two," the man said to the floor by his feet.

The form on the bed shuddered, moaned, and made a retching sound. Then he subsided.

Wade turned to his satchel. He inserted a thermometer in the man's mouth, checked his pulse, took his blood pressure, fitted a stethoscope and checked lungs and heart. Then he reached for a pen and paper. As he wrote he said, "This man is extremely weak. I must set up an intravenous drip to get some fluids into him." He tore off the sheet, handed it to the guard, said, "Have one of your men take this back to the truck and give it to my friend."

"Your own man—"

"My man stays with me," Wade replied firmly.

"They will never find your truck."

"Then you must go yourself."

The guard glowered at him, started to object. Wade cut him off with a strength he only found when working. "This man is very near death. I do not know if I can save him. Every moment is precious."

The guard spat a bitter curse, then turned and stomped from the room. With electric swiftness, the man who had spoken in English leapt forward, swept up the pen and paper, then returned to huddle in the far corner, his back now to the room. His companion sidled up closer to him and blocked his actions from view.

Outside the hovel the guard barked orders to his men, then marched into the night. Another man, shorter but broader in girth with arms as thick as Wade's thighs, came up and filled the doorway.

Wade prepared one injection of antibiotics and another to stop the nausea. The man made no protest as the shots were administered. Wade turned to the guard and said, "I need water and a clean towel."

The guard hesitated, then retreated a step. As soon as his motion carried him from the doorway, the other man was sliding silently across the floor toward him. But the guard had not left, rather simply told his companion what to bring. The man froze into his position beside Wade as the guard turned back around, then said in a tight voice, "Can you save my friend?"

"I will try," Wade replied, his heart in his throat. "Will you help me strip and wash him?"

"Of course." Together they rolled the inert form over, lifted off the sweat-stained clothes, then bathed the fever-heated body first with water and then with alcohol.

As they were finishing and covering the man with the cleanest of the blankets, the scarred guard pounded up the path. There was a moment's confusion at the door. Clearly the burly guard did not wish to enter too far into the room's fetid depths. As the two men traded places, the Russian slipped the square of paper from the folds of his clothes and into Wade's palm. Wade pocketed the paper with the speed of one handling a live coal.

He set up the drip, taped the needle into place, hung the plastic bag from a nail in the wooden part of the wall, and adjusted the flow. He set two further pouches beside the Russian and said, "You must change the drip when the level reaches here. Just turn this handle so, take off the empty pouch and replace it with a full one."

"I will do as you say," the man replied, his eyes never leaving Wade's face. They shouted a mute appeal.

"And bathe him once more with the alcohol," Wade

said, packing up his satchel, wanting nothing more than to be away.

The guard demanded, "Will he live?"

"I will return at dawn," Wade replied. "By then we should know."

Robards listened with the stillness of a hunting cat as Wade described the scene. He then rose and with casual ease checked their periphery. "All clear. The old man's on point guard. Let's see the note."

Wade plucked the slip of paper from his pocket. It was in Russian. He translated, "We were to be delivered to new guides here. They were supposed to pay the men who have brought us this far. They never arrived. We are being held for ransom, but there is now no way for money to reach us here. Save us. We will pay and pay well. Otherwise we shall die."

Robards pulled at his lip. "You say they didn't look like locals?"

"Definitely not. They were Russian. At least the one who talked with me was."

"Did he sound educated?"

"We didn't talk that much. But his Russian was proper, if you know what I mean. And he spoke at least a little English." Wade reread the paper. "Who do you think they are?"

"Hard to say. The question is, what do you want to do now?"

"What do you mean?"

"Still your show, sport. Long as you're paying for the dance, you call the tune."

Wade examined him. "I just don't understand you."

Rogue smiled. "You're still trying to fit me into some little cubbyhole, aren't you. Still thinking that a man who lives like I do can't be bound by anything as slim as his word."

"I've never met anybody like you in my entire life," Wade replied. "So I don't know what to expect."

"Yeah, well, that makes two of us."

"What's that supposed to mean?"

"You're only the second religious boyo I've ever met who hasn't made it his primary objective to stuff the meaning of life down my throat."

"Maybe it's because I don't understand it all that well myself," Wade confessed.

"That's not the way I see it," Rogue contradicted. "I've seen you working with sick people. You know. You just don't feel like you've got to use a megaphone to get the message across."

Wade hung his head, both embarrassed and pleased by the man's words.

"Okay, back to the subject at hand. Like I say, I offered you my services. If I understand you correctly, you want to take up my offer."

"I do," Wade confirmed. "Very much."

"Right. So that leaves us with three questions. First, where are we headed? And second, do we take these joes with us? We can dicker over payment once we figure out where we're headed."

"You think you can get them out?"

"We," Rogue corrected. "But let's stick to the ifs and the wheres just now and leave the hows for later."

"I think I want to go to Georgia and see if I can find the Red Cross survivors," Wade said slowly.

"I kinda figured that," Robards said. "Well, forward looks about as safe as backward from this point. I've checked the map. We're about as close to halfway as we can get."

"I hate the idea of leaving those men trapped there," Wade said.

"That's the spirit," Rogue said. "Dress up the chance to make a little extra change with some good old-fashioned morals, and all of a sudden the man grows some courage."

Wade threw him a look but did not challenge Rogue's statement. Instead, he confessed, "That guard with the scar really scares me."

"Good. Best chance to stay alive is to have your reflexes sharpened with a little fear."

"So what do we do now?"

"Turn in," Rogue answered. "Tomorrow's early enough to start working on a back door for our friends. You can take top duty."

As Wade was stretching out his bedroll on the truck's canvas roof, Rogue raised himself onto the top of the cab. He spent a moment watching the stars, then said, "I watched you with those folks. You've really got the touch."

Wade slid into the bag. "Touch of what?"

Robards dropped his gaze from the heavens and inspected Wade. "You remind me of somebody I once knew."

"A friend?"

"Probably woulda been," Rogue replied, "if he'd lasted long enough."

"He's dead?"

Rogue nodded. "Took a direct hit in Nam. One meant for me."

"I'm sorry."

"Threads had that way of caring for people. Like you. Had your religion, too. Big, gangly kid. Didn't talk much. All nuts and bolts of different threads, our lieutenant said. That's where he got his tag. Threads. Only time it all came together was when somebody needed help. Then he stopped looking gangly and started . . ." Rogue shrugged. "He just changed, is all. I don't know how else to explain it."

Rogue's features cut a sharp silhouette from the night's starry swath. "We were up on the line. All of a sudden the gooks were on us from both sides. The caps started going off like crazy. They lobbed in one of their homemade grenades, landed in a puddle maybe ten feet from me. Threads just fell on it."

Rogue's voice held the bleakness of a winter wind. "Man, what a waste. I always felt like something in me died with Threads that day. I came outta that war hating two things more than anything, waste and the lies people put on you to get you to do their dirty work. I decided I was done with waste and I was done with all the lies."

And then the words were there waiting for Wade, a gentle force too strong to be held back. "You could make the best of your friend live again," Wade said quietly.

The massive frame swiveled around. "What are you talking about?"

"By opening yourself up to his faith," Wade continued. "By figuring out how to live with that same light in your own life."

There was a long silence, then Rogue turned away. "Threads is dead. That's fact. It's late and I'm tired and we're sitting here jawing about stuff that neither of us knows anything about. That's fact, too."

He slid from the cab's roof. "Get some sleep. Tomorrow's gonna be a big one."

8

ALLISON AROSE BEFORE the day's heat became a burden. From some unseen grove came the fragrance of ripening fruit. The early morning air was alive with scents—nutty smoke, blooming herbs, dark bitter coffee. She opened her window as far as the stubborn hinges would allow and drank in the aroma.

The window faced east and south. Allison was able to look out over a series of rooftops and catch sight of a sliver of sea. The water looked impossibly blue, as did the sky. In fact, the whole landscape was brilliant with color. Silver-green olive trees softened distant hills. Tiny rivulets furrowed the dry earth, their paths lined by brilliant yellow flowers. Allison watched the dawn strengthen and felt an awakening sense of excitement over the beauty and mystery of this land.

She arrived in the kitchen after everyone else had eaten. A communal pot contained coffee of gluelike consistency. A metal serving tray was piled high with cold pita bread. A vat of butter and half-gallon jar of marmalade stood alongside, both covered by cheesecloth to ward against the flies.

As she served herself, someone glanced in, spotted her, and left. Soon afterward, Ben arrived and greeted her with a smile. "I hope you slept well."

Allison nodded around her mouthful. The bread was

utterly tasteless and had the consistency of boiled leather. "Fine. I had a visitor here a minute ago, but I scared him away."

"Oh, that was Fareed. He's a product of the old school. He will be friendly enough once he has been properly introduced to this attractive new foreign lady." He watched her set down the half-eaten bread and push the plate to one side. "If you are finished with breakfast, perhaps I can show you around the clinic."

Beyond the cramped waiting room, the clinic opened into a series of largish rough-hewn chambers. Ben led her down a side hall and explained, "This was formerly a tea warehouse, which was very good for us as it meant that at least a modicum of cleanliness was maintained." He pushed open a door. "This is your office."

The closet-sized room was jammed full with a desk, chair, and two filing cabinets. Papers were strewn about the desk, piled on every surface, littered across the tiny floor. There was no window.

"We lost our administrative assistant three months ago," he said. "I am afraid we have permitted things to get a little behind."

"A little," she agreed.

"We deal with the poorest of the poor," he went on. "People who are disowned by clan and society. Bedouins, Palestinians from the more impoverished sectors of several neighboring camps, illegal guest workers from other Arab states who cannot afford a licensed doctor's fee. Our money comes from various missionary and hospital associations. Forms for this, and the stock lists, will make up the majority of your work."

"At least around here," she murmured, wondering when she would find time for anything else.

"I make almost daily rounds through outlying areas, including the camps. I shall also expect you to accompany me."

She nodded her understanding. "Granting me entry to the areas denied to the little man and his friends."

In response, Ben pushed her gently into the office. By scrunching up beside her, he managed to close the door. In a low voice he said, "You would be well advised to say as little about that as possible."

She stared at him. "You have spies working in the clinic?"

"One of whom we know for certain. His name is Ali, and I alternate between thinking that he is a delightful young man and a pestilent little demon."

"But if you know who he is, why don't you get rid of him?"

"Because any outside group operating within the camps will be carefully watched. That Ali is both young and overly vocal suggests they consider us to be relatively harmless."

The thought of such subterfuge at close range chilled her. "But there might be others."

"Certainly others whose sympathies lie more with the fundamentalists than with the West," he replied quietly. "But they are both excellent workers and also willing to consider the Christian faith as an alternative to hatred. So I remain certain only about Ali."

"I'll be careful," she said solemnly.

"Good." He pulled open the door and ushered her back outside. "Now let me show you the women's and children's wards."

The wards were packed to overflowing, both with patients and families. Each bed had its own little gathering, and most gatherings carried on running commentaries among themselves. Talk ceased at Allison's entry, but with Ben Shannon at her elbow, she was quickly accepted and ignored. Ben showed calm courtesy to patients and families alike, gently resisting their pleas to join lengthy discussions. The nurses were introduced. They gave Allison friendly yet reserved greetings of those accustomed to taking time to inspect before granting full approval.

The flies troubled her tremendously—that and the

cries of the children. A little girl of perhaps five clung to a bearded, beturbaned grandfather and wailed as the nurse pressed a stethoscope to her bare chest. For an instant, Allison saw through the young girl's eyes; a strange, uniformed woman in this world of sharp lines and alien smells pressed a bright cold piece of metal against her body, while her beloved grandfather forced her to submit. It was terrifying.

Just inside the second chamber, a querulous little voice halted their passage. Ben sat beside the little form in the bed, accepted the fist which grasped his lapel with panic strength, and replied with a softness that for some reason brought a lump to Allison's throat.

Ben looked up at her and said, "This boy survives on strength of spirit alone. He was shot in the abdomen by a stray bullet during one of our fratricidal conflicts. There has been severe infection. He can rarely keep food down."

"Can't you do anything?"

Instead of replying, he bent over the boy, placed a hand on the flushed forehead, and spoke softly. The boy chirped a reply, his fever-bright eyes glittering. "He says he feels a song coming on," Ben told her quietly.

The boy began to sing in a cracked and wavering voice, the tonal changes making no sense to her Western-trained ear. But the sound brought smiles out from the two nurses working elsewhere in the room, and a few handclaps from other bedridden patients. The boy sang and sang, then his energy simply disappeared. He wilted like a flower under a desert heat; one moment he was bright and warbling, the next he was simply not there. His eyes lost their focus, his jaw slackened, his hands dropped like weights. Ben Shannon remained bent over him for a moment, stroking his forehead and whispering words not meant for Allison.

Then he straightened and gave her a weary smile. "Shall we continue?" He walked on down the ward.

Allison found herself unable to move. She was surrounded by need and fear and pain, and felt utterly helpless.

He returned to find her standing in the middle of the floor. "I thought you were following me." He stepped closer. "Do you realize you are crying?"

"No, I . . ."

He grasped her arm and gently steered her forward. "Come along. Let's make you a nice cup of tea. I'm afraid that's the strongest thing we can offer you here."

Ben settled Allison in her new office, brought tea, and seated himself opposite her. He did not speak, gave no explanations, did not try to explain it all away. When she was once again capable of thought, she saw the wisdom of his deed. There was nothing he could say to change the way things were here. Either she could accept them or she could not. It was her choice.

She took the time to study him. Ben was more comfortable with silence than anyone she had ever met. Not with remaining quiet. He was *silent.* It was an atmosphere which he carried with him, an invisible symbol of who he was and what he represented—whatever that was. Even when he talked, there was a part of him which remained unreachable. It was as though he dwelled in two worlds at once—one ruled by man, the other by stillness.

"Cyril was right," she eventually said.

"About what, my dear?"

"He told me I'd find you changed."

Ben did not deny it. "Did he give you a reason?"

"He said it was your wife and the desert."

"They were certainly important. But Cyril's description lacks what my wife calls the yeast of a well-lived life."

"And what is that?"

"Before I arrived here," Ben replied, "my life spoke so loudly of my faults that no one could hear what I was saying. But this land and these people are a quieter world than any I have ever known. Learning the lesson of silence forced me to see my life and my heart for what they were. Before, I walked across the stage of life like a poorly trained actor, reading hollow lines placed in my mouth by a preacher or a book or the Scriptures, but never really understanding what was being said. I simply lived my assigned part. I was desperate to avoid taking a long, close look at who I was on the inside. When I came here, the actor's role was stripped away, and suddenly the lie of my untested heart was exposed."

Allison's brow furrowed. Ben was speaking to her, and yet at the same time he appeared to be speaking *beyond* her. If there was anything in his voice besides a quiet desire to share, it was gratitude.

"The whole concept of mission to the Muslim world must be very low-key," Ben went on. "We tell all newcomers that you cannot evangelize on a street corner here for two days, because on the first day you would be arrested, locked up, in some places tortured, in others killed. No, you must show the love of Christ in word and deed and prayer. You share His mercy in public action until someone finally asks why, and then with an individual ready to listen you share in private word."

"That must have been tough for you," she replied. "Pop used to say that once you started on religion, if everybody left the room you'd have tried to convert your own shadow."

"That sounds exactly like your father." He toyed with his glass for a moment, then went on. "Living with silence teaches a great deal. When you cannot speak, you learn to share more from the heart. Instead of giving words, you give love. After having spent so much time here, it now appears to me that many Christians substitute words for love. They have mouths like foghorns and hearts like lemons. A year of silent service might teach them what is more important, a big heart or a big mouth. It certainly did me."

• • •

When Ben excused himself to see to his rounds, Allison sought refuge where she had always been most comfortable—in work. It was slow going at first, but by midday she was beginning to orient herself.

The first requirement was to establish order, and order was something she was very good at. A box was found. File drawers were inspected, and outdated files stored away. Then Allison began gathering the piles of paper littering her office, sorting them the best she could, and stowing them in the freed file space.

She was so involved in her work that the knock on her door made her jump. "Yes?"

The door creaked open to reveal a dark sprite crowned with a bounty of dark curly locks. "You Miss Allison?"

"That's right."

"I am Ali. Dr. Ben, he say, you no eat?"

Allison glanced at her watch. "I didn't realize how late it had become."

"You are hungry, yes? You wait, I bring."

Within a few minutes he was back, bearing a tray with a sandwich, some dates, and a Pepsi. Ali set it down, looked around the room, and observed, "You work hard, Western lady."

"Thank you for the food," she said, suddenly very hungry. "Do you know where I can find a broom and some cleaning rags?"

"Don't worry. I bring." But Ali stayed where he was. "You are American?"

"Yes?"

"Why you come here to Aqaba?"

She inspected the boy as she took a bite of the sandwich—processed cheese on white bread, no butter, no nothing. Ali was small and wiry, probably about eighteen or nineteen. Certainly not what she had expected as a spy. "My father and Dr. Shannon were friends."

"Ah." He nodded. Family ties were clearly something he could understand. "Nurse tell me you cry for boy."

Allison fought back another surge of emotion. "I thought it was very sad."

"The boy is martyr. He soon happy."

"You mean he is getting better?"

Ali shrugged. "*Insh 'Allah.* But I think no."

"Then how—"

"You no understand, Western lady. He is martyr. He goes to live on the highest level of paradise. There the green birds of the Garden sing to him forever. Is that not a glorious thought? He is alive while we are dead."

Allison fought back the argument that rose in her throat. Instead she confessed, "I just felt so powerless."

"We know power to be banned," Ali replied, not understanding. "To be arrested. To be disappeared."

"What do you mean?"

"We struggle against corrupt governments. They very strong, but we don't defeat at all. Real power is in Allah, not where they think, in official power. Our goal is to serve Allah. To do as Allah commands. We push them. We get power, and then we turn power over to Allah."

"Ah, I see Ali has decided to keep you company." Ben Shannon appeared in the doorway. "Unfortunately, it is time for my rounds in the villages, and I thought perhaps you would care to join me."

Allison finished her Pepsi and stood. "Thank you for the lunch, Ali."

"You good lady," Ali decided, taking the tray. "We talk more."

When they were alone, Allison said, "I think I just passed inspection."

"It would appear so," Ben agreed and handed her a plastic bag. "If it is not too much trouble, I would be grateful if you would please carry these extra supplies for me."

"Of course," she said, recalling his warning. "I have a case back in my room I could use."

"Please get it, then," he said, nodding.

"I'll be right back." She rushed away, excitement an electric shiver through her nerves.

It had begun.

9

THE NEXT MORNING Wade found his Russian patient much improved. The man was able to take a few spoonfuls of the stew Wade brought with him. "I think he is going to survive."

The guard showed no reaction, but the other Russian gave a feeble smile. "This is good news."

"I brought enough food for all of you," Wade said, indicating the covered pot. "Try and see if he will eat some more later. And give him as much to drink as he will take."

"I will do this," the Russian agreed. "Thank you."

"He is your friend?"

"No questions," the guard snapped.

Wade busied himself with his satchel. He gave the sick man another pair of injections, then brought out two boxes of medicine. "He needs to take one of these antibiotics three times a day for seven days. It will help protect him from secondary infection."

"Your Russian is very good," the man responded.

Wade handed over the second box. "These tablets should help dry him up when the sickness is upon him. Give him one every two hours for as long as necessary." He resisted the urge to glance toward the guard. Instead he looked directly at the Russian and said, "You must carefully read the directions on the box. This is very important."

"I understand," the Russian said, his eyes suddenly filled with the same appeal as the night before.

"Tonight I shall return for a final check." Wade stood. "Until then."

"It's not too late to turn back," Robards had reminded him earlier that morning. "Even if the money does sound attractive."

"It's not the money. I don't like the idea of leaving anybody trapped like that," Wade had replied. "But I'm worried about taking on anything else until I finish with this assignment."

"In the first place," Robards said, "you did what you were supposed to do. Far as I see it, whatever happens next is going to be a seat-of-the-pants deal anyway. In the second place, the money's always important. Always."

"Then why are you so interested in helping out somebody who might not even be able to pay you?" Wade retorted. "They're in this fix right now because their guide did not arrive with the money."

Rogue nodded. "I've been thinking about that."

"And?"

"And I think maybe we'd be in better shape to collect if we act as guides as well as help them escape."

"You mean, take them to Tbilisi?"

"Like I said," Robards replied, "it's your show."

Wade thought it over. "There's no reason not to take them along, since we're going in that direction already."

"My thoughts exactly."

"But what makes you think you'll be paid then?"

"We," Rogue corrected. "We'll be paid, all right. The boys were supposed to have been met by a guide here for the rest of their trip—somebody who from the looks of things decided to skip town with these other guides' payment in his own pocket. That means they have to have a contact at that end—somebody with dough. So we deliver them to their destination, collect for both jobs, then we're through with the guide-dog business. Simple."

"It sounds okay," Wade said slowly. "Who do you think those Russians are?"

Rogue busied himself with another mug of coffee.

"You know, don't you," Wade pressed. "Or you think you do."

"Just a hunch. Nothing that can't wait until we're safe and all have a little chat," Robards replied. "So what's it going to be?"

"How do we get them out?"

"Is that a yes or not?" It was Rogue's turn to push. "No need to get into details until the go-ahead's been given."

"Does that mean you think we can do it?"

"Wouldn't be wasting time talking about a target like this if I didn't."

"And we can get out of this alive?"

"Those are the only targets that count."

"We can't just leave them, then. Not if you really think we can help."

Rogue waited in catlike stillness, only his eyes showing the faintest glimmer of interest.

Wade took a breath, fought to still a sudden flutter of nerves. "You've got to promise me that nobody is going to get hurt from this."

"I've got no desire to be on the receiving end of a vendetta," Robards answered. "I've met guys like these before; they're the kind that'll follow you to the ends of the earth."

"Okay, then," Wade said. "I guess we should do it."

"That's the spirit," Robards said, rising to full height. "I've written a note that you need to translate and carry along when you pay your next call."

• • •

By dusk all was prepared.

Wade walked toward the prisoners' hut on legs that threatened to give way at any moment. The scarred warden grunted his customary greeting and prodded open the door with his boot. "This is your last time," he declared. "The man is well enough, and I will not pay for visits and medicines which he does not require."

Wade stood his ground and spoke as Robards had instructed. "You must give him boiled water and green vegetables. He remains very weak, and if you are not careful, he could still die."

The guard's customary suspicion weakened for a moment. Sullenly he agreed, "It will be as you say. Come."

Wade forced himself forward. He found the same lantern-lit tableau as the night before. The two relatively healthy men squatted in their corner, while the third sprawled on his filthy matting. But three pairs of eyes fastened upon him with singular intensity as soon as he came into view, and Wade knew the morning's note had been read.

The same man crawled over to help as Wade inserted the thermometer. His back to the watchful guard, he looked Wade square in the eye and nodded. Once.

Wade lifted the thermometer and squinted at numbers his nerves would not let him read. "You are doing better," he said loudly and for the guard's benefit. "If you rest and are careful, you will be well."

"Thank you," the sick man said, speaking for the first time. His voice was barely above a whisper, but it held surprising strength.

"I must give you one final injection," Wade said. "You are continuing with the tablets?"

"Just as you said," the helper replied. "Three times this day, one of each, taken with twice-boiled water."

Wade swallowed and resisted the urge to glance at his watch. Time seemed to be dragging by in milliseconds. "You must—"

At that point the promised diversion arrived.

A group of extremely drunken men, Ossetians all, staggered by the front of the hut. Some sang, some argued, others pushed and laughed and milled about and created a vastly noisy confusion.

The scarred lookout snarled a curse and turned to the door. The men staked out on the porch shouted threats and received a chorus of oaths in reply. The yelling became louder still, and the guard took a half-step outside the door.

It was the moment Wade had been waiting for. His heart in his throat, he whispered, "In three hours there will be another diversion. You must break through the back wall, the tent part. Someone will be there waiting for you."

The Russian helper glanced toward the guard, who gesticulated toward the drunken crowd with upraised weapon. The helper hissed, "I have leaned on the wall by the chamber pot. It is not just cloth, there is wood beyond. But it gave when I leaned. With luck we can make an opening."

"May luck be with us all." With hands trembling so badly he could scarcely force a grip, Wade reached into his bag and extracted a hammer, a short crowbar wrapped in cloth to keep it from clanking, and a long-bladed knife. "Once the opening is seen, others will be there to assist."

The helper stuffed the three implements under the bedding. The sick man lay and listened with a burning gaze. The noise outside reached a crescendo, then subsided as the drunks began to disperse. The helper asked, "When shall we know to act?"

The guard chose that moment to shift his bulk around. Wade tensed his muscles to still the trembling, lifted the syringe and ampule, and after two tries managed to fit the needle into the opening. He plunged the needle into the man's thigh, released the placebo injection of vitamins, swabbed the place with alcohol, and feared that at any minute the guard would notice the thundering beat of his heart.

But no alarm was sounded. Wade collected his articles, forced his legs to carry him aloft, and steeled himself to meet the guard's hostile gaze. "You must take great care that he eats only food which is fresh and cleanly prepared and drinks only twice-boiled water from a clean cup. He cannot survive a second illness."

The guard nodded. "And for payment?"

"Come and see me at the truck compound tomorrow," Wade replied as Robards had directed. "I have not yet calculated the cost of the medicines used."

As Rogue had predicted, the guard's gaze turned contemptuous. Here was a Westerner who cared so little for money that he put off payment, and thus could be easily taken. "It will be as you say."

The blast, when it came, lit up the entire northern sky.

Following Robards' directions, Wade had remained on guard duty by the trucks. The compound rocked to its typical nighttime revelry. A band of gypsy musicians played beside a great fire, their music rising into the chill night air along with sparks and shouts and drunken laughter.

From his post atop the truck cabin, Wade looked down over the heads of the gathered throng to where two lambs roasted on slowly revolving spits. The meat glistened golden-brown in the flickering light; the tantalizing aroma drifting up past the smell of diesel fumes and road dirt.

But Wade's nerves left no room in his belly for food.

Occasionally men and women whom Wade had helped approached, offered the formal greetings of highlanders, and invited him to join them. Wade declined with quiet thanks. They did not press. There was understanding among such as these for people tending watch.

And even more for people who sought the solitude of night.

Then the first flames leapt toward the distant heavens, and all revelry ceased with a series of shouts and cries.

The explosion was not loud, yet even at the distance where Wade sat it pushed at him with a powerful *whoof.* Then a great orange ball rose with deceptive slowness, illuminating the entire northern end of town before gradually dying out.

Before the light had faded, a second explosion followed. Shots rang out, sporadic at first, then with a long automatic ripping sound. Then a third explosion. A fourth. And a final, larger than all the others combined. The shots continued, and Wade worried for the man who preferred to take such risks alone.

By then the entire compound was moving. People leapt from trucks, grabbed for weapons, pointed, shouted orders, scooped up children and hustled them to safety, took up guard positions, or scrambled toward the slowly fading light.

Wade stayed where he was and doubted seriously that his heart rate could manage a single beat faster.

After what seemed an eternity, yet by his watch was only forty-five minutes, Robards came trotting into view. Wade resisted the urge to race up, grab his arm, and ask what happened. The big man stopped in front of Wade's truck, turned, and pointed back toward the darkened distance. "You see the fireworks?"

"How did it go?" Wade demanded quietly.

"Let's pretend," Rogue replied, his arm still pointing into the distance. "I'll play like I'm filling you in on the light-show, and you play like it's all great fun."

Wade stood on the massive front fender and shielded his eyes and searched the invisible distance. "I feel like a hood ornament."

"Better to play the fool than arouse suspicion," Robards said. "Never can tell when there are watching eyes."

"So how did it go?"

"Without a hitch," Rogue answered. "Long as I can wash off the smell of gasoline before anybody gets too close."

"Can I get down now?"

"Sure. How did it all look?"

"Like that whole side of town was being fire-bombed."

"Biggest Molotov cocktails I ever saw," Rogue said with a satisfied grin. "Like to have singed my eyebrows with that last one, though. Didn't make the rag long enough, and the bang was bigger than I expected."

"You smell like a filling station."

"Yeah, got to wash this off. Come on around back." Behind the truck Robards peeled off his shirt. "Your Ossetian buddies sure know how to follow directions. The gasoline canisters and the rags were right there at the back of the empty corral, which ain't no more, if you're interested. I set the canisters about thirty yards apart in a sort of semicircle around the front of the hut. Good thing that house was set out there by itself."

He poured soap and water into a basin, used his shirt to wash off his upper body, then stripped and doused all his clothes. "After lighting the last rag I skirted around back and watched the guards go blazing away at the night."

"I was worried when I heard the shots," Wade confessed.

"Aw, they were just shooting at smoke," Rogue said, slipping into his dry clothes, "and so blinded by looking straight at those exploding canisters they couldn't have seen me even if I'd walked up and shook their hands. I placed the second and third to either side of the porch. They did just what they were supposed to—sort of blew the guards out into the night before they had a chance to think what was going on."

"The Russians got out all right?"

"Yeah," Rogue said and allowed the satisfied smile to emerge again. "When I made my way round to the back of the hut, these great bearded giants were pushing in the back wall, making it look like all the work was done from inside."

"Just like you said," Wade offered.

Rogue nodded. "Might help us make a getaway in one piece, having it appear like they made it out on their own."

"So where are they now?"

"Somewhere safer than they were before, I expect," Rogue replied, rubbing his hair dry. "Where don't matter, long as they're at the pickup point tomorrow."

The weather was still with them the next day. Barely.

By the time the light solidified enough to be truly called another day, it revealed a sky blanketed by heavily laden clouds. The temperature did not rise as it had in mornings past; instead, the air held a biting, metallic feel. Neighboring peaks were lost beneath coverings that threatened to release their dangerous white loads at any moment.

Now there was a different quality to the compound's growing activity. Talk was muted. Men gathered and searched the sky with worried expressions. Children stayed close to their camps. There was none of the casual banter or easy loitering over breakfast fires. Gear was packed and stowed. Movements were purposeful, swift, pressured by what was clearly coming.

The scarred soldier and three of his fellows arrived soon after the dawn. They wore crossed bandoliers and fierce expressions. Two of the men stopped in front of the trucks, arms at the ready. The other pair walked back to where Rogue, Wade, and Mikhail were finishing a breakfast of bread and tea.

Wade stood to greet them. "You will take tea?"

"We will take what is ours," the man snarled in reply.

The old man rose in carefully rehearsed offense at

the threat in the man's voice. "My friend has done you a service, and this is how you reply?"

A whistle from the front pair swung the scarred man around. Wade followed his gaze and was surprised to find a delegation of perhaps a dozen armed men walking toward them. An elder whose child Wade had treated two days before for a strep infection called out, "All is well with you this dawn?"

"Thank you, uncle," Wade called back. "All is well."

"The clouds herald a change for the worse," the elder went on, drawing closer. "Which way does your course take you?"

"Over the pass and down to Tbilisi," Wade replied.

"Then a swift departure is advised," the elder counseled. "Even a dusting of snow is enough to turn the cursed road ahead to something from your worst nightmare."

"I am grateful for your advice," Wade said.

The elder nodded and turned to face the scarred man square on. In an even voice, he announced simply, "These men are friends."

The scarred man faltered. "I came only to pay for the healer's services."

"Strange that it takes four armed men for such an errand," the elder replied.

"We . . ." The scarred man hesitated, then continued. "We are missing something of great value. The healer was the only man who approached our house."

"And what might this thing of value be?"

The scarred man gestured toward Wade. "He knows."

Wade turned to Robards and forced his voice to remain even. "He is accusing us of having stolen something from him."

Rogue made an issue of carefully searching the sky before shrugging his unconcern and saying, "They can search the trucks if it'll speed things up any."

Wade turned to the scarred man and said, "The weather presses us. You are welcome to search our trucks if it will ease our departure."

"There is no need," the elder said, his eyes fixed on the scarred man.

"We have no objections," Wade replied, "if it will help maintain the peace."

The scarred man faltered, then motioned for his men to climb aboard.

"My clan will ensure your honesty," the elder warned. He gestured for several of his own men to move forward and keep watch.

"I thank you," Wade said solemnly.

"My child is much improved," the elder replied. "It is a duty for friends to share the road's burdens."

Within a few minutes the four men were again gathered at the back of the first truck. The elder demanded, "Did you find what you seek?"

"There was nothing," the scarred man muttered, his gaze smoldering. He started forward, beckoning for his men to follow, only to be stopped by the elder and his clansmen.

"There is now the unsettled matter," the elder said, "of payment for the healer's services."

Past winters had chewed great hunks from the road, leaving potholes of ominous depth and edges that were ragged and crumbling. The trucks climbed in an unending stream, grinding abused gears and belching great streams of black smoke that rose to join the clouds hovering overhead. Great razor-edged peaks jutted aggressively to every side.

They had long since left behind the last sign of green. On either side, in place of trees, loomed piles of crushed rock and scrabble, careless waste heaps left behind by departing glaciers. Their brethren glinted gray-white and ominous upon neighboring peaks, and watched the passing of men with timeless silence. This was their world, cold and harsh and as foreboding as the load that weighed down the clouds.

Wade spotted Mikhail's arm emerging from the truck window ahead to point them both into a lay-by. They passed two round-shouldered buses disgorging weary streams of passengers. In the distance the River Terek poured a milky-white waterfall between two great daggerlike sentinels and down into a chalk-colored pool. The water was almost lost beneath the thundering spume.

Rogue halted his truck beside a battered farm wagon pulled by a muttering tractor. Wade followed his lead and eased in close to the tractor's other side. He joined the pair at the pool's edge, and wondered at the calm with which both Mikhail and Robards looked out over the creamy waters.

Mikhail pointed far in the distance toward the two greatest peaks in the Caucasus range, twin edifices that rose and rose and were finally swallowed by the clouds. "Together they are called El'Brus," he said, "the king and queen of the Caucasus. Five thousand six hundred meters, and still volcanic. The highland Balkars lived at the base there since the dawn of time. But they were all shipped to Khazakstan by the butcher Stalin, may his name be erased. They are now trickling home in twos and threes, with fifty years of bitterness to unleash on those who now occupy their ancestral homes. Today the area belongs to the Karbardino-Balkarija Autonomous Republic and is a part of Russia. For how long, as the Balkar numbers grow once more, is in the hands of fate."

Wade translated for Robards, who nodded thoughtfully, as though taking it all in. He then turned around and said, "I think that should give them enough time."

"Who?" Wade demanded. "For what?"

"Let's hit the road," he replied. "We're racing nature today."

Wade walked to his truck, started the motor, backed out, then drew up to within inches of Robards' bumper. That way, the highway traffic would be forced to grant them both entry at the same time. Together they shouldered the trucks out into an empty pocket, and Wade rammed his way up through the complaining gears. The endless and ever-changing vista of rocks and ancient ice rose and fell before him as the road clambered up and up and up.

Suddenly the covering that separated the cabin from the back of the truck parted slightly, and a voice almost stopped his heart with, "It appears that you are as good at escapes as you are at healing."

Wade whirled about and saw it was the Russian who had helped him care for the sick man. He eased back and fought the wheel around yet another hairpin curve. "You made it, then."

"Yuri Bazarov, at your service," the man said. "And most certainly in your debt."

They encamped toward dusk under a sullen sky. Rogue parked them as far from the gathering of tired and dusty transports as the encircling river would allow. There were a few quiet greetings from some of the other trucks, but no more offers to draw nearer and join in the comfort of a larger group. By then their habits were known. They were marked as loners and left in peace.

While Mikhail made their evening meal, Rogue and Wade worked to construct three tunnels in Wade's truck, walled and roofed by boxes of medicines and floored with the extra beddings. A cramped space was also cleared at the back of the truck, where they could gather and sit upright.

The trio of Russians made no protest when Robards suggested they not show themselves, nor even leave the trucks, until well after dark. It was best to expect trouble, Rogue said through Wade, than to have trouble catch them unawares. Yuri spoke for them all when he replied in his rough English that the tunnels were a far better home than the one they had left behind.

After finishing his preparations, Rogue sidled over to where Wade was standing. "Hope you don't mind if I handle the business end of this setup myself," he said. "Having more experience in it and all."

"I've already told you," Wade replied. "I don't want anything."

Rogue inspected him. "What's gotten under your skin?"

"I just wish I knew who they were."

"Three guys on the lam," Rogue answered. "Nothing's changed since we cut them loose except their address."

Wade looked up. "Do you think they're criminals?"

"Not any more than anybody forced to try and survive under impossible conditions," Rogue rejoined. "Bad laws make the best of men crooks in somebody's eyes."

Wade turned his attention back to the fire. "I wish I knew that for sure."

"They're right over there, sport. All you've got to do is ask," Rogue said and turned away.

As Robards climbed into the back of the truck, a figure appeared out of the gloom. He wore the tattered yet clean shirt and trousers and mismatched jacket of a man making a formal call. He clutched the brim of a sweat-stained fedora with both hands. A heavy-duty flashlight protruded from one jacket pocket. "Healer," he called softly. "The blessings of Allah upon you."

"Peace upon you as well."

"My wife has been taken ill. She is with child."

"I am not a doctor," Wade warned, repeating the familiar litany.

"You are all there is," the man replied simply.

Wade reached into the back of his truck for his makeshift satchel. "I will be back as soon as I can," Wade said to a watchful Mikhail. He walked over to where the man was waiting. "Let us go."

It was over an hour before Wade returned, drained more from his lack of medical knowledge than from giving what little help he could. Wade ate dinner with the old man while a soft murmur of voices and the muted clink of dinnerware sounded from the back of one truck.

Wade set his dinner plate aside to find the old man's gaze resting steadily on him. "The man was Ingush," Mikhail stated.

"Yes."

"Ossetian and Chechen you treated at our last stop. And now Ingush. Do you seek to make friends of all the world?"

"I saw only need," Wade replied simply.

The old man inspected him. "You are a religious man?"

Wade's fatigue was the greatest truth elixir he had ever known. He shook his head. "I try to be. I wish I was more so."

"What does this mean?"

"I believe. But God has always seemed distant to me."

The old man turned his face back to the fire and was silent for a time. "My people are said to be the oldest on earth with lines that still run pure. Our elders tell how we are descended from the Narts, a tribe from before the measure of time, half giant and half human. There are said to be ruins of Nart villages hidden among our secret mountain valleys. These I have not seen, but my father, he walked as I rode by truck. He spoke of these as real, and I carried his stories with me. Now I am old and face the unseen door. And I seek what before I was content to leave in the hands of priests. I, too, find no answers, save one."

He aimed his gaze back toward Wade. "To seek is in itself a meritous act. And sometimes the One who is sought speaks when we are not listening. I have watched you as you work your arts of healing, and I have seen a face that knows what I know not. Perhaps you seek what others have found, while all the time the great Lord speaks to you in a different tongue and at a different time."

Wade offered hesitantly, "The Bible says that he who repents and believes in Christ is saved for all eternity."

"Yes," the old man agreed. "So the priest says as well. And I tell you truthfully, for we have shared both bread and danger, young stranger. When the night shadows gather and speak the tongue of those who are no more, this promise remains my only hope."

Their conversation was stopped by the sound of Robards calling from the back of the truck. Wade stood and walked over. Rogue said, "We had a little trouble in the beginning, but this guy's English improves with practice. He's got a question he wants to ask you."

There was a silence, then the one called Yuri spoke up in Russian.

"How do we know we can trust this man?"

"First, I want to know who you are," Wade responded, "and what you are running from."

"We flee an impossible life in a hopeless situation," Yuri replied vaguely.

"I have a right to know," Wade insisted stubbornly.

Yuri exchanged glances with the other two and received some form of silent communication, because he turned back and said, "We are all engineers. We have grown tired of working for ten different bosses, and being ordered to do work made meaningless. We are weary of being paid with paper which will not buy enough to feed our families."

A knell sounded deep and ghostly within him. "Where do you go?"

"We have been promised work," Yuri replied. "Work and enough money to offer our families a life. In the south. That is all we know, and all we know to tell." He nodded at Wade. "And now I ask my own question. How can we trust this giant of a man to do as he says?"

"He is a stranger to me as well," Wade replied. "I met him only a week ago and hired him on the advice of an ally to bring me here. He has done as he said, and more. I believe him to be a man of his word."

The three huddled together to converse among themselves. Then Yuri questioned, "And he will take us where we wish to go?"

To that Rogue replied, when Wade had translated, "Tell them if the price is right, I'll cart them to the gates of hades itself, long as I don't have to follow them inside."

He slid easily from the truck, arched his back, and said, "That's enough talk for one night. We got you gents out, we brought you here. Seems to me that's about the best answer you could find." Rogue inspected the darkness, then said, "Looks safe for you three to come on out and stretch your legs."

Yuri and the man who had been sick slid from the truck and followed Rogue out into the surrounding shadows. The third man, the one who had never spoken, walked around to the far side of the fire and sat looking out over the rushing waters. The cloud blanketed all heavenly illumination, leaving only the faintest of ghostly lights to show where the river was. The water's muted roar was a constant call, spoken in the language of the mountains, a tongue held forever secret from the minds and hearts of man.

Wade skirted the fire and squatted down beside the loner. "May I ask your name?"

There was a pause, then, "Ilya."

"You were a prisoner?"

Hard eyes turned his way. "Why do you say this?"

Wade pointed a hesitant finger. "Your hair. And you've lost a lot of weight. Your head looks shrunken around your eyes."

A smirk showed through the shadows. "You are observant. Too observant, perhaps, for your own good."

Wade did not know what to say, so he squatted there in silence. His knees hurt to remain in that position, but something told him it was best not to move just then.

"I was convicted of the crime of trying to leave a country that did not want me in the first place." The man's tone was mild, almost conversational. "I was a technician at one of the military air compounds. A civilian. When Estonia became independent, Russians like myself were suddenly like lepers. My wife could not go alone into the marketplace. Nobody would sell her anything. Passersby would spit upon her and my children. They held elections, and said that because we were Russian we could not vote. No matter that I had been born in Estonia. And my wife. And our children. No matter that I had no other home. We were aliens, and it was only a matter of time before we would be kicked out. So we decided to leave for the West. But when we arrived at the Finnish border, the guards took one look at my documents and sent me to prison."

Wade eased himself down into a more comfortable seated position, then ventured quietly, "Because you were a nuclear engineer trained to work on nuclear bombs carried by the Russian fighter aircraft stationed there."

"Too observant," the man repeated quietly.

"I have heard the stories," Wade persisted, "of how Arab states are offering great wealth to attract nuclear engineers. And how Russia and some of the other states have responded by making it illegal for their nuclear technicians to leave the country."

There was a long silence, then, "They took me to Patarei, an old czarist fortress on the outskirts of the capital, Tallinn. For three weeks I was kept in a cage too small for me to even stand up. They fed me slops from a bucket. There was no light, no blanket, a wooden plank for my only furniture. Then I was transferred to a cell with two others, a teenager jailed for three years for stealing twenty rubles and another lad sentenced to two years for stealing a tire. We were let out for fifteen minutes each day. We could walk around a yard with a thousand other men. They played rock music in the yard to keep us from talking. The music was so loud it left my head ringing all the rest of the day."

He fished a cigarette from his pocket. The lighter's

flame illuminated haunted eyes. "My wife made a tremendous fuss with the military commander, and he brought my case up before the local tribunal. Finally I was released. Three nights later we escaped into Russia. The Estonian border guards were only too glad to see the backs of one more Russian family. Our papers weren't even checked."

"And now you will go build bombs for the Arab terrorists," Wade said quietly. "And create more suffering for more people."

The Russian pulled hard on his cigarette, sucking his cheeks into hollow caverns. "Tonight my wife and children sleep in a refugee camp in Austria. The same is true for my two friends. We go to where we can make for them a home."

"And what of all the homes your work will destroy? What of the world your children will inherit?" Wade kept his voice quiet, insistent. "You no longer even have patriotism to justify your actions."

"Go away, little man," he said, tossing his cigarette into the fire. "Your questions I do not need."

Wade stood, turned around, and caught sight of Robards' gleaming eyes watching him from across the camp.

The night closed in upon them with a mist so heavy it was almost solid. Every open surface was swiftly drenched. The air was bitter with a wet cold that seeped to the bones. The river's muted roar and the call of other watchmen who could no longer see one another were the only sounds that pierced the stillness. Wade took the first watch and every few minutes emerged from the cabin's relative dryness to circle the trucks. He was careful to stay close enough to reach out and touch the cold metal. With each step, his flashlight's beam struck an impenetrable white wall.

The mist isolated him, for some reason making him think of home. It was a past so distant from that particular place and time that it felt as though it belonged to another person. Wade smiled to himself and knew it was both true and not true. He was different, and yet somehow the same. He carried his thoughts with him into his bedroll, and allowed the voices of his mind and heart to lull him to sleep.

While blackness still reigned, Wade shot awake to the sound of hammering and Mikhail's shout. He clambered down from the back of the truck just as Robards bolted over the neighboring tailgate, a flashlight in one hand and gun in the other. "What the blazes?"

They came around front to find the man whose wife Wade had treated the night before beating on the hood with the butt of his automatic rifle while Mikhail watched over him, gun at the ready. "There is little time," the man said. "I saw no movement about your trucks, and my wife said I should come."

Wade was still foggy with sleep. "Time for what?"

"The air begins to freeze," the man replied. "Death stalks above."

"Look!" Robards said. The beam of his flashlight reflected on tiny pinpoints of white. Frozen ice-motes began to dust the windshield. "This what he's talking about?"

"Yes."

"Tell him whatever debt he owed us has just been wiped from the books," Robards said, opening his door and swinging inside. "Let's move out!"

Wade turned back to the stranger. "My friend says—"

The man hefted his gun to stop Wade. "May Allah bless your way with safety, healer. Until our next meeting, farewell!" He turned and vanished into the night.

"Get that truck started!" Rogue yelled over the roar of his own motor.

Yuri's head protruded from the canvas curtain as Wade clambered aboard. "What is it?"

Wade stamped upon the starter pedal, pumped the gas, nursed the choke as the motor started, faltered, caught, and held. The engine bellowed, eased, roared again. Wade slammed the gears home as Rogue's truck started forward and then he shouted back over his shoulder, "Snow!"

10

ALI SHOWED UP just as Allison was opening her office door to begin another day. "So very nice to see you another time, Western lady. You are sleeping good?"

"Quite well, thank you."

"*Insh 'Allah Sulameh*—thanks be to Allah for your well-being. I am so very glad for you. Yes, so nice."

"And how are you this morning, Ali?"

"Thanks be to Allah, life is good. Yes. You will take something? A cool drink, perhaps?"

"That would be lovely. Thank you."

"Just a moment." He was gone and back in no time. "You like anything else?"

"Not just now, thank you."

"You need, you call me. I help." He surveyed the semblance of order which her office was gradually approaching. "All people here say you do big work. I think yes, is so."

"A lot needed to be done," Allison agreed.

"Yes, you have met with very little of difficulties. All is going very smooth." He nodded. "Allah must smile on your work, I think."

She picked up the first form in her box, surveyed the questions to be answered, and said, "I'm not sure how much Allah had to do with this."

Ali scoffed. "This is opinion of who? You? You are expert? You have witnessed all life?"

"No," she said, determined to work despite the interruption. Maybe he would get the idea and leave. "But I'm just not sure how the hand of Allah has been busy in this office."

"This is something not yet revealed," Ali agreed. "Maybe sometime in future, all will be told for you, but not yet."

Ben chose that moment to step into view outside her doorway. "Ali, are you bothering Miss Taylor?"

The young man looked positively offended. "I am only standing here. Bring cool drink. I wonder how you can throw on me such accuses."

"I think your services are required elsewhere," Ben said.

"You need helps, Western lady, you call, yes?" With that he was gone.

"Ali tends to linger where he is not wanted," Ben said.

"So I've noticed."

"I thought we would visit one of the local camps today. When can you be ready to leave?"

Suddenly the forms lost all interest. Allison stood from her desk and replied, "Right now."

"Camps like these are to some extent a microcosm of the entire Arab world," Ben told her. "They are small-scale, face-to-face communities, organized in many respects as villages were in the days of our Lord. The inhabitants live in wards or neighborhoods defined by kinship and marriage and destiny."

Fareed, Ben's driver, drove them in the clinic's only transport, a battered Land Rover. They traveled through the mountains encircling Aqaba and entered the dry desert reaches. Allison tried to pay attention to Ben, yet the surrounding images haunted her.

A lone woman in head-to-toe black djellaba and *chadar* head scarf walked through miles of utter emptiness, following a snaking yellow track down to the main highway. From where had she come? Where was she going? What was the life she led?

Razor-sharp sandstone ridges jutted aggressively from a blank desert landscape—from utter flatness to a thousand feet high and back to flatness in the space of fifty meters.

The silence. Even in a rattling car, with Arabic music blaring from the radio, the silence was not dispelled. They traveled in a tiny shell of noise through a vast kingdom of quiet.

And now, unforgettably, the refugee camp.

"What you see before you is true living history," Ben said, as Fareed parked the car in front of a noisome cafe and remained seated behind the wheel as they continued on by foot. "The attitudes of the people in these camps are the same as those of two thousand years ago. Long-suffering. Patient. Hard-bitten. Pessimistic. Shrewd."

No sign was needed to announce that they crossed an invisible barrier separating the town from the refugee camp. The buildings did not change, save by degree. Yet it was clear even to Allison that they were entering another world.

"As you probably know, the first Palestinian camps were formed in Lebanon and Jordan in 1948, after the founding of the state of Israel," Ben explained. "Nowadays the remaining Jordanian camps resemble enclosed, crumbling suburbs, with shops and apartments and families who have lived there for two generations. They no longer require papers. The strongest chains of imprisonment are invisible, down deep where none but the other camp inhabitants can see."

The road was hard-packed clay and lined with mud and refuse. The fences were rusted and crumpled, more lines of demarcation than barriers.

"The refugee camps are Middle Eastern ghettos at

their most brutal," he said. "And the greatest tragedy is that the money is available to transform them right now, this very day. But to do so would rob the Arab world of their greatest propaganda weapon against Israel and the West. So these Arab states who wallow in oil wealth and decry the Palestinian plight at every opportunity sit back and do nothing. They allow the people trapped here to remain pawns in the game of international politics."

The rubble grew and formed into crumbling walls. Gradually the walls tightened their grip upon the dusty road until its width was halved and then halved again.

"If the Palestinians' situation were to improve," he went on, "then Israel and the West could say, there is no need for us to do anything; they are all okay." He sighed a weary sadness. "There is a vast chasm between the human potential for change and the political reality of hatred between peoples and nations. By politicizing the situation, they have dehumanized the people trapped here."

The fitful breeze chose that moment to back around, surrounding Allison with the stench of rotting refuse. She stumbled, almost blinded by the reek.

"There is no drainage whatsoever and only the most rudimentary of sewage systems," he explained. "Whenever there is a heavy rain, the water turns these streets into filthy knee-deep torrents."

Buildings rose and sent corroding balconies out overhead, draping the street with shadows and trapping the fetid air. Mangy dogs and cats scurried furtively down alleyways so narrow that Allison could have reached out and touched both walls. At each turning, crowds of children scampered and played and watched her passage with young-old eyes. Oncoming cars and trucks announced their passage with blaring horns and black clouds of exhaust. Donkey carts added to the confusion. Wherever a doorway or building corner allowed a fraction of space, there sprouted a tumbledown stall selling fruit or dry goods or cigarettes or papers. Allison squeezed her way down the cramped, squalid way and felt eyes follow her everywhere.

The road was now so narrow that women could pass articles overhead from balcony to balcony. Old men sat on upturned crates beside crumbling doorways, smoking hookahs and cigarettes, sipping tea, eying the strange Western woman with blank expressions. Their faces spoke of a lifetime's experience at giving nothing away.

Allison glanced at her watch and announced, "It's the twenty-minute mark."

"Very well," Ben said mildly. They had agreed that Ben would note their surroundings, then tell her the address when they were in a less public place.

Their passage suddenly opened into a large, unpaved square. To one side, a large group of men were digging at the dusty earth.

"The local radicals do great good as well as great harm," Ben told her quietly. "They do not simply harangue crowds. Right now, for instance, they are gathering many of the jobless young men and putting them to work building a new communal mosque. They pay the families with food and medicines. They give the young men a sense of purpose, of belonging. And they use this time to draw them into the fundamentalist fold."

He stopped her with a single finger on her shoulder, pointed with a minute jerk of his head, and murmured for her alone, "There ahead of me. The most radical of the local imams. Sheikh Omar."

The imam was a white-robed older man crowned with a bright scarlet turban. He wore a long gray beard and carried a silver-tipped cane. When he spotted Allison he glared fiercely, shook his cane at her, then turned away in disgust.

"What was all that about?" she demanded.

"You are Western," Ben answered very softly. "You are infidel. You are female. By your very presence you challenge his hold over all the males and tempt them into sin."

"That is the most preposterous—"

"Come," he murmured. "It is no longer safe here."

They reentered the winding series of nameless alleyways. Allison walked as closely behind Ben as she could, fighting off a sense of suffocation.

They entered an apartment block festooned with black electric cables. They climbed crumbling concrete stairs up three floors. Their knock was answered by a young woman whose pinched features looked aged far beyond her years. She did her best to smile for the doctor, opened the door, and softly invited them in.

"This is Sarah," Ben said, "a special friend."

"It is the doctor who is special," she replied in softly accented English. "Would you care for tea?"

"Why don't you two see to refreshments," he said. "And I shall see to our patient. How has he been?"

"Better, thanks to you and the Lord above," she replied. "He awaits you."

When Ben had disappeared into the bedroom, Sarah led Allison into the kitchen alcove. It was as bare as the living room and just as spotless. The enamel top of the vintage stove had been scrubbed so hard and so often that the enamel had been worn away in places. Sarah asked, "You are American?"

"Yes. Are you Palestinian?"

"My husband is. I was born in Amman."

Allison glanced at the only adornment on the walls, a crucifix, and wondered at her own surprise. She had heard that many Palestinians and other Arabs were Christians. She asked politely, "Do you mind living away from your family?"

Sarah hesitated in the act of lighting the stove, then said quietly, "I have not returned to my home for twenty-one years."

"Why not?"

Again there was the hesitation, again a quiet reply. "Conversion is a very big problem for young Muslim women."

"You converted to Christianity?"

Sarah nodded. "In the strict Muslim world, the unmarried woman is not considered someone independent. She is just a part of her family. So for some who become Christian, the family simply makes her disappear."

Allison was not sure she had heard correctly. "What do you mean, disappear?"

"I have a friend who went to Bible study with me. We were caught together with the forbidden Book. I was locked away for nine months before I escaped and went to England. I never heard from my friend again. I have looked everywhere, as hard as I know how. She has simply disappeared."

"I—I don't understand," she stumbled over the words. "You were locked up? Like in a prison?"

"For nine months," Sarah repeated. "I was put in a room, and the door was locked. I was not permitted out at all. My brother was very young then, not even seven. One night he slipped in and told me that the family had been discussing plans to kill me. Because he loved me, he helped me escape. The church put me in a school in England because I could not stay in my country. But now my parents are dead, and I have come back to my homeland with the blessing of my brother, who is head of the family. But still I am not allowed to go home."

Allison was still trying to process what she had heard. "Your own family was going to kill you—just because you had adopted a different religion?"

"It is not all that uncommon," she replied. "We hear of such incidents at least once a month. A young woman converts to Christianity. She is locked in a room, and after a while, if she refuses to recant, her food is stopped." She nodded slowly. "Very common. In every church here there is at least one person whom they know for a fact has been made to disappear. Sometimes they die. Sometimes you never know. Perhaps she has been sold to a wealthy family in another country as a servant. So many people, you see, they become sick, they have a fever, and they die. Such a case does not come to the police. How could it? The police are Muslim, too."

Sarah was silent a long moment, then said quietly, "Forget the police. Forget the authorities. If you know of such a case, it is better that you dig a hole and bring them out."

As they left the apartment, Allison said to herself as much as to Ben, "I will never understand these people."

He smiled sadly. "She told you of her family?"

Allison nodded. "How could parents ever act that way toward their own child? I'm sorry, I simply could never understand that."

Ben was a long time in answering. "There are few places in the Koran where one finds the word *forgiveness*. The Islamic attitude is, forgive or not forgive—who knows? Even Mohammed had to keep asking for Allah's forgiveness. Mercy is spoken of in the Koran—but only Allah's mercy, mind you, not man's.

"Arabs love to discuss, to argue," he continued. "It is a favorite form of entertainment in a world where little else is offered, especially to the poor. In my own discussions, I find that many Arab Muslims simply cannot fathom the concept of Jesus. Why? Because they have little concept of holy love. There comes a point in such discussions when they say something like, yes, all right, so you tell me that God so loved the world that he what? He did what? He gave who? His son? No. That is simply beyond their understanding. Unless one first accepts the concept of infinite love, the gift of universal salvation is impossible to accept.

"In the Arab world," Ben went on, "the family is ruled by the father. If no father, then by the uncle. If no uncle, then the grandfather or the brother or the cousin. It is a male-dominated world, one where domination takes on meanings that cannot be fathomed in the West. Yet these same men have no command to *love*. Thus many of these families are dominated by *fear*. I hear so often when discussing with young men the response, no, I cannot think of such things, I do not know what my father would say. And this answer is not given out of family respect or honor or love, but rather out of *fear*.

"Family ethics are mirrored by religious ethics, you see. This means, for many in this society, that the primary command is not to love Allah but to *fear* Allah. Fear his judgment. Fear his condemnation. Fear his wrath. The very word Islam means to submit; Muslim means the one who submits. Almost no emphasis is given to the *why* of this submission, do you see? Fear, love, societal dictates—the key is not the internal basis, but the act. Submit to this fearsome Allah, and perhaps he will show you mercy."

A pair of clattering scooters drowned out further talk. Once they had passed, Ben continued, "You can see how this affects personal relationships. Where fear rules, how can a wife give her family a truly loving, joyful home? What urges a husband to grant his family loving compassion and heartfelt guidance? Thus for our Arab converts, the responsibility, the *command* for lifelong love is a whole new concept. It is the greatest challenge they face in becoming a Christian, to substitute love for fear."

Three hours later they finally returned to the car. Allison groaned her way into the seat and forced herself to return Fareed's welcoming smile. She was hot, dusty, tired, her feet throbbed, and her head felt swollen from all she had seen and heard. Twice young fundamentalists had shouted at her, their threat losing none of its force by being in a tongue she did not understand. Once a mullah had raised his staff as if to attack her. Each time Ben had responded with quiet calm, defusing the situation with open-handed respect.

Everywhere she had felt herself followed by eyes, trapped in silent hostility.

Once underway, she found herself unable to relax and release the day's images. She asked, "Why are the fundamentalists so violent?"

"Because," Ben replied, his own voice tinted with fatigue, "they live in the past."

"I don't understand."

"Napoleon's conquest of Egypt in 1798 marked the decline of the Ottoman Empire and the beginning of the Western colonization of Islamic countries," Ben explained. "For many fundamentalists the past two hundred years are not important. Their minds dwell in the period when Islam ruled their world. They see the humiliation and degradation of the past two centuries as something that must be changed. Fundamentalists insist that all Arabs must return to Islam and submit to Koranic law; then their star will once again rise in the East."

Allison watched the desert roll past outside their car. A solitary tree grew in the midst of dust and rock and lifelessness. The tree did not offer a gift of green. It merely heightened the desolate loneliness.

"Capitalism and democracy are being declared manmade idols," Ben went on. "Radical mullahs throughout the Middle East are openly calling for a jihad, a holy war, against Western modernism. The fundamentalist splits the world into two distinct segments. *Dar Islam* refers to the domain of the faithful. *Dar Al-Harb* is the domain of war. In other words, you either live as a devout Muslim, or you are an enemy. The Hezbollah faction is typical of this attitude. Hezbollah means Party of Allah; it comes from the Koranic verse meaning the Party of Allah is the victorious one. That same verse goes on to say that all who oppose the work of Allah's faction belong to the devil's world. The Party of Allah must remain in battle with the forces of darkness that dominate all the world not ruled by Islam. Their mullahs call the faithful to take the

Western sword of science and use it to cut the West's throat."

Allison stared through the cracked and dusty windshield, the beauty surrounding her at complete odds with Ben's chilling words. The desert landscape was anything but monotonous. She had never imagined there could be so many different hues of yellow. A single cloud flitting overhead transformed the earthbound canvas with its shadow.

" 'War, war until victory for Allah,' " Ben recited. "Perhaps the most chilling verse in the entire Koran. Up until now, the fundamentalists' numbers were limited and their power chained. But the turning point would be if they or one of their sponsoring countries were to obtain nuclear armaments. Small, portable nuclear weapons would be the ultimate terrorist weapon. Syria, Iraq, Iran, Libya—were any of these governments to gain control of such weapons, the West would not be able to sleep peacefully. Not ever again. Which is why, my dear," Ben said gravely, "we must absolutely not fail."

11

AS THE MORNING LIGHT strengthened into brooding grayness, the trucks crested a rise and confronted two vast cliffs. A narrow slit between the mountains grudgingly permitted passage to both the river and the road. At that moment the softly falling veil of snow lifted unexpectedly, granting passage to brilliant shafts of early morning sunlight. As though taking that for a signal, Rogue pulled his forward truck into a lay-by nestled close to the right-hand cliff.

By the time Wade climbed from his cabin, Mikhail already had the stove out and was cooking a pot of water for tea. Wade accepted bread torn from a loaf, took more to where the Russians sat in the truck, then joined Robards by the fire.

"Five-minute break," Rogue said, "then we make like the wind. Ask the old man how long the gorge is."

"Twelve kilometers," Mikhail replied when Wade had translated. "This is the Daryal Gorge, known among my people as the Gates of Alan. It is the entrance to South Ossetia, the lands now usurped by the Georgian bandits."

"Georgia," Robards remarked with evident satisfaction. "Does that mean the road starts descending on the other side?"

Mikhail poured tea into glasses and set them by the fire for the tea leaves to steep and settle to the bottom.

"Beyond the Gates lies yet one challenge more. After that is safety, at least from the beasts of ice and snow. But ahead we still have the two harshest tests of all. This one first. Here, the road climbs along one cliff wall. Soon it will be a thousand meters up to the heavens and a thousand meters down to the river. Wind blows through the gorge like a funnel, seeking to pluck us from the road and hurl us into the waters below."

"The old man's a real source of light and joy this morning," Robards said, picking up his glass and sipping noisily. "Notice there's no wind."

"Not now," Mikhail warned ominously, "but there is snow. And the highland folk say that one follows the other as smoke follows fire."

"Great," Robards said, not the least affected by the news. "Anything else?"

"Rocks," Mikhail replied. "The winter beasts pluck them from on high and hurl them at the unsuspecting. In the last century a rock fell that weighed a thousand tons and closed this road for more than two years."

Rogue grinned. "If we meet one that big, we won't have long to worry about it."

Mikhail did not wait for a translation. He pointed ahead to a castle perched on the Terek's riverbank just before the entrance to the gorge. "The Fortress of Daryali. A thousand years ago, a line of castles and towers reached all the way across the Caucasus. When invaders swept down from the Russian steppes, fires were lit on their flat roofs to warn the Georgian and Ossetian kings."

"A line of fire and stories from a thousand years ago told like they happened last week. How can anybody not love this place?" Rogue picked up the last three glasses and headed for the trucks. "If you want a second glass, drink fast. Time to go meet the wind."

As though on schedule, the moment they wheeled back into the staggered line of vehicles, the snow closed in around them. Just before entering the gorge, the road passed over a shaky wooden bridge. Beyond it, the pace of traffic picked up, as though all those who drove before them were pushing themselves to the limit, racing to make it through before the denizens of winter conquered all.

Twisting rock formations rose like guardians of the high kingdom, sweeping in and out of view as the snow danced a silent warning to their passage.

Then the walls closed in around them.

They emerged into another world.

Brilliant sunshine fell upon a wide-open valley of verdant green. A small village of ancient wood and stone spread out in the distance. A flag fluttered in the welcoming breeze, gaily announcing the Georgian border.

Wade slowed in time to Robards' truck and stared out in awe as gusts of wind blew the meadows into paths of frothy silver-green.

Five hours it had taken them to traverse the twelve-kilometer gorge. Five hours of heart-stopping drops, his wheels barely able to remain on the crumbling road. As Mikhail had predicted, the wind had started soon after their entry, and had grown steadily fiercer until it buffeted his truck with angry fists.

Passing other trucks became the stuff of nightmares.

Without warning the veil of blustering snow would part to reveal a marauding behemoth bearing down upon him, horn blaring, the driver's face pressed against the windshield just as Wade himself drove. He had no choice but to move farther and farther toward the verge and the three-thousand-foot drop beyond. Several times he felt the weightless sensation of tires scrambling for a hold on a crumbling edge.

And now this.

Gratefully Wade followed Rogue off the road and onto a lay-by crammed with trucks and people. Laughing, joking, gesticulating, jabbering people. Pointing back up behind them and shouting abuse at the closeness of their escape. Passing communal bottles around. Sharing cigarettes and tea and laughter. Joined together by the lightheaded freedom of having made it through.

There were several friendly cries as Wade opened his door and slid down onto legs that seemed barely able to support his weight. He recognized several former patients, including the Ingush driver whose wife had been ill.

He walked unsteadily toward them, grinning as their laughter turned toward his faltering gait.

The Ingush offered Wade his hand. "The blessings of Allah upon you, healer."

Wade accepted it in the manner of the East, barely placing pressure upon the man's fingers. "I would not do that again for all the tea in China."

That announcement brought an extended burst of hilarity. "It is far worse for the likes of us," said a stranger, whose own face was split in a gap-toothed grin. "We knew what it was we faced. You entered seeking only adventure."

Wade turned around and looked up at the malevolent peaks. They were enshrouded by clouds that reached from earth to heaven's heights. Here was light and air and the comfort of new friends. There was only darkness and danger.

"The upper realms are closed for yet another year," one spoke, his voice subdued as he too surveyed the higher reaches. "Winter has now come, and where she rules, none may enter and leave again."

"Take, healer," someone said, and offered him a bottle of vodka. "Give some warmth to your bones."

"I do not drink, but thank you just the same," Wade replied.

"If that's what I think it is," Rogue said, walking up behind them, "I'd sure like a slug."

The sound of a foreign tongue provoked yet more hilarity. Rogue grinned to all and sundry, took a long belt from the bottle, roared his satisfaction as he passed it on, and received back-thumping laughter in return.

"Ask your friend what he thinks of the Russian highways now," someone said.

"Not a bad stroll in the park," Rogue replied when Wade had translated. "Coupla times I thought I might have to grow wings real fast."

Wade noticed the Ingush driver standing beyond the group's edge and motioning to him. Wade excused himself and walked over. "Your wife?"

"She is better, thanks be to Allah. I wish to tell you, healer, there is a border station up ahead."

"I have seen the flag."

"Indeed, the Russian dogs who guard this side are eager to rob all who are not seen as regular travelers. Their bribes are heavy at the best of times, but strangers bearing two laden trucks and Western papers will be picked to the bone."

Wade sobered. "What would you suggest?"

"We are seven trucks," the man replied. "Join with us, near the middle, and let two of us drive. We will declare no more than usual, and you can pay your share of the bribes."

"Wait here," Wade said and turned back to find Rogue's piercing gaze holding steady upon him. At Wade's gesture Robards slipped from the group and joined them.

"It's a risk," Robards said when Wade told him of the man's offer, "that they'll save us from the Russians and rob us themselves."

Wade did not disagree. "Even if they don't, we'll pay more than our share of the bribes."

"So what do you think, sport?"

"I say go with them," Wade replied. "You ride in one truck, Mikhail in the other, and I'll hide out in back with the Russians."

"Sounds good." Robards inspected him with a grin. "Wish you could hear yourself."

"What are you talking about?"

"It's been coming on so slowly, you haven't noticed it, have you?"

"Noticed what?"

"You're growing up," Robards replied. "Getting confidence in yourself."

Wade took a step back. "That's silly."

"Sure it is." Robards turned back to the group and the bottle. "Go tell your friend it's fine by me. I've still got a thirst to work off."

They joined the endless line of trucks at the border crossing, one of a group of nine, all driven by dark-skinned Ingush traders. Mikhail sat uneasily in the passenger seat beside the bearded hawk-nosed stranger, showing with every movement of his ancient frame that he neither trusted nor wished to be near this man whose clansmen were his enemies. If the Ingush noticed Mikhail's unease, he gave no sign. He spoke not at all except to turn and solemnly greet Wade, who crouched behind the canvas awning where Yuri had formerly rested. All three Russians were safely holed up in their small tunnels, scarcely breathing.

Mikhail gave the warning with a faint hiss and ducked down under the dashboard. Hidden by shadows, Wade craned and caught sight of the scarred man standing with two of the other guards a few paces ahead of the border station. They eyed each truck with undisguised hostility, searching for alien Western faces. Wade ducked back into darkness.

The Ingush driver murmured, "Was he not one who came to your truck in the compound and accused you of stealing?"

"They are not friends," Wade whispered back. "Are they looking this way?"

"Why should they?" The Ingush showed vast unconcern. "We are just another cursed Russian truck, barely able to crawl forward another kilometer, driven by a simple trader, in line with his clansmen, bearing meager goods and too many hungry mouths."

"You say it well."

"It is the chant we use before all border stations," the man explained, "one I have heard since before I could walk."

Wade ventured another glance. He could no longer see the scarred man. "Are they gone?"

"They seek you farther back along the line. Who are they?"

"Chechen," Mikhail answered for them both.

"Then they would skin their own clansman for the dregs of his cup," the Ingush replied. "Did one of their own die after you treated him?"

"I don't know," Wade replied truthfully.

"Only two things would force a Chechen to brave the Daryal Gorge at winter's onset," the Ingush said. "Revenge or money."

"The healer is not a thief," Mikhail declared fiercely.

"That much is clear," the Ingush agreed. "Seldom have I seen such an honest face even upon an infant. What brings you to our land, healer?"

"The call of God," Wade replied, grateful for the shadows that hid his reddened face.

"Ah, a holy man," the Ingush said, nodding. "I saw the sign of peace upon you as you dealt with the pains and sicknesses of others."

Mikhail showed surprise. "A Muslim who pays homage to a Christian?"

"I saw what I saw," the Ingush replied stubbornly. "My heart saw as well. The healer is a man who gives from that which is beyond man's vision."

Wade let the flap fall and spent long minutes inspecting himself in the mirror of the Ingush trader's words.

• • •

The village of Kazbegi was rimmed by water and ringed by mountains. It crowned a graceful hillock at one end of the long green valley. Peaks so high they remained white all year round encircled the village, towering giants that glinted proudly in the afternoon sun. The village houses clustered up tightly together, seeking strength and solace from one another in the face of such overwhelming might. The dwellings climbed the hill in orderly rows, their rooftops making a series of ocher steps up to the three church spires.

"The Kazbegi do not care overmuch for us," the Ingush said as he drove on past the graceful village. "They permit our trucks space only beyond the village. They give us air and water, at least until they find a way to make us pay for these as well. For all else we are charged prices higher than the surrounding mountains. What we can do without, we leave until after the true descent is made."

The truck compound was nothing more than a large field too rocky to permit planting. A trio of armed men shouted orders which were lost in the motors' perpetual racket and pointed them to an unoccupied corner. The Ingush gathered their trucks in a tight cluster, with Wade's two trucks at the center. Only when the engines coughed their last did the first trader climb down on tottery legs. It was the man whose wife Wade had treated. Following close on his heels was Rogue.

The big man asked when Wade had descended, "Since we're all here and breathing, I take it the guys didn't spot you."

"I was in the back, and Mikhail was under the dash. What about you?"

Rogue grinned. "It's surprising what a tiny ball this body can make when it has to." He motioned toward the trader. "Tell the man we're in his debt up to our eyeballs."

Wade said to the Ingush, "Our gratitude will remain with us all our days."

"A day when the Chechen dogs are outsmarted is a

day to be remembered with great relish," the trader replied. "What did you do to gather such wrath upon your heads?"

Wade's Ingush driver answered for him. "He was gracious enough to treat one of their own, who did not have the grace himself to survive."

Rogue broke in and said, "I sure wish we had the cash to pay for all their bribes."

"I've got an idea," Wade said and ran back to his truck. He reappeared a moment later with a box under each arm, which he offered to the trader. "We shall never be able to repay your kindness. But please do us the honor of accepting this small token of our eternal gratitude."

The trader took one box, split the top with a practiced motion, and widened his eyes at the sight. "Medicines."

"Antibiotics," Wade agreed. "All within the dates of use, as the numbers stamped here state to any who can read the Western script. They should bring you a good price."

"As would gold itself in the right places." A murmur of agreement rose from the gathered traders. The Ingush straightened, accepted the second box, and said, "A worthy gift from worthy friends. I and my clansmen thank you, healer."

"Smart," Rogue agreed. "A good use of what we've got here."

The trader looked around the gathering of his fellows and apparently received an affirmative, for he said to Wade, "We shall rest here for an hour and then drive up and through the Krestovy Pass."

Wade translated for Rogue, who asked, "They'll take on the pass in the dark?"

The trader pointed toward the cloud-enshrouded mountains behind them. "Tonight the might of winter will reach out to ensnare all this valley and perhaps the pass as well. I would rather drive through a clear night than yet another day of snow, and this one at a thousand meters higher than the gorge."

"Sounds like good advice to me," Rogue said. "You up for another push?"

As Wade nodded, a thought struck home, one that felt as though granted from beyond himself. He turned back to the trader and asked, "We would be beholden if a place might be found for our trucks in your caravan."

"There is always room for friends," the trader replied.

"I have yet another request to make," Wade said. "We shall be perhaps the last convoy through this valley before winter. I would like to see if there is a doctor in the village in need of medicines and equipment."

As one, the traders showed astonishment. "You would give such as this away?"

"If he cannot pay," Wade said gamely. "These articles have been given to my charge in order to help doctors in need."

There was a moment's amazed silence, then the driver of Wade's truck proclaimed with pride, "It is just as I have said. Here is truly a man touched by God."

They took one of the Ingush trucks so as to draw less attention in case the scarred man and his fellows still scouted the road. Rogue and Wade refused the traders' offer of help with unloading the supplies. They used their movements as a chance to bring the hidden Russians news and food and water.

The Ingush driver of Wade's truck fought for the privilege of taking him into the village. His enthusiasm infected all the clan, even the children, and they were seen off with waves and happy chatter. Rogue watched the proceedings in brooding silence. His only comment was that if Wade wanted to spend free time driving some more, that was his choice. But it was clear he did not approve of Wade drawing unnecessary attention their way.

Wade hunched far down below the dash, keeping only his eyes up high enough to watch as the road narrowed and entered the hamlet. The streets were cobblestoned, constricted, and steep. Three times the Ingush stopped and asked for directions, only to be greeted with hostile suspicion. The fourth time, he explained in desperation that he bore a friend approaching death. This time he was pointed toward the hovel that contained the village's meager clinic.

"I would not have you lie on my behalf," Wade chided him as they drew up and stopped before a building whose wide doors indicated previous duty as a stable.

"Do not worry yourself," the trader replied cheerfully. "All men approach death with each breath, healer. You above others should know the truth of such words."

They scouted the street before descending and pushing open the stubborn door. They were greeted with a scratchy female voice declaring from a second room, "Too late, too late! My hours are known by all."

The trader began, "We do not—"

The woman remained unseen as she interrupted with, "I too must sleep and eat and breathe air not infected by the sickness of all. Come back tomorrow."

Wade looked around what apparently served as both waiting area and examining room. As with many of the clinics he had visited in outlying Russian villages, the chamber was pitifully bare. A metal dish contained two ancient glass syringes. The sterilizing tray held perhaps half a dozen needles and a few battered instruments. The medicine shelves were almost empty.

"You must not tell me that the patient shall not last the night unless it is true. I shall not be brought out on a fool's errand." An overweight woman in a stained white jacket strode into the room and stopped at the alien sight of an Ingush trader alongside a foreigner. "What do you want?"

"Only to help," Wade replied.

"You stay," the trader told him, and headed for the door. "It is not safe for you to be seen."

The woman showed growing confusion. "You are sick?"

Wade shook his head. "Do you need supplies?"

"Ah, another trader bearing the dregs of Russian medicine," she muttered bitterly. Shadows of fatigue gouged deep crevices under her eyes. "Save your strength. I have no money with which to buy even aspirin."

"Then I shall give it to you," Wade replied.

The hostility hardened into anger. "Do not joke with me," she snapped. "I face yet another winter with no news of shipments which are six months late. Six months! Do you know what it is like to treat people with hot water and herbs?"

"Yes," Wade said, and turned as the trader brought in the first load. "Here you will find analgesics. In these two boxes, sterile solutions. And here are two hundred disposable syringes. They can be boiled and reused, but only the needles can go into your sterilizer. The syringes will melt."

The trader departed with a broad grin for the doctor's growing confusion.

"Who are you?" she demanded.

"It does not matter," he replied. When the trader reappeared, Wade went on. "Ampicillin, one hundred doses. Another hundred sulfas. Urinary tract medicines, digestive tract, anesthetics, both local and general. Can you read directions in English?"

The woman sought support from the doorjamb. "You are giving these to me?"

"Yes."

"Do not jest," she pleaded, her voice touched by desperation. "I tell you, I have no money. These people are too poor to pay."

The trader straightened from setting down his load, and declared solemnly, "Woman, I am Ingush. The Ingush do not lie. I tell you truthfully, this is a man of God. Take him at his word." He turned and left the room.

"Here are a few instruments," Wade said. "Not many.

Thermometers, scalpels, probes, needles, and gut. I hope it is enough."

"Enough," the woman murmured, her eyes on the boxes.

"This is the last of them," the trader announced, depositing his final load.

"All I ask," Wade told her, "is that whenever a trader or his family enter here, be it night or day, winter or summer, you will give to them from the best of what you know and have."

A single tear escaped from the woman's eye and made its way down the broad features. She whispered, "It will be as you say."

They arrived at the entrance to Krestovy Pass just as the setting sun turned the gathering clouds to burnished gold. "The Georgians call this the Djvari Pass," the Ingush driver explained to Wade. "Djvari means cross. It is here that the Terek River, which flows into Russia, and the Aragvi, which flows through Georgia, are both born."

From his perch behind the driver, Wade saw glaciers clinging to every visible cliffside. Their passage had carved boulder-strewn scores deep into the alien landscape. From the glaciers' lower reaches poured great flows of whitish-green waters, which gathered in pools and lakes and streams in every direction as far as Wade could see.

The trader had proudly taken charge of Wade's truck before the final onslaught on the pass. Wade had protested, not from desire to drive himself, but for the sake of the three Russians who remained cooped up within their cramped tunnels. But the Ingush would have none of it. The man of God did not know what lay ahead, he had proclaimed. Otherwise he would not wish to see, much less drive himself. With a nod from Rogue, Wade had agreed.

Out of respect for his years, Wade had insisted that Mikhail take the passenger seat. After checking that the Russians were doing as well as could be expected after almost seven hours in their stuffy burrows, Wade lifted the canvas awning up and out of the way. This would allow more air to filter through and also grant Wade an uninterrupted view.

The road leveled out for its final advance upon the pass. They detoured around what before had been an avalanche tunnel, now smothered by a rockslide so large its lower stones dwarfed the trucks that crawled past. The road deteriorated to a crumbling track, often submerged beneath swiftly running waters. Twice there were great crashing booms as rocks loosened and fell somewhere out of sight. All jollity vanished from the Ingush trader. He drove at a snail's pace and with a white-knuckled intensity.

The road skirted a giant snowdrift frozen into place for countless decades, with only its tip carved away so that vehicles could crawl past. Then came a series of hairpin curves with drops so savage Wade had to struggle not to turn away. And then, with a shout of relief from the trader, the road began to descend. Even Mikhail sighed his relief as descent turned steeper and it became clear that in truth the highest reaches were now behind them.

It was then that the first snowflake descended through the deepening gloom to coast across their windshield. The trader laughed and pointed and said, "See, healer? This is your doing!"

"That is the silliest thing I have ever heard," Wade replied without rancor, glad only to be heading downward.

But the trader was not to be dissuaded. "Your God has protected us. This I know in my bones. Why else would the snows have been held back for our passage?"

Wade was saved from a reply by their line of trucks pulling into a rubble-strewn lay-by. Wearily he clambered down from his perch and took in great drafts of the icy-fresh air.

The Ingush trader approached. "Two hours ahead, the road enters the last Chechen enclave this side of the mountains."

Wade called Rogue over and explained what the trader had said. Robards directed, "Ask him what he would do in our place."

Clearly the man had given the matter great thought. "Two hours further descent will have you beyond winter's reach, so you should have no further need of our help. There is a track which turns off just before the enclave is reached; it is used by Ossetian traders who have no wish to deal with the Chechen."

"I know it well," Mikhail said, coming up alongside.

"There are wars and rumors of wars in these southern Ossetian lands," the Ingush warned.

Wade translated for Rogue, who nodded once. "Thank the man and tell him we'll take his advice."

"What about the wars?"

"If you've got to choose between the bogeyman you can see and the one you can't," Robards answered, "go for the one who might not even be there."

Wade turned back to the trader. "Our debt to you mounts with each passing hour."

The trader who had driven for Wade shouldered his way forward. "The tale of the man of God will brighten firesides for years to come. There is no debt. May your God guide your footsteps and light your path forever, healer. These days I shall carry with me to the grave."

12

AS USUAL, ALI WAS THERE to greet Allison when she arrived at her office that morning. "Hello, Western lady. We talk about democracy today?"

"No," she replied flatly. "This is the absolute last thing I want to hear before another cup of coffee."

"You sit, I make. My coffee is best, you see. American style, just like you want." Five minutes later he was back. As he poured coffee from the burnished copper pot into the little cup, he said, "The mullah, he say to look at Britain. Three hundred years ago was great power. But America was primitive. Now America is great, but Britain has lost power. The mullah, he say America will go like British Empire. They are corrupt. They have not strength to hold power. America has big army, powerful weapons. But America has not strength of belief. Yes. They have lost *inside* strength. They will continue for little while only, the mullah say. Then will come Islam. Why? Because we have this strength. We live for Allah. Not for self. Not for gold. For Allah. And Allah will win."

He set the tiny cup down in front of Allison and nodded happily at the thought. "Oh yes. Allah will win. We will defeat all enemies."

"I am an American," she said, sipping at the cup. Ali was right; his coffee was delicious. "Does that make me an enemy?"

"Oh no," he replied solemnly, shaking his head. "Enemies are governments. Not people. Never people. We wish to show you glory of Islam, to have you to join us. How can we do this if you are enemy?"

Allison reflected that she felt very much a part of her culture and certainly was working for her government. "So where is it you think you're headed?"

"Simple, Western lady. Arab nation ruled by Allah. This is the good future. Everywhere rule of *shari'ah,* law given by Allah in Koran. Islam is all one system; you cannot separate. All must be done together. All is one goal."

"It doesn't bother you to see the drop in Iran's standard of living since the fundamentalists came to power?"

He shook his head. "Listen, Western lady. I tell you great truth. People not go to paradise because of big GNP. We are not slaves to money and job and success. We are slaves to Allah, who created us. That is difference between West and Islam. Not one difference. *The* difference. Only difference.

"At the time of the Prophet, peace be upon him," he went on. "You have people who were sinful, people who were hypocrites. So government was important, to block ways of the wrong. That is meaning of good government. But now in West all is changed for the bad. Governments protect the wrong and hurt the right. The government is bad, you see. And we, the chosen of Allah—we are told to make it right."

"How?" she demanded.

He shrugged easily. "How does not matter. That we do is enough."

"You learned this in school?"

He gave his head a violent shake. "I went to European school. All I learned, I want to forget. School set up by colonial regime, taught me to be slave, not free, not Arab. All I learn at school was lie."

"Democracy was a lie?" Allison scoffed.

"You understand nothing," he replied scornfully.

"Try me," she retorted.

"Democracy is not suit. You not go to shop and buy. You build. You shape to people and nation. But we Arabs, we are old people. Older than time. Democracy is new, Western. You have vote, yes, but we have *Islam*. You take this path, walk two steps, change and go here, there, anywhere you like. We have Allah, and he say, you go *here*, you do *this*. Democracy we shape to will of Allah, not shape Allah to will of democracy." He looked triumphant. "Now, Western lady. You tell me, which is stronger way?"

"Democracy," she said flatly. "The only form of government that gives equal power to each individual."

Ben stuck his head in her door. "Ali, you are needed on the children's ward."

Ali stepped out and smiled back brilliantly. "We talk more tomorrow, yes?"

"I can't wait."

Ben entered and surveyed her progress in the office with a bemused expression. "I never thought so much could get done in such a little time."

The room was neat and orderly. All forms and correspondence not filed away were ordered into neat stacks—pending, questions, awaiting response, and so forth. Fragrant desert blossoms sprouted from a mason jar on one of the filing cabinets. Allison pointed at her overflowing out box. "All these need are for you to look them over and sign, and then I can get them in the mail."

"Later," he replied. "I want to take you into the desert today, and for that we need to make an early start. Like five minutes ago."

They stopped at several villages along the way, all cut from the same depressing mold. The houses were square and squat and flat-roofed, all constructed of concrete blocks. The wealthier dwellings were encircled by concrete block fences topped with broken glass. Around every house, goats and camels and donkeys searched for meager shrubs. There were no trees. Children in filthy djellabas played in the dust. Everyone stopped to stare at the strangers. Ben flitted from house to house, then quickly returned, and they were off again. Every twenty minutes, Allison made note of their whereabouts.

They were inspected twice, once by blue-shirted policemen and once by the army. In both cases the uniformed men spoke in gentle tones barely above a murmur. Fareed, Ben's driver, answered the same way. When Allison remarked on their almost effeminate voices, Ben replied simply, "It is the desert. Quiet breeds quiet."

Beyond the third village, they passed through the final army checkpoint and left the highway. Soon the world consisted only of rock and sun and sand and wind.

They traveled a washboard road, and the ride was too noisy to permit talk. They rattled and bounced their way between steep-sided mountains, the surrounding desert ever changing and ever the same.

At a spot where one of the gnarled akashi trees grew large enough to offer shade, they stopped. "Time for a breather," Ben said.

Allison got out, stretched her back, and gazed at a scene void of anything familiar. "You know," she said quietly, "I've heard about this part of the world all my life, and even studied it, but I never imagined what it is really like."

"I call this the land of thyme," he said. "Do you know your Plato?"

She shook her head no, her thoughts filled with the sound of wind.

" 'Just as bees derive honey from thyme, the strongest and driest of herbs, so too does man gain great rewards from mastering the difficulties of this world.' " He stood for a moment, sharing with her the vastness of their landscape, then turned back to the car. "We must be getting on."

The mountain faces were nature's artboards, molded

into fantastic dreamscapes and painted a thousand desert hues. Eagles called out their desert songs, as much at home in these empty reaches as the wind. Desert plants grew in scattered profusion, their twisted branches as white as bones.

"The rock is smoothed by sand, not water," Ben told her at their next stop. He pointed up to a semicircular cave. "Bits of sand become trapped in hollows, and over millions of years of wind carves out caves. The Bedouins use them as dwellings during the worst of storms, pushing their herds in before them."

He led her by foot around a spit of rock to where the mountains clenched in together. As they started into the cleft, Allison noticed a sweetness to the dry air. "What is that I smell?"

"Water. Even after just a few hours here, our senses become more attuned to its presence." He pointed to where the passage was blocked by barbed wire. "Up ahead is a Bedouin spring. Rights to its use have been passed through the local Hawaitaat tribe for countless generations."

He stopped before the remains of a fire and tested the ashes with his shoe. A plume of dust rose at his touch. "Stone cold. They haven't been here for days. All right, we must search elsewhere."

"You don't know where they are?"

"Of course I do." He waved an expansive arm, taking in the rocks and mountains and sky. "Somewhere out there."

Beyond the narrow passage, the mountains opened into a vast yellow sea of sand. Rock islands pushed up at odd intervals. For some reason, their presence amplified her sense of aching emptiness.

The Land Rover lurched its way over a sand track of dips and curves and bumps. Fareed released his two-handed grip on the wheel long enough to turn on the radio. Arabic music filled the car. Allison continued her vigil out the windows and found the music to be in harmony with all that surrounded her.

They spotted the camels first.

At the sound of their approach, the animals sauntered over a ridge, vanishing from view. Fareed topped the slope and cut off the engine. In the sudden silence, Allison heard the bleating of goats and the shrill calls of children.

There were perhaps a dozen tents, each about thirty feet long and half as wide. A cluster of akashi trees marked the presence of water. A trio of old trucks were pulled up nearby.

"In twenty years this way of life may be gone forever," Ben said, leading her toward the camp on foot. "As the old generation dies off, more and more of the Bedouins are choosing to settle in permanent villages like the ones we just visited. It is a far easier life, but I for one will be sad to see this world disappear."

Allison followed Ben into the central dwelling, where a toothless old grayhead croaked a welcome and waved them in. Ben shook hands with a hawk-nosed younger man, whom he introduced as Mahmoud.

"He is the effective leader of the clan," Ben explained, seating himself gracefully on the carpet-covered ground and motioning for Allison to join him. "His father rules in name only."

At the center of the tent was a rectangular dugout lined with coals, over which rested the ever-present brass coffeepot. A woman entered, murmured greetings to Ben, knelt, and poured them thimble-size cups. Allison accepted hers and tried not to stare at the intricate tattoo that ran across the woman's forehead and down over the bridge of her nose, and across her lips, ending at her chin. She was perhaps nineteen or twenty years old.

"Tradition requires you to accept three refills," Ben

murmured. "Shake your cup from side to side when you have had enough."

The two Arab men wore the *keffiyeh*, or checkered headdress, and Western-style jackets over their robes. An interminable discussion ensued, all in Arabic. Allison sipped her coffee, watched the men talk as much with their hands as with their mouths, and took in her surroundings.

Around the tent's periphery were low cushions covered with soft carpets. Taller square cushions were set at intervals, upon which arms and bodies were leaned. The tent's interior was surprisingly cool.

Abruptly Ben stood and announced, "Time to begin."

They made their way from tent to tent trailing an entourage of chattering children. With each woman and child patient, Allison stood in quiet attendance. When the sick person was a man, she waited outside. As they walked through the camp, Ben told her quietly, "They have heard of new smugglers operating through the desert routes."

"Smuggling what?" Allison stopped. "Going where?"

"Walk with me, please." When she had caught up, he went on. "They can only find out so much without forcing dangerous attention their way. The smugglers and the local Bedouins live an uneasy truce. Those camels you see out there are nowadays kept more as signs of wealth than as a means of transport. The only time they are worked is when the Bedouins become competition for the smugglers. Camels are harder to track on radar than trucks and do not leave tire treads on sand. A full-grown camel can carry five or six televisions roped to each side."

"That's what they think the new smugglers are carrying?" Allison asked. "Just televisions?"

Ben shook his head. "Not this time. Smugglers tend to specialize—one tribe takes radios and televisions and computers to Saudi Arabia, another carries Lebanese hashish to the wealthier Gulf states and sometimes for the West, and so on. But these new people are different. Mahmoud called them shadows, since he had not seen any of them, only signs of their passage. This he finds most troubling." Worriedly Ben rubbed the side of his face. "And there have been visits from strangers—Hamas, he thinks—fundamentalist terrorists who receive financing from the oil-rich states to the south. They have warned him to stay away from certain southern routes which have been his clan's property for generations. The only positive development from all this is that their threats have made Mahmoud so angry he is now willing openly to help us."

"But what—"

"Enough for now," he said, flipping up the tent flap. "We shall talk more back at the clinic."

They had worked their way around perhaps half of the encampment when a shout stilled all activity.

Ben straightened over the woman he had been treating and rushed through the entrance. Allison followed him out. "What is it?"

Ben shushed her with a chopping motion. He stood poised as though sniffing the air. Allison looked around, saw that men stood still and alert by almost every tent.

Then she realized that the wind had died. In its place was a sense of breathless waiting. Again there was a shout, this time by a pair of voices. Allison followed their pointing arms, saw a white plume rise from the desert floor and spiral gently upwards. It looked like lazy smoke from some distant fire.

Then out of the distance there rose a low moan.

Immediately the camp exploded into action. Men and women raced for flocks and children, and frantically herded them toward tents and nearby caves. Ben shouted to Fareed, who ran toward the Land Rover.

Ben sprinted after Fareed, shouting to Allison, "We must hurry!"

"What's the matter?"

"Khamsin!"

"What?"

"Sandstorm. Be quick!" He skirted a pair of men hobbling camels made skittish by the panic. When they reached the vehicle, Fareed was pouring water from his canteen onto long cotton cloths.

Ben took one and handed it to Allison. "Take this."

"What for?"

"Just in case. Climb in."

Fareed ground the motor and started off. Nobody in the camp took time for even a glance in their direction.

Fareed geared up to a punishing speed. Allison grasped the roof-strap with both hands and hung on for dear life. Water from the damp rag trickled down her arms.

They were halfway back across the great yellow sea when she saw it. A ballooning cloud rose before them, the color of old ivory and fine as mist. It filled the valley from side to side. The cloud was topped by a yellow mountain ten times the height of the surrounding peaks, a solitary behemoth that shifted and molded and reformed in slow-motion grandeur.

Fareed stopped. Both he and Ben leaned forward and studied the cloud with a look of worry.

Finally Ben shook his head and pointed toward the nearest cliffs. *"Jallah!"*

Immediately Fareed wheeled the Land Rover around and caromed cross-country at speeds that had them bouncing around like Ping-Pong balls. Arriving at the cliff face, he pulled the vehicle as far into a shallow cave as he could, partially blocking them from the rising wind.

"Is your window rolled up tight?"

Allison checked. "Yes."

"Wrap the cloth around your face," Ben ordered. "Cover your mouth and nose and leave a fold free for your eyes."

The wind rose to a shrieking pitch, buffeting their car. Then the dust cloud struck them, and Allison watched the world disappear.

13

THE ROAD AWAY from the Chechen stronghold was little more than a goat track in places, but being on the downhill journey put them all in good spirits. They camped in a meadow an hour or two from the turnoff. When they continued their journey at dawn, Rogue announced that the Russians no longer needed to travel as hidden cargo. The news was received with vast relief.

As they descended into the southern Caucasus, all the world changed—birds, animals, trees, weather. Where the north had been dry and dusty and either overly hot or cold, the south was welcoming. They descended from the dead of winter into a balmy autumn of golden leaves and warm sunshine. The change was staggeringly sudden. In the space of a half-day the world was transformed, and they with it. Birch and fir mounted the steep slopes in friendly welcome to the weary travelers. Wild tulips lined the paths of cheerful streams. Coats were shed, the grim squint through icy winds was lost, the ability to smile returned. For some.

"Now there will be trouble," Yuri muttered when they stopped for a cold lunch of stale bread and goat's cheese and water that tasted of the metal container.

"Don't borrow worries," Robards replied easily. "Keep your weapons ready and hope for peace, that's my motto."

"At least we are avoiding the accursed Chechen," Mikhail agreed when Wade translated, and pointed westward. "All the hills you see in the direction of the setting sun they claim as theirs. The other tribes disagree, of course, we Ossetians most of all. The battles between us have continued for over seven hundred years."

"Yeah, these religious wars always last the longest," Rogue said.

The old man shouted his laughter. "They drink whiskey, these Muslims. They eat pork. They do not pray. How could they call their war anything but what it is? They fight Christians for war's sake. Why? Because they are Chechen. There is no other reason required."

"And you, my friend," Wade probed, surprised at his own boldness. "What about you?"

The old man's gaze turned guarded. "What are you saying?"

"You call yourself Christian. But do you pray? Is the Christ real for you?"

The Russians watched and listened with utter absorption and guarded eyes. Mikhail tossed it aside impatiently. "I leave such things for the priests. That is their job, no?"

"What is he saying?" Rogue asked.

"He says," Wade replied quietly, his eyes on the old man, "it is not a religious war."

"To say that took so long?"

"He says that war with the Chechen is inevitable."

"Correction," Rogue said. "War is inevitable, here or anyplace else."

"What does the warrior say?" Mikhail demanded.

When Wade had translated, the old man grunted. "He speaks a truth. War is man's curse and his destiny and his beginning and his end. I am an old man and have seen much and know there is no other answer."

"I am young," Wade replied quietly, "and yet I believe you are wrong. With respect, I must say that I feel you are wrong."

The old man turned glittering eyes his way. "Yes? You say the answer lies with the priests?"

Wade shook his head. "With Jesus."

"What are you two talking about?" Robards asked.

The old man kept his eyes fixed upon Wade. "Tell the warrior that this is a land where time is not measured as elsewhere. Here the Khevsur tribesmen still have shrines to their tree gods. Here the Eti fought in chain mail and great swords until Stalin swept through here in the thirties and showed them that modern war has no concern for battle honor, only blood."

Robards accepted this news in silence. "What was your little tiff about?"

"It wasn't—"

"Tell him these mountains contain the great fortress of Shatili," the old man continued, his sharp gaze now shooting from one to the other. "The only fortress in the world never taken in battle, although the Chechen, their mortal enemies whom they call the Kistebi, tried for more than eight hundred years to overrun its defenses. Tell him that here the word of honor dominates all else. Disgrace and offenses to the family name are held as matters of revenge for three and four and five hundred years. Here men still show their strength as warriors by abducting brides from enemy villages in the bright of day."

Instead of being troubled by the news, Robards leaned back against the stone wall, crossed his legs, and released a satisfied sigh. "Been looking for a place like this all my life and never thought I'd find it."

"So tell me," Mikhail demanded of Wade. "Where does this religion fit into my world, except hidden behind the priests' doors?"

Wade met the old man's level gaze and quietly replied, "In the hearts of believers."

Silence fell among the group for long minutes. Then Robards stood, dusted off his trousers and started back toward the lead truck. "Okay, let's make tracks."

• • •

They traveled through a countryside that spoke vivid tales of bygone days.

Tucked here and there amidst the green landscape and softly layered hills lay deserted villages, ruined by passing wrath and conquering armies. Piles of rubble buried what once had been cobblestone thoroughfares, the cinders and sorrow gentled by forty years of weeds and wind and rain. Here was the final testimony to Stalin's determination to wipe out all vestiges of allegiance to anything save the great Soviet Empire.

And yet elsewhere remained hamlets of a dozen or so houses, untouched by the red tide of Soviet power. They were peaceful places, rich in produce and beautiful to behold. Vineyards glistened in the early sunlight, their orderly rows pointing toward ancient villages. Chapels nestled beneath trees so old that their girth could not be spanned by six grown men. Churches and monasteries crowned distant hilltops, majestic in their timelessness. The houses had been built before Western Europe had formed itself into nations and had served as homes to more than twenty generations, often of the same family. Living history dwelled among the citizens of such places, reminders of what was, beacons to what was yet to come.

Women sat in doorways and hand-spun the hair of goats into thread, most of which would be used within the community. The local wool, Mikhail told them at their next stop, made clothes with the softness of silk, yet was waxy enough to keep skin dry through the hardest of storms. Wade waved as they passed and wished them well from the fullness of an adventurous life.

Yuri and Mikhail rode in Rogue's lead truck, while Ilya and Alexis, the man who had been ill, traveled with Wade. Ilya remained the loner, content to stay in the back of the truck and doze. Alexis, on the other hand, reveled in his regained good health. He was thin by nature, and his illness had left him little more than skin and bones.

He bore the air of an esthetic, his light blue eyes glorying in all they saw, his cheeks sunken and arms almost skeletal, his copper-colored hair and three-day growth in unnoticed disarray.

As they drove, Alexis turned from gazing out the side window to demand, "You are a religious man?"

"He is a fool for God," Ilya called from the back, speaking for the first time that day. "He seeks to grow peace in soil where only war can take root."

"My mother was religious," Alexis said, taking no heed of Ilya's bitterness. "I thought of her often when the illness had me."

"Do not listen to the fool's talk," Ilya shouted over the road noise. "He will only ask you questions for which there are no answers."

"There is but one true answer to all questions," Wade countered, wondering at the sureness which his voice carried. It was not like him. Not at all.

Ilya cursed and subsided, yet Alexis replied with a smile, "My mother, she used to speak words just like those. I never understood her, and yet I found comfort in her strength."

"Most of the time," Wade admitted, "I do not understand much."

"And yet you believe?"

"In Christ's salvation I have no doubt," Wade replied firmly. "It is my rock."

Alexis nodded slowly. "It would be nice to have such a rock."

Ilya groaned and said, "Another fool in the making!"

There was a silence until Alexis announced quietly, "I lived in Polygon."

"I don't think I've ever heard of it," Wade replied.

"It is Russian for nightmare." The sunlight streaming in the truck window turned his stubbled features into a deeply shadowed visage. "And if it is not, it should be."

"Where—"

"Moscow 400, that was our only address. We were

more than two thousand kilometers from the capital, but letters went first there, even if sent from a neighboring village. Every letter was screened by the KGB. A telephone call to the outside world meant applying for a pass and waiting a day, a week, sometimes months. Travel outside was tightly restricted. Everything was restricted."

"Why did you stay?" Wade asked.

"Because I was ordered to." Blue eyes glinted with bitter humor. "Of course, that is something one raised in a land of freedom like you would not understand."

"Perhaps not," Wade agreed.

"Life was not so bad. We were well paid, by Soviet standards. We had good housing, by Soviet standards. We had access to goods that were not available to the average citizen. My work was granted high priority, which meant that almost anything I felt was required, I received. There were twenty thousand of us, all either specialists or soldiers or spies. We used to joke that Polygon was a comfortable model of the great Soviet state—a prison within a prison."

"What did you do there—I mean, what was your work?"

Alexis replied simply, "Object 100."

"What?"

"A miniature nuclear reactor. A propulsion system for an atomic-powered rocket." He stretched his legs out as far as the cabin area would permit. "Your American scientists had such a project, but it was dropped in 1979 as too costly. There were also environmental questions, although we have since proven them to be unfounded. We were on our way to Mars. We were just ten years away, and then . . ."

"And then everything changed," Wade said.

"Before I left, we had teams of American scientists visiting, looking, taking pictures, asking questions." His tone turned bitter. "We were required to stand and be polite because suddenly there was no more money. Our research was at a standstill. Our stores were empty. Our homes had no heat. The Americans walked around as if they were shopping at a local bazaar. Then they left, and we heard nothing further. We wondered if perhaps they had decided to take all our years of research, return to their warm comfortable homes in America, and do their work in bright new American factories. We asked, and we wrote, and we begged, and still we heard nothing."

"What shame you must have felt," Wade offered softly. "What humiliation."

"So now you ask why I go to build bombs for strangers, yes?" Alexis smiled sadly. "Tell me, have you ever watched your life's work lie in ruins? Have you ever had to beg for assistance, only to have it ignored? Have you ever seen your children go hungry?"

Slowly Wade shook his head. "No."

"Then what right have you to judge me?"

"None," Wade said quietly. "I have no right."

"No?" Alexis turned back toward the front windshield. "Then why do you bother me with the questions in your eyes?"

"A hope only," Wade said. "That you would stop and think of other families, families who also only wish to live in peace."

Alexis was silent so long that Wade thought the conversation had ended. But as the truck bounced and rumbled its way around yet another bend, Alexis said to the window, "Can you also tell me why I hear such questions asked by my heart to my head? Can you tell me why there are no answers?"

They approached yet another nameless hamlet as the sun softened and cooled and touched the highland peaks. Robards pulled from the road and pointed. Nearby fields had been torn apart by dual troughs, which ran in irregular patterns around the nearest houses. "Tanks."

Mikhail walked ahead on foot and returned in the last light of day. "I have found us safe refuge," he announced.

"The trucks?" Rogue demanded when Wade had translated.

"There is a stable," Mikhail replied, swinging into the truck. "Come. My belly is becoming too neighborly with my spine."

The village houses were constructed of rock slathered with concrete and laid roughly in place. The roofs were all jagged slate. Other than the single main road in and out of town, the tracks were mud layered by stones upon which donkeys and people could find safe footing. At the high point of the village rose an ancient watchtower. A church huddled up against it, as much in abject submission to the region's brutal ways as for protection against invaders.

The house where Mikhail led them was of concrete and brick. One side of the house was in shambles. A deep trench split an old oak standing between the house and stables. The trench continued on through the living room wall and ended upon the opposite wall, a violent fiery comet whose reddish tail splashed up and around the ceiling.

"Three weeks ago we were hit by a rocket attack," the woman of the house told them dully. Her five young children clustered about her with expressions of weary sadness. "The rocket did not explode. Otherwise we would all be dead. My aged father and mother came and dug it out while we waited in the woods. They said their lives were closer to an end, and so they took the risk of it blowing up in their faces."

Robards inspected the plastic tarp that covered the gaping hole and asked, "Where is her husband?"

"Away," she replied through Wade. "Fighting these past four months."

Wade did not need to ask for details to explain further, "When Georgia declared independence from the

Soviet Union, South Ossetia declared independence from Georgia."

"That was asking for trouble," Rogue commented.

"I do not know where he is," the woman went on in her toneless drone, "or even if he is alive. I have no way of finding out. When the Georgians last came through here, they demanded that I hand over my husband. When I said that he was not here, they did this and ordered me to leave my own homeland."

"Ossetia was split up by Stalin," Wade continued to Rogue after translating. "The lower half was joined to Georgia to split up the patriotic Ossetians and to make the Georgian border look straighter. They don't have the same language as the Georgians, not even the same alphabet. North Ossetia has been made a semi-independent enclave inside Russia. South Ossetia wants to join up with its other half."

Wade gestured at the ruptured wall. "The result is war. All of South Ossetia has been split into villages either full of Georgians or Ossetians."

"You are speaking of my lands?" Mikhail demanded.

"Yes," Wade replied, and explained what he had said.

"How is it that you know so much of our struggle?"

"I listen," Wade said simply.

"You listen and you hear with compassion," the old man corrected. "It is a pity that others do not do the same."

Wade thought that over. "I must tell you," he said, "the compassion is not my own."

For some reason that shook the old man. Hard. "Such talk from one who is not a priest," he muttered.

"I tell you all," Ilya scoffed from his habitual place in the corner. "He is a fool for this God of his."

Rogue stepped up in front of Wade and demanded with some irritation, "What's got their wind up?"

The woman saved him from answering by declaring, "There is little in our house to eat."

When Wade translated, Robards replied, "Tell her

we'll eat from our stores, and we'll leave her more food in return for lodging. Ask her if there is bread to be had in this village."

"For those with money," she replied.

Wade handed her a few rubles. "We have little cash, but we will pay for your hospitality with goods that can be easily traded as well as with food."

She nodded, and then volunteered, "The next three villages are Georgian held, and they shoot anyone coming from this area. You will need to go south on a trail I can show you in the morning."

"For such information," Wade replied, "we shall pay even more."

She handed the money to her daughter, who leapt up and ran out the door. She then turned and spoke sharply to her eldest son, who nodded and left without a word. She explained, "He will go and sleep in your trucks."

"I was planning to do that," Robards said when Wade had translated.

"Do so," she replied. "But let him be there also. He has the eyes of a night bird and knows all who live here, who is foe and who friend. There are not many friends."

After the meal, the woman and her children retired to the back room, leaving the men sprawled about the drafty living chamber with its single flickering bulb. The three Russians smoked their foul-smelling *papyrosi* cigarettes, enjoying the moment's relative freedom. Robards cast a glance at the wall's open wound and declared, "This whole region's a patchwork quilt of little wars."

Wade translated for the others, and there was no dissent. "It is the same story over much of the former Soviet Union," Yuri said, speaking in Russian so all but Rogue could understand. "The local tribes have suffered much."

"Not to mention we Russians," Ilya muttered.

"The usurpers to ancient tribal lands have no rights,"

Mikhail countered, but without heat.

"I, a usurper?" Ilya snorted. "I was born in Estonia. My parents were forced there, given fifteen minutes to pack and shoved upon a cattle car and sent off on a voyage that lasted two weeks and almost killed my mother. I am the product of modern Russia, a man who belongs nowhere."

"The villagers have never been concerned with Tbilisi or Moscow or politics or the world," Yuri said. "They live life on a different level. They want to know, what is the price of bread? How will I heat my home this winter? Will there be medicine for my sick child?"

Rogue demanded, "How has the military been handling the crisis?"

Yuri looked at him with a cynic's eye. "You wish to know if it would be possible to add product to your cargo of people and carry over bombs as well?"

"Not bombs," Robards replied, unruffled by the man's tone. "Too heavy. And not this trip. Maybe later, though. A little material, maybe. Something small enough to carry."

"Just go to the right gate and ask the right person," Yuri replied bitterly. "The one with hunger in his eyes."

"I've heard things were bad," Rogue said conversationally.

"Listen, and I will tell you how bad," Yuri's voice was overlaid with venom. "For I was stationed at a military compound meant for collecting and holding these nuclear weapons."

"Sounds like I've come to the right man," Rogue said easily.

"Families with cash bribe those sent to look for absent conscripts," Yuri continued. "The officers responsible for rounding up draft dodgers put down one illness or another, because they too see hunger stalking their doorsteps. Those conscripts who do show up find there are no uniforms, no weapons for training, and little food. An admiral was imprisoned for starving naval conscripts to death, and his response was, how can I give what I myself do not have? Every base in Russia overflows with men brought in from former Soviet lands, and none of them have clearly assigned duties. It is chaos. Total chaos."

Yuri nodded to himself, his face etched deeply by the shadows of the room and the memories of what he fled. "You want to steal weapons-grade nuclear materials? Fine. Go to such a base, carry dollars, and seek out the hungry man."

Rogue chewed thoughtfully on his twig. "Sounds to me like a good time to get out."

"A normal country, that is all I seek," Yuri replied.

The next morning Wade accepted his cup of tea and hunk of breakfast bread from his unsmiling hostess and took it out to where Alexis stood by the cracked oak. The man looked more haggard than usual. When he was up close Wade asked him, "How are you feeling?"

Startled, the man swung around, "Oh, it's you. I did not hear you approach."

"Are you sick again?"

"No, thanks to you," Alexis gave his gentle, sad smile. "I simply found my sleep disturbed last night by your questions—and by ones rising within my own heart."

Wade sought a response. "I have always felt that my whole life is full of unanswered questions and unsolved mysteries. I think that is why the single truth of Christ's salvation means so much to me."

"Yes," Alexis murmured, his eyes returning to the bomb-shattered tree. "It would be good to have something so certain."

"When I am faced with what I do not comprehend," Wade persisted, "I seek my direction in the Word of God. I may not understand what I am shown to do, but there is always something which I can use."

"This is true?" Alexis traced the rocket's trail toward

the house with bleak eyes. "Always?"

Wade nodded. "It should be quite a change," he offered tentatively, "working in the desert."

Alexis raised his eyes and examined him. "You have visited the great northern steppes?"

"No."

"In winter it is so cold that snow freezes hard and sharp as broken glass. The ground is like iron, the wind a knife that tears through your skin. There is nothing to see for hundreds of miles in every direction except snow and ice and more snow and more ice." He returned his gaze to the damaged house. "I do not think the desert will be so great a change."

Wade hesitated, but found an unseen force was pushing him so hard he had to ask. *Had* to ask. "Where are you going, Alexis?"

It was as though the man had been waiting for the question. There was not even a moment's delay before he demanded, "Do you know the city of Aqaba?"

"I don't think so."

"I found it on a map just before my departure. It is in Jordan. We were intended to rendezvous there for transport to Baghdad. The guides who failed to meet us were to bring us to Tbilisi. From there transport was supposed to be a matter of buying a ticket."

Wade stared at Alexis. "You are to go and build bombs for Iraq?"

The man's eyes were haunted, his reply without strength. "Iraq or Iran, Russia or America—what difference does it make so long as my wife and child are fed?"

"You really don't care?"

"A flight to Amman via Istanbul," Alexis replied, his voice echoing the doubts that plagued his gaze. "A night there, then down to Aqaba—just another Russian tourist taking in a few days by the sea. There is a group operating there, far from the listening ears and watchful eyes in Amman. They will transport me along desert ways to Iraq. Either that, or a boat to Iran. Or so it appears."

"But do you really want to do this?" Wade pressed.

"Yes," Alexis replied. "And no." The sadness in his eyes threatened to spill over. "This I have agreed to do, this I must do. There is no other way."

"Couldn't you—"

"No more questions," Alexis interrupted. "Please. My head and heart are full to bursting." He turned and walked away.

Wade started at the sound of approaching footsteps, and turned to find Rogue towering over him. "What'd you say that got him so worked up?"

"Nothing."

"Didn't look like nothing to me."

"I just asked where he was going," Wade said. "And why."

"He's going where he's going," Robards answered. "That's all you need to know, long as we get paid."

"Yes, I know you're here for the money," Wade accused. "But what about the casualties? What about all the pain and grief and hardship that happens when worlds end and bombs blow up? What about cities blown apart and families torn up and little children starving or killed? Doesn't that bother you even a little?"

Robards inspected him with a strange mix of amusement and irritation. "What happened to the shy little guy I started this trip with?"

"I don't know what you mean."

"Sure you do. You're speaking up. Charting your own course. And it's not one I care too much for, either. What's gotten into you?"

Wade took a moment for introspection, and confessed the only answer that made sense to him. "I think I'm learning to trust in God's strength where my own isn't enough."

"Yeah, well, your God better keep his nose out of our business, sport. We got too much riding on this to start digging around where we don't belong."

The tone rankled deep. "I thought you said I was calling the shots here."

"Sure you are, long as you don't start aiming to shoot yourself in the foot. Might end up shooting me as well."

"I don't think that's what I'm doing."

"Maybe that's the problem." Rogue changed course with, "Were you planning on giving medicines to the old lady to help pay for our stay?"

"Yes."

Rogue shook his head. "Bad idea. It'd be leaving a clear trail for anybody who might be after us."

"She won't tell anybody."

"Maybe not, but it's a risk we don't need to take. You've got cash left. At least enough for my second payment."

"Not much more than that."

"Go ahead and use it now," Robards urged. "I'll take my share in medicines. It's safer."

For some reason he could not explain, Wade found himself resisting the idea. "I planned to keep the cash with us—for a crisis."

"Brother, if traveling through a war zone ain't a crisis, I don't know what is."

"I'm also planning to stop at every village with a doctor and leave supplies," Wade said stubbornly.

Robards inspected him, his face set in lines as hard as granite. "If you were a man under me—"

"But I'm not," Wade said, marveling at his sudden certainty. "Shouldn't we be getting under way?"

14

ALLISON FOUND IT A delight to awaken.

Mornings in the desert dawned cool and clear. The air was perfumed with smoke from cooking fires and mysterious spices. Allison brushed her teeth while gazing out her window and across the rooftops, where her little slice of sea joined with the cloudless sky.

Downstairs, the delightful sense of strangeness continued long after she had learned the routine. The smiling cook handed over her usual glass of Nescafe. Today Allison pointed to the blackened vase-shaped pot resting on the open flame. The cook beamed his approval and poured her a thimble-size cup of Arabic coffee.

She sniffed the cup. Yes, there was a distinctive fragrance, just as she had smelled in the Bedouin's coffee, something strange yet appealing.

"Cardamom," said a voice beside her. "It comes from dried fennel. We grind it up and spice our coffee with it." Allison turned toward an olive-skinned woman whose unlined face and youthful gaze struck an intriguing contrast to her graying hair. "I am Leah, Ben's wife. You must be Allison. Come sit with me.

"All the staff are talking about how good you are at your work." Leah led her to the corner table. "Ben was so afraid that once you saw the state of your office you would change your mind and leave us."

"It was in pretty bad shape," Allison agreed, wondering how much Leah knew of her true purpose in Aqaba. "You are Palestinian, aren't you? Where did you learn your English?"

"In America. My family emigrated from Beersheba after the '67 war. That is where most of the Palestinians in Aqaba come from—Beersheba and the southern villages. My father had a brother working in Baltimore, and we emigrated there."

"Are you a nurse?"

"No, I run a series of Bible study programs and mediate between our work and the local established Christian churches. I try to stay as far away from Ben's clinic work as I can. This is the only way he will ever escape from his work." She inspected Allison's face. "Ben tells me you had quite a day yesterday."

The sandstorm. Allison had spent half the night hearing the wind howl through her dreams. "This whole place is like something out of a dream—it never stops surprising me."

Two hours waiting for the storm to pass, another hour digging themselves out of the drift, then three hours back. The road had disappeared in places under the drifting sands. Often they had been forced to get out and push the car while Fareed raced the engine, and showered them with dust from the spinning wheels.

"Yes, my country is that way," Leah agreed. "Harsh and unyielding one moment, but then suddenly rain falls on the desert, and the land is transformed into paradise."

"That's a word I would never have thought to use for here," Allison said, and then stopped. "I'm sorry. I didn't mean to offend you. I mean, I really think it's beautiful."

Leah only smiled. "I think after your experience you deserve the afternoon off. Why don't you meet me here at lunchtime, and I will try to show you a little of Jordan's other face."

• • •

Fareed took the gulf road southward toward the Saudi border. Beyond the port area the road rose and fell along a slender plateau, lined on one side by jagged peaks and on the other by the Gulf of Aqaba.

Leah possessed the calm tone of one who could ask almost anything and receive a truthful answer. "Do you mind working so far away from your world?"

"Not at all." Being so distant from the world she knew granted Allison a welcome opportunity to draw out aspects of her life and examine them in safety.

As though reading her mind, Leah asked, "Do you have someone waiting for you back home?"

"My boyfriend and I broke up a month before my departure."

Leah examined her. "Should I be sorry?"

Allison turned her face toward the ocher hills. "Probably not," she sighed.

From the safety of these distant lands, it seemed to Allison that the men in her past were a little less than her. A little less bright, a little less witty, a little less successful. She was the driving force in the relationship. The men depended upon her. But in order to reinforce their own masculinity, they spent time putting her down. As a result, even though she knew she had a lot going for her, she wound up being the weaker partner. She was the one who sat by the phone. She was the one who waited for hours when the guy was late, then accepted weak excuses for inexcusable behavior, only because she knew that was all she was going to get. She *accommodated* them. And tore herself down in the process.

Leah took Allison's diverted face as an answer, and granted her silence. Allison found herself thinking once more about the last relationship, which had been with a sociology student at the University of Maryland. He had been in his seventh year of trying to complete his master's and had worked for a roofing company in his spare time. She had liked him because he was cute and funny. Her best girlfriend had taken one look at him and proclaimed him the worst of a long string of losers.

One night he called her up and said she had to come over, he needed to talk. This after almost three weeks of not being able to find him at all. Allison replied truthfully that she could not come, she had to work late on a project due the following day. Then the computer system went down unexpectedly, and she had the bright idea to go out and surprise him. She arrived with a bagful of Chinese takeout and a video. He answered in a state of borderline panic, and despite his best efforts to block her view she saw over his shoulder that another girl was draped on the couch.

The next day during lunch Allison unloaded to her best girlfriend. Her girlfriend responded with something more than the standard pep talk. I'm so glad you're finally rid of that jerk, she said. Why do you keep wasting your time on all of these losers? You're bright, you're beautiful, and you deserve better. Look what you've done in your career. You set a goal, and then you went for it. That's exactly what you should do in your love life—set a goal, and stick to it. Allison returned to work dry-eyed and determined to pick her men more carefully.

And then came the offer to leave it all behind and fly off to London and places beyond. She did not hesitate for a moment.

The question now was, what would she return to? What had she learned?

A few miles later, a crescent-shaped beach emerged from the waters. They pulled in through the main gate and started down toward the water's edge. The sand was hard enough to drive on. Great metal parasols sprouted from the sand every twenty meters or so. All of the other visitors were Arabs. Many had erected Bedouin-style tents using the parasol as a base. People emerged from the shade to play in the water, then returned to their little camps. The absence of sunbathers left the beach looking strangely empty.

As they unloaded and set up camp under their own

shelter, Leah explained, "It is unwise for women to come to such a public place without a male escort. Also, some of the fundamentalist police have begun to give women drivers a very hard time these days, if one happens to stop us. Now I take Fareed with me almost everywhere."

"Stuff like that really makes my blood boil," Allison said.

Leah did not disagree. "The problem is, nowadays many people are beginning to lump all Arabs together under the fundamentalist banner. This is very wrong, and it is very dangerous. Ben and I have many good Muslim friends, people for whom we have the deepest respect, whom we would trust with our lives. The fundamentalists are still a minority. But their numbers are growing, and the people they tend to attract are the vocal ones."

Allison settled herself down on a towel and began to rub sunscreen on her arms. The breeze was just strong enough to bring in a sweet coolness from the water. "The discontented," she said.

"Exactly. In most of the Arab world, the poor are trapped and held down by the system. These are stagnant societies, ruled by corrupt governments. The fundamentalists feed from this angry pool just as the Nazis did in Germany after the First World War. They set themselves up in the poorest quarters of the large cities and in the small villages that are struggling to survive."

Leah motioned toward Fareed, who sat leaning against the parasol's center pole. "Fareed is from a Christian family, but his father named him after his closest friend, a Muslim. This is a living example of how our two cultures once coexisted." She then asked the quiet man, "Would you tell our new friend what happened in your village?"

The driver was a very compact man, his age more evident from his graying hair than from his strong unlined face. "I remember before twenty years," he began, then stopped. "Please to excuse my English."

"It's fine," Allison replied. It was the first time she remembered hearing the man speak to her.

"Before twenty years, Karak was still old village. We all live in tents. Christian, Muslim, all together. Peace and good life. Government come, make wells better, build houses; we use tents only when take animals different place. We have many Christian families. Some of them, they come from Palestine very long time. Was quiet village."

He stirred, made uncomfortable by what he remembered. "Then new mullah come to mosque. New mullah talk, talk. My family, we like to stay. But mullah talk many bad things. We decide city is safer. My family, we rather live in village. Maybe someday go back. But not now. Mullahs no let us."

Allison asked, "You don't like living in the city?"

Fareed continued to look out to sea. "In springtime and autumn, village have very nice wind. Also the sun not too hot. Always nice wind in village. In city, wind trapped. Village quiet, no noise all time like city. Very good life in village, very safe, nice for children. But no more."

"I don't understand," Allison said. "The mullahs forced you to leave?"

"No, not force. Never say go. Just talk hate. Everybody, they worry, what comes next?"

"What did the mullahs say?"

"Hate things," he replied impatiently. "Anger things. Not good for me, for family, for whole village."

"The atmosphere in your village was changing."

"Yes, yes, whole village change. No more village where I born. Now is new village. Mullahs rule new village."

"There are many such places nowadays," Leah offered. "Some struggle against it, but others relish this supposed inspiration from Allah to rise up in anger and hate. In many places, the tide is running in the mullahs' favor."

"This mullah talk, it not good," Fareed declared. "Muslim friends, they also not understand. They come to me and say, we not follow this way. We believe in Allah, yes, but we want peace." Fareed was silent for a time, then, "Why this come? I not understand."

"A lot of people don't," Leah agreed. "And even more wish it could be stopped."

"Is hurt for many people," Fareed told them. "Too much anger, too much talk for fighting."

They all sat without speaking for a long moment, then Leah rose to her feet. "Enough of this. We're supposed to be having an afternoon off." She turned to Allison. "Do you know how to snorkel?"

"I've done it before."

Leah reached into a sack by her towel. "Good. Come along. I have a surprise for you."

Allison followed her down to the water's edge and stared at the world of contrasts. Both behind her and across the gulf's other side rose stark desert peaks. The water was crystal clear and as blue as the sky. The sand was the color of crushed pearls.

"Here, put these on." Leah handed her a snorkel and fins. "Be sure to stay close enough that we always have each other in sight."

They walked out to where the water was waist deep, then lowered themselves and began swimming out. With her first glimpse under the surface, Allison gasped into her mask.

Sunlight cascaded through the sea as through a prism, turning the sandy bottom into an ever-changing rainbow. As they swam farther out, the bottom dropped off, and up rose a fairy-tale undersea kingdom. Fan corals formed a series of gateways, rising twenty feet and more from the bottom. Smaller versions clustered on rocks and ledges, sculpted into fantasy shapes of orange and rose and purple. Brain coral fifteen feet across crowned underwater peaks. Schools of fish as brightly colored as the coral swam everywhere.

Allison swam for almost an hour, until her shoulders began sending warning tingles of too much desert sun.

She signaled and followed Leah back to the shore. "That was incredible."

"We say that all Jordan is like this," Leah replied. "With much beauty hidden just beneath the surface. All you have to do is make that little extra effort to search it out."

Toward evening, Allison returned to the clinic dormitory to find that a note had been slipped under her bedroom door. She opened the buff envelope and took out the single sheet of paper.

She read, "Meet me in Petra tomorrow. C."

15

THE TRUCKS ARRIVED at the main road to Beloti around midafternoon. Fifty yards before the turning, Rogue halted the trucks and waited. Once an hour, their hostess had told them, Russian-led convoys drove through, headed for villages still controlled by the enemy. Otherwise, the roads belonged to the Ossetians.

They took a late lunch and waited behind the high hedges until a deep rumbling announced the convoy's arrival. They watched through the leaves as a pair of Russian tanks rolled into view. Behind these came several armored personnel carriers, and following them was a hodgepodge of vehicles—trucks, buses, autos, ambulances, farm transports piled to the brim with produce, even an occasional horse-drawn wagon.

"Russian troops were brought in to protect the enclaves held by non-Ossetians," Wade explained in an undertone. "Stalin emptied a lot of villages. He hated the Ossetians' patriotism, so he shipped more than a hundred thousand either to Siberia or Kazakhstan."

"And imported Russians to fill in the holes," Rogue finished.

"Georgians, too," Wade added. "Stalin wanted to scatter them around as well."

"So why don't the Georgians have something to say about these Russian troops being around here? Didn't you tell me they claimed this territory for their own?"

Wade nodded. "It's not as simple as that."

"Yeah, I kinda figured."

"The Georgians are tied up fighting a civil war with the Abkhazi tribe farther to the east. That area has been a part of Georgia for more than a thousand years, and the Abkhazis make up less than fifteen percent of the total population. This trouble started before Georgia actually became a nation, and the Russian troops arrived long before independence. So the Georgians sort of turn a blind eye to the Russians' still being here."

"From the sound of it," Rogue agreed, "they need all the help they can get."

Wade translated this conversation for the impatient old man. The Russian engineers listened with the intensity of ones whose fate rested in the hands of others.

Mikhail nodded his agreement to Wade's explanation and added, "Thus the conflict of South Ossetia has neither front nor cohesion. The Russians have no way to plan an attack. The Ossetian militia fights roving battles. Newly returned transportees gather arms and attack whatever village had once been their own. There is no central command. We are a hundred different armies, unified only by our desire for an Ossetian homeland."

"With a lot of old hatreds added in just to make things interesting," Robards amended, watching a third tank roll by at the end of the convoy. "Okay, road's clear as it's going to get. Let's head out."

At the village outskirts Rogue pulled over and waved Wade in behind him. Just ahead, a pair of battered jeeps had been parked to partially block the road. Heavily armed men clustered around them. Wade cut his motor and walked over to Rogue. They watched as Mikhail approached the men, calling out loud greetings and proffering all their papers in outstretched hands.

Wade asked, "Is everything all right?"

"We'll find out soon enough. Get a load of the man in charge."

The soldier examining their papers had a distinctly raffish air. Instead of a helmet, he wore a black Stetson with its wide brim pulled down low over his eyes. His hollow cheeks bore the three-day growth cultivated by Western male models. He wore a hand-stitched leather hunting vest over a dark green flannel shirt, with regulation camouflage trousers tucked into lace-up doeskin boots. Over his back was slung a machine gun. Around front hung a machine pistol with polished burl handle.

Rogue snorted. "He looks like the Marlboro man, Russian style."

"He's not Russian," Wade corrected. "He's Ossetian."

"Doesn't matter," Robards said easily. "What you see there is just another trendy trekker. Anybody that concerned with looking the part isn't a problem. If he started shooting, his first concern would be how to keep his hair neat."

The man was taking his time over their papers. Wade swallowed nervously. "Looks dangerous enough to me."

"Aw, he's just another style bandit. Look over there, see the guy in the black leather gloves with the silver studs?"

"Yes."

"Another wannabe warrior. These days, you find them around every little war. They're mostly guys bored with the normal life. These are probably all locals, Russians or Georgians or Ossetians, but you see the type everywhere. Yugoslavia's full of cowboys these days." Rogue pointed with a jutting chin. "Look, see that one? Black outfit, matching boots and blackened bayonet, probably got some local woman who washes and presses his uniform at night. They get these Skorpion machine pistols and wear them down real low, like a Dodge City gunslinger. Problem is, every time they have to run anywhere the doggone thing gets caught between their legs."

Robards waved cheerily as a cluster of guards walked toward them. "Gucci warriors, the lot of them. Look at the black bandanna. Means take no prisoners. Reason is, the first sign of trouble they'd be raising dust from here to Moscow. Take a look at those aviator shades—gold Ray Bans. Probably set him back a year's pay."

Wade glanced at Robards. "What's the difference between them and you?"

"Ten years and a lotta miles," Robards responded easily. "I guess you could say I've been distilled. I'm the essence of what these guys wish they could be."

"A mercenary."

"I prefer realist. Besides, life on the edge has its advantages. Take an honest look at yourself. Tell me the last time you've ever felt so alive."

The search was perfunctory, with Mikhail proclaiming friendship in the searchers' own tongue and Rogue hovering around with smiling menace. The three Russian engineers were too cowed to appear a threat and received less notice than did the two Americans, which was not much at all. Clearly the Ossetians saw them as just another strange group attracted by the rough-and-tumble lawlessness of a world at war. Two bottles of vodka were passed over, apparently the customary bribe from the way they were accepted, and the trucks were waved through on their way.

They entered the village a few minutes shy of the next hour, in time to watch all life vanish. Rogue followed suit by pulling over to the curb and waving Wade in behind him. They hunkered down below the dashboards and waited for the Russian convoy to pass. When the grinding of the tanks died away, the streets returned to bustling activity.

Every so often they came upon the burned-out hulk of a truck or bus or car, pushed far enough to one side so as not to impede traffic. At least one building in each block had been bombed to smithereens. Children played in the ruins, while vendors filled the front spaces with their stalls.

Everywhere were signs of life without order. Cars careened down streets with total disregard to lanes or speed or traffic signs. Occasional bursts of machine-gun fire ripped through the air; pedestrians stopped in mid-breath, searched their surroundings, then returned to matters at hand. Motorcycles zigzagged down sidewalks at thirty or forty miles per hour, the pedestrians simply stepping aside. Cafes took advantage of the fine autumn weather by moving tables out onto the sidewalks and into the streets; customers paid little heed to the cars and motorcycles and pedestrians who threaded their way among the tables.

Twice their own progress was halted by roving bands of armed men who threatened the lead truck. Mikhail's loud exhortations and Rogue's imposing presence eased them through.

The town's only hotel was situated on the central square. They rented the only room with a private bath—not because anyone would sleep there, but so they all could get clean. Rogue and Wade pulled the trucks into the neighboring alleyway, and Robards offered to take first watch. Mikhail and the three Russians headed upstairs to wash. Wade asked the desk clerk for directions to the city's clinic, then returned to the trucks.

Rogue demanded, "Why aren't you upstairs getting clean?"

"I'm going to see if the local doctor needs anything," Wade replied. "If there is a doctor."

Robards shook his head. "Not a wise move. All you'll be doing is telling every gunslinger within a hundred miles what we've got on these trucks."

Again there was the unfamiliar sense of being granted unbidden certitude. "I guess I'll have to take that chance. People are fighting and dying all around here; they need this stuff. What if you were wounded and in danger of losing a limb because there weren't any antibiotics? What if you had to have surgery and there weren't any anesthetics?"

"I'm not," Robards replied with his false ease. "I'm here and I'm fit and that's all there is to it. A man can't build a life on worrying about all the what-ifs."

"And have you ever considered the possibility that there might be something more important than yourself?"

Rogue leaned his back against the near truck and sighed up at the heavens. "Don't I recall having pretty much this same conversation with you the other day?"

"You're doing great now," Wade persisted. "But what happens when your own strength isn't enough?"

"Then I'm dead," Rogue said flatly. "That's part of the price you pay for living a real life."

"Carting people around so they can go build bombs for terrorists doesn't seem all that real to me."

"Oh, it's real, all right," Rogue drawled. "You know what your problem is, sport? You never had enough confidence in yourself to make it on your own. You went off and made up this God of yours so you can have somebody else to blame."

"I don't blame him for anything," Wade replied. "But I am learning to find strength in him."

"Man's born alone, he lives alone, he dies alone," Rogue stated flatly. "Anything else is just baloney dished out to people who don't want to face up to reality."

"Reality is salvation through Jesus Christ," Wade replied steadily. "Reality is recognizing that death is nothing but a passage into eternity. Reality is living each day with compassion for others."

"Sick, sick, sick," Robards replied. "Shame we don't carry any medicine for delusions."

There came at that moment a sense of tearing apart. Of an invisible turning, a new course being set in place. Wade said quietly, "I am going to go see if there is a clinic in need of supplies."

Robards inspected him for a moment, then declared,

"If you head out on this goodwill mission of yours, all bets are off."

Wade did not understand what was meant, but all the same felt an answering knell deep within. He nodded his acceptance and headed for the truck. "I'll see you when I get back."

Once again, the doctor's gratitude was almost pathetic. He was a slender man with the long graceful fingers of a classical pianist. His dark eyes opened to the size of saucers as Wade led him to the back of the truck and pointed out the various things on offer. His two aides rushed to unload the chosen boxes, moving as fast as they could, determined to take everything possible before this crazy man returned to his senses and demanded a payment they did not have.

All I ask in return, Wade had said upon departure, is that you do not speak of this for several days. The doctor had nodded an abstract reply, unable to see beyond the largess which littered his waiting room. Yet when Wade turned to leave, he noticed that one of the aides was nowhere to be seen. He returned to the hotel with a faint sense of disquiet.

When he pulled up alongside the hotel, Wade discovered that the other truck was not there. He was almost certain his comrades had gone in search of gasoline, but no amount of internal reassurance could still his jangling nerves. He bounded up the stairs, rushed down the dimly lit hall, pushed open the door, and felt his heart stop when all he found to greet him was a note propped upon the crumpled bed.

With shaking hands, Wade lifted the paper and read, "I gave them a choice, sport. Everybody decided to come along when I announced I was pulling out. Mikhail says Tbilisi is a hundred klicks or so straight down the south road. I've taken the truck and its load as payment in full. Rogue Robards."

Voices from outside drew him to the open window. He stuck his head out and felt his blood freeze at the sight of a dozen or so armed men crowding in and around his truck.

He shouted a protest and was answered by the clinic aide, who turned and pointed and shouted back. Four of the men broke off and headed for the hotel's front door.

Wade fled out the door and down the hall, but stopped at the sound of heavy boots clumping up the stairs. He craned and searched and realized there was no other way out.

He turned to the nearest door, twisted the knob and pushed. It was locked. The boots clumped ever closer. He tried the next door, and when he found it locked as well, gave a panicked shove with his shoulder. The flimsy lock gave with almost no noise. Wade then leaned his weight against the door and listened as the men hastened up the final stairs, fearful that his breathing was loud enough to alert them.

When the footsteps had passed his door, Wade turned and flew to the window. Ten feet below protruded the roof over the hotel's dining room. Wade slid himself out. He hung from his fingers, then released and dropped the final two feet with a thud he was sure would be heard in the next village.

He stumbled over to the roof's edge, shifted and slid and dropped to the street.

Feeling every instant that the cry of alarm would be raised, Wade fled as fast as his feet would take him.

16

THE NAME PETRA, Allison learned from her guidebook, was derived from the Greek word for rock, and never had a city better deserved its name. The ancient ruins were reached by way of a *siq*, a narrow chasm two miles long, in places no more than six feet wide, with walls rising four hundred feet above her head.

Although much of the city had been destroyed in the earthquake of A.D. 747, what remained was still one of the most spectacular sights Allison had ever seen.

Eight- and nine-story buildings had been carved from the surrounding cliffs. Temples, treasuries, granaries, spice markets—all such designations were guesses, as the Nabateans had left few records. Allison did not mind the mystery; it granted her the freedom to walk, explore, and imagine for herself what life might have been like in this rock-bound city.

The larger halls had been carved from multicolored sandstone, as had the pillars and building edifices. Lanes were further canyons extending from the central valley. Caves that had once been used as pantries for rock-hewn houses now served as teahouses and museums.

Allison was picking her way up temple steps more than three thousand years old when a voice beside her said, "Let us join that tour group over there, shall we?"

She jumped and spun around. It was Smathers, the

little man from the British Embassy. "You scared me."

"No more theatrics than absolutely necessary, all right? Just gather with the other gawkers and pretend you're having a good time."

"One theory," droned the English guide at the front of the group, her voice bounding off the distant walls, "is that this temple was intended for funerals of high officials. This lower level where we are standing was for humans, the upper levels for spirits only. That would explain the absence of stairways leading to the higher floors. Templegoers would have left their libations in these basins you see carved in the floor here and here. Upon death the bodies would be dried in the sun, then the desiccated remains would be deposited up above, to dwell with the spirits."

As the group was herded back out into the sunlight, Allison whispered, "What am I doing here?"

"A perfectly acceptable question." As the group emerged into the glare, the little man slipped a floppy white hat from his pocket and plopped it onto his peeling head. "And one which I asked myself a dozen times already this morning. Stay close to the group, please."

They walked down the main valley, the guide stopping to point out various tombs along the way. "The Nabateans were famous traders," she explained, "and over the centuries they borrowed architectural ideas from quite a variety of lands with whom they dealt—Egypt, Persia, Greece, even China. You will see the results grafted onto the tombs, which became increasingly intricate over the centuries."

She raised her umbrella aloft, signaling the group forward. As they walked, she continued in a voice trained to carry over distances. "Then came the Romans, and even here the wily Nabatean traders did not give up easily. There was one local hero by the name of Sikarius. When the Romans under Augustus tried to take control of the region, he pretended to be a traitor and offered to lead them into this fortified city by a secret back route. He led them around in circles for six months, then left them to die in the desert. The Jordanians hold Sikarius up as their sort of David against the Goliath of other, greater nations. What they don't bother to mention is that Augustus responded to the trickery with a Roman style of economic sanctions; he moved the spice and silk route so that it bypassed the Nabateans entirely. In thirty years the Nabatean Empire was decimated, and they accepted incorporation into the Roman Empire, coming to be known as the state of Arabia Petra."

Smathers stopped Allison's forward progress with a hand on her arm. When the tour group had departed, he pointed up a set of stairs that mounted the rise behind them. "Up there, if you will."

"After you."

"I was not invited," he snapped.

"First I want—"

"Oh do go on; that's a good girl. You can play the stubborn American some other time."

Allison bit back her reply. She turned and started up the stairs, anger speeding her climb.

The steps were carved from the mountainside, and had been smoothed by millions of feet over the previous three thousand years. They climbed up one cliffside, made a series of sharp turnings, and continued on to breathtaking heights. Every supposed pinnacle proved at its summit to be nothing more than the base for yet another climb. The steps numbered well over a thousand. With each sharp turning the views became more spectacular and her breath harder to find.

She finally crested the last rise to find herself standing in a flat space carved from the very top of the mountain. Cyril rose from his seated position and dusted off his trousers. "My dear Allison, how lovely to see you. Do come sit down."

She allowed herself to be guided to the ledge and seated, her lungs still pumping like overworked bellows. Her shirt was plastered to her back, her hair sticking to the perspiration that streamed down from her sun hat and down her neck and face. Cyril looked neat as a pin and untouched by the heat. She could have shoved him over the edge.

"We are now standing in the triclinium," he said, politely ignoring her efforts to compose herself, "a three-sided gathering place for worshipers. The carved stone there at the center of the forefront dais area is called a *djinn,* or god-block. Probably in the late Mesolithic or early Neolithic times, people began taking the unformed stones which they worshiped and dressing them. From these crude square blocks later came the formation of statues and idols. But not here—at least, not as far as we know. Here it appears that the people remained content to offer their sacrifices upon the *djinn.*"

Allison turned and looked over the ledge at the magnificent vista. "I feel as though I can see to the ends of the earth."

"Probably why the high places were originally chosen as places of worship; the view granted people the feeling that they were closer to their gods." Cyril pointed again to the god-block. "Of course, this is a perfect example of one of the high places destroyed by King Josiah. Do you know your Bible, my dear?"

"No."

"It is one of the many gifts I have received from knowing Ben. Although I do not share his strength of faith, I have certainly granted it a greater place in my life from having seen the invisible live through him."

Allison lifted her hat and pushed the hair back from her face. The desert wind had already dried her skin. "Why did you bring me here?"

Cyril pointed back down the stairs. "Security, my dear. Anyone following you up the ceremonial way, as it is called, would have long since shown themselves. Our dear Mister Smathers is stationed at the bottom to watch for anyone who might have followed."

Allison stood and walked over to where she had

emerged from the stairway. "Who would they be following, you or me?"

"Do come back and sit down by me, my dear." Cyril raised a thermos from his carry-sack. "Would you care for some tea?"

"I would prefer some answers."

"Very well." He replaced the thermos. "I can only tell you what I know. We think you are being trailed, but we cannot say for sure. We had thought that perhaps this little trip today would flush them out."

She nodded. Her suspicions of the past week were becoming as solid as the surrounding peaks. "You're using me as bait."

"My dear Allison, I would never dream of referring to you as anything so crass as bait."

"I don't know what else to call it." Now that it was out in the open, she found she did not really mind. "I've been trying to figure out why you needed me. Ben is perfectly capable of carrying around that little machine by himself. You wanted to draw attention to your search and see what or who pops out of the woodwork."

Cyril did not bother to deny it. "You are clearly your father's daughter," he said approvingly.

"I just hope you are keeping a careful eye on me."

"Rest assured," he replied. "You are better watched than the crown jewels."

She continued her guessing game. "I also give Ben a convenient out, don't I? If all of this ever comes to light, he can deny all knowledge of anything."

"His work helps so many," Cyril agreed. "It would be a great pity if his assistance with our efforts forced him to make an untimely departure." He reached into his sack once again and extracted a thin circular object about two inches in diameter. "I think it would be a good idea if you were to carry this upon your person at all times."

Allison accepted the object and inspected its smooth

black surface. The only marking was a switch embedded into one side. "What is it?"

"A homing device." Cyril pointed to the switch. "In case you are ever unsure of your safety, you should immediately switch this on. Do not hesitate, my dear. It would be far better to have a few false alarms than to have you wait once a bit too long."

"All right." She agreed, and slid the object into her pocket. "So what do we do now?"

"We wait. Wait and hope that our efforts will not go unnoticed."

"And if you flush them out?" Allison pressed. "What then?"

"Then you flee," he replied gravely, "just as fast as your feet will carry you."

17

WADE ARRIVED AT THE OUTSKIRTS of Tbilisi, footsore and filthy, three days after his narrow escape.

His pack was a burlap feed sack, compliments of the farmer who had picked him up outside Beloti. Wade had raced out of a side alley, almost colliding with the farmer's donkey cart, and had pleaded a ride with the urgency of one frightened for his very life. The farmer had been returning from market, more than a little drunk. His cart had been empty of anything worth stealing, so he had waved Wade on board and offered him a drink from an almost- empty vodka bottle. Wade had politely declined, and had crammed a tattered straw hat he had found under the seat down hard on his head. The farmer had thought that hilarious. Three minutes later, a jeep had roared by in pursuit of a young man now masquerading as a farmer's helper.

After a night in a smelly barn with a donkey for company, Wade bathed in the horse trough and walked back to the main road. While waiting for a ride, he opened the money belt still firmly attached to his waist, pulled out a few dollars, and rolled them in the dirt. This gave them the look of Western currency hoarded for years and given up only as a last resort.

As he expected, the truck driver who stopped demanded money for the ride. In such lands where gasoline was scarce as diamonds, drivers often stopped for paying passengers. Still standing on the road, Wade argued the price down to half the asking price—to do otherwise would attract attention. The driver heard his accent and asked if he was a Latvian down seeking work. Wade responded with a half-nod, half-shrug. The driver snorted his derision at a fool who would travel in any other direction than westward, but he opened the truck door for Wade to clamber in.

The road leading into Tskhinvali, the capital of South Ossetia, was barricaded with sandbags and barbed wire and guarded by machine guns and mobile rocket launchers. To Wade's astonishment, the barricades came in two distinct sections—the first guarded by the Russians and the second, a hundred meters later, by the Ossetians. When asked about the double barricade, the driver replied that the Russians wanted to pretend they controlled the capital city, and the Ossetians were not fool enough to openly attack the Russians—not yet, anyway.

From Tskhinvali, Wade obtained, with more rubles, a ride in what once had been a proud Communist limousine. A hard life and countless kilometers had reduced it to a rattling junk heap with fenders held in place with baling wire, two plastic sheets for side windows, no lights, and a faulty exhaust that sent continuous foul puffs up into his face as he wallowed on the springless backseat.

The town of Gori was thoroughly Georgian and relatively safe. It was best known for having produced the half-Georgian, half-Ossetian man named at birth as Josif Vissarionovich Dzhugashvili, and whom the world knew as Joseph Stalin. Wade used a few of his dollars to obtain a bed and his first decent meal in two days. By then his clothes resembled those of the Georgians around him, dirty and nondescript, and in this land of swarthy features and numerous accents he was taken simply as another northerner. The dollars he offered were enough to erase further questions.

After eating, Wade stretched out on the first bed he

had felt since Grozny. His time at the clinic now seemed like ages ago. He stared up into the darkness of a strange room in a strange town, more alone than he had ever been in his life, and wondered at all the mistakes that had brought him to this point. Yet as he lay and tried to condemn himself, some invisible force as all-enveloping as the darkness closed in, granting him a peace he could not understand.

As his eyelids grew increasingly heavy, he found himself seeing his life anew. The convoluted path that had taken him from a small town in Illinois to this strange room south of the Caucasus Mountains was not simply a series of errors, but a means of both testing and hardening him for something that lay ahead.

Wade drifted in and out of the first layers of sleep and found himself thinking that although the idea of being guided made no logical sense at all, there was indeed great comfort to be found in the hope that it was so.

When he arrived at the outskirts of Tbilisi, Wade was of two minds. On the one hand, he had no idea what he should do next. On the other, there was a growing sense of ordered process, of a clear purpose rising from the chaos and confusion of his circumstances. Wade sat in the rear of the empty produce truck, jounced heavily by every bump in the road, surrounded by choking clouds of dust and diesel fumes, thirstier than he had ever been in his life, yet still retaining the sense of abiding peace that had led him into sleep the night before.

Tbilisi's architecture spoke of two distinct and clashing cultures. Ancient buildings climbed the steep-sided hills in the pattern of formerly walled enclaves, covering every possible inch of available land. Streets were narrow and winding and ever in shadows. The multistoried dwellings were brightly painted and well kept. Delicate balustrades curved into ornate balconies. Yet sharing the streets with these fairy-tale houses stood newer Communist structures, squat and stolid and featureless as a tombstone. The newer buildings dominated much of the city like the foreign rule they represented—alien, unwanted, hated, scorned.

The buildings along the main thoroughfares showed scars from recent conflict. Windows blown to gaping holes. Facades stripped of paint and punctured by thousands of bullet holes. Whole structures reduced to ashes.

Also along these main streets were shops where men gathered and smoked and drank innumerable glasses of spiced tea. The truck halted outside a tumbledown department store. Wade climbed down, thanked the driver, and headed into the cool depths of the nearest cafe.

Everyone spoke simultaneously. Faces were grim yet spirited. There were few smiles, yet none of the resigned hopelessness Wade had often seen in Russia.

Wade accepted his bread and tea from the counter and carried it back to a table by the wall. His arrival brought the usual frank stares. He responded with a greeting in Russian, this time strengthening his American accent as much as he knew how.

His efforts had the desired effect. After a proper pause for him to sip his tea and taste his bread, the nearest man, a grizzled elder with the nose of a hawk, asked, "The stranger is not Russian?"

Wade shook his head. "American."

"Ah." The news brought around the head of the other person at the old man's table, a younger man with the wiry strength of an underpaid day worker. The old man continued his queries. "Truly you are from the United States?"

"Yes." Wade took another tentative sip from his steaming glass. "Forgive me for not speaking your own language, but I have just arrived in Georgia."

"My own language was seldom heard outside the home for many years, and even now I speak the Russian tongue better," the old man confessed. In the ways of his world, too many direct questions would be an offense, so he simply commented, "I have never had the pleasure of speaking with an American. Is it normal for Americans to know the tongue of our former oppressors?"

"I come from Grozny," Wade said, supplying the desired information. "I worked with the injured and sick and wounded."

This the old man could understand. "We have many such in these troubled times."

"My own brother lies wounded in the central hospital," the younger man confirmed. "He has just this week been returned from the Abkhazi front."

"It is a difficult time for our nation," the old man agreed. "And yet at least we are a nation once again."

"I have heard that yours is a land with a long and glorious heritage," Wade said politely.

"Sarkatvelo, it was known in the dim reaches of man and memory," the old man replied, his eyes alight. "The land of the Kartvelian tribes. It was the very first of the northern lands to accept Christianity, when our king was converted in the year 337. Since that time, Georgia has had its own Orthodox church, its own Patriarch, its own struggle against foes who sought to bury its name and its nationhood forever."

Through the open door Wade could see a fire-blackened shopfront before which rested the remains of a burned-out bus. "You have had a hard struggle."

"Indeed. Schevardnaze now rules not one nation, but twenty, with all the old tribes now saying, since we cannot trust Tbilisi to govern us fairly, then we will govern ourselves."

"Civil war," Wade interpreted.

"Chaos," the old man moaned. "Chaos and bloodshed and hatreds from which this land may never recover."

Wade finished his tea and asked, "Where would I find the main hospital?"

"Just off the Rustaveli Avenue, not a kilometer from

here," the younger man replied. "And may you bring peace and healing to those who are in need."

Before the trauma of independence, Rustaveli Avenue had been a main artery of Tbilisi. Its great trees had shaded thousands as they took their regular evening strolls. But recent battles had transformed the city's heart. Rustaveli Avenue was a bombed and gutted ruin, its length still littered with the smoke-stained hulks of cars and buses and tanks. Scarcely a building was left unscarred by shells and smoke. The central government building at the avenue's end was little more than a blackened skeleton.

Wade turned off the main boulevard and a hundred meters farther entered the central hospital's main gates. After an interminable wait he was allowed to see one of the head doctors, a heavyset man with the girth and hands and rumbling voice of a human bear. Swiftly Wade explained his mission and asked if Red Cross personnel had appeared from the highlands.

"They were here," the man replied, his eyes bearing the same fatigue smudges as every doctor Wade had met in these war-torn lands. "But they returned to the West."

"When?"

The man shrugged. "Soon after they arrived. One was slightly wounded, and they stayed until she was well enough to travel on." Clearly the exact date was unimportant to him. That they had left was all that mattered. "Are you a doctor?"

Wade shook his head. "A nurse."

"Yes?" Gray eyes took on renewed interest. "We have much need for trained personnel. You will be staying?"

Wade hesitated, but not for long. The sense of being drawn forward was too strong. "If I do, I would be honored to work with you."

"Honored, yes," the doctor sighed. He understood the answer for what it was. He rose to his feet. "You must excuse me, then, I am seeing to the work of ten."

Wade made his way out of the hospital and stopped

when he arrived at the road. He understood it then. He did not like it, but he understood. He had arrived at the fork in the road, and the choice was upon him. Even to hesitate meant to choose. He could not back away, could not turn around, could not ignore that simple fact.

He could certainly refuse the challenge. He could pretend that it was none of his concern and do nothing. He could turn away from the silent call.

But he was too honest to lie to himself, to believe that anyone else would pick up the fallen staff. It was him or nobody.

It was hard to cast off the blanket of anonymity that had sheltered him all his life. Harder still to see the cliff's edge there before him, and step off, and rely on God to hold him aloft. Hard to know that he alone could not do what was required, to understand that the odds were infinitely against him, and yet still to go ahead and try, trusting in God to see him through.

So very hard.

18

THE PLANE FROM ISTANBUL was delayed, so Wade arrived in Amman long after the last bus had departed. The plane ticket had cost him almost every cent he had left, leaving him enough for bus fare to Aqaba and perhaps a few sparse meals. He purchased a sweetcake and Pepsi from one of the airport vendors and settled himself as comfortably as possible in a corner.

After the final tourist hordes had been processed and gathered and sent to their hotels, the airport belonged to the Arabs. Desert travelers too poor to afford city prices bedded down in family clusters. From time to time one of their number would approach a short-tempered clerk to whine and plead and shake fistfuls of grimy tickets and beg for things that Wade could not understand. Each departing traveler was escorted by huge extended families who had brought comfortable-looking carpets, copper-lidded food containers, radios, and even several goats. The air was full of smoke and talk and wailing babies. Wade ate his sugary supper, leaned back, cast a final glance around the cluttered hall, and fell asleep.

He awoke the next morning with every muscle complaining from the hard floor. Bright sunshine lanced through the smoke-filled air. The hall was already filled with bustling, jabbering, scurrying figures who paid scant attention to yet another road-worn traveler.

Wade collected his meager belongings and made his way to the toilet. After scrubbing his face and the back of his neck he raised his head and stopped. For a long moment he stood and stared in the mirror, and wondered who was staring back.

Dark brown hair had been slicked back by countless motions of grimy hands too busy to bother with a brush. The bandanna knotted around his neck was matted with sweat and dirt. Hard travel and poor diet had honed down his features, giving his face a leaner, tougher cast. His nose and cheeks were splotched by multiple bouts of sunburn. His five-day growth covered a jaw set in alien, determined lines.

But it was his eyes that held his attention. They burned with a resolute light. There was none of the doubt that had plagued his life for so many years, none of the hesitant worry. There was no room for any of that.

He had been called to take sides, and his choice was there in his eyes for all to see. Even himself.

The wind still blew from the southwest—never varying, never ceasing. All the clinic staff spoke of it and complained of the accompanying heat. To Allison, the reddish dust, blown in from the distant African plains, was a far greater trial. It was red and fine and irritated her throat and nose. Her eyes looked as though she suffered from a perpetual cold. She kept a plastic bottle of mineral water by her at all times, so that she could sip continually and ease the dryness caused by breathing dust. But the bottle had to be kept tightly capped; otherwise a thin red sheen would quickly appear across the water's surface. The dust coated every surface, even her papers, and left her hands and face and clothes feeling perpetually grimy. The dust made the hottest part of the day almost unbearable.

The knock did not raise Allison's attention from the

dusty pile of forms. Someone was always coming by, asking in that pleading tone she hated for things she could not understand. She was in the middle of counting down a long line of figures, so when the knock was followed by the sound of someone clearing his throat, she impatiently waved the person away.

But when the unseen stranger spoke, the sound of an American accent pushed the numbers from her mind. "What?"

"I asked," the bearded, dirty young man asked, "if you were a doctor."

"No, I'm, that is . . ." She hesitated. The young man exuded mystery. His clothes were battered beyond belief. His features were chiseled, his air raffish, his look tremendously determined. "Who are you?"

"My name is Wade Waters." His voice was soft, almost apologetic. "I was wondering if you needed help—at the clinic, I mean."

His appearance was a strange mixture. Piercing eyes, yet gentle voice. Rugged good looks, a determined presence and an air of urgency.

She immediately assumed he was a doctor. "You are American?"

He nodded. "I've just—"

"I am Doctor Shannon," said a voice from down the hall. "Can I help you?"

The young man turned and said, "I was wondering if I could work for you."

Ben stepped into view, surveyed the young man, and asked, "Why?"

"I'm trained as a nurse, and," the young man hesitated, then finished, "I'm hungry."

Ben smiled. "That we can remedy. Forgive me for pressing, but a young American nurse appears out of nowhere seeking work—you must admit that a few questions are in order."

"I trained in Illinois," Wade responded. "I have a BA, a BSN, and two years experience at a U.S. hospital. For over a year now I have been a missionary nurse . . ." Again the hesitation.

"Where," Ben pressed.

"Grozny," the young man replied, almost a surrender. "It is in the Chechen-Ingush area, north of the Caucasus Mountains."

Dr. Shannon's eyes widened considerably. "In Russia?"

"Yes."

"Not exactly a place from which I might obtain a recommendation."

The internal struggle subsided. "I am a good nurse, Doctor Shannon. Personal reasons have brought me here, that's all I can say. I don't know how long I will need to stay, probably several months. But I will work hard at whatever duties you give me."

"We are terrifically understaffed," Ben admitted. "But I cannot pay you anything more than room and board."

"That is enough."

"You will be watched carefully," Ben warned, "and not allowed to take on a number of duties unattended."

"I understand."

Still the doctor hesitated. "You are Christian?"

"Yes."

"It is very dangerous to speak openly of such things here," he warned. "Dangerous both for you and for others."

"I have worked among Muslims before," Wade replied.

"Well, I am tempted, but I shall have to think more on this before making a decision. In the meantime." He turned to where Ali had appeared and waited just outside the door. "Take this young man over to the house and have Esa prepare him something to eat."

"And soap and a razor, if possible," Wade added quietly. "All my belongings have been stolen."

"Really? At the airport?"

"No." A moment's indecision, then the softly spoken words, "Near Tshkinvali."

"I beg your pardon?"

"It is the capital of South Ossetia. I was delivering Red Cross supplies to clinics along the battlefields, and my truck was stolen."

"And you came here from—what was that city called?"

Wade shook his head. "I flew to Amman from Tbilisi."

"And that is?"

"The capital of Georgia. Via Istanbul."

"So you traveled all the way from a war zone in Georgia to Aqaba in southern Jordan," the doctor said, and waited. But the young man gave no reply.

"I see," the doctor murmured. "Well, I suppose it will not hurt anything to offer our mysterious young man a meal and some soap. Ali?"

"This way," Ali said.

"You won't regret this," Wade promised as he turned away.

"I hope and pray not, young man," Ben Shannon said doubtfully. He gave an eloquent shrug to Allison and walked back down the hall.

Allison leaned back in her chair and cast a bemused look around her empty office. Suddenly everything seemed so quiet, as though a powerful and unexpected storm had just passed through.

Mentally she caught herself and pulled back hard. Allison returned to her work with a sigh. First a roofing worker, now a male nurse.

She always was attracted to the wrong sort of man.

19

WADE MADE HIS WAY from the clinic toward the souk, the truck compound's central market, hoping that at least a little of what he had gained from his time in Russia would apply here as well. If so, then the market would not be simply a place to buy, but a focal point for community life, a magnet for all, a central gathering place for both people and information.

What he could possibly learn, neither knowing the language nor having the first contact, he had no idea. But he had to try.

The foremost ranks of stalls catered to the tourist trade—in this case, truckers from distant lands. There were the usual sorts of mementos on display—coffee urns, etched plates, brightly colored blankets, hookahs, rugs, hats, straw camels, leather gear, carvings. Wade walked past these offerings and searched for he knew not what. His obvious lack of money saved him from the worst of the sales pressure.

Past these outer ranks was the heart of the old market, row upon row of spindly stalls selling a vast variety of items. Sheep and goats and chickens kept up a panic-stricken cacophony at the row of butcher stalls. Fruit and spices and animals colored the enclosed air with intense fragrances. Flies swarmed everywhere. Dust settled on everything and everyone. The heat was fierce.

The cramped alleyway opened into an ancient central square. Tired donkeys and a few camels were lined up under a makeshift straw shelter. Some munched from feedbags; others drank from leather buckets held by ragamuffin youths in threadbare robes. A series of tea shops lined the opposite wall. Wade counted through his meager change and decided one glass would do no harm.

But before he could seat himself he felt a hand grasp his elbow. "Not there, Mister Wade. He will cheat you and serve bad food, make you sick. Come here, over here. My friend, he treat you better."

"I only wanted a tea," Wade protested. The young man from the clinic was called Ali, that much he recalled.

"Here, over here," Ali insisted, and led him to the corner shop. "What you like, I order for you."

"Just tea. I don't have much money."

"Is okay, Mister Wade. Today I buy; another day you do same, yes?"

Wade shrugged. "Another day I still might not have money."

"Okay, okay, you buy when you can."

"Fine," he consented. "Whatever you say."

"Good." When they were seated, Ali launched a barrage at the hovering waiter, who remained utterly unmoved. When Ali stopped, he scooped up the dirty glasses littering their table, ignored the overflowing ashtray, gave his filthy towel a single flick at the covering of dust, and slouched away. Ali turned back to Wade with, "Is good place, you see."

"The clinic pays you enough for you to eat in restaurants?" Wade asked.

The young man's eyes flickered everywhere but directly at Wade. "I already tell you. My friend, he own this place. I get special price."

"I see."

"For you too, when you come back. Just say you are friend of Ali, and all will be first-rate. You see."

"Thank you for your kindness," Wade replied.

Dark eyes turned and searched suspiciously for sarcasm, found nothing, and darted away. Ali reached inside his robes, extracted a pack of cigarettes. "You like?"

"I don't smoke, thank you."

He lit one for himself, drew on it with fierce intensity. He pulled his hand back in a jerky arc, threw the ashes out into the street with impatient gestures. Blasted the smoke from mouth and nose, paused to make smoke rings, drew again. An adolescent bundle of nerves. "You come from Russia, yes?"

"How did you hear that?"

"I hear," Ali assured him proudly. "All things in clinic, Ali know."

"I see." Wade nodded his thanks as the waiter deposited a glass of steaming tea in front of him, the mint leaves floating on the top, and a piece of rock sugar set upon the saucer. He had seen this in several Muslim cafes, where the men would place the sugar in their cheeks and suck on it as they drank their tea.

"Russia is far from Aqaba," Ali persisted. "Why you come?"

Wade knew the question had to be asked and answered. He knew also that he would not, could not, lie. But there was no way of knowing for whom Ali asked—for the clinic, or for others. "I am looking for a man," he said.

The smoking grew more intense, the eyes darted ever swifter. "Arab man?"

"No," Wade replied. "An American. He stole something from me. Something important."

"Money?"

Wade shook his head. "A truckload of medical supplies I was supposed to use to help the poor. And the truck."

"Whole truck of medicines," Ali mused aloud. "Worth much money."

"It was very hard to bring those supplies in," Wade

continued. "A lot of people in dire need could have been helped."

"So why you look for American man in Aqaba?"

"A rumor," Wade replied. "It is all I have to go on."

The cigarette was already down to the filter. Ali took a final drag and flicked the remains out into the sunlit square.

"Maybe I help," he offered. "What he look like, this man?"

"Big," Wade replied. "Two meters tall, heavy, dark hair, blue eyes, very dangerous. Trained as a soldier."

Ali was not impressed. "There are many soldiers here. Some in army, most not. What his name?"

"Robards," Wade replied. "But most people call him Rogue."

Allison went through the motions of preparing for bed, but her mind remained fixed upon the day—and on the strange young man called Wade.

She could find no reason whatsoever to justify her interest, except perhaps the mystery surrounding him. He had cleaned up to reveal a fairly attractive person with nice, even features. The only remarkable thing about him, as far as she could tell, was the single-minded intensity that surrounded all his actions—that and his silence.

The one time she had seen him discard his reserve was when he had worked that afternoon in the men's ward of the clinic, where he had been assigned as assistant to the ward nurse. Ben had allotted Wade only the most menial of duties—changing sheets, prepping patients for surgery, bathing and feeding them—and those only under strict supervision. He was not to approach either the children's or the women's wards nor to touch any medicines. He was never to be left alone for an instant. Wade had accepted it all, including the ward nurse's evident hostility, with apparent indifference.

Yet when Allison was restocking cabinets that afternoon, she had caught sight of the ward nurse looking back toward the end of the hall, a bemused smile on her face. The nurse was a battle-hardened ward sister seldom given to any expression except a perpetual grimace. Curious, Allison had risen to her feet and looked down the hall to see Wade seated beside an old Bedouin trapped in the fever dreams of pleurisy. The old man had dribbled a broken stream of Arabic; Wade had responded with a continual croon of English, bathing his face and upper body with a cooling mixture of alcohol and water. His motions had been calm, steady, and patient—infinitely patient.

But it was the expression on his face that had captured her. The naked compassion reminded her of the way a mother might watch her own newborn. Allison had watched as the old man calmed, quieted, drifted into deeper sleep. Only then had Wade relaxed from his bent-over position, dropped the sponge into the basin, gently pulled up the sheets, and risen to his feet.

Instantly a querulous voice had reached out from another bed. Again Wade had responded with gentle patience, clearly not understanding what the man was asking, but in no hurry to leave until the request was discerned and answered.

"He says his bandages are uncomfortable," the nurse called out, making no move to approach.

Wade looked around and spotted a metal basin on a nearby table bearing new bandages, scissors, antiseptic, and tape. He did not roll the patient over as much as help him turn at his own pace, soothing the occasional groan with a murmur of his own. Only when the man was resting comfortably on his side did Wade begin the laborious process of pulling away the soiled bandage. Blood had clotted the cloth, sealing it to the skin. Wade comforted not with words, but rather with his entire being. He plucked, waited, spoke, sponged, pulled again, his face filled always with a compassionate sharing of the man's pain.

By then the families gathered at neighboring beds were watching, many faces bearing the same gentle smile as the nurse. They murmured their sympathy as the man jerked in response to Wade's last pulling tug. The man basked in the attention and relaxed under a touch he had come to realize would give him not an instant's more discomfort than was absolutely required.

The ward nurse happened to glance over at Allison. Something in her expression caused the nurse's smile to alter to a knowing smirk. Allison blushed without knowing why and fled back to her office.

Within a few minutes Ali was lounging in the doorway. "What you think of this man, this nurse?"

"I have work to do, Ali," she replied automatically.

"I ate with him," he announced. "We talked. He told me things."

She resisted the urge to raise her head. "What things?"

"Things," he repeated. "He comes from Russia."

She had learned it was best not to show too much interest in what Ali had to say. If she did, he treated it as a negotiable property, only to be traded for something in return. "I already knew that."

"Sure, Western lady. But did you know he was here looking for a man?"

She inspected a paper she scarcely saw and replied in a bored tone, "I don't think he mentioned that."

"American man," Ali confirmed. "Stole his truck. And medicines. This man Wade thinks is here."

"Seems strange that he would follow another American from Russia to Aqaba," she ventured idly, drawing designs on her pad.

"Yes, I think, too. Is crazy. Just another Western man with no idea of where he go in life." Ali turned from the door. "I tell Doctor Ben."

Allison carried that bit of news and the look on Wade's face with her through the rest of that day. She thought of it as she washed her face and brushed her hair. But it was only after turning out the light and climbing into bed that a new thought struck her. It came unbidden, and she could see no logical reason for it. But it came with such force that it left her shaken and unable to sleep.

The thought was that this young man would change her entire life, if only she would let him in.

By the end of the week, Wade's presence in the clinic was an established fact. He worked the long hours, accepted the basic conditions and standard fare and lack of pay without complaint. Constant emergencies and an overworked staff soon dissolved his restrictions. He moved freely through the men's and children's wards, carefully avoiding the women's rooms out of respect for the clinic codes. This too won looks of approval from the other staff. He handled medicines with precision, gave careful attention to duties both major and menial, accepted orders without argument, yet also showed he could think on his own. By week's end, even Dr. Shannon was calling him a godsend.

The mysterious errand that had brought this young man to Aqaba was much discussed. Opinions varied. Some thought him foolish, Ali included. Many of the nursing staff, however, took note of his abilities and his quiet demeanor, and accepted his single-minded determination as just another part of his makeup.

Wade was assigned to the morning shift, which was by far the busiest; it included both breakfast and lunch, the doctor's morning rounds, surgery prep, processing new patients, bathing and cleaning and dressing wounds. Wade finished sometime between two and five each afternoon, depending on how the day progressed. Then he returned to his room, changed clothes, rested, ate, and began his endless searching in the cool of the dying day.

He had registered his complaint with the local police, whose only interest was sparked by the idea of one American following another American from Russia to the tail end of Jordan. Now he mostly walked and looked—and daily resisted giving in to the futility of his search.

Dr. Shannon called Wade in after the clinic's Sunday worship service and asked him to be seated. "I have heard, as has everyone here, that you are here looking for another American who stole a truck from you in Russia."

Wade nodded reluctantly.

"And you really think the man you seek is here?"

"It's all I have to go on."

"He told you himself where he was going?"

"No." Wade hesitated, then added, "It was one of his companions."

"Then he's not alone?"

"I'm not sure, but I don't think so."

Ben Shannon examined him carefully. "The Arabs are the world's experts at saying much through the silences between words, so I have become skilled at listening for what is not being said. I have the distinct impression that you are leaving out more than you are telling."

Wade tensed, then forced himself to relax. "I have told you all I can."

"Tell me this," Ben insisted. "Is it possible that your search could endanger this clinic?"

Again there was the inward struggle, then Wade conceded, "Rogue Robards is a very powerful man."

It was Ben's turn to deliberate. "You are one of the finest nurses I have ever had occasion to work with. That much is clear after just five days. And it is true that the workload here is pushing us beyond our limits. But before I can allow you to remain, I must have your solemn word that you will do everything possible not to endanger our work."

"You have it," Wade replied earnestly.

"Wait, there's more." Ben bore down on him. "I also

have the impression that more is involved than just a stolen truck. If I am to trust you with the lives of my patients, I feel I have a right to ask what this is."

Wade dropped his eyes to his hands, and replied quietly, "I'm sorry, but I just can't tell you."

The ensuing silence forced Wade to raise his gaze. To his surprise, he found the doctor with bowed head and closed eyes, enshrouded in a veil of stillness. Eventually Ben opened his eyes and spoke calmly. "Tuesdays and Thursdays I make rounds within the local camps. I want you to come and assist. I want you to observe me very carefully. After you have gone with me, if you decide that I am worthy of your trust, I ask that you tell me what you are leaving unsaid. However, if you feel that I cannot be trusted with your secret, then I must ask you to leave at the end of the week."

"I guess I don't have any choice," Wade said bleakly.

"On the contrary," Ben replied. "Choice is all we are speaking of. For you, and for me."

Wade left the doctor's room in a quandary of doubt and indecision. He knew he needed help, but to share his secret with a man so closely linked to the Arabs was a risk he dared not take.

20

THAT NIGHT WADE ACCEPTED last-minute duty to replace an ill staff member. He slept late the next morning and ate his breakfast alone. Heavily burdened both by the sense of futility and the impending choice, Wade took a purposeless walk down into the souk. At the central square he took a table just inside the shop's open doorway. When the same bored waiter appeared, he purchased his seat for the price of a tea.

He sat and watched the dust drift in the brilliant sunshine, while various half-formed ideas flitted through his troubled mind. Overriding every thought was a feeling as intense as the rising heat—that it was all a mistake. That he had no business being there. That he had listened to false voices and fooled himself from the beginning.

Which made the sound behind him even more shocking.

"You're making yourself a real nuisance, sport," said the unseen man. "There's a knife aimed at your gizzard. Calm and easy, now, I want you to—"

Wade acted without conscious thought. In a single electrified movement he threw his glass back over his shoulder and dived through the doorway.

Behind him echoed a roar of rage and pain. Wade did a three-point scramble in the dust, arms akimbo and legs flailing wildly, and fled down the nearest shop-lined alley.

• • •

Allison was just climbing into the clinic's battered Land Rover when a very dusty Wade came racing into view. "Where are you going?" he demanded breathlessly.

"Just our normal supply run to Amman. Why?"

"Take me with you," he burst out. The focused power to his gaze shone with feverish intensity.

"What's the matter?"

"Please," he said, pressing with more than just his words. "It's really important."

"Are you in some kind of trouble?" Allison had a sudden thought. "Did you find that man?"

He shot a glance over at where Fareed sat stoically behind the wheel. All Wade said was, "Please."

Allison pondered briefly. It was standard policy for all clinic staff to be granted lifts wherever official business took anyone, so long as there was room. "We'll be stuffed to the gills on the way back."

"No problem. I'm used to cramped quarters."

She shrugged. "I guess it's okay, then." She cast a glance over his rumpled form. "Do you want to change or anything?"

"No, I—" he stopped. "My passport! I'll be right back."

Allison stared after his departing back and felt a faint tingle of alarm. The only place she could think of where a passport would be required for entry was the American Embassy.

The new United States Embassy in Amman was a cross between an Arabian Nights palace and a functional American office building. The exterior was covered in desert stone, with rose-tinted borders around numerous windows. The structure dominated an entire hilltop in a newer suburb of town, and afforded a wonderful view over Amman's old quarter.

Judith Armstead strode impatiently into the guardhouse, where all nonembassy personnel were required to sign in, and greeted her friend with "What took you so long?"

"I was lunching with the ambassador and the foreign minister," Cyril Price replied. "What on earth is the matter? Our meeting with Allison is not for another hour."

"You'll see." Judith managed a quick glance at her watch as Cyril surrendered his passport and signed the passbook. She was a stern, no-nonsense woman with clear gray eyes and a very direct gaze. She wore a navy-blue skirt and jacket of severe lines, no jewelry, and little makeup. Her gray hair was cut short and worn straight. Her expression was as determined as her stride. "Come on, we've got to get this finished before Allison shows up."

He nodded his thanks as the Marine guard waved him through the security gate, then crossed the open parking lot and hurried up the embassy stairs. "Don't tell me there's trouble."

"I'm not saying another word," Judith replied. She hustled her British counterpart through the main entrance, across the foyer, and down the long hallway. "I want you to hear this straight from the horse's mouth."

She opened the door leading to the small conference room and let Cyril enter first. Seated within was a decidedly scruffy young man, dusty and sweaty and clearly the worse for wear. But his expression was resolute and he measured Cyril with a steady gaze.

"Wade Waters," Judith began, "this is—well, let's just leave out any introductions for the moment, okay? This man is the primary contact in these parts for activities such as what you have been describing."

"If I'm to trust him," Wade replied, his voice as steady as his gaze, "I want to know who he is."

"Cyril Price at your service," Cyril said, taking a seat across from the young man. "Judith says you have something of interest to tell me. I have known Judith for a number of years and have learned to trust her implicitly."

"Cyril's the real thing," Judith said, seating herself beside Cyril. "Why don't you just take it from the top and tell him exactly what you told me."

When Wade finished, Cyril sat in stunned silence. "I confess," he said finally, "I am at an utter loss."

A smile appeared on Judith's face. "That is a first."

"Would you permit me," Cyril asked, "to return to a few minor points?"

"Sure," Wade replied.

"Judith, how much time before our next appointment?"

"Fifteen minutes, tops."

"We shall simply have to reconvene another day. Would you mind returning to Amman later in the week, Mr. Waters?"

"If I have time off," Wade replied. "And if I can find enough money for the trip."

"That's right," Cyril recalled. "You spent virtually every cent you had after losing your truck in . . . what was the name of that town once again?"

"Beloti," Wade replied. "About twenty-five kilometers north of Tskhinvali."

"Ah, yes. And that is . . ."

"The capital of South Ossetia," Wade replied. "A contested region currently held by Georgia."

"You do not, I hope, take offense by my returning to such points," Cyril said. "My memory, you understand—an attribute of age."

"I understand perfectly," Wade replied calmly. "I have spent more than a year in places where strangers are tested as a matter of habit."

Cyril's gaze turned keener. "Ah, yes. You were in Grozny, I believe." And with that he switched to a passable Russian. "You were no doubt instructed in the local tongue."

"Many of the locals," Wade countered, also in Russian, "would dispute your calling this language their own."

"Indeed," Cyril said, returning to English. "Most interesting. Well, I suppose that brings us to asking for a description of the three men."

"Four," Judith corrected. "Don't forget the American. I was just finishing up the descriptions when you arrived."

Wade asked, "Is there any chance you could find me a job or something where I can earn my keep?" Swiftly he explained the problem with Ben Shannon.

"It so happens that I know Dr. Shannon," Cyril replied, avoiding any eye contact with Judith. "Quite well, as a matter of fact. I shall write a note for you to carry back with you to clear things up."

"That would be great," Wade said, visibly relieved.

"If I were in your position," Cyril went on, "I should trust Ben Shannon with everything you know. He is both well connected and extremely trustworthy."

"I was worried that somebody that close to the locals might pass on word."

Both Cyril and Judith shook their heads to that. "Not a chance," Judith stated flatly.

"I quite agree," Cyril said. "Ben Shannon positively loathes the activities of terrorists. You will do well to trust him with your secrets, young man."

"While we're at it," Judith interjected, "it probably wouldn't hurt to supply you with a little pocket money."

"An excellent idea." Cyril rose to his feet. "I am afraid that a prior appointment forces us to end our discussions for now. I suggest that we plan to meet again on," he thought for a moment, then asked, "Would Thursday suit both of you?"

"Thursday's fine with me," Judith said.

"If I can get off work," Wade said.

"Trust Ben Shannon with your secret," Cyril said, "and

you will find any number of impediments disappearing from your course. And rest assured that we shall in the meantime make every effort to seek out the men you have described."

He offered Wade his hand. "As my colleague mentioned, it is very seldom that people surprise me. You, young man, have succeeded in doing so. I shall look forward with anticipation to our next meeting."

After Wade's departure, the pair stood and watched the closed door for a time before Cyril murmured, "Most remarkable."

Judith took that as her cue. "You're going to use him as bait too, aren't you?"

Cyril nodded. "Now that all else has failed, it may be the only way to draw the lion from its lair."

"You're not going to warn him to stay out of harm's way?"

"Oh, I am certain he will remain enclosed and relatively safe for a time." Cyril smiled frostily. "Perhaps even as long as a day or two."

"And then?"

"Then the same determination that has brought him this far will push him out into the open yet again."

"They'll be waiting."

"And so shall we. You must double the guard at the clinic."

"That will just about strip the cupboard bare."

"The cupboard has up to now produced nothing of substance," Cyril replied. "Let us place all our resources where we have the best chance of succeeding. Allison and this lad must be watched every step of the way."

Judith smiled. "I know that look."

"What on earth are you talking about?"

"You do have plans for this young man, don't you?"

"Yes, well. It is so very seldom these days that one

finds a person who combines a talent for adventurous derring-do with an ability to think on his or her feet."

"What about Allison?"

"Oh, our young lady has all that and more." He gave a fond smile of remembrance. "Her father would be so very proud of her."

Judith watched him with wise eyes. "They would make quite a team, wouldn't they?"

"I find it is best not to raise my hopes too high," Cyril replied. "But yes, I admit the thought has crossed my mind. And yes, they would make a truly formidable pair."

"So will you tell her about him?"

Cyril thought it over. "I think not. This is Ben's turf, at least within the clinic. It should be his decision." The glint of humor resurfaced. "Besides, not telling them should grant our dear Dr. Shannon yet another reason to be irritated with me. That should please him no end."

The three-hour trip back to Aqaba that afternoon was long and hot and far too quiet. The Land Rover's air conditioning provided a fitful stream of stale air that blew only when the truck was coasting downhill. The trip left Allison feeling sticky, dirty, and frayed around the edges. But that was not what bothered her the most.

It was Wade's total lack of interest in her that really hit where it hurt. Not that he was anything like her ideal man. Yet here she was, upset because Wade sat and stared straight ahead, not speaking with her, not noticing her at all.

She didn't know anything about him. He probably had a girlfriend. Maybe he was even married. She checked as unobtrusively as she could—no ring. Not that it meant anything these days.

Allison looked out at the arid landscape and could almost hear her girlfriend's condescending voice. A male nurse—are you kidding? The bartender at Clyde's would be a big step up. Yet she could not deny she was attracted to him.

Since Wade's attention remained focused outside the car, Allison took the opportunity to furtively inspect him.

Nice hair. Beautiful green eyes—his best feature, really, with that strong, purposeful gaze. Not too strong a chin, but he was so determined it was hard to notice.

Clearly not a snappy dresser. But Aqaba was not a place that attracted men from the pages of *GQ*.

Great teeth. She wondered what his smile would look like.

Then she recalled his caring attitude toward the patients, and felt that little catch to her breath once more.

Was she really interested in a relationship with him? She pushed the thought away as hard as she could. Definitely another Mister Wrong, to be avoided at all costs.

And yet there was something to him that she could not put her finger on. Something that called to the still, small voice of her heart. Something that would not be denied, no matter how hard and loud her mind might object.

Allison risked another furtive glance at her silent neighbor and wondered at the emotions welling up inside.

Wade was immensely relieved when they arrived back at the clinic. As soon as the Land Rover pulled up to the main gates, he bolted as though flung from an ejector seat.

Sitting next to Allison the entire way to and from Amman had been sheer agony.

She was without a doubt the most beautiful woman he had ever met. And because of that, she was utterly beyond his reach.

Wade had tried as hard as he could to hold his attention to the matters at hand, but with Allison beside him it had been impossible. The fact that she had been so close and yet so unreachable had left him hollow.

Wade found Ben in his cramped office, working his way through a pile of forms. He knocked on the open door. "Can I bother you for a moment?"

"Only if it's good news," Ben replied, giving him a tired smile. "I've had one of those days."

"I'm not sure whether this is good or not," Wade ventured doubtfully. "Maybe I should wait until tomorrow."

"What, and leave me free to worry all night?" Ben shook his head. "Too late for that. Come in and sit down." When Wade had done so, Ben asked, "What's on your mind?"

Wade offered him the note from Cyril. "Maybe you ought to read this first."

"Read what?" Ben opened the letter. He read the note a second time, growing grimmer by the minute. Finally he said to no one in particular, "Is this his idea of a joke?"

"He told me you would understand."

"Oh, I understand, all right. I understand my old friend suffers from an overdose of international intrigue." He focused on Wade. "Go find Allison and bring her here, please."

"But I'm not—"

"Now," Ben said.

Wade departed in utter confusion. He found Allison in the dining room, glumly passed on the message, and responded to her query with a shrug. He followed her back into Ben's office and allowed himself to be guided into a seat.

"All right," Ben said. "I will start the ball rolling. Allison Taylor is here at the request of Cyril Price." He ignored Allison as she bolted upright in her chair. "She is assisting British and American Intelligence in trying to track down smugglers of weapons-grade nuclear fuel."

Allison protested, "Why are—"

Ben stopped her with an upraised palm, his eyes never leaving Wade's face. "Now it's your turn."

"I'm not sure—"

"I am," Ben interrupted. "These shenanigans will not extend to cat-and-mouse games inside my clinic. Now then." He folded his arms across his chest. "You trust me, you trust her."

Resigned to his fate, Wade gave them a scaled-down version of his experiences over the past month. When he finished, he risked a glance at Allison. She stared at him in open-mouthed shock.

Ben, on the other hand, responded with a grin. "That tale is far to wild to be a lie."

"I've told you the truth," Wade responded quietly.

"Yes, I believe you have." Ben eyed him with new-found respect. "And what would you call the coincidence that has brought you to this particular clinic at this particular time?"

"A miracle," Wade said softly, warmed by Allison's uninterrupted gaze.

Ben nodded slowly. "Then I suggest we three join with the Maker of miracles in prayer, and see where He takes us from here."

21

FOR THE AVIATORS and sailors manning the United States Gulf Convoy that fall, Iraq was not the worst enemy they faced. First position was reserved for the heat.

For five long months, the convoy surrounding and protecting the aircraft carrier USS Independence had sweltered in heat which by noontime rose above 120 degrees Fahrenheit, and often hit 140 by midafternoon.

Their orders had been to send warplanes over southern Iraq, enforcing the air-exclusion zone south of the thirty-second parallel. This had been intended to protect the Shiite Muslim minority in Iraq and diminish Saddam Hussein's hold over the region. But the Iraqis had held back from challenging the Americans' overwhelming might and had let the heat do battle for them.

On the aircraft carrier alone, a dozen people a day collapsed from heat exhaustion. Staff meetings began and ended with the order to see that all sailors force-fed their bodies with liquid, which was difficult, as everything on the ship was bath-water warm.

Air-conditioning units, designed to both cool the air and chill incoming seawater, barely made a dent in either. Machinery shops, laundries, kitchens, lower storage holds, all rarely fell below 110 degrees. Officers sat beneath a/c vents and felt the sweat continually drench their bodies. Sleep in the poorly ventilated noisy holds, where 200 sailors crowded together for their six to eight hours of off-duty, was impossible.

For the aviators, the heat created unforeseen dangers. The sea water was so hot that the slightest weather change caused thick swatches of impenetrable mist to boil up, reducing visibility to less than three hundred feet—very little distance for an incoming jet to calculate a safe landing. Radar was little help, as the shifting mist and hot-air streams were a misery to their sensitive machinery. Among the pilots, landings were known as controlled crashes.

But the snipes, or low-level engineers, had it worst of all. Temperatures around the engines, boilers, and generators daily rose to over 150 degrees. Pipes burst for no reason. Machines became stubborn as mules. Welded plating blew its seals without warning. Stairs and railings grew so hot that they burned one to the touch.

But by early October, when the missile cruiser USS Arapahoe was sent on a solitary top-secret mission, temperatures had cooled to the point that officers lingered on the bridge at the end of the watch to survey the alien landscape.

The ship passed well clear of Aden, the capital of Yemen, before entering the Red Sea via the narrow strait of Bab el Mandeb. They steamed north by the Dahlak Archipelago, then passed between Port Sudan and the Saudi port of Jeddah, heading for the Gulf of Aqaba. They maintained strict radio silence, sending a single burst by satellite each morning and evening—not to their fleet, strangely enough, but back to Washington. Or at least that was the scuttlebutt on board.

That October afternoon, Lieutenant James Ferguson was lingering on the deck after his watch, when the horizon suddenly disappeared. He backed into the windowless radio chamber, with its surreal lighting, and called out, "Wind's on the rise, Cole!"

His friend Samuel "Ears" Cole, a great reader of old travel books, had made Ferguson promise to keep watch for the mistrals. Cole was out of his seat in a flash, earphones still hanging around his neck. "Let's go, Fergey boy."

"No rush, no rush. Looks like it'll pass us on the other side of the horizon."

"It wouldn't dare. And if it would, I'll just have to have words with el capitano. Respectfully ask him to get the lead out."

They thundered down the stairs and raced to join the crowd gathering in the bows. Cole pushed his way through to the railing. "First come, first served, Ears," somebody complained. "Shove me again and you're shark bait."

"The only reason you're out here is because I told you to watch for it," Cole replied and made room for his buddy at the rail. "Get a load of that, Fergey."

"Okay," Ferguson said, trying to match Cole's casual drawl. "So just what is it I'm looking at, anyway?"

Their ship was out of the wind's course, so they stood in bright sunshine as a golden-red cloud billowed from the sea to the distant sky. It was immeasurable, a power of nature beyond any human scale.

"This is the first of the season," Cole said, his words carrying over the awestruck crew, "so it probably won't last more than a day. But the winter mistrals blow as long as a couple of weeks—always steady, never budging an inch off course. A first cousin to that cloud you see there ahead will deposit Sahara sands as far away as the Alps."

Throughout the remainder of that day, the gathering along the railing waxed and waned as the ship altered course to remain just beyond the khamsin's steady bearing. Giant tankers and container vessels regularly emerged from the cloud, reduced to the size of fleas by the cloud's mammoth proportions. There was surprisingly little talk. The jibes and ribald laughter that normally sparked the crew's conversation was stilled by the khamsin's majesty.

In late afternoon, the lowering sun touched the

cloud's upper lip and sent pillars of light shooting across the sky. The sudden pyrotechnics drew a gasp from the crew and brought every senior officer out onto the bridge.

As abruptly as it had appeared, the khamsin vanished. Toward sunset, the last tendrils of gold-red dust floated northward. The sky grew utterly clear, the sea glassy calm. Cole and Ferguson stood on deck and watched the desert horizon reappear. Ahead stood the narrow Straits of Tiran; beyond them stretched the Gulf of Aqaba. The only movement was the flight of a few sea birds and the continual flow of cargo traffic. It was as though the wind had never existed.

For once Cole's habitual nonchalance escaped him. "I am going to remember that for the rest of my life," he said quietly.

"That was incredible," Ferguson agreed. "What—"

The moment was shattered by the ship's sirens whooping out the call for battle stations. For a heartbeat the crew gathered on the bow decks were frozen solid. Then discipline took over, and they raced away.

Ferguson followed Cole up the ladder to the bridge, hitting every third rung. He entered the bridge's controlled bedlam, slipped into his helmet and gear, drew out a pair of unused binoculars and fastened his gaze on the horizon. Nothing.

"Full speed ahead, mister!" the captain rapped out.

"Aye, aye, sir. Full speed ahead."

"Snook surfacing, Captain," the sonar specialist called out.

"Anybody see anything?" the captain demanded, straining to catch sight of the submarine that sonar had picked up. No one replied.

Then Ferguson caught sight of the telltale ripples and the first sign of a black object rising to the surface. "Got him, sir! Just under the cliffs, about eleven o'clock."

"Good eyes, mister. Alter course to bearing one-one-eight."

"One-one-eight it is, sir."

"Must have thought the wind would hide him," the captain said to nobody in particular. "Let's see what he thinks of our little reception committee. Tell the forward lookout to hit the lights."

"Aye, aye, sir."

"Anybody care to confirm the class?"

As the submarine's upper bridgework came into view, what Ferguson saw pushed the spectacle of the desert wind into the realms of distant memory. "Kilo class, sir. Russkie."

"Full marks, mister." The captain turned to the open radio-room door. "Send a scrambled message that sighting has been made and confirmed. Request instructions."

"Aye, aye, sir," Cole replied.

"Use open lines and start demanding that they identify themselves. Keep it up until I say otherwise."

"Aye, aye, sir," Cole replied cheerfully. "Verbal abuse starting now."

Ferguson squinted at what appeared to be an apparition on the side of the submarine. "Sir, I know this sounds crazy, but that snook's got its name written in Arabic."

"Farsi, mister," the captain corrected grimly. "Same alphabet, more or less. But we're talking Iran here."

The bridge grew still as rumors and paper briefings took on chilling reality in the day's fading light.

News that Iran was purchasing Russian attack submarines had struck a note of alarm in U.S. naval forces from Yokohama to Chesapeake Bay. The United States government had been so panic-stricken by the news that they had approached the cash-rich Saudis and asked them to offer a substantial bribe for the Russians to abandon the project. When that failed, they then tried to pressure the Russians directly, also to no avail. The Russian Foreign Minister had bluntly told acting U.S. Secretary of State Lawrence Eagleburger that his country simply had to have both the cash and the jobs generated by the sale.

The first two submarines had set sail for the Persian Gulf in 1992. Three more were reaching completion in the United Admiralty Sudomekh Shipyards of Saint Petersburg. Iran had used proceeds from international oil sales to pay more than three hundred million dollars for each Kilo-class submarine. Agreements had been reached for unemployed Russian naval officers and crews to man the submarines until Iranian crews could be trained.

The Iranian government planned to utilize the subs as pickets in the strategically vital waters of the Gulf of Oman, the Arabian Sea, and the Strait of Hormuz. They would also, it was rumored, be utilized in their international terrorist activities.

Kilo-class submarines carried a payload of eighteen torpedoes or twenty-four mines. Fully loaded and charged, they could operate on super-quiet battery power for six days without surfacing and could carry sufficient provisions to remain at sea for sixty days. They were considered by many to be the quietest subs in the world. The complicated weather patterns and heavy shipping traffic of Middle Eastern waters would magnify their extraordinary stealth qualities. And they were designed to both carry and deliver nuclear warheads.

The West had every reason to be worried.

"You still peppering that snook with demands for identification?"

"Yessir. Nothing back." A pause, then, "Sir, we are instructed to maintain visual contact but not engage. Repeat, avoid engaging if at all possible."

"There it is, ladies and gentlemen," the captain replied grimly. "Diplomacy at work. Ears, confirm that we will play watchdog only."

"Aye, aye, sir."

"Sir!" Ferguson's voice took on the hated squeak of

tension. He deliberately calmed himself and said, "The snook's submerging."

"Got the eyes of a hawk," the captain said approvingly. "Keep bearing down on that sub."

"Sir, is that a dhow under the cliffs?"

"Where?"

"Ten o'clock. You can just see the mast sticking up above the rocks."

The ancient fishing vessels of the Arabian peninsula were a constant threat to the fleet's maneuvers. Lying low to the water, made almost entirely of wood, they were extremely difficult to identify either by radar or eye, especially when the sails were lowered. Larger dhows were powered by antiquated diesels, and often their columns of smelly smoke were visible for miles. But the older vessels, still used for net fishing and pearling, were powered either by sail or oar.

"Four guys rowing like mad," Ferguson reported. "Pulling for what looks like a small cove."

"Get the lights on them," the captain ordered, "and alter course to intercept."

"Aye, aye, sir."

"You better be keeping sonar contact with that snook, Ears," the captain barked, "or you'll be missing your next birthday."

"He's switching to electric," Ears reported. "Sounds like a dive."

"He can't go too deep in these waters. Stay on him. How far to the dhow?"

"Eleven hundred yards and closing."

"They're dumping something!" Ferguson shouted. "Looks like metal cases."

"Order the seals to prepare for a night dive," the captain commanded. "And radio headquarters that it appears we intercepted them before the handover could be completed."

22

ALLISON WAS AWAKENED by a knock on her door. "Sorry to trouble you so early," Ben said. "How do you feel?"

"Feel?" Allison struggled to cast off the fog of sleep. She had sand impacted in her nose, her ears, and under her eyelids. At least ten pounds of the stuff seemed to be in her hair, despite three washings that had turned the shower floor brown. Other than that she felt, "All right, I guess."

"There's been a change in plans. Could you be ready in ten minutes?"

"I guess so."

"I'll have someone bring you a cup of coffee," he said, turning away. "Please hurry."

The afternoon before, the skies had darkened and shadows lengthened and dogs howled, and evening had descended four hours early. Then the week-long southwest wind had delivered the Saharan Khamsin, a deluge of fine red dust that made her own desert sandstorm appear a tempest in a teacup. The dust storm which had swept across the Red Sea blanketed them for ten solid hours.

The clinic had been as prepared as it could be. Windows had been shut and taped, doors wedged with rags, food and drink wrapped in plastic and shut in cabinets, all instruments and dressings and medicines locked away. Still the dust had gathered everywhere. It was finer than sugar frosting, lighter than face powder, and it covered everything. Within the first two hours, every flat surface—floors, desks, cabinets, shelves, beds, and patients—was layered with the stuff. The clinic staff was kept frantically busy trying to keep damp cloths over the mouths of patients—an almost impossible task, since a perfectly clean pail of water was polluted with silt ten minutes after being filled.

Late that night, when the skies had cleared and the howling wind began to settle, they found the dust would not. The slightest footstep sent great rust-colored plumes rising to the ceiling. The only way to clean it up was with a damp cloth, on hands and knees, scouring away at everything. Stripping all the beds. Washing down every surface. Sterilizing all the equipment. It had even managed to infiltrate half of their refrigerators.

Allison had finally pleaded exhaustion and stumbled to bed around two in the morning.

She arrived downstairs to find the three men already in the Land Rover. When she appeared in the doorway Fareed fired up the motor. Ben asked, "Did you bring everything?"

"Of course." She slid into the backseat beside Wade, taking a little satisfaction from the fact that he looked as tired as she felt. "What's going on?"

Wade shrugged a weary reply. Ben waved Fareed on and said, "We have to hurry. The boat leaves in less than half an hour."

"What boat?" she asked, then gave up when Ben ignored her question. The engine bellowed and cut off all further talk.

They flew down the hillside, weaving in and out of traffic, driving as much by the horn as by the wheel, scattering dogs and people. Women hiked the hems of their djellabas and scampered to safety, children in tow. Allison saw no angry gestures at their passage, only waves, and decided the people around here had grown accustomed to the doctor's quick getaways.

Buildings grew higher and streets broader the closer they came to the sea. Hotels sprouted balconies and names in both Arabic and English. Trees rose alongside the boulevards. Shops bore signs advertising Swiss watches and Italian suits and French perfumes. White-limbed tourists paused to inspect prices and take one another's pictures. Allison felt as though she was catching a fleeting glimpse of the world she had left behind.

They took the main boulevard around to the port. Traffic ground to a halt behind an endless line of trucks. Ben threw open his door, said, "We'll have to go the rest of the way on foot."

"But where—"

"No time!" Ben was already striding down the sidewalk, motioning for them to follow."

She looked a question at Wade, who spoke for the first time. "I don't know any more than you do. But it looks like if we're going, we'd better do it now."

"Be quick!" Fareed gestured for them to take off.

They slid from the Land Rover and hastened to catch up with Ben. Their path edged past three battered steamers unloading sacks and bales of goods, both by crane and by endless lines of sweating men. Ben dodged through the lines, hustled down a long, littered passage, and finally stopped at a windowless gatehouse. Beyond swarmed a mass of humanity. Farther still rose the filthiest boat Allison had ever seen.

The officers staffing the guardhouse clearly knew Ben. All three rose from their sullen lethargy and offered smiles and outstretched hands. Ben returned the greetings, motioned Wade and Allison forward, talked rapidly in Arabic.

At that moment the ship's whistle wailed. The people

not yet on board responded with a cry of their own and surged forward. Over the clamor Ben indicated that they wanted to board. Allison looked from Ben to the struggling, shouting people and from them to the foul boat. She opened her mouth to say they could give her place to somebody else. But before she could speak, two of the officers hefted long wooden batons and gestured for them to follow. Allison grabbed for Ben's shoulder, wanting to turn him around and tell him she had changed her mind, that she would wait with Fareed in the truck. He mistook the gesture, grasped her hand tightly with one of his, and stepped forward. Immediately Wade moved up close alongside her, grasping her with one hand and Ben with the other. She was well and truly trapped.

The two officers used their batons to form a wedge. They pressed forward, shouting fiercely. Turbaned men and kerchiefed women turned angrily to see who was shoving them, recognized the uniforms, and stepped meekly aside. Ben drew himself and Allison and Wade up close behind the officers, so that they moved in virtual lockstep. As soon as they passed, the opening closed up behind them, swallowing them up into the noisy smelly throng.

People closest to the gangway held money and tickets and passports aloft, screaming continuously at the two sailors barring their way. The officers pressed grimly forward until they were directly in front of the gangway. The noise was deafening. The sailors were not impressed by the guards' uniforms, and gesticulated that there was no more room. But the officers had not come that far only to be turned away. Angrily they pushed the sailors aside and formed a narrow passage between them. Ben ducked his head and slipped through, pulling the pair of them along behind.

The sailors shouted a protest but were kept from following by the crowd, who saw an opportunity for themselves and massed forward. Arriving at the top of the gangplank, Allison looked back to see the horde funnel into the gap, carrying both officers and sailors with them. But three more sailors pushed by Allison to join their mates, and together they forced the crowd back down. The whistle hooted once more, the sailors retreated, the gangplank was removed, and the boat chugged away.

"Because smuggling has become so serious a problem, they have limited all sea travel between Jordan and Egypt and Saudi Arabia to these ferries," Ben explained once they had all caught their breath. "Those who did not make it onto this boat will have to wait and try their luck again tomorrow." He gestured for them to follow. "Come, we'll be more comfortable in the bow."

Once the boat was well underway, the clamor died. Those who had made it on board swiftly settled into the relaxed activity of people long used to endless waiting. Bedrolls and prayer rugs and frayed carpets were laid out, marking clan territory. Lines formed at the two kiosk windows selling lukewarm drinks and coffee and platters of unidentifiable food. Men lounged and chattered and smoked. Women gathered and tended children. All eyes marked the Westerners' gradual progress toward the bow. Allison did not see another white face.

Conversations stopped as they approached the bow, and everyone turned to stare. Ben responded with a nod, a wave, and words in Arabic that resulted in a blooming of delighted smiles. Room was made for them at the railing. Ben had been right about one thing; here the air was indeed better. It blew directly off the sea, uncontaminated by the countless bodies crowded in behind Allison.

When curiosity about the three white passengers abated, Ben turned to Allison and Wade. "Are you both all right?"

Wade nodded. Allison declared, "I never want to go through anything like that, not ever again."

"I am truly sorry," Ben replied. "It is always such a press for these ferries, and with the new travel restrictions the situation has become almost impossible."

"Where are we going?"

"Nuweibi. It is an Egyptian port on the Sinai Peninsula, about halfway down the Gulf of Aqaba. The full name is Nuweibi al-Muzayyinah." Ben motioned at the boatload behind them. "The people you see here come from Egypt, Sudan, Libya, Chad, Niger, Mali, even as far away as Morocco. They come from small desert villages that are often a hundred miles from the nearest electric light or running water. But still they hear of the money to be made in these richer lands. So they hoard their pennies or sell their livestock or barter a prayer rug that has been in their family for generations. They walk the days or weeks to the nearest big road, buy a ticket for the bus or the train, and make their way to Nuweibi."

"How long does it take," Wade asked in his quiet way.

"For some a week, for others up to three months. They gather there, where corrupt agents squeeze out the people's last remaining pennies in exchange for work contracts the majority cannot read. These agents of course collect their commissions from those hiring, but such agents do not rise to the rank of flesh peddlers unless they are utterly consumed by greed."

Ben's face grew stern, his eyes lost their light, his voice cut like a rapier's sweep. "So the guest workers board the ferries and go to work as street sweepers and janitors and dishwashers and ditch diggers. They work six, sometimes seven days a week. They are paid a pittance, but it is a fortune by the standards of their homelands. They often do not return until their contract is completed. They do not see their families for as long as ten years, and their families are almost never allowed to join them. They often live in appalling conditions. But they have no recourse, no one to turn to. No local or international agency sees to their rights. It is a practice that has existed for a thousand years, and is accepted by almost everyone here. The argument is that the guest workers are so much better off here, even under these circumstances, than they would be at home. And because this is tragically true, the people keep coming."

"I don't understand," Allison said. "If it's so bad, why are we going there?"

Ben's features resumed their habitual calm. "I received word this morning of a possible shipment that went amiss. It originated from the Egyptian side of the Gulf, or so they seem to think."

"They? You mean Cyril?"

"Nuweibi is a natural starting point for us to check, if the information is correct," Ben went on, ignoring her question. "The police there are trained to look the other way." He turned to Wade. "It was suggested that if product was involved, people might be as well. Do you understand?"

"Yes."

"I will do a quick check of the four local clinics and pharmacies. That is normal for me; I try to come over every few months to see what they need. We must be extremely careful not to become separated."

The voyage was long and hot and monotonous. Allison watched hill after desert-colored hill pass until the sun's glare became too strong. Ben then found them a place to sit and doze by a shaded bulkhead.

When they arrived at the port, the chaotic scramble occurred in reverse. At Ben's direction they hung back and watched passengers push and shove and shout and scramble off the boat. When the worst of the crush was over, he slipped away, then returned a few minutes later and motioned them to follow.

"Where did you go?" she asked.

"To ensure our return passage. We must hurry. There isn't much time."

The port area was a series of dilapidated metal and concrete warehouses lining a red-clay street. Their way was often blocked by crowds gathered about hawkers who had set up impromptu stalls wherever foot traffic was heaviest.

The dust was as fierce as the heat. Following Ben, they sidled around packed throngs of gawking Arabs and Africans. Their shirts were plastered hard to their backs and coated with the reddish sand. Where possible they stayed to the shadows; entry into daylight meant being struck by hammer blows of heat.

Nuweibi looked just like what it was—a poor Egyptian village that had been absolutely overwhelmed by the flood of humanity. The original blockhouse structures were now merely a centerpoint to a sprawling city of shacks and shanties and tenements. There was little electricity, less running water, the most rudimentary of sewage. The only saving grace for most of the people was that they would not be staying long. Those who lived there permanently were drawn from life's very dregs.

Allison passed gatherings from three dozen different tribes representing the length and breadth of Africa. Many of the darker men and women had faces deeply marked with tribal scars—patterns cut into cheeks and foreheads with ritual knives during coming-of-age ceremonies. Headdresses varied as widely as stature and faces and dress, ranging from simple rags to elaborate coiffures of brightly colored cloth and beads and silver pins.

Ben knew exactly where he was going, and he did not tarry. He led them past great open spaces where men harangued gatherings and waved papers bearing fancy script. He ignored the cries of stall holders and the smells of cooking and the plucking arms of beggars. When Allison announced the twenty-minute mark he paused momentarily, looked about, nodded, and strode on. His calls on the clinics were in-and-out affairs. He was clearly uneasy being in Nuweibi, and was determined to cover the ground in the least amount of time possible.

It was while he was in the third pharmacy that the bandits struck.

Like many of the older structures, the pharmacy was one of a line of businesses built upon a raised foundation that lifted them away from the street and the worst of the mud during the rainy season. A narrow sidewalk fronted the businesses. The walkway had not been built to handle the foot traffic now inundating the town. Stopping and standing proved difficult because it forced people to travel around them. Allison did so anyway, as the sidewalk offered a little shade while she waited for Ben.

At first the tug on her black bag was so gentle that she simply took it for someone's robe having snagged it in passing. But when she pulled back, the tug became sharper. She tightened her grip and jerked, then felt the grimy hand weaseling around her fingers.

Allison tried to reach over with her other hand, but the crowd was especially thick just then, and suddenly there was another body blocking her movement, another pair of hands reaching for a hold on her arms.

Her call for help almost came too late. But the knife's blade caught a glimmer of the sun. As her grip loosened, Allison folded in and around the bag and screamed as loudly as she could.

Suddenly a whirlwind erupted around her.

The pull on her bag loosened as swiftly as it had come. The crowd parted, no match for the force that assaulted it. Allison looked up, still tensed into her half-crouch, and saw Wade shove a second man off the sidewalk and into the dust, then turn and barrel into a third.

It all took place in less than three breaths.

Ben appeared in the doorway. "What is—"

"Come on!" Wade shouted. He reached and plucked up Allison with a surprising strength for his slender frame. "Back to the boat!"

While the crowd was still collecting itself, Wade drew Allison up next to him and jammed them through. Not quite a run, but fast enough to jar. Aggressive. Hard and sharp and as determined as his gaze. The crowd parted before them.

"What happened," Ben demanded, hustling to keep up with Wade.

"A thief tried to take my bag," Allison said, gradually recovering. The vision of the knife blade still swam before her eyes, and she was grateful for Wade's supporting arm.

"It wasn't just a grab," Wade said, not slowing down. "And it wasn't just a thief. There were a lot of them, and it was slick. They separated us before I even knew what was going on. Just a tight group of people, sliding us apart one half-step at a time, and if she hadn't yelled I wouldn't have noticed what was going on until too late."

"Take this left," Ben directed. "How can you be so certain it wasn't just a thief taking advantage of the situation? We haven't finished covering the ground yet."

"I don't know how I'm sure," Wade said stubbornly. "But I am. And I'm not going to let her risk staying around here any longer."

Let me risk staying. Normally Allison would have bristled at the sound of someone looking out for her like that. But just then it sounded nice. Warm and comforting. Something a friend would do. Let her be weak for a moment. *The knife.*

"I'm still not clear—"

Wade slammed to a stop so sharp that Allison almost lost her footing and Ben rammed into them from behind. Ben protested but was cut off by Wade's upraised hand. "I thought I heard something," he said, and squinted into the shadows of a rank and narrow alley.

Then Allison heard it too. A voice. Speaking in a tongue she had heard before but could not understand. Soft and sibilant and musical. Wade answered in kind.

She asked, "Is that Russian?"

The voice from the shadows said once more, "Can this be the man who has robbed me of my nights?"

"Alexis," Wade said, his heart hammering hard. "Is that you?"

The Russian stepped forward far enough to reveal himself, then slipped back again. "All night I hear your voice, my friend. There alongside the calls of my wife and child. Asking me questions for which I have no answers."

"What are you doing here?"

"Yes," Alexis agreed. "That is one of them. And others. Many others. Too many. I find I cannot go on, but I also do not know where I might go instead."

"Are they after you?"

"If they already know of my escape," Alexis replied, "then you are speaking to a dead man. I saw you and your friends from my window, and I slipped out. They leave me alone much of the time, you see. I have not been well. I lie in bed much of the day, trying to regain what you have taken from my nights."

"Will you come with us?"

Still he hesitated. "I am defeated. I cannot go and do what I know is wrong. It would kill me. But where else can I go? You have given me so many questions, now answer one. What can I do? I will not go back to Russia, that is certain. Where else is there for me? How can I bring my family together again?"

"I don't know," Wade replied honestly. "But I will try to help."

Alexis thought on this, and decided. "Then I will come."

A cry was raised behind them. Wade started, wheeled around, and saw the man he had shoved from the sidewalk heading a gang that stalked the alley toward them. "We must flee!" he cried, for a moment not even aware that he still spoke Russian. "To the boat!"

Whatever the language, they all understood. They raced down the alley and across the central square, dodging through the throngs gathered about the various job peddlers. And it was the crowd that saved them. Where four white-faced foreigners were given the leeway to scramble through, a gang of local ruffians were caught like a beast in quicksand. One pushed someone, who hit another, who pushed back, and soon the entire clearing was a mass of cursing, heaving, jostling humanity.

Together the four of them raced down the central port road, skirted the hawkers, rushed past the guards, and ran up the gangway to the boat.

And safety.

23

THE NEXT AFTERNOON, Allison found Wade waiting in Ben's empty office. "Did he call for you too?"

"Oh." At the sound of her voice, he leapt to his feet. "I mean, hello."

His shy uncertainty was back in place. Such an incredible difference from the take-charge attitude he had shown the day before. "I'd like to thank you for what you did yesterday."

"I didn't really do anything . . ."

"Don't say that," she said, determined this time not to be put off by his reserve. She waved him to a chair and took the seat next to him. "If you hadn't moved so fast, I might not be here today."

Wade looked down at his hands. "I don't know what came over me," he said quietly. "When I heard you call—"

She repressed a shudder at the memory and said lightly, "A lot of good my homing device would have been."

"Your what?"

"Oh, something Cyril gave me. He said I should switch it on if I was ever in trouble." She sobered at the reality of how close the encounter truly had been. "I could have been—"

"Don't say it," Wade told her. "Don't even think it."

"All right." More softly, "At any rate, I do thank you."

"Oh good, you're both here," Ben Shannon said briskly, entering and closing the door behind him. "I have something to discuss with you."

"Did they find anything in Nuweibi?" Allison demanded.

"As I understand it," Ben replied, seating himself behind his desk, "the preliminary search last night was unsuccessful. But with the information Alexis supplied, the Egyptian authorities are again combing the area, and no doubt they will soon have everything under lock and key. Alexis himself is now safely ensconced in a hotel in Amman, where he is busy helping the authorities, as they say."

"But they haven't found anything." Allison settled back in disappointment.

"Not yet. Be that as it may," Ben persisted, "I now feel that your work here at the clinic has come to a close."

Allison found herself with nothing to say. She looked at Wade. The young man observed the doctor with quiet intensity and said, "You were frightened."

Ben Shannon did not deny it. "On the boat ride home last night, thoughts kept running through my mind. What if something had happened to either of you? Could I have lived with myself?"

"But you knew about this risk before we started," Allison protested.

"I did," Ben concurred. "Yet I did not truly come face-to-face with the possible danger until yesterday. I am in the business of running a clinic, not chasing after international smugglers and terrorists. I have grown very fond of you both. I could not sleep last night from the thought of what might have happened."

"We're willing to take that risk," Allison responded. "At least, I am."

"Perhaps, but I am not," Ben replied. "Not any longer. This operation has already taken far longer than I had expected. I had hoped that either the contraband would be swiftly uncovered or the rumors proved untrue. Instead, we have worked on this for weeks now, and what have we accomplished?"

"We have discovered that there really is a danger," Allison retorted. "And that they really are trying to smuggle in nuclear engineers—and probably material for bombs as well."

"Yes, from another country where we have no business being." Ben sighed. "Now these terrorists in Egypt know of us and probably know of my clinic. Whose lives have we put at risk? What will keep them from attacking us here?"

"We understand," Wade said quietly. "We'll pack and be gone by this afternoon."

"We will?" Allison demanded.

Wade turned her way and nodded slowly. "Could you really stay if he doesn't want you here anymore?"

"You both are wonderful people," Ben said quietly, the worry tightening his features into unaccustomed lines. "Allison, your administrative work here has been impeccable. And Wade, you are one of the finest healers I have ever had occasion to work with. I would love to keep you both on in these capacities, and simply ask you to stop with the searches. But I can't. I hope you understand that. It has gone too far. I simply cannot put you or my patients or my other staff at risk."

Wade stood and lifted Allison with his gaze. "We understand. You have other responsibilities."

Ben did not rise. He kept his gaze on his desk, clearly unhappy with the turn of events. "I will stop in and see you both again before you go."

Wade followed her from the room. Once the door had closed behind them, she demanded, "Why wouldn't you let me argue with him any more?"

"Because it was tearing him apart," Wade replied softly. "His mind was made up. He was doing what he thought was correct, and he was doing it for valid reasons. What right did we have to try and force him to do something different?"

They walked outside and entered the brilliant sunshine. "I guess I better go pack," Wade said.

"Wait," said Allison. Someone was standing by the front gate, talking with Fareed and gesticulating urgently. "I think I know him."

"Who?"

Then it came to her. "That's Mahmoud. He's a Bedouin leader and a friend of Ben's." She started walking. "Come on."

Mahmoud was so fiercely involved in his discussion that he did not notice their approach. Then he saw Allison, shouted, and waved her over.

Allison demanded of Fareed, "What's he saying?"

"Mahmoud, he say he must talk to Doctor Ben and right now."

"The doctor's tied up," Allison replied. "What's the matter?"

"He say, men come at dawn, set up camp. Another truck arrive later. He not know them, but say maybe are people you seek."

Allison shot a glance at Wade, then said, "Ben is going to stay tied up pretty much all day. Ask Mahmoud if he will take us with him now."

"But Doctor Ben, he say—"

"It's all right," Allison assured him. "We just spoke with him. He can't be disturbed today; he has a lot to think about. So we'll take care of it. Ask Mahmoud if that's okay with him."

Fareed posed the question. Mahmoud responded by turning and striding toward where his dusty truck was parked. "Tell him I have to write Ben a note and pack a couple of things," she said to Fareed, then to Wade, "Let's get moving."

"Where are we going?" Wade said, hurrying to catch up.

"The desert!"

• • •

Night painted the desert with a mystic's brush.

The half-moon competed with a billion stars for their attention. The sands glowed as though lit by soft, silver fires. The mountains were great dark djinn, silver and still as the night, watchful as the stars, timeless as the wind.

Wade sat with his back to the camp, so he did not know of her approach until he heard the soft footfall. "Can I join you?"

He nodded, then realized she could not see him. "Please do."

"It's so beautiful," she said, sinking down beside him. "Like another world."

"It is another world," he said quietly.

Mahmoud had brought them to the Bedouin camp just before sunset. Together they had paid respects to his father, talked with several of the men, arranged for Allison to bed down in one tent with the women and Wade in another, then Mahmoud had taken off again. He had not yet returned.

She looked at Wade. The campfire behind them cast half her face in the softest golden hues. "Are you afraid?"

It took him a while to answer. "Yes," he said finally, "but I've been frightened for so long that I guess I've grown used to it, like it's normal to be at least a little afraid all the time."

"I don't think I could ever grow used to fear—or want to," she replied, then asked, "Would you tell me the whole story of how you came to Jordan?"

Because she asked with the tone of a friend, because they shared the exquisite aloneness of an empty desert night, because their fear was a bond between them, he told her. All of it.

She watched him intently while he talked, her gaze large and solemn, so quiet that Wade did not notice her shivering until he was almost done.

He interrupted himself with, "You're cold. Why didn't you say something?"

"I'm fine, really. Please don't stop."

But he was already up and moving toward the camp. He returned with a heavy blanket, which he flipped open and draped around her shoulders. "It's amazing how cold it gets out here at night."

As he settled back down, Allison lifted the edge toward him. "Come share."

Wade slid closer, and allowed her to drape the blanket around his back.

"Okay, now finish your story."

He did so, acutely aware of her warmth and the memory of her touch on his shoulder. He spoke, but scarcely heard himself. He was too full of her closeness and the night and the scent of her hair.

"So you used the church's money and followed them down here," Allison said when he fell silent. "Amazing. And you're sure it was the same man behind you in the Aqaba souk? What was his name?"

"Rogue Robards. And yes, I'm sure." Once again he was chilled by the memory of Rogue's words. A knife. He pushed the thought away by telling her the whole story of Alexis.

After a silence, Wade heard a new tone. With the voice of a woman-child, Allison asked him, "Did you leave a girl behind in—whatever that city was called?"

"Grozny." And because of the vulnerability in her voice, and because of the night and the stars and the wind, Wade found the courage to speak from the yearnings of his heart. "I've never had a girlfriend. Not someone I really, you know, loved."

She backed off far enough to inspect his face. Wade turned to meet her gaze, although it was hard. Then he saw the open, questioning, longing look in her own eyes.

"Why?" she asked, her voice no stronger than the wind's gentle whisper.

By then more than the night's chill was clenching his

chest and causing his entire body to tremble. He could only manage the words, "I'm very shy."

And with a gift of womanly wisdom that transcended his feeble words and her own awkwardness, Allison's gaze opened even farther, filled with compassionate understanding. And slowly, ever so slowly, she drew closer to him, stopping now to study his eyes, finding the reassurance she sought, moving closer, closer still, until her lips met his.

Wade awoke to a desert choir in full performance.

Donkeys brayed. Camels groaned. Goats bleated. Desert sparrows relished the power the echoes gave their chirps. Behind his tent a group of men chanted their morning prayers. Other voices murmured and called and even sang in their desert tongue. Baby goats cried like a band of hungry young children.

He rolled from his bedding, looked around, saw that all the other men of his tent were up and started with their day. He combed back his hair with his fingers, tucked in his shirt, flipped back the tent cover, and blinked in the glare.

"Good morning, sleepyhead." Wade squinted and saw Allison approach with a smile and a glass of tea. "I was just coming to wake you up."

Gingerly he accepted the steaming glass, grasping it around the rim. "How long have you been up?"

"Oh, hours." She smiled. "Truthfully, about fifteen minutes. Mahmoud wants to tell us something. He's waiting in the main tent."

Wade sipped his tea, struggled to find the proper way to say, "Our talk last night was, uh, really..."

"Me, too." The touch she gave his arm was as soft as her gaze. "But we probably should save the rest for later. Mahmoud looked like a man in a hurry."

At their approach Mahmoud rose and offered them a

formal greeting, to which they nodded in thanks, then he waved them to seats. His father blessed them with a toothless grin and chanted words they could not understand.

Mahmoud gestured with hands to the side of his head, asking how Wade had slept. Wade leaned forward and patted the stones lining the tent's central fire. Like a rock. The old man cackled with delight, then heaved his chest full with a deep breath. The desert air. Wade nodded his agreement and sipped at his tea. It was good to be alive.

By the tent's outer corner an older woman sat where she could remain in the shadows yet still watch the children play. She combed shreds of thick goat's hair with a pair of wire brushes, then gathered the strands and spun them into thick black thread on a portable spindle. Beyond her, children laughed and squealed and rolled a pair of inflated goatskins back and forth between them. The children were beautifully bright, their intelligent faces so full of character that they looked more like miniature adults than true children. Wade thought they were playing a game until he heard the sloshing liquid inside the skins and realized they were making curds from goat's milk.

Mahmoud brushed the sand before him flat and smooth, then drew a line and pointed to the eastern hills. He made a humping motion. Up and over to the other side. The old man nodded and spoke a running commentary as Mahmoud drew a slit running partway through the line—a narrow passage leading to the mountain's other side. Here he drew a circle, then pointed around him. A camp.

Next Mahmoud pointed to his own truck, pointed at the sun, drew a wavering line toward the sun. Then he pointed higher in the sky, drew another wavering line from a different direction. A third time the finger raised to point directly overhead, then a third line drew in toward the camp. Wade nodded and spoke to Allison, "I think he means he watched trucks come in yesterday at different times, from different directions."

"A meeting point," Allison said, slightly breathless with the sudden excitement.

Again Mahmoud pointed at his truck, then showed an open palm. Five vehicles. He then tapped the nearest stone, hands held over his head, squinted, looked around, shrugged. This time Wade looked confused; Mahmoud repeated the gesture. Then Allison understood. "He's saying the chasm has ledges so that the camp can't be detected from above."

Wade asked Mahmoud, "Bedouin?"

Mahmoud balanced his hands in the air. He was not sure. Then he pointed to his chest and shook his head. Definitely not of his tribe. He pointed at Wade and nodded vigorously. "Foreigners in the camp," Allison said.

Mahmoud stood. *"Jallah?"* We go?

Wade rose to his feet, and Allison followed. "Jallah," he agreed.

Before starting out, Mahmoud had them don old Jordanian army jackets—camouflage against prying eyes. He then brought out a pair of men's headdresses and insisted on fitting them both personally. The white-and-red-checked *keffiyeh* was set on the head, then held in place with a black thong twisted into a figure eight and folded into a double loop. Mahmoud pointed from it to the camel's hoofs, indicating that it was also used for hobbling the animals in an emergency. Then the *keffiyeh*'s two tasseled ends were crossed behind the head and tucked into the hoops.

By that time most of the camp had gathered to watch and see them off. The men smiled and murmured approval when Wade was equipped and joined the women in delighted laughter when Allison's headdress was set in place. They laughed even harder when the camels were led up.

Mahmoud showed them how to mount the animals, sitting side-saddle with their front leg cocked up and around the wooden saddle horn. The camel rose in stages, rocking like a small craft buffeted by heavy seas. They shared smiles as the Bedouins lifted hands and shouted *"Humdi-'lah"* in approval, their grins as bright as the sun.

Their passage over the desert took the better part of the day, a lurching journey over terrain that was a world removed from the distant Caucasus, yet in its own way just as harsh and beautiful.

The wind was a constant force. It buffeted. It probed. It etched. It moaned a sibilant voice into Wade's ears, teaching him of the desert in a tongue only his heart could fathom.

The wind and the sun and the camel's rocking had a stupefying effect. Wade's whole body swayed in time to the motion. He found it increasingly difficult to keep his eyes open. At one point he drifted off entirely, only to be startled awake by a tap from Mahmoud's riding crop. The Bedouin pointed at the ground in warning. It was a long way to fall.

They stopped twice for water and unleavened bread and olives and goat cheese. Mahmoud would not let them tarry long, however, and made his fingers walk up while pointing to a setting sun. They must climb the hills ahead of them before dark.

The desert shadows were already slanting when they entered a maze of interlocking chasms. Mahmoud motioned to his lips—from here on they should not speak. As the cliffs closed in around them, they were granted welcome relief from the sun. Wade soon understood why they had not taken the truck; the sandstone walls tightened so that he could touch both sides at once.

As the sky began to darken overhead, they entered a

sand-bottomed cul-de-sac containing an almost empty pool and a single tree. When Mahmoud made his camel kneel, Wade sank gratefully to the ground and walked about loosening his sore muscles. He glanced at Allison. Her face was set in tired yet resolute lines.

As the camels slurped greedily at the pool's scummy water, Mahmoud pointed at one of the cul-de-sac's side walls and traced the upward passage they were to take. Wade immediately saw why they had raced the sun. Their climb would start up a crevice fashioned into irregular stairs, then continue along a slender walk which had crumbled in places, reducing it to narrow toeholds. From there a kind of rough rock ladder ascended another forty, perhaps fifty meters.

Wade swallowed hard and refused the urge to simply sit down and give up.

Mahmoud turned to Allison and motioned that she should stay with the camels.

Although her face had turned pale beneath its coating of dust, she whispered, "I'm going with you," and pointed sharply first at herself, then at the wall.

Wade protested quietly, "Two of us—"

"Save your breath. I'm going, and that's all there is to it."

Wade turned back to Mahmoud, who responded with an eloquent shrug. He then walked to the crevice and started to climb.

The steps in the crevice were waist high and far from level. Wade climbed with hands as well as feet. Because the stone had been shaped by sand and wind instead of by water, the rock was very porous and offered good grips.

Mahmoud stopped them at the top of the stairs. Wade leaned his back against the rock and looked out, up, across—anywhere but down.

"Are you all right?" Allison whispered.

"I don't have much of a head for climbing," he admitted.

She bit down hard on a smile. "My pop would say this will either kill you or cure you."

"Thanks a lot."

Mahmoud hissed them to silence and started out along the ledge. Wade forced his muscles to unclench and followed. The ledge narrowed, then narrowed further, until they were progressing in a sideways crawl with their faces crammed up against the rock and their heels over the edge. Wade fought for meager handholds.

Then Mahmoud began to climb again, ascending the rock ladder. Wade clung grimly to the ledge until Mahmoud's boots were up above his head, then started up immediately. Anything was better than hanging on where he was.

One moment Mahmoud's boots were scrambling up above him, sending a shower of dust and stones down on his head with each step, and the next he was gone. Wade scrambled up the last few rungs, grateful for the strong arms waiting to help him over the ledge, then he was up. Sitting in safety. Helping Allison over the cliff's edge. Willing his legs to stop their trembling. Breathing great gulps of desert air and feeling the wind on his face. Safe.

They sat upon the roof of their desert world. The sun's ruddy orb touched distant peaks and began to dissolve into another evening. A thousand hues of orange and red and violet and deep blue painted the sky. Besides their own rasping breaths, the only sound they heard was the wind. Wade looked about, waited for his stuttering heart to quieten, and gloried in the boundless view.

Mahmoud turned from his inspection of the sunset to give them both a gold-toothed smile. He whispered, "Goot, yiss?"

"Good," Wade softly agreed. "Very, very good."

Allison nodded and looked around their plateau. It was a level space about twenty feet to a side, as though the peak had been sawed off. She pointed to the carved blocks set to one side and whispered, "This looks like another high place."

"A what?"

"You know, for sacrifices." Her brow furrowed in concentration. "Like the ones the king—I forget his name—struck down."

"Josiah," Wade replied, looking at her anew. "So you know the Bible?"

"Not as well as I probably should," she replied truthfully, and quietly changed the subject. "I thought that last ladder looked as if it was carved by hand."

"That last ladder almost stopped my clock," Wade murmured. "Are you—"

Mahmoud hissed from the plateau's opposite side, motioning for them to move over and stay low. They walked at a stoop, then sank to their knees and looked over the edge.

A narrow path crept down the mountainside from where they lay, making a series of jinking turns as it descended to where the chasm's sides joined. There a broad stone shelf jutted out, forming a natural protective barrier from any low-flying planes.

Allison pointed to the path and whispered, "The ceremonial way. The worshipers probably came up this side."

Mahmoud silenced her with an upraised hand. He then motioned with one finger to his nose, and breathed in. Wade smelled the wind, and nodded. Smoke.

Mahmoud pointed back to where the sun had descended behind the clouds and made a motion up and over the sky, then pointed down and traced a trail leading away from the rock overhang. When it was fully dark, the trucks would drive away.

They watched for a time as the darkness gathered. Twice Wade heard the muffled clank of metal upon metal; once he thought he heard the murmur of voices. But no one came into view.

Then he had an idea, and before fear could stop him he whispered, "Do you still have the homing device?"

"Yes, but what—"

"Give it to me."

Allison looked a question but did as he asked. He then sidled along to where the path started its descent. Mahmoud started as though to rise up and protest, but Wade stopped him with a look. Confused and worried, the Bedouin sank back down.

Wade crept down the path, his heart thundering so loud he feared the men down below might hear. His hands kept to the cliffside, holding tightly onto nooks and crannies in case he slid. He did not. He made it down to the overhang just as the moon's first sliver appeared over the far peaks.

Wade dropped to his belly and slid toward the lip of the overhang. Holding his breath, he gradually eased himself out the last few inches until the hoods of five trucks came into view.

They were parked facing outward and crammed in so closely together that they completely filled the chasm's mouth. There was just enough light to see that the sandy ground leading into the gorge had been brushed to clear away the truck treads. A single guard sat on the hood of the central truck, busily eating from a tin plate in his lap, a carbine resting on the hood beside him.

A voice called softly from the unseen spaces behind the trucks. The guard swiveled, and instantly Wade slid back out of sight, holding his breath, steeled against the call of alarm. But he had not been seen. He heard the tread of boots over metal, and after a wait he risked another look.

The guard was gone.

From the back came louder sounds of people moving about, objects being shifted, murmured conversation. In the dying light Wade could see an old-fashioned metal lockbox welded to the front bumper of one truck. It was open, revealing tools and an oil canister and rags used for emergency repairs.

Moving quietly, pushed to hurry by the fading light, Wade slid over until he was perched directly above the truck. He leaned backward, slipped off one shoe, and slid off his sock. He pulled the homing device from his pocket, thumbed the switch, and slipped it into the sock. Then he balled the sock up tightly, reached over the ledge, held his breath, and took as careful aim as he could. Then he let go.

The sock dropped into the box with a muffled thud.

Wade slid back out of sight, rolled over, and lay looking up at the stars with his mouth open, breathing great silent gasps and feeling the sweat trickle down the sides of his face toward his ears.

The noises gathered, and metal scraped against metal as the trucks were rocked against one another by bodies sliding up and into place. Then one by one the motors started, roaring loudly in the confined space. Then the first one moved out, followed by its fellows. Traveling slowly, without headlights.

Wade waited until the engines' noise had drifted away, then rose to his feet and began his slow return to the top.

Judith Armstead and Cyril Price arrived at the American Embassy within moments of each other. He demanded, "Do you know what this is all about?"

"No," she replied grimly. "But if it's another false alarm, you are about to witness the demise of last night's duty officer. In any case, it appears that your bait has slipped off the hook."

"Yes," Cyril agreed tiredly, nodding to the Marine who passed him with a salute. "A bit tedious, that. I can only say how relieved I am that I don't have to face Allison's late father with this news."

"That's right. You used to work with Dr. Taylor, didn't you. Back in the good old days."

"Those days were many things, none of which I would describe as good." Cyril climbed the embassy stairs and held the great doors open for her. "Yes, John and I happened to be quite close. But he had a way of dressing one down that practically flayed skin from bone, all without raising his voice."

"I seem to recall an instructor who shared that ability," Judith told him. "It made the experience all the more painful to have it done in such genteel tones."

Cyril nodded. "I shudder to think what he would say to the news that I had managed to lose his daughter."

"In the Jordanian desert, no less." Judith keyed in the elevator doors. "How is Ben Shannon taking it?"

"The poor man is pulling out what little hair he has left. Fareed traveled out with our people and finally located the Bedouin encampment, far to the east of their normal grazing territories. The pair were nowhere to be found. Interestingly enough, their leader, Mahmoud, was also not there."

"It sounds—"

The door to the nearby stairwell slammed open. A young technician with glasses and tie askew announced, "We've got a reading on the homing transmitter!"

Cyril bolted forward as though electrocuted. "Tally ho, lads! The prey has gone to ground!"

24

WADE AND ALLISON DINED that night at a sidewalk restaurant near the gulf.

They had spent the night before in the high place, huddled together against the cold and watching the stars parade overhead in timeless grace. They had dozed, and awakened, and dozed again, warmed by each other's closeness and by the knowledge that everything possible had been done. The hunt was out of their hands.

At daybreak they had climbed down and started the long journey back to camp. Toward midmorning the desert stillness had been shattered by eight helicopters thundering by in close formation. Two hours later one had returned, circled them, then descended to earth. Cyril had alighted amid the rotors' noisy hurricane.

Two Russian nuclear scientists had been captured, he reported, and the men matched the descriptions Wade had supplied. Along with the scientists, they had seized three truckloads of components for making bombs and several lead-lined containers holding what he suspected was weapons-grade fissionable materials. Quite a haul.

When asked about Rogue Robards, Cyril had shaken his head. Several of the Bedouin guides had managed to escape, so perhaps he had escaped with them. The interrogations would tell them more.

Cyril had been on his way back to Amman, where the

scientists would be held for questioning. He offered the pair a ride back to Aqaba. They had bid Mahmoud solemn thanks and farewells, then returned to the port city by chopper.

"I'm a little sorry it's all over," she confessed. "It's been the most exciting time of my life."

"I'm sorry, too," he agreed, his eyes locked on hers, "but for different reasons."

The remains of their repast had been pushed to one side so that a way was clear between them. People smoked and talked and walked about the tables. In the street next to them, traffic hummed by. In the distance, great cargo vessels and tankers vied for places in the crowded port. They saw none of it. Their attention moved no farther than the borders of their table.

"All that's happened," she shook her head. "I wonder if I'll wake up in a couple of weeks and decide it was all a dream."

Wade was silent for a moment, then said, "The only way I've been able to make sense of all I've been through is by my faith."

"What do you mean?"

"In the eleventh chapter of Genesis, the world was split by languages. But I guess you know all about that."

"I'm not sure," she said weakly, suddenly very ashamed.

"Man's motivation for building the tower of Babel was pride, and his purpose was power. He wished to make himself like God. In chapter ten, it says that originally God gave us unity. This was taken from us only when we took those gifts and turned them against God. We claimed them for ourselves. God then reclaimed His power as His own, and scattered His peoples because of our rebellious pride.

"Then what happens, but the Creator offers us the gift of redemption. In the second chapter of Acts, the Holy Spirit unites all the races back together again. At the gathering where the Spirit first entered into the believers, they turned and began speaking to the crowds, each in their own language. The barriers which separated all the nations were dissolved."

Allison watched as much as she listened. She saw a new light enter his gaze as he spoke, one full of the excitement of internal vistas she could hardly fathom.

"God divided the nations of the world so that man would rely on God's power and not his own," he went on, unaware of the effect his words were having. "The character of the age we live in is marked by divisions, wars, and rumors of wars. Yet we have in this passage the blessed assurance that man will ultimately live united. Man will know lasting peace. Man will live as a single people in a single city with a single ruler. Yet we are shown that this will come about because of His work, not ours. That is our hope. That is our purpose. To be a part of His Kingdom, not our own."

Allison listened, and felt a new awakening within herself. A yearning. A call she had never before heard.

Wade looked at her, yet saw inwardly. "A Christian is granted the opportunity to see the world through the vision of God's holy Word. We can understand this divine promise of peace through God-inspired unity. We have all inherited Adam's attitude of separation from God, and with this comes friction between those who should offer each other only love. But with a change of each heart, and an indwelling of His Spirit, we shall see a coming of everlasting hope."

"That's very beautiful," she said quietly, not completely understanding, but wanting to.

With her words his shy awkwardness returned. "I don't know what's gotten into me. I usually don't talk this much."

"You make it seem so *alive,*" she said. "Religion has always been something I'd see in my mind's eye as sort of dried up and covered with cobwebs." She stopped. "I hope that doesn't upset you."

He shook his head. "It's only come alive for me in

these times. Before, well, it was a part of me, but it didn't really live." Wade looked at her for a time. "Can I ask you something?"

"Anything."

He hesitated, then asked, "Is there someone waiting for you?"

"No." She smiled without humor. "I'm afraid my love life has been sort of a mess."

"Do you want to tell me about it?"

Hard as it was to confess openly what she was just coming to understand deep inside, Allison returned his gift of honesty with the same. "I guess it's like the song says, I was looking for love in all the wrong places. More than anything, I just wanted to feel wanted. I didn't understand that having a man want you because he loves you is different from having him want you because he's weak and lazy. I guess it's easier for that type of guy to find a woman who'd be there for him than to solve the problems inside himself."

Wade listened with the watchful silence of one intent on sharing. She found his gaze reached deep within her, helping her to see, to express, to share. "Before, when I was with a man, I always defined myself by what he needed. You know. Typing his résumé. Cleaning up his apartment. Buying his birthday gift for his mother. Always ready to help out when he ran short of cash."

She swallowed hard. "I thought I was instilling a sense of love and gratitude. But really the guys just withdrew from me. They left me trying too hard to overcompensate for the fact that they really didn't care that much at all. Caring takes effort. Caring means responsibility. And those are things a lazy sort of guy avoids at all costs. I was left feeling weak and dependent on someone who didn't want to help me, since that meant too much effort as well."

Allison stopped, her head down, raw and ashamed and hurting by the confession, sure that he would either laugh or leave.

Instead he asked softly, "So what about giving to someone who needs you and loves you as well?"

"That I've never managed," she replied softly, still unable to lift her head, and now having trouble forcing the words around an oversized heart. "I've dreamed about it, though."

He reached out, took her hand, enveloped it in both of his. "What about someone who needs your strength but wants to give back from what little he has himself?"

"You have more than you give yourself credit for," she said, raising up now, finding his gaze as open as her own. "But to answer your question, I think I'd be a little afraid that I was only kidding myself. That I was only repeating the same old patterns and that sooner or later I'd drive this person away too, just like all the others."

"No chance," he said softly. "No chance at all."

They sat without speaking for a long moment. Then she asked, her eyes luminescent, "Tell me about your dreams."

"Just now," he replied, "it's hard to see much beyond the dream here in front of me."

"Tell me," she pressed.

"I think I want to go back to medical school. There's so much more I need too learn. But . . ." and there he hesitated.

"But you're afraid."

"Very," he admitted.

"At least now," she said, "you won't have to take that step alone."

They paid and rose and clasped hands. He asked, "Do you want to walk awhile?"

"Sure." Reluctantly she let go of his hand. "Just a moment, I'll be right back."

But when she returned from the restaurant's interior, Wade was no longer there.

• • •

Wade stood waiting for Allison at the restaurant's periphery, intoxicated by the night. The traffic was thinning with the hour, yet each time a car passed he had to resist the urge to smile and wave. His feelings were almost too powerful to hold inside. He had to share them, and since Allison wasn't there just then, anyone would do. He had happiness to spare.

Then came the hand in the dark, gripping his throat with the pressure of a vise. His feet were lifted almost clear of the ground. His hands clutched at an arm as solid as a steel girder.

The voice. "Time for paying dues, sport."

And then blackness.

25

"UNTIL THE MOMENT WE HAVE all information," the Jordanian officer crossly informed his three Western visitors, "we wait."

"What if you wait too long, and," Allison could not say it. To even come that close to the thought pierced her heart with an ice dagger.

She had searched the restaurant and the street, calling his name with increasingly frantic strength. The waiters in the restaurant where they had eaten had observed her theatrics with growing concern. Finally one of them had approached, fearful, knowing without being told that he took great risk involving himself even this much. Still, he had observed their talk and their affection, and now he observed her panic and her pain.

The waiter had not spoken much English, just enough to say that Wade had met a man. Big man. Yes, English man or American, but big. Very big. And strong. No, he had no idea where they had gone. Only that Wade had vanished into the night, taken by the big, big man.

Fareed and Ben had driven her to Amman that very night. Judith Armstead and Cyril had gathered at Ben's request, and the search had begun. In Allison's mind, there was no room for question. Wade had been taken by Rogue Robards. Kidnapped.

Because the crime had taken place on Jordanian soil,

Cyril had felt obliged to inform the local authorities. The Jordanian general had been most sympathetic. After all, Allison and the missing young man had been largely responsible for the international coup that already was reaping such benefits as press visits and interviews and urgent cables from Washington and London and elsewhere. The general had assigned an officer whom he claimed to be his best man.

But the man assigned did not want to look for a missing young American. He wanted to be involved in the uncovering of the cache of nuclear weaponry. And he did not like Allison at all. He was Jordanian, he was Arab, he was military, and he had no time for her borderline hysterics. He treated her with the contempt he reserved for pushy American women.

And Allison had started off on the wrong foot from the very first moment. She had almost screamed at the officer when confronted with his reluctance even to move from his office. Allison had caustically pointed out that the two Russian scientists were being held in the same military compound; why couldn't they ask them if they knew of safe houses anywhere in Jordan where Wade might be held.

The Russian scientists had responded to their questions with sullen silence, and the Jordanian officer had been vastly pleased by this result.

They were now standing in the front hall of the compound's main building. Arguing. Getting nowhere fast, while seconds ticked away, and Wade might be hurting.

"I cannot see any problem to wait," the officer announced pompously, his gaze brooking no further argument.

Allison was having none of it. "No problem? He's been kidnapped and you see—"

"Yes, kidnap. Is much kidnapping here. Question is, for what did this? Is only one answer."

"Ransom," Cyril said quietly.

"Is correct." The officer nodded in Cyril's direction as

if to say here, look, observe a professional. "If you add this plus this, is only one answer. For money."

"And if you're wrong?" Allison found it painfully hard not to scream the words. "What if he wants something else? Like revenge?"

"We already have this before many times," the officer replied laconically. "Almost never are problems. Your man here say he pay. We set up for pay only for the live man. He gets money, we gets man. Is almost never problem."

Allison turned to Cyril and pleaded, "Can't you get him to understand?"

"Yes, yes, I see very clear," the officer snapped. "Is everything out in open now. Now you do what should be first day, you talk to Jordanian military. Is Jordanian matter. Has always been."

"This is an international issue," Cyril argued, "involving Russians and Americans and possibly Iraqis—"

"On Jordanian soil," the officer finished for him. "So now we do what Jordanian military say, with experience over years. We wait." He pointed at Allison. "Why this woman come along? She is civilian, yes?"

"She happens to have been in on this since the beginning," Cyril replied. "She is a field agent working with both our governments and has been indispensable in ferreting out these criminals. Miss Taylor has as much right to be here as anyone."

The officer glared first at Cyril, then at Allison. "I say who has right. I say this woman not belong."

"Your superior officer happens to feel otherwise," Cyril replied at his frostiest.

That did not sit well at all. "I am speaking with them this day. Then we see."

"Indeed we shall. Now, can we please get on with the matters at hand?"

"Yes. We do." The officer drew himself up and pronounced, "We wait."

"Fine," Cyril acquiesced. "We will do our waiting at

the American Embassy, in case the man attempts to contact us there. You won't object if we stop by the hotel where the third Russian is being kept and ask him a question or two? No, of course not." Not allowing the officer time to respond, Cyril ushered the two women toward the doors. "Come along then, we mustn't keep the busy officer any longer. Good-day to you, sir."

But Alexis had been equally unhelpful. He had spent the entire time staring blindly from his window, responding to their questions only with silence. Allison thought his own sorrowful face mirrored how her heart felt.

"We have so very little to go on," Judith Armstead told Allison on their way back to the embassy. "Unless this Robards slips up and lets himself be seen—"

"No chance," Allison said morosely. "Wade always referred to him as the professional's professional."

"—or tries to take Wade out of the country, we just have to wait." Cyril had succumbed to the heat and the morning's pressure, and folded his coat in his lap and loosened his tie a notch. "We can only hope that this fellow will seek to gain from us what he failed to receive from our opponents."

"And if he doesn't?" Allison pressed. "What if his motive really was revenge?"

"In that case, my dear," Cyril shook his head and turned toward the window. There was nothing more to be said.

The car slowed and halted at the embassy's guarded entry. Allison used the temporary stop as an opportunity to throw open her door and alight. She leaned back down and said, "You two can hang around here waiting for the phone to ring. I have to at least try to do something. I *have* to."

When the door had slammed shut behind her, Judith asked, "You're going to let her go?"

"We can hardly hold her against her will," Cyril replied. "Besides, she and her young man have already worked wonders. Perhaps she can once again uncover what remains lost to us."

Neither the Western security men nor the two Jordanian military guards questioned Allison's right to visit Alexis in his downtown hotel room a second time. Allison had already appeared once that morning with Price and Armstead. So when she showed up by herself and asked to speak with Alexis alone, a note was made in the logbook, the door was unlocked, and she was permitted entry.

Alexis was not actually under arrest. He had broken no laws except that of leaving Russia, for which he could not be extradited under international law. He was therefore not held with the other two scientists, who had been caught transporting weapons-grade nuclear fuel. He was not, however, free. A half-dozen nations clamored for the chance, according to Cyril, to grill him and his companions for what they knew about the international nuclear arms smuggling operations—how had they heard of the jobs, what form the offer had taken, who, where, when.

When Allison entered the hotel room, Alexis was sitting just as she had left him an hour earlier. The room's single comfortable chair was pulled up close to the window, angled so that he could remain hidden from view and still watch the street below. His face wore the only expression she had seen on him—that of blank despair. Life held little hope for him and less purpose. He remained motionless as Allison crossed the room, pulled up a straight-backed chair, and seated herself. He appeared totally unconcerned as to whether she came, went, stayed, sat, or danced on her hands. He was lost in the defeat that filled his gaze.

"I need your help," she said, filling her voice with all

the quiet urgency she could muster. "Not the government. Not the others. Me. Just me. I have to find him."

"Slow, speak slow," Alexis said. "Little English."

"Wade has talked to me about how you met. He saved your life."

"Yes? Save from what? For what? What I do now with this life he save? What about my wife, my child?" Alexis turned back to his window. "Too much questions."

"Alexis, please. I . . ." She had to stop and swallow hard. "I love him."

That brought his gaze back to her. He searched Allison's face long and hard before saying quietly, "He good man."

"I know," she said and blinked back hard at the sudden burning in her eyes.

"Not just good. In old Russia, we have *staret.* Not know English word. People with problem, they go to—what is church where people live?"

"Monastery," she offered.

"So. People with big problem, they go there and speak to staret. Sometime he answer with words, sometime with silence. But the people, they come back with answer in heart, because staret share wisdom. Is from heart to heart." Alexis showed her the agony of his choice. "Your man, he show me first answer, but now I have new questions. Too many."

"I want him back, Alexis. I need him back." *I* need *him.* I *need* him.

"Perhaps he come and speak with me again, yes?"

Allison felt the first electric thrill of hope. "Or perhaps we can arrange for you to go and speak with him."

"I can go? I free? You do that?" A spark of hope surfaced. "You bring me to family?"

"It's not my authority. But I will do all I can to see that you are freed. On that I give you my word."

"What about note?"

"You want me to get a message to your family? I will try, Alexis. I promise."

Once more he searched her face. "I think maybe you good person for him. Good woman. Good friend."

"Please," Allison whispered. "Help me. I don't know where else to turn."

Again his gaze returned to the scene outside his window. "Trucks."

"What? I don't—"

"Many, many trucks. Outside Aqaba. Is big market there for people on trucks. You know?"

"Yes," she said, fighting to hold herself down, seated, still. "The souk for the drivers. Of course."

"Was building on main road from trucks to port. Big building with apartments, highest I see. Near market. We stay in cellar many nights."

"The tallest apartment building on the main road running from the truck depot to the harbor," she repeated, struggling to find the breath to speak. "And not far from the souk. Is that right?"

"Yes. Except for first night here in Amman, we stay there whole time until Nuweibi."

"Amman? You spent a night in Amman?"

Alexis looked at her with naked appeal. "You not forget promise?"

26

"I FEAR I HAVE NO CHOICE but to go with the major to Aqaba, and follow up this lead Alexis gave you," Cyril said distastefully. He clattered down the HQ stairs, accompanied by Allison and Judith Armstead. The army convoy stretching out before them was in the final throes of preparation. "We all happen to be walking on very thin diplomatic ice just now. After all, it is their country."

"But to put all of your resources into searching one place?" Allison protested. "It just doesn't make sense."

"It does to our little Napoleon," Cyril replied. "And his commanding officer informed me in no uncertain terms that the major is responsible for our search."

"I understand," Allison said. "I just have this feeling that Wade is here in Amman."

"My dear, we have been through this twice already." Cyril raised a laconic hand toward where the officer strutted and shouted. "I concur one hundred percent. I have seen your so-called hunches pay off too often already to insist otherwise. But as I said, I must accompany the major to Aqaba, so I must leave it to you to do what you can here in Amman. However, Miss Armstead has agreed to accompany you, and she is the best there is at this business."

"Second best," Allison countered.

"Yes, well, it is indeed kind of you to say so, considering our current state of affairs." He offered her his hand. "Now I really mustn't try the major's patience any further. Do take care, my dear. And may we meet again under far more joyful circumstances."

Amman was a sprawling, mostly modern metropolis with an overriding quality of sameness. Virtually all the buildings were constructed of concrete blocks, then finished in either white stucco or white-dressed stone. A few of the larger dwellings had lawns or landscaping, but the vast majority looked planted in unfinished construction sites.

Some of the structures were truly palatial, residences of wealthy Jordanians who had worked in the oil-rich southern lands. But the closer Allison and Judith Armstead came to the center of the city, the older the more cramped the quarters became.

And the more talkative their driver grew.

Judith Armstead had insisted they take a taxi for their search, in order to remain anonymous. The driver had started off in silent concentration, but the closer they drew to their destination, the harder he sought to keep hold of his Western clients.

"If you like," he offered, "I make special price."

"No thank you," Judith Armstead replied crisply.

"Why not, hey? How you know next driver not take you wrong way, maybe leave you far in desert?"

"Not likely."

"So is first time you are in Amman? You are welcome." He was a grizzled man in dirty robes and filthy headdress. "You come with group?"

"No."

"You come for business? You government officer from embassy?"

"Just drive the car, please."

"Is good to be government officer. They pay you and

you pay me, yes?" He turned far enough around to see them both, then swung back when a horn warned him of impending doom. He swerved, braked, stuck his head out the window, and shouted oaths at the innocent driver. Then, "You must to hire other driver to return, pay much more, maybe driver not so honest like me. I take you safe. Come, go, special price. Many accidents was happened on this road. But I am always safety."

"So happy to hear it."

"Yes. Am safety driver. So why you not let me take you come, go? I have all the good roads. Old roads. Special ways. Am born here, have all life in Amman. Know all good roads."

Allison leaned forward. "Do you know a road that climbs a hill behind the old Roman amphitheater?"

"Is many hills in city. Amman built on hills. You like tour of Amman city?"

"Forget it."

"Wait, wait." His brow furrowed in concentration. "Hill from ampitheater? Old city?"

"We can find it just as easily on foot," Judith Armstead said.

"No, no, not easy. Old Amman very tricky place; roads all go in wrong direction, take you out, lose you in desert. Wait. Hill in old city. I thinking."

"We are looking for a pair of apartment buildings built side by side, and there is a view looking down across the rooftops and over the Roman amphitheater," Allison told him, relating all the information Alexis had given her. He had been granted one brief time out on the roof. The remainder of his stay, he had said, had been spent in the building's cellar. It had been dark and windowless and smelled of wet laundry. More he could not say. "He was looking out over the amphitheater to some old ruins."

"He?" Driver demanded. "Who is he?"

"None of your concern," Judith replied.

"The roofs were flat," Allison continued, "and both of

the buildings were old. There were maybe five or six stories, but he was not sure."

"All roofs flat in Amman old city," the driver retorted. "All buildings old."

"But two buildings built together," Allison pressed. "So close that he could easily step from one roof to the other."

Again the brow furrowed. "I thinking. You pay good tip for help, yes? I wait, drive you come, go?"

"We pay a very good tip," Allison assured him.

"You've just designed an Amman taxi driver's dream day," Judith Armstead informed her. "Take two rich Westerners on a tour of the old town, look for something they're not too sure about, drive anywhere you like. This is going to cost us the moon."

"No, no, not moon," the driver protested. "I honest man. Do good safety driving."

He pulled up at the edge of a large parking area. In front of them stretched a white parade ground colonnaded along one side. To the right of that, the amphitheater climbed its way up a steep hillside.

The driver pointed to his right. "Jabal Al-Jawfa. Jabal mean hill. There Jabal Attaj. And there Jabal Al Qal'a. Now, where we start?"

Allison pointed toward the remains of what appeared to be an ancient Roman circus. "He said the ruins were behind the amphitheater. That means it would have to be the hill over there."

"Jabal Al Qal'a," the driver said. "I think maybe yes too." He ground the gears and raced the engine. "Now we start."

It was extremely hard to eat with his hands tied behind his back. Especially when the room was pitch black.

Wade had awakened to find himself crammed inside a jouncing coffin so small he could not stretch out his legs. Then he had recognized the sound of a roaring motor and realized he was stuffed into the trunk of a car.

The air was stuffy but breathable. His muscles ached, his head hammered, and the more awake he grew the more frightening his predicament became. So he did the only thing possible under the circumstances. He went back to sleep.

He awoke a second time to find a bright light being directed into his eyes. "Wakey, wakey, sport. Time to rise and shine."

"Why are you doing this?" he mumbled.

"If you hadn't slept the whole way you'd have figured that out for yourself already." Wade watched as the flashlight was handed to someone else standing beside Robards. Then strong hands pulled a black stocking down over his head and plucked him effortlessly from the trunk. "Stretch out your legs."

He did, and groaned as the circulation revived in areas long left dormant.

Robards showed no sympathy. "Okay, turn around." When Wade did not move fast enough for him, Rogue spun him about, leaned him roughly against the car, and tied his hands behind his back. "All right, let's move."

Wade started to tell him that he couldn't get away with it, then stopped. By the looks of things, he already had.

Robards led him up a set of crumbling steps, through a door, and down a flight of stairs. A key rustled and turned, a heavy door opened, and Wade was shoved inside. He stumbled against the rough concrete floor and fell heavily, landing full force on one knee. He cried out sharply and rolled to his side.

"There'll be somebody outside this door all the time," Robards said. "Make any noise and you'll spend your days with a towel stuffed down your throat. Make any trouble and it's the last trouble you give anybody. That clear?"

"My leg," Wade groaned.

"Hey, I'd be a little more sorry if it wasn't for all that's gone down." He stepped into the room, ripped the stocking from Wade's head. "People don't find it profitable to get in my way, sport. For two cents I'd stomp your head in. So count your blessings and keep it quiet."

Robards returned only twice after that, both times in the quiet before the world awoke. Both times he jammed the stocking back down over Wade's head and led him limping down the corridor to a rudimentary toilet. Then he brought him back to the cellar room, retied his hands, and left him with two tin plates set on the bare floor. One held water, the other a portion of the poor man's food of the Middle East, a concoction of cold beans and onions and garlic called *foul.* The only way Wade could eat or drink was by kneeling and bending far over to lap it up like a dog. The pain in his swollen knee made doing so pure agony.

Wade counted the passage of hours by the sounds that echoed down from above him. Children crying, mothers yelling, dogs barking, a few cars passing, muzzeins' call to prayer, music being played from a dozen radios. Occasionally he thought of shouting, then recalled the cold detachment in Robards' voice and knew that if he did it would be the last sound he would ever make.

Allison knew from the first moment of their search that they faced an almost impossible task.

The hill called Jabal Al Qal'a was inundated with apartment houses, none of which were more than five or six stories high, and all of which were old. The roofs she could not tell much about, as the roads were winding and narrow and snaked back and forth in confusing, interlocking array. The taxi was airless and almost unbearably hot.

The only one pleased with their state of affairs was

the driver. Every now and then he would break into a single-note warble, tapping time on the steering wheel as he ground slowly down one street after the other.

"I think we've already come this way," Judith Armstead announced. "Five or six times."

"No, no, lady. This new road. See? That house, you not see that house not ever before. And this one, maybe this the house, yes? Two up close, see how built?"

"No," Allison replied, marking a larger house looming up on the road's opposite side and blocking the view. "Definitely not this one."

"Okay, all what you say is okay. We take this road now, yes? You see, I good safety driver. Take all day and help what I can."

"They're all jammed so close together," Allison said, "I can't even tell if we're still above the amphitheater."

"Oh, yes, yes, you see, this why important you have honest driver. I know. Amphitheater just down there. We stay right where you want."

"Our driver," Judith Armstead murmured, "is going to be telling the story of this day to his great-grandchildren."

Allison pointed through her window. "Stop here."

"Sure, sure, anything you say. We stop here right now."

Judith climbed out beside her. "What is it?"

"See those two buildings? No, not these, up higher. The next road. See how they stick up over the tops of these others?"

"Maybe," Judith said doubtfully. "They all look the same to me."

"Me, too," Allison confessed. She sighed. "Maybe we should have gone with them to Aqaba."

Judith looked at her. "Is that the sound of defeat I hear?"

"Then if they hadn't found anything, we could have tried to convince them to come back this way."

"Come on," Judith said, climbing back in the car. "Let's go check it out."

"What are we supposed to do when we get there?" Allison asked, suddenly burdened by doubt. "Go up and knock on doors and ask if they've happened to see any kidnapped Americans lately?"

Judith Armstead was not the least concerned. "It's early hours yet. Ninety-nine percent of our work involves eliminating possibilities."

Allison pointed out her side window. "Can you take us to those buildings up there?"

"Sure, sure, no problem. I take you anywhere, you see."

Once they were again under way, Judith told Allison, "I met your father once, by the way."

"You did? When?"

"Oh, it was some time ago." For a moment her strong exterior softened. "I was just getting started. Your father had an almost mythical reputation in those days. He was giving a lecture, and afterward he took time to chat with me. I was young, a complete unknown, and yet here John Taylor was, surrounded by all these officers and bigwigs, treating me like I was somebody important."

Allison felt a sudden kinship. "I never knew anything about that side of his work. I still don't, actually."

The taxi driver pulled over and stopped. "See? Just like you ask. I know all special roads."

"Wait here, please." Allison climbed from the taxi and surveyed the twin structures, asked, "What now?"

"Let's go see." Judith strode determinedly up to the first building, pushed at the door, found it unlocked. A moment's hesitation, then she walked inside. "The cellar, you say?"

"That's where Alexis was held." Allison answered breathlessly.

They walked down the stairs and entered a dank and moldy corridor with wires and cables strung overhead. Most of the rooms had no doors; the hallway opened directly onto fusty-smelling chambers full of refuse and old washing machines.

"At least he had the smell right," Allison murmured. She walked over to the one sealed door, hesitated, then knocked and whispered, "Wade?" She pressed her ear hard to the surface.

"Hear anything?"

"Nothing."

"They probably wouldn't leave him unguarded. Let's go try next door."

The cellar of the neighboring building was identical except for two women busy gossiping over a laboring washer. They looked up and gawked in utter astonishment as the two Westerners stepped into view. Their eyes opened even farther when Judith addressed them in Arabic. One of them answered her with a question. Judith replied at length, motioning around the chambers. The two women looked at each other and howled with laughter. Judith smiled in reply and waved a goodbye.

"What did you tell them?" Allison asked.

"The only thing I could think of. That the embassy was looking for downtown living space, and we needed a large basement for entertaining guests in safety." She pointed up the stairs. "Let's go take a look at what we can see from the roof."

At that height, there was at least a little wind. Laundry flapped in the sultry breeze. Allison gulped deep breaths and surveyed her surroundings. The taxi driver was correct; he had managed to bring them in a relatively straight line directly up from the amphitheater. Allison turned around, visually searching the other buildings. "We should have done this in the beginning."

"Everything is much clearer," Judith agreed.

"How about those two over there?"

Judith nodded, pointed to her left. "And those."

"And the two a couple streets higher. To my right."

"Try to fix them clearly in your mind. Things will look different from down below."

They returned to the taxi, pulled the driver from his car, pointed, and explained where they wanted to go. He agreed with the genuine willingness of one whose fortune was assured.

The next pair of buildings proved to have roofs separated by a high wire fence. Alexis had not mentioned anything of the sort, so they merely noted the location and left that building for later. The following pair of buildings had cellars as empty as the first ones. The next set were located on a street so narrow the taxi was twice forced to backpedal in order to permit through traffic. No sunlight filtered into the manmade chasm.

Allison climbed from the taxi and said, "I don't see how you can keep up your enthusiasm for a job like this."

"By having one in a thousand searches pay off," Judith replied. "Don't give up hope."

The first cellar proved to be one vast chamber sectioned off by ankle-high concrete partitions.

The second building greeted them with a locked door.

Judith did not hesitate. She rang the top two bells, waited, and when nothing happened took the next two in line. This time the door-speaker squawked. Judith put her face close to the box and said in English, "We're the Avon ladies, come to see if you received your samples this week."

The box squawked and rattled and stuttered. "That's right," Judith agreed. "A free car."

Allison looked at her. "We're what?"

"These things don't work half the time," Judith explained. "And I doubt seriously that anybody on the other end speaks a word of English."

In reply, the buzzer sounded. Judith pushed her way inside, stuck her head up the stairway, and called, *"Shokran,"* thank you. She then guided Allison down the cellar stairs.

A leather-skinned Arab dressed in rumpled Western clothes and sporting a three-day growth rose from his chair as they stepped into view. He shouted vehemently at them and pointed back up the stairs. Judith started off in Arabic, but the man was having none of it. He started toward them, making sharp shoving motions at the air.

Allison took one step back onto the first stair and screamed at the top of her lungs, *"WADE!"*

It was impossible to find a comfortable position.

Standing was all right, except that his knee complained louder the longer he remained on his feet. Sitting up was best, with his back resting on the wall and his hands drawn up into the small of his back. But that eventually grew tiresome. Then he had a choice of either lying on one side or the other, with his head at a downward angle on the floor—and the floor was cool and mildly damp and extremely hard. Lying on his back meant crushing his hands, and they were already numb from restricted blood flow. Lying on his belly meant mashing his cheek into the moldy concrete.

And his knee thundered painfully with every heartbeat. Not to mention the agony he knew every time he knelt to drink.

Between dozing and staring into the darkness, Wade tried praying, to no avail. And yet he did not feel abandoned. It was strange how he could remain sitting here in the dark, utterly isolated, and yet not feel the least bit alone. There was great comfort in that mysterious fact, for fact it was. He was not alone. He felt no surge of peace beyond understanding, no breaking of his earthly bonds. Just the simple knowledge that he was not abandoned.

It was almost enough.

The sound woke him from a fitful doze. For a moment he thought it had been part of a dream. He struggled upright, hoping against hope, opening his mouth to still the noise of his breathing.

There it was again. Shouting. Just outside his door. And then the shrill cry. It was her.

He stumbled to his feet, overturned his food, yelled, "I'm in here!"

"That's his voice!" Allison started forward, only to be slammed up against the wall as the Arab strong-armed her into the concrete. She felt the breath whoosh from her lungs by the force of his blow, and thought her legs would give way.

The Arab snarled and reached inside his coat, then froze. Judith Armstead had two-armed a small blue-steel pistol directly up his nose. Her voice was as cold as ice.

The Arab hesitated. She snapped out a second command in Arabic, and he stepped reluctantly back.

"Take his gun, Allison," she ordered.

With trembling hands Allison reached inside his coat, drew out the pistol stuck into his belt, held it aloft with two fingers.

"Get a good grip on it."

The gun was surprisingly heavy. She pointed it at the Arab's face, found herself unable to hold it steady even with two hands.

"Go try the door."

Keeping the gun trained on the Arab, Allison sidled over to the door. She saw Judith take one step back and motion with her own gun for the Arab to move to the wall. He did not do so fast enough for her. Again the whipping sound of her voice, and with a snarl of his own the Arab complied.

Allison released one hand from the gun and knocked. "Wade?"

"Is that really you?" The voice was muffled but clear.

She caught the sob that rose in her throat and fought it back down. Allison glanced at the bolt set at chest level in the door. "It's padlocked shut."

"Tell him to back off and lie down. Then shoot the hinge," Judith snapped. "And hurry. We're sitting ducks."

"I heard," came Wade's muffled reply.

Allison aimed the gun and fired. The recoil popped her hands up over her head, and the boom reverberated like a cannon in the enclosed surroundings. The smoke burned her eyes. As soon as the ringing diminished she heard screams and cries from throughout the building. The Arab snarled a curse and started to move, only to find Judith's gun jammed into the nape of his neck. She screamed a command in Arabic and then in English, *"Move!"*

Allison hit the stubborn bolt with the butt of her gun. Then she grasped the door handle and pulled with all her might. The door groaned, then gave.

Wade stumbled into her arms.

"Out of the way!" Judith hustled the Arab over and into the chamber, rammed the door back home. She whacked the broken hinge as much back into place as she could, then took the Arab's chair and slammed it up under the handle. She yelled, "Let's go!"

They raced up the stairs as fast as Wade's injured knee would allow, Allison supported him with one arm; the other still held the pistol. They saw fingers pointed at them from the floors above, then just as swiftly disappear with a chorus of screams.

Allison threw open the outside door and rammed straight into the arms of Rogue Robards.

It was the only thing that saved them.

Rogue's startled pause from having an unknown woman suddenly in his arms gave Wade just enough time to shout, "It's him!"

Judith Armstead rammed the gun into his throat. "Barton Robards, you are coming with us. The authorities wish to speak with you in regards to charges of kidnapping, extortion, and the smuggling of—"

"No!" Wade shouted, surprising them all, and jostled Judith from behind, surprising them even more. Judith stumbled and lowered her gun a fraction.

"Run!" Wade shouted at Robards.

Rogue did not need to be told twice. He leapt from the stairs and moved so fast that he left behind only empty space.

Judith searched the empty street. "What the—"

"What did you do?" Allison cried.

"Let him go," Wade replied.

Further screams from inside the building sparked them into action. The Arab.

"Quick!" Judith cried, hustling them across the street toward the taxi.

Allison fell on Wade in the backseat. Judith clambered into the front and screamed, "Drive!"

"Wait, wait," the driver stammered. "I no drive for people in such dangers. We stop, you find new taxi, yes?"

Judith Armstead raised her gun. "Think again."

The driver moaned and ground his gears. The Arab slammed the apartment door opened and raced out, fists waving. "Quickly," Judith urged.

"Yes, yes, is speed now," the driver said, swerving to avoid the fast-approaching Arab. "All the day is slow and here and there and careful, and now is speeds and dangers. This not Gunsmoke. You no need for pistols."

"Can somebody untie my hands?" Wade asked.

"Lean over," Allison said. Then, "Why did you let Robards go?"

"My thoughts exactly," Judith Armstead added.

Wade winced as he rubbed the circulation back into his hands. "I owed him," he replied.

"He is a thief and a smuggler and a mercenary," Judith snapped. "Not to mention the fact that he kidnapped you."

"Not here," Wade said. "Before. Back in Russia."

"Didn't you tell me he stole a truckload of your pharmaceuticals?" Allison demanded.

Wade nodded, and glanced out the back window. "He also taught me courage."

The silence held for a moment. Then Allison ran a soft hand down one side of his face. "Are you all right?"

He captured her hand with his, and said, "Take me home."

Epilogue

We Have Been Warned

The recent availability of used MIGs comes as very bad news. . . . Former Communist nations are now selling them at deep, deep discounts. "They're advertising used MIGs for as low as $25,000 and $50,000. You can't even buy a Beechcraft Bonanza for that."

The Wall Street Journal
August 5, 1992

The Foreign Office official said that before the Soviet Union disintegrated, there were strict controls [on sophisticated arms sales to other countries], "although we did not like where they were exporting equipment such as Scud missiles." Today, however, apart from a degree of central control in Russia, there was no legislation in place to check arms sales, the official said.

The Times of London
October 10, 1992

Red mercury . . . is a potential source of cheap nuclear weapons. The substance, a compound of mercury and antimony oxides, has been seized by customs all over Europe en route from Russian laboratories. . . . It is one of the most sinister and dangerous materials ever developed, a substance that could transform the regimes of Saddam or Gadhafi into nuclear powers overnight. It is supposedly easier to manufacture than the complex types of device deployed by the West, and has the added advantage that it is even more compact. Eugeny Korolev, a politician in Ekaterinburg, central Russia, which is a center of the traffic, claims: "With red mercury, Saddam Hussein can make a bomb the size of a grenade that could blow a ship out of the sea." It is known to have fetched up to one million pounds [about one and one half million dollars] a pint. . . . Samples have been confiscated in countries as diverse as Ethiopia, North Korea and South Africa. In almost every instance, the original source of supply has been found to be military plants in Russia. Last April, Ukrainian police announced they had arrested thieves near the border trying to smuggle out 180 kilograms of red mercury.

The Sunday Times
October 18, 1992

German police have launched a nationwide search for up to 20 kilograms of deadly weapons-grade uranium smuggled into the country earlier this week by a team of Polish entrepreneurs. The uranium—enough to build a small nuclear bomb—and other highly radioactive materials are part of a consignment smuggled to the West from the former Soviet Union by five Poles and a German woman accomplice. Police had been on the lookout for smuggled radioactive material since a tip-off last month from a Swiss doctor who treated a Pole for severe radiation sickness. Last weekend a German fire brigade unit in protective clothing seized up to 200 grams of extremely toxic radioactive caesium–137—said to be one of the most toxic substances known to man—and radioactive strontium–90 from a luggage locker at Frankfurt's main railway station.

The European
October 22, 1992

A British businessman was arrested in Germany yesterday on suspicion of smuggling 80 kilograms of plutonium from Russia. Such a quantity of plutonium, if enriched, could be used to make several atomic bombs.

The Times of London
November 4, 1992

Thousands of Iranians, celebrating the thirteenth anniversary of the seizure of the US Embassy in Tehran, joined in a vocal "Death to America" message to President-elect Bill Clinton on Wednesday. "You know Bush has lost and Clinton won," a speaker told the rally marking the day in 1979 when Iranian students took over the embassy. "What we have to say to the new administration is: 'Death to America.' "

International Herald Tribune
November 5, 1992

State-of-the-art technologies are pouring into Iran as European, Asian, and US companies rush to profit from Tehran's attempt to infuse its Islamic revolution with modern science and to rehabilitate the economy. Much of the technology being transferred to Iran in the export boom is categorized as militarily useful by the US government, but relatively little is being held back. That is because of policy differences on Iran between Washington and its allies. . . . The technology reaching Iran includes radar testing devices, navigation and avionics equipment, oscilloscopes, logic analyzers, digital switches, high-speed computers, remote sensors and jet engines, according to these sources.

International Herald Tribune
November 11, 1992

White-robed Islamic militants gathered, in defiance of a government ban, to call for revolution. "Islam is at war on many fronts!" a speaker shouted, seated under a banner urging his followers to kill all nonbelievers. "We must rid ourselves of the infidels who rule this country, the Jews, the Christians, and the Communists! All are different, but all are united in their determination to exterminate Muslims!" . . . It was a signal that Egypt, with one-third of the Arab world's population, is in danger of losing its struggle against the regional spread of militant Islam.

New York Times Service
November 13, 1992

Ukrainian leaders have threatened to hold up approval of the treaty sharply reducing intercontinental nuclear missiles unless their new nation receives a substantial increase in Western aid. With Ukraine's economy faltering badly, leaders of the government and parliament have declared with growing determination in recent days that they will not part with strategic missiles "for free." . . . Diplomats said enriched uranium scavenged from the warheads could bring hundreds of millions of dollars.

International Herald Tribune
November 14, 1992

Egyptian fundamentalists will keep up their attacks on tourism because of its corrupting influence, a spokesman for the underground Islamic organization Jamaa Islamiya said. "Tourists bring alien customs and morals that offend Islam, especially the attire of some women," he said in Cairo. "Tourism must be hit because it is corrupt."

Associated Press
November 25, 1992

The world may be sitting on top of the next nuclear crisis without even knowing it. That is because at least five Middle Eastern countries—Iraq, Iran, Syria, Libya, and Algeria—are working to develop nuclear weapons. . . . They are buying strategic technologies from Western companies. They are also attempting to acquire nuclear materials from the former Soviet Union.

Editorial in the New York Times
November 26, 1992
Kenneth R. Timmerman

Nuclear materials have probably been smuggled out of at least one former Soviet republic, rasing new alarms about proliferation of weapons of mass destruction, the chairman of the Senate Armed Services Committee said Wednesday. Senator Sam Nunn, Democrat from Georgia, who just returned from a trip to five former Soviet republics, said that senior officials in Belarus—one of the four former republics that still has nuclear weapons on its soil—told of "several cases" of intercepting uranium as smugglers sought to take it across the border into Poland.

International Herald Tribune
November 26, 1992

Investigators looking into a recent rash of European criminal cases involving illicit smuggling and sale of radioactive materials say they have found evidence of thefts from former Soviet and East European nuclear plants, both commercial and nuclear. . . . Evidence in these cases suggests that freelance con artists and small groups of criminals are crossing borders opened after the end of the Cold War in search of quick profits from potentially dangerous radioactive contraband, and that the smugglers are using routes and methods adapted from Europe's heroin and illicit cigarette trades. . . . Uranium of the sort being seized in the smuggling cases could prove useful to a nuclear bomb manufacturer if acquired in large enough quantities.

Washington Post Service
November 30, 1992

U.S. intelligence analysts are divided on the issue of what Iran's $2 billion-a-year military buildup—including its nuclear program—means, and whether Iran could replace Iraq as an aggressive, expansionist military threat in the Gulf region in the coming years. . . . The new report also draws strong conclusions about the leadership in Tehran, asserting that President Hashemi Rafsanjani has built a team of nuclear experts, many of them educated in the United States, to direct a nuclear program. Based on their activities, as well as on Iran's nuclear research and development programs, the study concludes that there is more certainty about Iran's intentions. . . . The worst case scenario for Iran has been articulated by Mr. Gates. He said in an Associated Press interview published last week that Tehran could pose a threat to the United States and its allies in the Gulf within three to five years.

New York Times Service
December 1, 1992

Saudi Arabia has been thrown into an open struggle between the ruling al-Saud family and the increasingly powerful religious establishment. King Fahd has been forced to make the unprecedented move of dismissing more than half of the country's religious council because of its implicit support for a petition criticizing his rule. . . . Though Fahd is an absolute ruler, his political legitimacy is based on his claim to rule an Islamic society. . . . This latest upsurge of religious extremism dates back to the Gulf war, when Fahd allowed 500,000 allied troops into Saudi Arabia. Ultra-conservatives opposed the presence of "foreign infidels."

It also attacked the kingdom's foreign policy for accommodating "interests of Western governments."

The Sunday Times
December 13, 1992

Federal authorities arrested a suspect Thursday in the bombing of the World Trade Center and said others were being sought. The man arrested was a member of a Muslim fundamentalist group.

International Herald Tribune
March 5, 1993

As long as they have nuclear weapons, and as long as there is a market, you will probably see people in Kazakhstan—not necessarily the government, but maybe the entrepreneurs or unemployed apparatchiks—who will try to turn a quick buck through the sale of weapon components. . . . Given the political entente, it would surprise me greatly if nuclear weapons cooperation had not only been discussed, but deals actually consummated, where Kazakhstan has provided nuclear weapons to Iran.

Frank Gaffney, Center for Security Policy
Washington, D.C.
Interviewed on BBC-TV Dispatches Program
May 12, 1993

To make an atomic bomb, a terrorist or a would-be proliferator would need to get hold of only 5 kg of weapon-grade plutonium or 15 kg of weapon-grade uranium, less than you would need to fill a fruit bowl. At present the world probably contains about 250 tons of this sort of plutonium and about 1500 tons of the uranium. To lose one bomb's worth from the stock is the equivalent of losing a single word from one of three copies of The Economist. But the loss would be harder to detect. The world's stock of nuclear explosive material is dispersed and hoarded. Almost none of this material is covered by international nuclear-accounting rules. And more than half of it is inside the chaotic relic of the former Soviet Union."

The Economist
June 5, 1993

With the help of a confidential informer operating inside a suspected bombing ring, federal agents recorded many private conversations of Sheikh Omar Abdel Rahman, the Egyptian cleric who has been blamed for inspiring terrorism in Egypt and the United States. . . . Six of the eight men arrested on Thursday in a plot to assassinate political leaders and bomb the United Nations, the FBI's New York headquarters and two commuter tunnels, were followers of the sheikh. . . . As a loosely knit organization, Al Fuqra turned to Mr. Hampton-El and perhaps a few others in the Black Muslim community to provide it with weapons and expertise in carrying out attacks, the detective said.

International Herald Tribune
June 28, 1993

Q: Do the New York bombers represent the tip of an iceberg?

A: I think so. What worries me is this: One would have thought that the rapidity with which the FBI cracked the World Trade Center bombing case would have sent a powerful message to terrorists that the United States is a tough place to operate in. Rather, it has done the opposite. The people arrested last week used it as an excuse to carry out an even more audacious terrorist campaign. They have gone from killing a handful of people at the World Trade Center to contemplating mass wanton murder, such as the destruction of two tunnels. One can only shudder to think what the next group is going to contemplate.

Interview with Bruce Hoffman
Director of Strategy, Rand Institute
International Herald Tribune
June 28, 1993

Eighteen months after Algeria's military leadership canceled the country's first free parliamentary elections to prevent Islamic fundamentalists from coming to power, the already violent struggle between security forces and Muslim guerrillas appears to have entered a more ominous phase. Islamic extremists appear to have embarked on a new terror campaign in the past three months. . . . The killings have already sent shivers of fear and suspicion through Algeria's middle-class professional community.

Washington Post Service
June 28, 1993

The visions were apocalyptic: bomb blasts spreading fire and smoke through United Nations headquarters and a lower Manhattan skyscraper that houses, of all things, the New York offices of the FBI. Other explosions the same day in the Holland and Lincoln tunnels under the Hudson River, crushing motorists inside cars turned to twisted junk, killing many more by spreading intense heat, smoke and noxious fumes throughout the enclosed space of the tubes. Thousands dead, thousands more injured, the nation's biggest city in a wild panic. It was supposed to happen this week, stunning America with a new and ghoulish kind of pre-Fourth of July fireworks display.

Time
July 5, 1993

The Islamic Group, led by Sheikh Abdel Rahman, vowed in Cairo for the first time to launch a retaliatory terrorist campaign against US targets in Egypt and the United States. "We will hit American targets," said a leader of the Islamic Group in the militant stronghold of Imbaba, "and not just American targets in Egypt, but throughout the Middle East, Europe, and the United States." In a sign of concern Saturday about possible retaliation, the Federal Bureau of Investigation opened the command post that it uses to keep watch over crises.

International Herald Tribune
July 5, 1993

The true security nightmare is a nuclear weapon locked in a trunk in the parking lot at Washington's Union Station. Even a crude atomic bomb could level buildings for miles around ground zero. The resulting fireball would radiate at the speed of sound, incinerating every bit of steel, concrete and human flesh in its path and igniting a holocaust that would make Dresden look like a birthday candle. What's keeping a terrorist group from going nuclear? Building an atomic bomb requires two things: knowledge and material.

Newsweek
July 12, 1993

A nightmare scenario confronts Western governments trying to grapple with the problem of fundamentalism in Egypt: the government of President Hosni Mubarak falls, to be replaced by an Islamic regime; Egypt joins the Islamic government in Sudan to subvert the already shaky regimes in Algeria and Libya and then turns east to undermine the Gulf states, including Saudi Arabia. By the end of this century Israel will be surrounded by radical governments, millions of refugees will have fled to

Europe (further destabilising already weak economies), leaving Europe, the Middle East and North Africa in a state of armed confrontation which has not been seen since the Second World War. For the past few months the intelligence community and policy makers have been trying to measure the enormity of the challenge posed by the spread of Islamic fundamentalism. What is now understood is that unless action is taken to combat the growing political and military power of the fundamentalists, there will be serious economic and political consequences that could undermine the entire international community.

The Times of London
August 22, 1993

On Sunday Gadhafi invited the world's two most notorious Palestinian terrorists, Ahmed Jibril and Abu Nidal, to visit Tripoli, perhaps to set up headquarters there. The Libyan leader told a cheering crowd in the town of Azizia that the invitations were meant to defy the United Nations. . . . Intelligence reports link Jibril and his General Command organization to the planning of the Pan Am massacre, which cost 270 lives.

Washington Post
December 15, 1993

Criminal groups are already trafficking in nuclear materials and could conceivably acquire nuclear weapons one day.

Newsweek
December 13, 1993

(This book went to press in early 1994.)

"I looked and there before me was a pale horse!
Its rider was named Death,
and Hades was following close behind him.
They were given power over a fourth of the earth to kill
by sword, famine and plague."

Revelation 6:8

Acknowledgments

I would like to use this acknowledgements section not only as an opportunity to express my thanks to the many people and organizations who helped me in the development of this book, but also to share with readers some of the challenges of this research. In order for this story to ring true, three very difficult topics had to be researched—the conflicts of the Chechen-Ingush region, the current threat of dissemination of nuclear armaments, and the rise of Islamic fundamentalism. I am thankful I did not realize how much work would be involved before beginning this project, but God blessed me throughout.

In addition to library and archival research, most of my novels are based on scores of personal interviews. This requires developing a huge pool of potential contacts. In preparation for *Riders of the Pale Horse,* I approached dozens of organizations with experience in evangelical efforts in the Middle East and North Africa. What surprised me was how difficult it was to find even *one* person involved in Middle Eastern evangelism who was willing to speak with me. The reasons for this reluctance were some that I had never faced before. Perhaps the reader would find it of interest to hear of three of these experiences:

In late 1992 a conference took place in London entitled "Islam and the Suffering Church." Authorities on the Christian movement in Muslim countries were brought in from various Asian, Middle Eastern, and African states. In order to attend, a request had to be made at least two weeks in advance, and had to include the name of the participant's local pastor. Only after the pastor was contacted would a ticket be issued. Arriving participants were required to present both ticket and passport in order to gain entry. No late entries were permitted, no matter what their credentials.

The General Secretary of one Middle East evangelical organization told me bluntly that his missionaries had insisted that nothing be either stated or written about them, as it endangered both their efforts and their lives. In view of this fear, they had disbanded their magazine eight months before.

My publisher in the United Kingdom was able to make a contact for me with an Anglican missionary who had just returned from Jordan the previous month. The interview was done by telephone, and the man used an assumed name. I was required to promise in advance that I would not attempt to name either him or the organization that had sent him overseas.

Over thirty contacts were made, and resulted in only five interviews, all of them under clandestine conditions. When I asked for reasons behind their caution, I was presented with the polarity of the situation. On the one hand, *every missionary with whom I spoke* repeated over and over how kind and hospitable and friendly the vast majority of Arabs were. The dangers, they related, came from a small but very lethal minority. It was essential, they told me time and time again, that if I wished to have my story reflect the truth in today's Middle East, I could not describe the Arabs as generally being either dangerous or evil or anti-Christian. It would be as incorrect as describing every American as being a member of the Ku Klux Klan.

Those with whom I was able to speak related numerous conversion stories, many involving entire families. They also spoke of many other cases where families were quite happy to accept a new Christian convert within their clan. They described how essential it was for young Arabs, who now saw the burning fanatical anger offered by Islamic fundamentalism, to be shown a grace-filled alternative. They discussed the joy that filled their lives when they saw the living God awaken a new heart.

But they also spoke of the danger.

Danger caused by a minority, yes, but still a danger. And as the number of fundamentalists grows, so too does their threat. I offer three examples:

A missionary working in Pakistan and the Central Asian states told me that after several of his converts had been discovered and murdered, they had decided to structure their church in the form of cell units, as was utilized by war-time underground armies. It assured that if any were caught and forced to talk, they would only be able to implicate a few of their fellow believers.

In the late summer of 1992 a group of Philippine guest workers were arrested in Saudi Arabia and flogged until they bled. Their crime was attending a Christian service. I discussed this with several missionaries, as the Saudis were generally considered to be tolerant about the worshiping habits of guest workers. The general consensus was that they had become very vocal in their worship service, praising God and singing loud enough to be heard outside the hall. One staunch fundamentalist with political clout who overheard them was offended enough to insist on punishment. Laws calling for such punishment still exist in Saudi Arabia. It is also a crime for a Saudi to convert to Christianity—under penalty of death by beheading. It is also a capital crime to publicly proselytize for Christ.

When one person who had tried to set up a meeting for me was met with a stone wall, he apologized by relating the following story: Some years ago, three sisters converted to Christianity in an unnamed Arab state.

When their mother learned of this, she responded by putting strychnine in their food. For many missionaries who had experienced such atrocities firsthand, to openly discuss their work was to invite unnecessary danger.

Once again, it must be stated that this is the work of a minority. To condemn all Arabs because of the fanatic fury of a few is not only ludicrous, it is wrong. I have tried very hard in this work to clearly differentiate between the threats presented by a minority and the tolerant acceptance shown by most Arabs. While they may not choose to adopt our faith, the majority of Middle Eastern citizens are most willing to listen. And discuss. And argue. All of this is a part of both their nature and their hospitality.

The danger, both to Christian evangelism and to the Western world as a whole, rests within the radical minority. This hazard is growing as the power base of Islamic fundamentalism extends itself wider and wider. This is the threat that must be vigilantly watched. This is the danger that must be clearly understood. This is the threat that must be checked.

Dr. Robert Parsons is the former director of the Russia desk of the BBC World Service, and now runs their Moscow office. He lived in Georgia a number of years and traveled extensively in the Caucasus region. He proved a most able teacher, both in regard to the current conflicts sweeping the region, and the mentalities and cultures behind the various factions.

Yuri Goligorsky is the BBC Editor for Russian Current Affairs. In the midst of the Russian parliamentary crisis, he was kind enough to walk me through the various cultural and political currents at work in the Caucasus.

Because of the four different wars enveloping the Caucasus region, travel up into the highlands was dangerous. I was able to fill many of the visual gaps thanks to the very able staff of the British National Film Archives, a part of the British Film Institute. Their archives contained documentaries on the region dating from as far as 1928 to as current as two months ago. I would like to thank in particular Simon Baker and Bryony Dixon, who first led me through the extensive research catalogues, and then placed a chamber at my disposal for the hours and hours required to review the work.

Mr. Roy Gonzalez is a telecommunications engineer with Science Applications International Corporation, which among other things is partly responsible for the current renovation of the Pentagon's communications equipment. The idea for Rogue Robards came from a conversation with him about his experiences in Vietnam.

Dr. Christoph Bluth is Professor of International Politics at the University of Essex, and one of the world's leading authorities on strategic and tactical nuclear armaments. I am most grateful for his careful and thorough introduction to the current dangers of nuclear proliferation.

Dr. Edwina Moreton is Diplomatic Editor at The Economist, and is one of the magazine's chief authorities on the current political and economic struggles in the former Soviet empire. She was most helpful in drawing together the myriad of details and separate incidents into a cohesive whole.

Dr. Sugden is Director of the Oxford Center for Mission Studies, a library and study center for over two dozen graduate theology students from almost as many countries. Their beautiful facility contains a wealth of resources, most especially in the persons who study there. The gentleman with whom I worked mostly, who must remain unnamed, is a perfect example. He is training to go back as a missionary to a Muslim population in Asia. I am indeed grateful to Dr. Sugden for opening his center to my research activities and for making the required introductions.

Professor F. Jahanpour of Oxford and Reading Universities proved to be a rare find—someone capable of taking historical events and trends and shaping them into a logical succession that led to the events of today. His summary of the roots of current Islamic fundamentalism was both clear and exciting. He truly made both the people and the circumstances live for me.

In February 1993, a symposium was held in London on Islamic fundamentalism and power-sharing within their countries. I was the only American attending, and one of only four or five Westerners. It was a conference by Islamic fundamentalists and for fundamentalists. The issues included whether or not democracy was a principle permitted by the Koran, and whether fundamentalists should be willing to form coalitions with nonbelievers. This high-powered meeting took place in London because it was one of the few places on earth where the speakers could safely assemble. Representatives included top-level political officials and academics from Jordan, Algeria, Tunisia, Kuwait, Egypt, and other Islamic countries. Much of their discussion is reflected in portions of this book concerning the fundamentalist attitude toward democracy and the West. While their disagreement over the place of democracy was fiery, their attitude toward the West seemed universally hostile.

As I mentioned above, making contact within Middle East missionary programs was enormously difficult. As the rise of Islamic fundamentalism results in an increasing risk to the missionaries themselves, their families, and their converts, they have begun steadily closing all doors to disseminating information. Even magazines or newsletters about their work are now being closed down.

I am therefore tremendously thankful that five missionaries were willing to put aside their justifiable concerns and speak with me at length. My heartfelt thanks must also go to the three dozen people who acted as both my advocates and my introduction to these people. It was an enormously time-consuming practice for all involved, and the process taught me almost as much as the interviews themselves. Naturally, no names will be given here. These people taught me at a multitude of levels, both in the development of this book and in my own spiritual growth. I can only hope that as they read this novel, they will feel that I have portrayed them and their work with honesty and admiration.

All of the stories of Christians presented in this book are true. They come to me from people who experienced them firsthand. For obvious reasons, their names cannot be given here. Nonetheless, I wish to offer my sincere thanks for speaking to me so openly, and my prayers for their continued safety.

It should be noted that Aqaba does not have a major Palestinian camp in its vicinity. The Palestinians who emigrated there from Beersheba and other southern Israeli towns after the '67 war have more or less been fully assimilated into the society. For the sake of this story, a camp situated on the outskirts of Amman was relocated here. Conditions are as they were described in these pages.

My travels in Jordan were enlightening, if not always easy. I was particularly transfixed by the desert reaches surrounding Petra. Like the character of Leah, I found Jordan to be a place of fierce beauty, warmly hospitable people, and brilliant contrasts. As with my travels elsewhere, I remain indebted to all who assisted and taught me, both named and unnamed.

Cyril Price is in truth a grand gentleman whom I met during my first trip to the Sudan. At the time, Cyril was Middle East Director of Tennant Guarantee, now an arm of the Royal Bank of Canada. Unlike the character in this book, Cyril remained involved only in business, and only in governmental intrigue where it related to his business. Cyril guided me through the treacherously murky waters of Middle Eastern and African affairs. He and his wonderful wife Nancy have remained very dear friends over the years. It is a great pleasure for me to have this chance to enrich my book with the polish and unruffable calm with which he approached his work. Thank you, Cyril. I shall carry your lessons with me always.

As with all my books, this one bears my wife's loving imprint on every page. She assists at every step, from initial research to final polish. Thank you, Izia, for helping to make this dream reality.